STORM'S PERIL

AMELIA STORM SERIES: BOOK TWO

MARY STONE
AMY WILSON

Mary Stone

To my readers, who are the best ever. You mean the world to me.
Thank you from the bottom of my grateful heart.

Amy Wilson

To my one and only, my husband and best friend, and the best boys
a mother could dream of, who all worked with me to make this
story possible.

DESCRIPTION

Knowledge is ~~power~~ peril...

In a city as large as Chicago, the wicked never sleep. When an undocumented migrant teenager goes missing, military veteran and Special Agent Amelia Storm teams up with her partner to take down what could be the most shocking forced labor and sex trafficking ring her hometown has ever seen.

The case reeks of mafia involvement, but even with an investigative reporter as an informant, there's little in the way of leads. Suspicions cast a wide web, and the stakes climb when the boy's sister and their journalist informant also disappear. Still, no one is talking, and every second counts if they hope to find them alive.

As sinister secrets are unearthed, Amelia won't stop until she frees the innocent from the evil that lurks in the shadows of her beloved city. What she discovers hits a little too close to home. Was her brother involved? She needs to know, but some answers are better left unasked.

From the dark minds of Mary Stone and Amy Wilson comes Storm's Peril, book two of the Amelia Storm Series, where you'll be tempted to peek through the curtains to be sure evil hasn't chosen you.

1

What was that?

Javier Flores whipped around, peering into the night while attempting to locate the loud bang that had startled him so badly. The sound came again, much less distinct this time, and he relaxed a little as an ancient truck with a rusted fender backfired once again.

Pull it together.

Javier rubbed the back of his neck and shifted positions on the uncomfortable metal bench he'd been sitting on for what felt like an eternity. Since leaving the farm early that morning, he hadn't been able to shake the nagging sensation that someone was watching him...following him.

In his youth, he'd been stricken with the same paranoia after watching an R-rated horror film while his parents worked the night shift and his little sister was in bed. But that was four years ago. He wasn't a twelve-year-old boy anymore. Now, at the ripe old age of sixteen, he could watch a scary movie in the dark by himself without relying on the protection of his security blanket.

The source of Javier's anxiety tonight wasn't the thought

of ghosts or demons. Those were make-believe. The men he'd left behind at the farm? They were real.

Glancing around the bus station, Javier tightened his grip on the battered backpack holding his meager belongings. Aside from a young man and woman two rows down from him, an older man with a cane across from them, and the clerk behind the ticket booth, the bus station lobby was empty.

He was alone.

Again.

A blessing and a curse.

How had it come to this?

After his father died two years ago, money had been tight for their little family of three. Javier had witnessed his mother's tears, watched her go hungry so her children could eat. He'd wanted to help, and the plan had been so perfect. He'd get a summer job to make some extra money for his family until the school year started again.

When he and a friend had learned of a company that hired employees with little-to-no prior work experience, he thought he'd found a solution that would keep their household afloat. Well, at least until he graduated high school. He hoped.

According to the human resource person he spoke to, the job was labor-intensive but simple. The work wasn't glorious, but the pay was decent.

Or so he'd been told.

Maybe the paychecks he'd received each week would have been *decent*, but the company—whose official title Javier had never learned—tacked on extra taxes, fees, and penalties for expenses over which the workers had no control.

Each week, the company had saddled him and the other workers with more debt. Penalties for broken equipment they'd never even seen, fees for late payments on prior debts owed, interest for loans they'd been forced to take out to pay for those fees. The list went on.

Even when Javier had tried to control the costs, he'd been unsuccessful. He'd felt like he was trying to stem the bleeding for a wound that would never close.

In his eight weeks as a laborer on the farm, Javier had heard stories about men who were beaten for trying to leave before paying their debt to the company. There had been whispers among the workers about others who had disappeared after attempting to skip out on what they owed. Whether they'd been deported or killed, no one knew for sure. Any of those who had been reprimanded by the boss were closemouthed about what they'd experienced after the public beating.

He had no choice but to throw money at the company until the balance listed on his checks was zero.

The venture had taken more than two months, but Javier had finally done it.

For the first time since his arrival, Javier's debt was paid. He was debt free and intended to make the most of the reprieve. They couldn't keep him there if he didn't owe them anything, and they had no reason to reprimand him. He was done with that god-awful place and would never go back.

Still…he was scared.

You shouldn't be, he told himself in a voice as stern as his father's had once been. Javier was careful. Meticulous even. He'd been more thorough than those who had come before him. He had paid all his debts to the men who ran the farm. He was sure of it.

But try as he might, Javier couldn't scratch the incessant itch on the back of his neck. The one that told him he was being watched, that he was in danger.

The shadow of a man moved just at the edge of his field of vision, and Javier snapped out of his downward spiral of paranoid thoughts. Tightening his grip on the backpack, he angled his head to the side to get a better look.

Dread and fear swirled in his stomach.

As the first hint of the man's pungent cologne assaulted his nostrils, Javier's pulse rushed in his ears. Though none of the farmworkers were permitted to address that man by his first name, Javier had heard the other managers refer to him as Carlo.

White fluorescence caught a silver ring on Carlo's index finger as he ran a hand over his close-cropped hair. Under the harsh light, his receding hairline was even more prominent than usual.

Blowing out a long breath, Carlo turned disappointed brown eyes to Javier. "We've been looking for you. Are you planning on going somewhere?"

Javier cursed himself.

He should have waited in the bathroom or in the shadows of night outside. Maybe he could have sat next to the couple at the other end of the room, and then the man would have left him alone. Or maybe he could have just walked all the way back to Chicago. He could have hitchhiked, could have hopped on a train like he'd seen characters do in movies.

His throat was like sandpaper as he attempted to swallow. Movement caught his eye, and when he spotted a second man step up to the bench, the edges of Javier's vision turned dark.

The newcomer was called Matteo, the assistant manager of the place. The big man's forearms rippled with muscle as he grasped the back of the bench with both hands. Stubble darkened his face, but his clean-shaven head glinted as he tilted his chin to look at his prey. The crooked smile that split his lips sent an involuntary shiver down Javier's spine.

Nothing about the two men's presence was right.

Carlo, who called himself the shift manager, heaved

another sigh. "I really hope you weren't planning on leaving tonight. You know, I try to keep my feelings out of work, so I treat everyone the same, but I have to admit," his eyes bore into Javier, "I was starting to like you. It'd be a shame if you went and mucked that up by trying to leave."

As much as Javier wanted to believe the placating remark, in his gut, he knew the man was a liar.

Holding up both hands, he forced his voice to work. "I paid all my debts. I'm quitting, and I'm going home. I have school soon."

Matteo clucked his tongue, the corners of his lips turning up as if he'd heard a sordid joke. "School? That's not for another month."

Javier clenched his jaw until he thought his teeth might break. When he found the will to speak again, he forced himself to lift his chin and meet their dark gazes. "It doesn't matter. I can still leave. I paid everything I owed."

Carlo thrust his hands in his front pockets, causing his leather jacket to separate and reveal the dark shadow of a gun. His grin grew wider as Javier paled at the sight of the weapon. "You signed a contract, boy. You can't just walk away from that. You know that, right? If you want out of your contract, you have to talk to the boss. It'll cost you, though."

Straightening his back, Javier ignored the sweat that beaded on his brow. The station was air-conditioned, but in the presence of the two managers, he might as well have been back out in the late July heat.

"Then I'll pay it when I get home. I'll send a payment."

Carlo's laugh held more malice than Javier had ever heard. "That's not how this works, kid. You work for us, and that's a legally binding contract. You can't leave without paying."

Javier squared his jaw. His was the internet savvy generation, and he'd done enough research to know that minors couldn't enter into a legally binding contract. It had been a fail-safe he'd hoped he wouldn't have to use, but they had given him no other option. "You're right. I am just a kid. Which means no contract is legally binding."

As Carlo removed his hands from his pockets, his expression darkened. "Okay, smartass. You want to talk about what is and isn't legal? Your mom isn't here legally, is she? It'd be a shame if we had to report your mom to the authorities."

"I hear deportation happens quickly these days." Matteo shrugged his broad shoulders. "It would be a true shame if immigration had a reason to look at your mother's citizenship status."

He should have known.

His mother and younger sister weren't legally documented citizens. Neither was he.

So much for his backup plan.

Javier had only been four years old when his parents had taken him and fled their home country of Guatemala. Neither of them had offered much detail about the decision to undertake such a dangerous journey, but Javier's online searches about the country and the time period had given him an explanation.

A thirty-six-year civil war had left a lasting mark on the populace, and his parents had rightfully feared for their lives.

His parents had worked so hard to build a better life for him and Yanira. He couldn't cast away their sacrifice just to void a contract so he could quit a job. Even if that job was grueling, and even if the treatment of the workers was akin to slavery.

They had obtained temporary residency in the past, but his mother, Mari, hadn't been able to afford to renew the documentation after his father's death. His little family had flown under the radar since then. Javier didn't understand all the details, but he knew enough to realize the implications of Carlo's threat.

He couldn't do that to his mother and sister…or to the memory of his father.

Dragging a hand over his face, Javier slumped down in his seat, defeat a heavy weight on his shoulders.

"Tell you what, kid." Carlo's knees popped as he shifted from one foot to the other. "You come back with us, and we'll talk to the boss about waiving some of those fees."

Javier dropped his hand back to his lap and met Carlo's expectant stare. He didn't know what to say. Or do. He no longer knew anything at all.

Carlo glanced to Matteo before turning back on Javier. "Or we can get ahold of our lawyers and report your breach of contract. The choice is yours."

But the malevolent glint in Carlo's eyes told Javier all he needed to know.

There was no choice.

WHEN THEY ARRIVED at the expansive farm, Javier had dared to let himself hope he'd be allowed to return to the workers' apartments so he could sleep. Their shifts started before the sun rose, and they weren't allowed to rest until the day's quota had been filled. Fourteen to sixteen-hour workdays were common.

His sliver of hope was dashed as Matteo and Carlo prodded him toward one of four warehouses.

In the dark of night, the white, windowless building seemed to glow beneath the harsh light of the lampposts that dotted the property. Gravel crunched underfoot as he took one agonizing step after another.

The closer they grew to the side entrance, the more jumbled Javier's thoughts became.

How had his desire for a summer job gotten him here? All he'd wanted to do was make some extra cash to help his mother and his sister.

When the school year started in the fall, he'd been bound and determined to send himself and Yanira back to class with stylish new shoes and clothes. For once, they'd be dressed in jeans and shirts that weren't hand-me-downs. And for once, his mother wouldn't have to pick up extra shifts to pay for their school supplies.

Instead, he was here, stuck at this godforsaken farm that had consumed more than just his time and energy. The weariness from his eight weeks in this place ran deeper than what sleep alone could resolve.

Javier was tired all the way down to the core of his being. All he wanted was to see his mother and his sister again, but as their steps toward the warehouse went on, he became more and more certain that his life plans were about to be permanently derailed.

As they neared the metal door with its rusted hinges, Javier wondered if he could outrun the two men. If he could disappear into one of the cornfields, he could lose their tail and find his way to the main road.

He knew the fields better than Carlo or Matteo. There was no way they'd be able to find him in the maze of tall corn stalks.

Desperation causing his legs to shake, Javier glanced over his shoulder to the field. As a night breeze blew past them, the leaves of the corn plants swayed together as if they were a single entity.

"You might be thinking about running right now." Carlo's gravelly voice was tinged with a mixture of amusement and malevolence that made Javier's skin crawl.

Javier jerked from his moment of contemplation and turned to cast a wide-eyed stare at Carlo.

How did he know?

His chuckle was even more sinister this time. "You wouldn't be the first to try, kid. But..." he dropped a hand down to the lever of the old door, "you might want to wait a second before you do that. The boss doesn't take kindly to his employees trying to skate on what they owe, you understand?"

Shaking his head, Javier opened his mouth to speak, to remind the men that he owed no debts. Before the words could form on his tongue, a flicker of movement at his side was followed by a sickening crack. White light exploded in his left eye as pain seared its way through his cheekbone like the venom of a snake. His head snapped to the side as the taste of iron filled his mouth.

In the split-second that followed, Javier wasn't sure what had just happened.

The blow reverberated all the way to the bridge of his nose, and he squeezed his eyes closed against the tears that burned like acid.

Throughout his time in school, he'd always been polite and kind to his classmates. He'd been caught in a couple disagreements between friends, but he wasn't the type to get into a fistfight.

He was the good kid, the kind who broke up the fights, not one to *start* them.

Pressing one hand against his wounded cheek, Javier forced himself to turn to face the source of the blow.

Matteo loomed like a malevolent shadow as his broad-shouldered frame blocked the glow of the nearest lamppost. He was only a few inches taller than Javier, but the hulking man was easily double his weight. From snippets of conversations he'd overheard, Matteo's free time was often spent in a boxing ring.

Javier didn't have a chance to ask what he'd done to deserve the unexpected blow before Matteo rammed his fist straight into Javier's stomach. Before he could scream or say a word, the air was forced from his lungs. Javier hunched over, wheezing for a breath of air he desperately needed. With fingers that were mostly numb, he groped at the sight of the blow, sure he'd feel his intestines hanging out.

Matteo was relentless. The brute landed another punch to his chest, and then another, and another, until Javier finally gave in.

Dropping to his knees on the sidewalk, Javier threw his arms up to shield his face before crumpling to the ground.

Between his choked gasps, he thought he heard Carlo speak, but he couldn't make out the words. Any time he tried to take in a deep breath, he was greeted with a sharp pain in his ribs. His vision blurred as he tried to open his eyes, and bile clawed its way up the back of his throat.

The pain had become a living thing. It pinned him to the ground with the force of a professional wrestler, and its searing grasp on his ribs made each breath a near impossibility.

He'd never experienced pain like this.

As much as he wanted to tuck his knees into his chest, to curl into a little ball and meld into the concrete, his stomach lurched, and the bitter sting of bile filled his mouth.

He barely managed to pull himself out of the fetal position before the first involuntary heave overtook him. Each time he wretched, the pain from Matteo's heavy punches reignited. Despite that, Javier continued to vomit, emptying what little had been in his stomach into the strip of grass next to the sidewalk.

"Give him a second." Carlo's voice was tinny and distant

through the ringing in Javier's ears, almost like the man had spoken through an old CV radio.

"This pissant's a waste of our time." Matteo nudged Javier's leg with the toe of his boot. "Get up, you little shit. The boss is waiting for you."

Had Javier not been so preoccupied by the waves of pain that alternated with nausea, he might have felt an impending sense of dread at the spite-filled announcement. But in those moments, there was only pain.

Sharp pebbles from the sidewalk dug through his jeans, biting into his knees. He felt a tickle on the back of his hand as an ant or a beetle crawled over his skin.

Spitting out as much of the foul taste as he could manage, Javier finally took in a breath of the humid night air. A skunk had sprayed somewhere around the warehouse, but he was grateful to fill his lungs all the same.

He'd only just caught his breath when a rough hand clamped down on the back of his t-shirt. Though Javier tried to push himself upright before the man could pull too much, the collar dug into his throat like a rope.

"Get up. The boss is waiting." Matteo's order was more a growl than a series of spoken words.

This time, despite the trickle of blood from the cut on his cheek or the persistent sting of his damaged ribs, a cold rush of dread prickled the hairs on the back of his neck.

If the boss was waiting, then his night was far from over.

Carlo pulled open the rusty door, his scrutinizing eyes fixed on Javier as Matteo gave him an unceremonious shove through the doorway.

Though the overhead lights had been dimmed, Javier still had to blink to adjust his vision. His left eye was blurry with the tears that continued to well up from the pervasive sting in his cheek, and when he glanced down to his plain gray t-shirt, the front was dotted with dark splotches of crimson.

Javier did his best to wipe the blood from his face as they headed to a concrete hall. He'd never stepped foot into this part of the warehouse. He'd always assumed that the side entrance led to a set of stairs to the overhead catwalk, as well as a couple management offices, but assuming was as far as he'd ever gotten.

The area was reserved for Matteo, Carlo, and whichever other managers might have been present that day. The only workers he'd ever seen escorted through the side entrance were the ones who rarely spoke.

Maybe Carlo and Matteo brought the workers in here to kill them so they could be replaced with robots. Maybe Javier was at the start of a dystopian science fiction nightmare.

Halfway down the hall, another corridor branched off to two rooms. Though one door was closed, white light streamed onto the dingy floor from the other doorway across the hall.

Goose bumps rose on Javier's arms as he made out the voices of at least two more people, but before panic could rise in his chest, he was shoved into the doorway. His attention landed on the wall-mounted television beside a vending machine. To his relief, the screen was the source of the unknown voices.

That sense of relief was short-lived.

As soon as Javier's eyes settled on the boss, he wished he was still curled up in a ball on the concrete outside. Flickering light from the television caught the man's shiny black dress shoes from where he'd propped his feet atop a wooden table.

On a workday, the boss's attire matched the jeans, boots, and button-down shirts of Matteo and Carlo. The sight of a man in a dress shirt, slacks, and polished shoes was unusual in a place like the farm.

With his attire and neatly styled ebony hair, the boss

looked like he might have just walked out of a men's fashion advertisement.

The boss popped a chip in his mouth, crumpled up the bag, and then tossed it to a nearby trash can. Swinging his legs away from the table, the man brushed off the front of his pressed white shirt and settled his dark brown eyes on Javier.

Where Javier had expected to see the same flicker of hatred Matteo had shown him, the boss's lips curved into a slight smile. Scratching at the stubble on his cheek, he leaned back in his office chair. "So, I hear you went for a little late-night adventure, is that right?"

Carlo clapped a hand on Javier's shoulder, and it was all he could do to keep from crumpling as the dull pain once again overtook his upper body.

As Carlo looked from Javier to the boss, a matching smirk made its way to his face. "Sure did. We found him at the bus station. Had a ticket and everything."

The boss lifted his eyebrows. "A ticket? Wow. That's farther than most of you people make it before we catch you."

Though Javier wanted to plead his case and assure the boss that he'd paid his debts before leaving, one glance at Matteo reminded him what would happen.

Instead, he clenched his jaw and lowered his eyes.

Clapping his hands, the boss rose to his feet. "You know, I was a little pissed off that I had to leave my sister's wedding reception early to come here, but honestly..." he shrugged, "they didn't even have an open bar, so no harm done. Especially with what I've got waiting downstairs."

Javier fought against his furrowing brow, attempting to hide the look of confusion and keep his expression neutral as he watched the boss. Until now, he hadn't even known that the warehouse *had* a downstairs.

As the boss rested his hands on his hips, he looked ready

to speak again. But at the last second, he waved a hand and grinned.

"You know, I was going to go on about what the consequences are if you decide to leave your work here before we give you the okay, but I think we ought to just head downstairs so you can see those consequences firsthand. What do you think, gentlemen?"

Carlo's chuckle was filled with all the malice of hell. "I think we ought to head downstairs."

The boss clapped his hands again, the devious smile still on his lips. "Good. Come on, kid. I've got something to show you."

As the heart-pounding rush of adrenaline spread through Javier's battered body, the pain from his injuries was all but forgotten.

He didn't have the first clue what the boss meant when he said that he had something to show him. But with each step he forced himself to take back toward the landing, he felt certain he was walking to his death.

Once they got to the square landing, the boss shoved open a door that led up to the catwalk. The hinges gave the same rusty creak of protest as the side entrance, but the door swung closed quietly behind them.

Motion sensor lights flickered to life as they descended to the basement floor, and the boss's shoes clicked against the concrete. Matteo and Carlo flanked Javier as they strode down a wide hall with closed doors on either side.

As they reached the second door on the right, the boss stopped and retrieved a set of keys from his pocket. He flashed one more of those wicked smiles at Javier before he unlocked the latch and pushed the door inward.

With an outstretched hand, he beckoned Javier forward.

Javier half-expected to come face-to-face with a medieval

torture device—some relic leftover from the Spanish Inquisition or another brutal event that he'd learned about on the History Channel. An iron maiden, maybe, or a rack. Or maybe just a hitman with a good old-fashioned handgun and a silencer.

What he saw instead sucked any last semblance of defiance from his tired bones.

The cramped room might have once been a storage unit, but its purpose had clearly been altered to function as a prison cell.

A dingy mattress had been pushed against a wall at the far end of the space, and the stained surface had been mostly covered with a set of pink and blue sheets. On each corner of the bed sat a neatly arranged pile of stuffed teddy bears and rabbits.

Seated at the edge of the mattress, her cheeks wet with tears, was Javier's little sister.

"Yanira?" He croaked the word. His throat dried with the air it had taken to say her name. Javier swallowed hard, feeling as if a million shards of broken glass lined his esophagus. "Yanira, are you okay? How did you get here? Did they hurt—"

Matteo's fist rammed into his ribs, cutting short his series of questions. The blow reignited the fire from the beating outside.

Yanira let out a cry of surprise.

Javier took in a sharp breath and hunched over. It was all he could do to remain on his feet. He couldn't let Yanira see him crumple.

"Enough of that." Matteo clamped a hand down around Javier's upper arm and jerked him upright. "Shut your damn mouth, or I'll do worse than just punch you."

Gritting his teeth against the newest onslaught of pain, Javier lifted his chin to meet Yanira's frightened eyes. The harsh glow of a battery-powered work light glinted off the tears streaking down her cheeks.

They used the same lights around the farm when their work continued after dark, but the lamp's presence in this cramped room was all wrong.

There was electricity in the basement, and Javier had no idea why they'd set up such a bright light in a single room. In addition to the work light, he couldn't figure out why they'd surrounded his sister with stuffed animals.

Yanira had just turned sixteen, only ten months younger than Javier. Even when she was very little, she'd never been keen on teddy bears or rabbits. She'd always preferred model cars and someday dreamed of becoming a mechanic.

She hated wearing dresses too, but for some reason, she was wearing a pastel blue sundress, one that Javier had never seen.

His thoughts spiraled in a desperate effort to puzzle together the pieces of the scene before him as the boss strode across the room, took a seat next to Yanira, and draped an arm around her trembling shoulders.

Carlo strode to a metal folding chair halfway between the closed door and the mattress, and that's when Javier noticed the video camera and tripod.

The pieces suddenly fit into place.

Yanira's outfit, the stupid stuffed animals, the cutesy sheets, the work light.

Another round of nausea rushed up to greet him with the force of a charging bull. His vision swam as he swallowed repeatedly against the bile rising in the back of his throat. If he threw up again, Matteo would beat him.

Or worse, they would hurt Yanira.

Wrapping both arms around himself, Javier reined in his expression as he fixed his gaze on his sister. As well as he could, he tried to convey some semblance of strength, but despite his efforts to control his emotions, his eyes had already begun to burn with tears.

He wanted to tell her that everything would be okay, that he'd find a way out of here for both of them, or that he'd find a way to get the men to leave her alone.

He wanted to assure her that he could help her, but part of him already knew their fates were sealed.

Their fates were sealed the second he'd accepted this job, then once again when he'd stepped foot outside the property. He shouldn't have tried to leave. Whatever happened in this dingy room, it would be his fault.

"Here's how this is going to go." The boss tightened his arm around Yanira's shoulders to pull her closer.

"Please don't hurt her." The words slipped from Javier's lips before he could stop himself. Tears streamed down his cheeks, but he didn't care if the three men saw him cry. "Please, just take me instead. Do whatever you want to me, but please don't hurt my sister."

Matteo took a step closer to him, his right hand closed into a fist.

The boss lifted a finger. "No, Matteo. It's fine."

Though Javier should have been grateful for the intervention, his blood turned to ice when the boss's gaze settled on him. A knowing smile flitted across his predatory expression.

One thing had become crystal clear to Javier. The man was evil.

"He's taken enough of a beating. He still has work to do, and he won't be able to do it if he's in a coma, will he?"

Matteo grunted out a few words under his breath and lowered his fist.

Javier barely heard the bald man. His attention was fixed on his little sister.

The boss must have sensed Javier's sudden disconnect.

With the same hand he'd used to call off Matteo, he snapped his fingers until Javier turned to face him.

"You're going to listen to me very carefully." His voice barely registered above a whisper. Each word was delivered with a slow precision and clarity that allowed no misunderstanding of his meaning. "Do you understand me, Javier?"

Javier's limbs felt weighted down with lead. As he nodded, even lifting his head was a monumental task.

"Good." The unnerving smile returned to the boss's lips. "You tried to break your contract with me tonight, Javier. You tried to leave here without my blessing. Do you mind telling me why that is? Are you unhappy here?" Rubbing one hand along Yanira's upper arm, he brushed a few strands of ebony hair from her face with the other.

As Yanira's lower lip trembled, Javier fought off another round of tears and slowly shook his head. "No. I-I h-have school, in a…in a f-few weeks."

One of the man's dark eyebrows arched. "School? Did you not think I'd let you go back home to go to school?"

Javier opened and closed his mouth, but no sound escaped.

The boss's hand settled on Yanira's thigh, just below the hem of her dress. "I don't know what would have given you that impression, but it's too late to go back now. There's a reason we keep tabs on your family members when you start working here. After everything I do." The boss clucked his tongue. "After all the food I provide, the housing, not to mention the job itself, this is how I'm repaid. And believe me, you're not the first."

Of course he wasn't.

Javier took in a half-breath as he was struck by a sudden thought.

The quiet workers. The men and women who had been

escorted to the side door, the same side entrance Javier had been shoved through that night.

They'd all come back *different*. Quiet.

Broken.

Now, Javier knew why.

The boss pressed his nose into Yanira's hair and inhaled deeply. "Here's what's going to happen. You tried to fuck me over. And I don't like to be fucked, unless it's by a pretty girl."

When the man turned his eyes back to Javier, he froze, no longer able to control his body.

Maybe he was dead. Maybe he'd drifted outside himself and was now merely a spectator to his own life.

The boss extended a free hand, and Carlo leaned forward to pass him an item Javier couldn't quite make out.

Panic welled up in Javier's chest. Was it a gun?

He blinked to clear his vision and focused on the boss's hands.

No, it wasn't a gun. It was made of fabric. A blindfold, maybe, or a towel. Javier blinked again, but he still couldn't be sure. Once the item rested in the boss's lap, the man returned his grip to Yanira's leg.

"You said something about switching spots with your sister, but I'm afraid that's not the way this works. You see," he squeezed Yanira's thigh, "your sister here is worth much more than you could ever dream of being worth. Sure, there's a niche for teenaged boys out there, but that's not my area of expertise. No offense, but you don't *do* anything for me."

On a normal day, Javier would have been grateful that the man found him unattractive.

Today, he desperately wished the opposite were true. If given the opportunity, he'd take his sister's place. Without hesitation, he'd put himself in front of that pervert and his camera if it meant they'd let Yanira go.

But as the boss had said, that wasn't the way this worked.

As the boss slid his hand up another inch, the sickening smile returned.

"Now, you can't take her spot. That just won't work, logistically speaking. But…" Another inch. Another squeeze. "Her fate is in your hands. We've got demand for all sorts of different things. Some violent, some gentle. Loving, even. How you perform *your* job determines *her* job. That seems fair, doesn't it?"

Javier swallowed more bile and tightened his grip on his damaged ribs. Nothing here was fair, but he knew that wasn't the answer his boss wanted.

The boss wanted a nod, and that's what Javier gave him.

"Good. I'm glad you understand. You work for me, Javier, and only me. And you'll work for me until you die, or until I tell you that you can leave. Whichever happens first. If you try to fuck me over again, you know who'll pay for it?" With his eyes fixed on Javier, the boss leaned in and brushed his lips along Yanira's ear. "I bet you know, don't you, sweetheart?"

Yanira whimpered, tears falling from her eyes in thick streams. But she didn't move. In fact, she looked frozen to the spot.

"I won't." Javier shook his head for emphasis. "I won't. I'll do my work. I'll do whatever you need."

The corner of the man's mouth turned up in a self-satisfied smirk. "Good. Now, just so you don't think I'm a liar." He reached for the item in his lap—a mask.

He waved the material, letting it flap in the air before pulling the black fabric over his head. Once it was fixed in place, he chuckled.

"Start the camera."

2

S pecial Agent Amelia Storm resisted the urge to rub her tired eyes. If she did that this early in the morning, she'd have to reapply her eyeliner or look like a raccoon for the rest of the day. She didn't have the time or the patience for either, so she willed herself to focus on consuming more coffee instead.

After draining her second cup, she went back to the mindless paperwork that took up the majority of her time. She'd been putting it off to do a little research after a call she'd received the night before. She hadn't slept well following the disturbing conversation, and her mind kept drifting back to Vivian Kell. Now, she just wished her partner would get to the office so she could talk through everything with him.

As she tossed the paper cup into the trash, she forced her eyes away from the twin monitors on her desk, giving them a rest. As her eye doctor had recommended, she focused on a point in the distance for a full twenty seconds. That's when she noticed how dark it was inside the office.

Scanning past the cluster of cubicles to the wall-spanning

windows on the other side of the room, she frowned. A dark tint was meant to keep out excess light and prevent outsiders from looking in—never mind that the Organized Crime Division was on the sixth floor of the FBI's Chicago field office.

Today, all it did was darken the lazy gray clouds that preceded the morning's predicted rain. Once she looked away from the windows, Amelia could have tricked herself into believing she'd come into work at nine at night instead of seven in the morning.

Not long ago, Amelia and her fellow agent, Zane Palmer, had worked a bizarre combination of their normal shift and the night shift while one of their colleagues recovered from a brutal beating she'd sustained in an undercover operation.

Now, even though they were a month and a half removed from the swing shifts, Amelia continued to struggle to read-just her internal clock. The long summer days didn't even help.

Stifling a yawn, she glanced down at the porcelain cat figurine that held sentry between her monitors. One paw was raised, always prepared to wave at onlookers, while the other held a gold coin painted to resemble currency in Feudal Japan. *Maneki-Nekos*, or Lucky Cats in English, were common staples in businesses and homes throughout Japan, and she was seeing more and more of the fake ones here in the States.

More than two decades ago, Amelia's father had brought the cat home from where he'd spent six months stationed on a naval base in Japan. Though he'd brought wooden *Maneki-Nekos* for Amelia and her older brother, Trevor, this porce-lain creation had been a gift to Amelia's mother. Before she succumbed to lung cancer, Bonnie passed the cat on to Amelia.

As she picked up her tote to grab a piece of gum, Amelia

noticed a familiar figure approaching. His gray eyes settled on hers, and a tired smile crept to his unshaven face.

Zane Palmer's light, sandy brown hair was fashionably slicked back, somehow managing to remain that way without an abundance of shiny gel too many men seemed to choose. His black suit was tailored to fit his lean, muscular frame, and his white dress shirt was as neatly pressed as always. The man was fastidious about almost every aspect of his appearance—except when it came to shaving.

In truth, Amelia was grateful for the little imperfection. Otherwise, on most days, she'd be convinced that she was working with a man who had just walked off a movie set. She was far from slovenly, but lately, she felt like she'd been forced to step up her fashion game lest she feel like a slob.

Then again, fashion and anything remotely expensive came more easily to him. Zane Palmer came from money, and Amelia didn't.

She glanced down and smoothed the front of her pastel blue blouse. Amelia usually didn't care about her appearance, which had been a good thing since she'd spent so many years in camo fatigues. Fortunately, her fashion-forward hair stylist sister-in-law had taken her underwing when she'd left the military.

If nothing else, Amelia's hair and makeup always looked neat and tidy. Maybe not exactly the height of fashion, or *on point*, as her twelve-year-old niece would say, but good enough that she didn't embarrass herself on most days.

The chilly breath of the building's air-conditioner brought a series of goose bumps to her exposed forearms. Even at the end of July, she always tucked a cardigan or a zip-up hoodie into her handbag.

Though the temperatures outside—not to mention the persistent humidity—approached blistering, the FBI building always felt like a walk-in cooler. Before another chill could waft over her, Amelia pulled a gray knit sweater from her handbag.

Shrugging on the cardigan, she forced some semblance of organization back to her thoughts as she stifled a yawn.

"Still getting used to the morning life again, huh?" Along with a touch of his native Jersey accent, amusement tinged Zane's tired voice. He held up a paper coffee cup. "Thought you could use this."

Amelia grabbed for the cup with greedy fingers and nearly burned her upper lip on the first sip. "Thank you. I've only gotten two cups in me so far. I might live after this one."

He held up his own thermos, and they tapped them together. "Rough morning?"

She wrapped both hands around the warm cup. "Yeah, you could say that. It was a late night too."

Even though Amelia was glad that her partner had finally arrived, she found herself blinking a few times as a yawn she couldn't control took over. The coffee needed to kick in and quick.

He arched an eyebrow. "I thought you had yesterday off? Did something happen?"

She fished her phone out of the tote and swallowed another yawn. "Kind of. Yes. More or less."

Eyes narrowed, Zane tapped his temple. "Is it just me, or did that not make any sense?"

The corner of Amelia's mouth twitched. "No, it didn't make any sense. At least, I don't think it did. Hold on."

Sitting her coffee down, she unlocked her phone and navigated to a news article. As she searched, she made her way around the end of the row of cubicles to stand at his side.

He leaned against the edge of his desk and accepted the phone she held out to him. "What's this?"

"A news article written by Vivian Kell. It's an investigative piece she did on sex workers in Chicago." She reached out to scroll to the woman's picture at the bottom of the article. "Look familiar?"

Zane's eyes went wide. "Holy shit." He zoomed in on the image. "Yeah, she does. That's the Viv woman from that nightclub." He snapped his fingers, like the clicking noise would make his brain bring up the name. It seemed to have worked because he smiled. "Evoked, right? We went there to follow up on a lead in the Leila Jackson case."

"Exactly." Amelia accepted the phone as Zane held it out to her. "Vivian Kell was indeed Viv, but instead of being there to hook couples up, she was there doing some semi-under-cover thing for a story. She was looking into prostitution rings in the city."

Scratching his chin, Zane blew out a long breath. "So, she wasn't just some other creep hanging around the place? Is that why you had a late night last night?"

"More or less." Amelia tried and failed to pocket her phone. Fashion designers for women's apparel seemed to think pockets were merely a decoration, not meant for actual use, and were almost always a farce. Clutching the device in one hand, she crossed her arms instead. "She called me last night. She'd been following the Leóne case, and she picked my number up somewhere along the way. She wasn't all that specific on the phone, but she asked if she could meet with me today. Naturally, she wanted to meet up at eight in the morning, so here I am."

He peered out of the window as the pattering of rain-drops grew heavier. "She wants to meet you? Where?"

Amelia tapped a foot on the carpeted floor. "Here."

Reaching for his coffee thermos, Zane flashed her a curious glance. "Well, we've got about thirty minutes before she'll be here. Assuming you didn't call Larson in bright and early?"

She didn't miss the hint of derision in his question.

Even after all the time she'd spent working with both Joseph Larson and Zane, Amelia was no closer to understanding the reason the two men disliked one another.

No time like the present to find out.

"No, I didn't call him into work. I figured you'd be here since you usually show up before eight. I rarely see Larson in here before nine." She scanned the vacant cluster of desks for good measure before lowering her voice. "What exactly do you guys have against one another, anyway? I keep waiting for this shit to level out, but it just keeps going. Did Larson steal your car or something? Sleep with your ex-wife? What's the deal, Palmer?"

Amelia had never cared much for exploring personal office dynamics before, but since learning a rat—one who was loyal to the Leóne family—lurked somewhere in the Chicago field office, she'd made a point to pay more attention to how her fellow agents interacted with one another.

Otherwise, the Special Agent in Charge of the Chicago field office, Jasmine Keaton, had taken on the task of locating their rat. Amelia hadn't heard much from the SAC in terms of investigative developments, but she hadn't let her guard down.

As much as her instincts told her she could trust Agent Palmer, not to mention the work he'd put into capturing Emilio Leóne and Brian Kolthoff, Amelia remained vigilant.

Blowing out a sigh, Zane returned his coffee to the desk and looked around the room before he spoke. "This seems like it might not be the best office conversation, you know?"

Amelia held her hands out at her sides. "Then where are we supposed to have it? At a bowling alley?"

"No, we've been over this. I don't bowl." Zane picked his thermos up to take a quick drink. "When I was in seventh grade, we went bowling for a couple weeks for gym class. I thought I was starting to get pretty good, but then my thumb got stuck in one of the bowling balls as I was throwing it down the lane." His gray eyes were fixed on her as he wiggled his thumb for emphasis.

Clamping her teeth together, Amelia fought against the laughter she knew was inevitable.

Zane had no shortage of embarrassing stories from his preteen years, and for reasons that eluded Amelia, he was more than willing to share them if he thought the tale would elicit a laugh.

"When I threw it, instead of going down my lane, it bounced two lanes over and almost took out some little kid who was going to get his ball after it had gotten stuck. And I mean a little kid." He held a hand out at waist height. "That bowling ball probably weighed as much as that kid, but it barely missed him. Then it bounced off the bumper, rolled down the lane, and knocked all the kid's pins down. I haven't been bowling since."

Even as she started to snicker, Amelia made a show of rubbing the bridge of her nose. "My god. I can't take you anywhere. Come on, let's just go wait in the lobby downstairs in case she gets here early."

He shot her one of his patented charming smiles and tilted the thermos in a silent *cheers*.

Before heading to the elevator, Amelia grabbed her coffee and stuffed her handbag under her desk. The FBI office was undoubtedly among the safest places to leave a purse or wallet unattended, but old habits and paranoia died hard.

With a sip of the still hot latte, Amelia leaned against the handrail as Zane tapped the button to take them downstairs. The doors slid closed with a soft ding, and Zane assumed the standard elevator stance...facing the front, eyes on the digital display counting down each level.

Amelia stood taller than the average woman at five-eight,

but she always felt as if she'd shrunk when she was next to Zane's six-three. She'd learned in the past few weeks that Zane's mother was almost six-foot, so the source of his height was no mystery.

"To answer your question about Larson," he leaned his shoulders against the wood-paneled wall, his eyes fixed straight ahead, "I don't have anything against the guy. He's just...he's obstinate. It seems like there's only about four people in this building he'll listen to, and I mean *actually* listen to when they disagree with him." Glancing at Amelia, he tapped himself on the chest. "And I'm not one of them. You know how they say you have to give respect to earn it, right?"

He had Amelia's undivided attention. This was more than she'd heard either Zane or Joseph share regarding their obvious contention.

He cracked the knuckles of one hand with his thumb. "Well, I've been in this office as long as you have. What are we at, four, almost five months?"

Though she felt like a robot, Amelia nodded.

"I have yet to see that guy be respectful when he and I disagree on something. He's always right, and no matter what I say, he's still going to be right. So, I'd say my problem with him is that he doesn't respect me. And if I had to guess, you've never seen that side of him because, by all appearances, he seems to respect you. Maybe it's a military thing, or something he's got against me because I was a civilian before joining the Bureau. I don't know."

Amelia was surprised by his disheartened tone. Then again, if she'd spent four months butting heads with a coworker who didn't respect her, she might feel that way too.

As Amelia pressed her finger against the edge of her cup's plastic lid, two floors ticked away in silence. She turned to meet his curious eyes. "I'm sorry."

Zane looked surprised. "Sorry? Why?"

She sighed. "I always thought you two were in some kind of territorial pissing match, something where this office wasn't big enough for the both of you. I guess I don't pay very much attention when you're arguing with each other, or maybe I'd have picked up on it by now."

"It's not your fault. What is it the kids say? 'Sometimes it be like that.'" He tipped his cup at her and took a sip of his coffee.

"Yeah, makes sense. You're totally justified in not liking him. And you're right. I've never noticed him acting that way to me. I'll try to back you up more often around him, then maybe he'll start to break out of whatever stubborn ass shell he's been hiding in." Amelia pushed the paper sleeve around her cup. "You know, provided you actually *are* right."

He huffed in feigned indignation, but his lips had already curved into a smile. "There's always a caveat, isn't there?"

By the time the elevator dinged, and they arrived at the horseshoe-shaped reception desk, Amelia felt lighter. Now that she knew the source of the bad blood between Zane and Joseph, she could finally take steps to put an end to it.

During her ten years in the military, she'd been in Zane's situation more times than she cared to count. Though she'd busted her ass to get through sniper and airborne training, earning respect amongst male peers was an uphill battle.

Since Amelia rarely had anyone to back her up in the early days of her military career, she'd come up with her own method to combat the constant doubt and second-guessing that had been hurled her way. Before she'd turned twenty-one, Amelia had developed a level of assertiveness that bordered on abrasive.

In layman's terms, she'd been an asshole.

But she'd been an *effective* asshole. And when she left the Armed Forces, she'd been a Lieutenant Asshole. She'd toned down the attitude after she became a civilian, but in her work at the FBI, there were still some instances where she had to let a little of her old self shine through.

Though the tactic had worked for her, she didn't want to encourage Zane to be a jerk to Joseph. But if she backed Zane up a few times, maybe Joseph would get the point.

She was lost in contemplation as they took a seat on a bench with a view of the main entrance. Though the room felt massive with its two-story-high ceiling, Amelia had only ever seen a handful of people in the lobby at the same time. In-person visitors to the FBI office weren't as common now that online communication had become more prevalent.

They'd been sitting for less than five minutes when the double doors at the far end of the room swung open.

Shaking out a blue umbrella, the familiar woman offered a few words of greeting to the security personnel before emptying her pockets and setting her handbag in a basket beside a conveyer belt. The FBI's security wasn't quite as stringent as what Amelia was used to in airports, but the metal detector and x-ray scanner were still thorough.

Once the woman had retrieved and shouldered her hand-bag, Amelia and Zane rose to stand. Vivian's hair had grown out of the asymmetric bob she'd sported when Amelia and Zane had gone undercover at the seedy nightclub Evoked, but her blue-green eyes were just as sharp as Amelia remembered.

Vivian's high heels clicked on the tile floor as she strode over to where Amelia and Zane waited beside the reception desk. With her smart gray pencil skirt and off-white blouse, she looked every bit the part of a competent reporter.

Her vivid blue eyes flitted from Amelia to Zane and back as she stuck out a hand. "Agent Storm, it's nice to meet you again."

Amelia clasped Vivian's hand in a businesslike shake. "Good morning, Ms. Kell. I'm glad you could make it."

"Of course." Vivian smiled as she peered up at Zane. "And this is…your husband?"

"Partner." Zane accepted Vivian's handshake, and Amelia could tell he was suppressing his amusement. "Case partner, Special Agent Zane Palmer. Shall I call you Viv?"

"Vivian is fine." Vivian pressed her lips together, but her eyes held a smile she couldn't conceal. "I guess that makes you the very definition of a work husband, doesn't it?"

Amelia liked Vivian right away.

Vivian turned somber. "But I'm right, aren't I? You both worked on the Leila Jackson slash Emilio Leóne case?"

Amelia wasn't surprised that Brian Kolthoff's name hadn't made Vivian's list, though the omission was like a punch. "That's right."

Until a couple months ago, Brian Kolthoff had been known simply as The Shark. Amelia still hadn't figured out exactly what acts had earned him the moniker, but she'd been able to safely rule out practicing law.

Based on his vicious reputation—a reputation the Bureau still hadn't officially tied to Brian Kolthoff—the nickname had its roots in bloodshed.

She swallowed the bitter taste that always came to her tongue when she thought about Kolthoff. He should have been charged with sex trafficking of a minor like Emilio Leóne had been, but his team of expensive lawyers had whittled away at the charges over the last month.

As the case dragged on, she was forbidden from discussing the details and charges with anyone other than the agents who had been assigned to the initial investigation, even though she wanted to rage to everyone she saw about the unfairness of it all.

She'd been so sure that they'd caught The Shark high and

dry, but even after they'd searched every millimeter of the yacht he owned, they'd found nothing...nada...absolute zero evidence to tie him to a trafficking ring.

It still pissed her off, and Amelia had been tempted to hire her own boat and inspect every single yacht in the sea. Which would have been illegal...and probably futile...and would have taken all the rest of her life.

But one day...

Forcing her mind away from Brian Kolthoff, she focused back on Vivian Kell. According to the reporter's phone call the night before, she'd uncovered a potential lead into another human trafficking ring.

Gesturing to the curved desk, Amelia shook herself free of the bleak thoughts. "Here, let's get you a visitor's badge, and then we can head upstairs to talk."

The three of them made casual conversation as they waited. Since the topic of conversation was Emilio Leóne's conviction, Amelia couldn't quite call the discussion "small talk."

One of Vivian's coworkers at *The Chicago Standard*—a branch of a major media conglomerate devoted exclusively to Chicago—had covered Emilio Leóne's trial. Because of that connection, she'd been filled in on many of the court-related details.

In all honesty, Amelia was surprised at how closely Vivian had kept track of the trial. As they all stepped into the elevator and ascended to their floor, Amelia reminded herself that Vivian wasn't just another reporter. She was an investigative journalist.

Though she made much of her living by writing online articles about the daily goings on of the city, her real focus was unraveling major stories, many of which were mired in controversy.

Finally, at the end of a quiet hallway just beyond the

elevator, Zane pulled open a heavy wooden door and waved Vivian through. Amelia followed behind, and as she stepped over the threshold, she met Zane's gaze.

With his hand still on the door, Zane lowered his voice. "Seems like she's pretty interested in the Leónes. We'd better watch what we say to her."

Amelia offered a stiff nod in response. She didn't think the Leóne family would add a reporter to their payroll, but she also wouldn't have thought they'd manage to weasel their way into the FBI office, either.

But here they were.

Clearing her throat, Amelia stepped through the doorway. The room wasn't lavish, but the space was far more comfortable than the areas they used for questioning suspects. With its warm lighting, solid chairs, and file cabinets of office supplies, the ambiance was closer to a professional meeting space than an FBI interview room.

Once the door latched closed, Zane took his seat at Amelia's side. He propped his elbows on the table and folded his arms. "So, Ms. Kell, my partner tells me that you've got a lead on a potential human trafficking ring, is that right?"

Vivian's gaze shifted between Amelia and Zane as she set a manila folder atop the wooden table. "Yes, that's right. I didn't want to discuss it too much on the phone just because," she paused and shuffled through a handful of papers tucked neatly inside the folder before returning her attention to Amelia and Zane, "it's...complicated."

Zane chuckled. "Well, you're in luck because complicated is just about all we deal with around here."

Watching the other woman carefully, Amelia pulled open the middle drawer of the file cabinet. After a couple seconds of rummaging, she retrieved a half-used legal pad and a pen.

Vivian's expression was neutral as she absently fingered the edges of the pages in her folder. "That would be why

I'm here and not at the Chicago PD. I've covered enough crimes and trials to understand the difference between local and Federal jurisdiction. Believe me, if I didn't think this warranted the FBI's scrutiny, I wouldn't waste your time."

Amelia and Zane exchanged a curious glance as Vivian pulled out a few printed photographs. Most of the people who contacted the FBI didn't vet the jurisdiction of the crime they were reporting.

At Vivian's attention to detail, Amelia couldn't help but wonder how long she'd had the information she was about to present to them.

"We appreciate your diligence." Amelia felt like a customer service answering machine, but the response was the best she could manage.

Glancing up from the pictures, Vivian offered them a slight smile. Though Amelia was sure she intended to come across as reassuring or confident, the way her eyes flicked back and forth between the pictures and the door told an entirely different story.

Vivian Kell was nervous.

Before Amelia could open her mouth to ask a follow-up question, Vivian turned over one of the pictures and slid it closer to her and Zane. With a quiet sigh, she did the same for the other two prints.

"I always include pictures in the longer pieces I write. I think it helps the readers visualize the more complex stories, which helps them understand what I'm trying to get across." She tapped the first photo. "I figured I'd do the same today."

Resting her arms on the table, Amelia leaned in to get a better look. The young man peering up at her couldn't have been any older than seventeen. Clad in a Chicago Cubs t-shirt, he rested a wooden baseball bat over one shoulder as he grinned for the camera. His ebony hair was windblown, and his tan complexion told Amelia that he enjoyed spending time outdoors.

Vivian tapped the top of the picture with a manicured finger. "This is Javier Flores. He's sixteen, and he'll be a junior when school starts up next month. From what his mom told me, he's a huge baseball buff, and he loves to go fishing and hiking."

Amelia and Zane held their silence as Vivian slid a second picture into view. A teen girl, maybe fifteen or so, wore a grin that bore a striking resemblance to Javier's. Her glossy black hair was pulled back in a ponytail, and her cheeks were smudged with dirt. In one hand, she held a wrench that was about as long as her forearm, and in the other, an orange pumpkin basket. When Amelia took a closer look at the girl's gray jumpsuit, she spotted a name tag that read *Bubba*.

"This is Javier's younger sister, Yanira Flores." Vivian's expression turned wistful. "This was from last Halloween. She dressed up as a mechanic." She stared Amelia straight in the face as she pointed to the third and final photo. "And that's their mother, Mari Flores. Mari's husband passed about a year ago from natural causes, and the family has been struggling financially ever since."

The truth was there. Even through the photogenic smile, Mari's tired eyes displayed a type of weariness that went beyond physical exhaustion. Amelia knew that fatigue all too well. She'd seen the same shadow in her father for close to seventeen years.

Amelia pushed the thought aside, refusing to let her mind wander away from the small family in front of her.

Vivian gestured to the photo again. "Mari and her husband came to the United States about twelve years ago when Javier was four. They both got temporary work visas, but when those expired, they couldn't afford to either renew them or apply for permanent residency."

Zane leaned back in his chair. "Permanent residency can be expensive, and it's complicated to apply for. A lawyer is almost always required, especially if the applicant isn't a native English speaker. Even without a lawyer, it's still a few grand, depending on where you are."

"Right." Shadows beneath Vivian's eyes became more pronounced as she looked back at Mari's picture. "That's why I'm here, and not Mari. She came to my office yesterday, and she was almost in tears. She said that she and some of her friends had read a few of my articles in the past and they thought I'd be a trustworthy person to turn to. She thought if she went to the police, she'd be deported."

Amelia scribbled the names down on her notepad. "That's not an unreasonable fear. I get why she came to you instead of going to the cops."

Vivian let out a relieved chuckle, and her shoulders relaxed as did the tension that had been apparent in her face. "That's good. That means we're on the same page."

Tapping her pen against the notepad, Amelia offered a polite smile. "We are. Why was Mari there?"

As she cleared her throat, Vivian's professional demeanor returned. "I'll start at the beginning of her story and go from there. It makes a little more sense that way." She tapped Javier's picture. "Her son was trying to get a summer job so he could make a little extra money for the family. Mari tried to tell him that it wasn't necessary, but you know teenage boys."

Zane grinned. "I sure do."

Though brief, Vivian returned the expression. "He was insistent, but he and Yanira are both in the same predicament as their mother. All three of them were born in Guatemala. None are technically legal citizens. It hasn't been an issue so far since he's just a high school student, but it limited the places he could look for a job."

Amelia stopped writing, already knowing where this story was headed. Though Jim Storm never went into much detail, Amelia knew that her mother had been in a similar situation after her family emigrated from the Soviet Union. Bonnie, like Mari and Javier, had been an illegal immigrant.

"Mari didn't know a lot about this part of it." Vivian folded her hands together atop the table, her fingers twisting together. "But Javier came across a man who was looking for workers to help out with some farm labor. It was the type of thing you don't need experience for, and apparently, they were willing to pay under the table. It seems suspicious to us, but to a sixteen-year-old boy whose family is broke and who can't work a legal job, it was like a godsend."

Amelia couldn't help but wonder if her mother had been approached by one of these so-called recruiters. Had she been pushed into the position and been exposed to the carcinogens that had ultimately ended her life when Amelia was ten?

But even though she could relate to Mari Flores and her children on a personal level, Amelia kept the notion to herself.

One of Zane's eyebrows arched sharply. "He took the job?"

"He did." Vivian sighed. "Mari saw him once after he first took it, and she said that he just seemed rundown. But he'd tell her that everything was fine, that he was making money, and that he'd be done with the work in time for the school year. But after that short visit, she didn't see him again. That was about four weeks ago, and all she's gotten since are a few emails saying that he's doing okay."

As she set down the pen, Amelia sorted through the multitude of questions in her head. "What about the money he was making? Did she ever see any of it?"

Vivian's expression darkened. "No. Javier told her that he

was saving it for when he was able to come back home. Mari, however, never saw any of it. She said she wasn't even sure that he was being paid as much as he claimed."

Zane cast a sidelong glare at Amelia. "That sounds like a pretty common tactic that labor traffickers use."

"Common, yes." Amelia's fingers found a lock of hair that had come loose from her braid and began twirling. This was hitting too close to home. "But it's common for a reason. It's effective."

Vivian looked grim. "I've done research on forced labor and human trafficking before, and that's what I thought too. But it didn't seem like Mari was fully aware of the types of things traffickers do to lure people in." She heaved a sigh as she pushed the photo of Yanira closer to Amelia and Zane. "But I think she is now. The day before yesterday, Yanira went missing. She went to soccer practice with her friend but never came home."

The room lapsed into silence. Amelia continued to twist the lock of hair until it had tightened so much it tugged at the roots in her scalp. The truth was something she didn't want to put into words.

When a trafficking victim's family started to go missing, there were only a couple probable explanations.

Either the family member was being used as collateral, or the traffickers were expanding by force.

3

Extending both arms above his head, Alex Passarelli stretched his back until he felt a light pop. He'd paid a lot of money for a computer chair that was comfortable for long periods of time, but even modern ergonomics couldn't fully combat the bizarre weariness that came with sitting in front of a computer screen for hours on end.

It was his honor to serve as a capo of the D'Amato family, one of the major Italian crime families in Chicago. Generations ago, the Passarellis joined forces with the D'Amatos and a few other families, knowing that strength came with numbers. But with those numbers came the headache of management. Still, Alex was proud of his position and enjoyed the monetary benefits it offered.

As he turned to look out the wall-spanning windows on the other side of his office, he squinted against the rays of sunlight that had finally pushed through the mass of gray clouds. Blinking away the bright light, he reached for a slender remote at one edge of his matte black corner desk.

Alex preferred the bleak, cloudy skies that came with the Midwest's summer storms. If he controlled the weather, every day would be dreary to match his perpetually sour disposition.

He hadn't always been so irritable, but over the past weeks, he'd been hard-pressed to find a reason to pretend to be cheerful.

Ever since the day Amelia returned.

In the back of his mind, he'd always hoped she'd come back to him, but he couldn't have anticipated the pain their reunion dredged up. Rather than rekindling the spark between them, the circumstances that had brought them together echoed all the pain and loss he'd been forced to endure.

Amelia hadn't wanted him. She'd needed information to help find a missing girl. A girl with the same blue eyes and raven hair as his own lost little sister, Gianna.

If only they had been searching for her.

A decade had passed since Gianna went missing. Kidnapped. But unlike the raven-haired girl Amelia was searching for, Gianna's captors had left no clues to follow. Whispers had suggested a shark of a man might have been involved in her disappearance, but as the years rolled on, the idea seemed more and more farfetched. None of the D'Amato family's enemies went by that moniker.

He knew the chances of Gianna being alive were slim at best, but Alex couldn't help holding out hope. The alternative was just...

He couldn't let himself finish that thought.

She'd had a bright future ahead of her. Smart, beautiful, and coming from a powerful family pedigree, Gianna should have achieved all she wanted in life and more.

The drive to know her captor, to bring justice to the person who had dared to touch his precious sister, had become an obsession. He would have vengeance.

Until he had confirmation, one way or another, of Gianna's condition, she would live on in his memory.

Gianna had always been mother and father's perfect little angel. At least that's how she behaved in public. A perfect little mafia princess. Well mannered, educated, and groomed to show the appropriate respect around members of the family. With Alex, however, she could get away with anything.

Devious as she was adorable, Gianna had wrapped Alex around her little pinky. She knew exactly how to employ the etiquette that had been drilled into her as a manipulation tactic, and Alex had always been her patsy.

He smiled as a memory surfaced, bringing a tear to his eye.

Mother and father had tickets to a show, and he'd been stuck with babysitting duty. Bedtime had come and gone, yet Gianna refused to go to sleep.

Frustrated by her refusal and annoyed that he couldn't get five minutes of privacy to call his girlfriend, Alex had shouted a few choice words.

Not his finest moment.

The normal response would have been tears, or maybe an angry threat of telling their parents how poorly Alex had treated her.

Not Gianna. That wasn't her style.

Instead, she smiled sweetly. Batting her eyelashes, she dropped to her knees. Making an elaborate show of deference that would have won her an Oscar, the mite of a girl took his hand in hers and kissed his ring finger.

Treating Alex as if he were The Boss, Gianna offered a humble request for his approval.

As darkness descended on his living room, Alex could swear he heard echoes of her tiny voice.

"Please, Boss, grant to me this day, your formal consent to

watch the movie Fright Night. *If you do this thing, I swear my allegiance to you and shall not utter another word to disturb your evening. This I pledge."*

Though his heart ached, Alex chuckled at the memory. Growing up in this life and being part of a powerful family, the siblings had been destined to one day take on the roles they playacted. But Gianna did it with unmatched flair.

If given the chance, she might have one day risen in the ranks herself and become the first woman capo of the D'Amato family.

Even so, he could never say no to her. Not that she ever asked for anything truly outrageous. Innocent kid that she was back then, Gianna would only want to stay up late, watch movies she shouldn't, or maybe sneak an extra slice of cake. More often than not, she simply requested to tag along whenever he went to see the love of his life...Amelia.

Alex closed his eyes as her name echoed in his mind.

Gianna had been best friends with Amelia's little sister, Lainey. Their friendship offered Alex the perfect excuse to escort Gianna for playdates. While the two girls did whatever little girls do, Alex got to enjoy a little private time with the girl who had stolen his heart. It had been a win-win for all.

"That was the past." Alex blew out a heavy breath. Replacing the remote, he returned his attention to the two glowing monitors. Though much of his work as a D'Amato capo had been shifted to the digital realm, his screen time over the past few days had been split between work and his newest pet project. "Better days."

He hadn't seen his baby sister in nearly a decade, and Amelia was no longer the love of his life. She'd returned to him as a federal agent, a position diametrically opposed to his own, with no hope of rekindling lost affection.

But, through helping Amelia find the girl she'd been

searching for, Alex had learned the name Brian Kolthoff. A man who, in some circles, was known as The Shark.

Alex had made it his mission to learn all he could about the bastard. If this Kolthoff was the same shark that had been rumored to have kidnapped his baby sister, it would be worth all the pain of seeing Amelia again. Alex might finally have the vengeance he'd long sought.

Kolthoff was a successful venture capitalist turned D.C. lobbyist. As a venture capitalist, Kolthoff had funded several tech startups that had become massive online platforms. The man's net worth was in the billions, and he owned one of the top one-hundred largest yachts in the world.

Despite his lucrative career in venture capitalism—a practice with which Alex himself was no stranger—Kolthoff had kept a low profile for most of his adult life. He'd been involved in a scandal that had to do with insider trading in Washington, D.C., but his name had long since been cleared.

Even after Alex's meticulous digging, he'd come no closer to uncovering a blemish on Kolthoff's professional record.

But Alex didn't particularly care about The Shark's business achievements. The information he sought was much darker and more difficult to unearth.

Fortunately, the D'Amato family wasn't strangers to the world of technology. In addition to Alex and his software engineer uncle, the D'Amatos employed more than a handful of talented hackers at any given time.

Alex had dug deep, and after all the tedium of sifting through travel records and old business itineraries, he'd established a timeline for Brian Kolthoff for the weeks leading up to and following the disappearance of Gianna.

She had gone missing more than a decade ago, and Alex had been operating under the assumption that Gianna had been kidnapped out of revenge or as part of a feud between the D'Amato family and a rival. However, no one had stepped up to claim responsibility for the act.

To any other person, the idea was normal enough. After all, who in their right mind would admit to kidnapping a thirteen-year-old girl?

In an ordinary world, the answer was simple. No one would willingly admit to a kidnapping. In Alex's world, however, an act of revenge was pointless if the recipient didn't know who sought that vengeance in the first place.

Which brought him back to Gianna.

The D'Amato family had no shortage of enemies. The fact that their lucrative criminal empire was based around low-risk enterprises, like selling counterfeit goods, hadn't exempted them from rivalries with other syndicates.

Why then had no one claimed responsibility? Not the León family, not the Russians, not even the Armenian mafia.

Someone like Brian Kolthoff—someone who was a friend to both the León family and the Russians—wouldn't have made a show of abducting Gianna. But if Brian Kolthoff *was* involved, like some whispered rumors suggested, then his involvement begged the question...why? What bad blood had been stirred up between the D'Amato family and Kolthoff that had led to him kidnapping and doing who knew what to a girl who was essentially mafia royalty?

Alex drummed his fingers against the desk.

His most recent source of information was more consistent with the traditional image of a mafia capo. Years earlier, his father, Luca Passarelli, had enlisted the help of a seasoned Chicago police detective to seek answers or locate Gianna.

For that, they'd turned to a trustworthy source, a detective who had been on the D'Amato family's payroll for more than five years and had a personal connection to the Passarellis. Detective Trevor Storm.

Being Amelia and Lainey's older brother, his family was deeply entwined with Alex's, and the added element of personal affection ensured his discretion. He'd been the perfect resource to tap. That was until his untimely death two years ago. Killed in the line of duty, the last remaining connection tying their families together seemed to have been severed.

Until Amelia walked back into his life.

Alex considered his options. He had little hope of starting fresh with Amelia. Given his position with the D'Amato family, any romantic connection would be strictly off-limits. But professionally, they might still be of use to each other. And seeing as she was the one to arrest Brian Kolthoff, she'd no doubt have all the dirt on him. Especially the stuff that had been deemed inadmissible in court.

There was just one problem. Was the pain of being around Amelia Storm, knowing he could never have her, worth the information she might provide?

4

The FBI frowned upon its agents using an entire conference room for a single investigation. Though Zane and Amelia had compiled evidence for Leila Jackson's case in a bright meeting room near their desks on the Organized Crime floor, for this latest case, they had been relegated to a remodeled interview room several levels below.

SAC Keaton claimed to have reserved the space for them a few weeks earlier, but she'd waited until they'd come across a fresh case to break the good news.

It was a far cry from the setting Zane had expected. As he glanced around the room, he wondered if the area had actually been used to conduct interviews or to store brooms.

The beige drywall was dented and scuffed with marks from furniture that had been rearranged, and the rugged carpet squares covering the floor had seen better days. But they had a whiteboard, a matte black table, a cluster of half-broken office chairs to choose from, and outlets for their laptops. The overhead fluorescent fixture was dead, but the recessed lights above the whiteboard were bright enough for the shoebox-sized room.

Despite the obvious flaws, the space had one important feature.

The windowless door locked and could only be opened with a six-digit code that was exclusive to him, Amelia, and SAC Jasmine Keaton.

After the discussion with Vivian Kell, Zane and Amelia gave SAC Keaton a high-level overview of the case. They had caught her right before she was due to a meeting, so she had assigned them the case and advised that she would stop by later that afternoon to go over the investigation in more detail.

Based on Keaton's normal hands-off style of management, Zane assumed she had more to discuss with them than just the Flores family.

Zane taped the picture of Javier Flores to the wall-spanning whiteboard and stepped back to admire his and Amelia's handiwork. "What are you thinking? Any ideas on who might've recruited Javier and then kidnapped his sister?"

Amelia blew out a sigh as she dropped into an office chair that was missing an armrest. "As far as the *who* goes? I'm not really sure. Whoever they are, they're organized, so this is definitely a case for us."

Zane leaned against a patch of drywall that had been installed to cover what was once a two-way mirror. His eyes settled on a list of known criminal enterprises written on the right-hand side of the board. He rubbed his chin as he made a mental note of each name.

He needed to shave. Zane hated shaving, but he also hated how itchy his face got when he tried to grow a beard. Caught between a rock and a hard place, at least this problem could be solved with a simple decision. Their case, however, still so new and with little to go on, promised to be a harder challenge to overcome.

Dropping his hand to his side, he shifted his attention back to Amelia. "How sure are we that the names we crossed out over there aren't involved in something like this?"

She stretched her legs out and leaned into the chair's back-rest, narrowing her eyes as it squeaked and groaned with her weight. "Honestly? With a scenario that's this specific, where an undocumented teenager is lured into a hard labor position, and then his sister is kidnapped..." her forest-green eyes flicked up to his, "it makes the most sense to look at the groups that have the infrastructure capable of large-scale labor trafficking. Small-time traffickers aren't going to go to the extent that these guys did. They don't have the organization or resources to kidnap a girl right from underneath everyone's nose."

"True. That's why I only put five names up there to begin with. We crossed two of them out, so that leaves us with the Russians, the San Luis Cartel, and the Leónes." He lifted an eyebrow at her. "You're sure that there's no way the D'Amato family or the Irish are involved in this?"

"Fiona was undercover with the Irish for a while, and from what she's said, they're all drugs and guns. The D'Amato family." She drummed her fingers on the single armrest. "They're more technologically advanced, I guess you could say. White-collar sort of stuff."

He didn't have to press the issue to know that there was more to Amelia's knowledge of the D'Amato family than met the eye.

Though subtle, Amelia always perked up at the mention of the prominent crime family. Zane had wondered at first if he was associating two unrelated occurrences, but after the past two months, he was certain that the observation wasn't a coincidence.

Then again, there were plenty of reasons Amelia's interest might be piqued by the mention of the D'Amatos. She reacted with equal enthusiasm at the mention of comic book superheroes and hip-hop music.

As far as criminal organizations went, the D'Amatos weren't uninteresting. Their use of technology to make low-risk money in illicit industries like counterfeiting and online theft was unrivaled by all but a few.

Plus, they weren't leaving a body count across the city of Chicago. Well, not that he knew of.

One day, Zane would ask Amelia what had piqued her special interest in the D'Amato family, but today was not the day, and their cramped workspace was not the place.

He resecured a pushpin on the corner of Alex D'Amato's picture. "Yeah, you're right. This isn't D'Amato's style."

She glanced up, and Zane could have sworn he saw a glint of relief in Amelia's eyes. "What about the San Luis Cartel? You dealt with a cartel when you were in D.C., right? Which one?"

Zane turned back to the whiteboard. "No. What we dealt with out in D.C. was part of the Veracruz Cartel. Their main base of operation was in New York, but they maintained a noticeable presence in D.C. too." He scratched at the stubble on his chin. "It's ironic, actually. The Veracruz and San Luis Cartels hate one another. Weird that I'd go from one cartel to their arch enemy."

Before he could speculate further on cartel rivalries, a few quiet beeps and a metallic click drew both his and Amelia's attention to the windowless door.

SAC Jasmine Keaton entered, and her dark eyes shifted from Zane to Amelia before resting on the whiteboard. "Looks like you're all settled in your new home. How do you like it so far?"

Zane made a show of glancing around the dim room. "It's...cozy."

"Yeah, sorry about that." The SAC eased the door closed behind herself.

Amelia's chair squeaked as she shifted in her seat. "Why exactly do we have a room, anyway? Not that I'm...well, I shouldn't complain. We could probably do a lot worse."

The SAC lifted an eyebrow. "How so?"

Humor deepened the fine lines at the corners of Amelia's eyes. "We could be outside."

With a snort, SAC Keaton set a couple manila folders on the scuffed tabletop. Resting both hands on her hips, her lips formed a hard line as she looked over the cluster of half-broken chairs in one corner and then to the burnt-out light fixture overhead.

"I guess it's been a while since I was last in here." She pulled a chair from the corner, wincing when its squeak was louder than the one Amelia was sitting in. "It was in much better shape the last time I saw it. This was an inter-rogation room back when I was a field agent, but I guess the Bureau felt it served a better purpose as a chair graveyard."

Laughter bubbled out unrestrained from Amelia's mouth.

A strange response for her, at least in the presence of a senior agent. Zane watched his partner attempt to stifle her mirth as it threatened to turn into boisterous cackling.

Very curious.

"Agent Storm?" SAC Keaton must have found Amelia's burst of humor curious too. Her eyebrows lifted to almost meet her hairline. "Did we miss something?"

Squeezing her eyes closed, Amelia coughed into her hand and shook her head. "No." Based on the smile that tugged at the corner of her mouth, she hadn't finished her fight against the laughter.

Uncontrollable laughter wasn't a normal part of Amelia Storm's repertoire. With all his smartass comments and their ongoing friendly jabs at one another, Zane usually only got a chuckle or maybe a grin out of her.

Just when he thought he'd figured out Amelia's brand of humor, she took an unexpected left turn.

Amelia cleared her throat a second time, patting her chest as if she could whip the humor into submission. "No, I'm sorry. It's been a long week. I didn't get much sleep last night, and I'm running on coffee and fumes right now. 'Chair graveyard' made me picture a chair ghost, and…" she faked a yawn, "yeah, not a lot of sleep."

"Well, I think we can all relate to the lack of sleep." SAC Keaton brushed both hands down her white dress shirt as she turned to face the whiteboard. "Looks like you got started on the Flores case. That's good. Has anything jumped out at you so far?"

Intent on giving his partner a few more moments to compose herself, Zane pushed away from the drywall as he gestured to the list of criminal organizations beside the pictures of Javier and his family. "Nothing has jumped out quite yet, but that in and of itself is enough to tell us a little about what we're dealing with. The boy, Javier, has not been in contact with his mother in weeks. And the girl, Yanira, has been missing for about forty-eight hours now. The mother hasn't heard a word about her disappearance. No ransom request or threats."

Amelia's amused outburst seemed like a distant memory as the usual sharpness returned to her eyes. "We think she was taken as collateral. We've ruled out just about everything else."

Zane nodded. "It stands to reason that whoever lured Javier to work for them and has prevented him from contacting his family might also be connected to Yanira's disappearance. The lack of a demand or ransom here is very telling. And based on the information we were given by

Vivian Kell, this looks like a classic case of forced labor trafficking."

The SAC pointed to the list of names. "And these are who you suspect so far?"

"Initial suspect list. Whittling down our focus." Zane watched Amelia from the corner of his eye. "We ruled out the D'Amato family and the Irish. Neither has any history of human trafficking. That leaves us with the San Luis Cartel, the Russians, and the Leóne family."

Keaton tapped the manila folders. "The Leóne family. That's actually what I wanted to talk to you about earlier. Before I had to go to that meeting."

If the topic of their discussion hadn't been so grim, Zane would have chuckled at the hint of irritation that crossed the SAC's face when she mentioned meetings. SAC Keaton was a former field agent, and even if she didn't come out and say it, her disdain for office politics was plain to see.

As his direct superior pulled the mesh-backed office chair closer to the table to sit, Zane made his way to the cluster of chairs beside Amelia.

In the moment of silence that followed, Zane racked his brain in an effort to figure out what Leóne related topic SAC Keaton could have come to discuss.

Had Emilio convinced one of his lawyers to file a civil suit against the Bureau? Specifically, against Amelia and Zane?

At the thought, a slew of four-letter words threatened to leave his mouth. He bit them back.

He and Amelia had been the ones to question Emilio Leóne about the time and meeting place where Brian Kolthoff—then known only as Mr. K—was slated to pick up Leila Jackson, the sixteen-year-old girl who had been kidnapped when she was twelve. According to Amelia's sources, the girl had stirred up controversy among the ranks of Emilio Leóne's prostitution ring. A prostitution ring that pimped out a number of underage girls.

Most of the underage girls they'd found at the Leóne house had run away from abusive home lives. Their stories were sad but common among street workers.

They'd fled their abusers only to wind up homeless on the streets of Chicago. To most of them, a creep like Emilio offered just enough of a hint at salvation to lure them into a life they'd likely never leave.

But then, there was Leila. Abducted in Janesville, Wisconsin on her way home from a friend's house at age twelve, she was sold into sex slavery until she matured too much for the tastes of the pedophiles who bought her. To keep their profit margin as high as possible, the traffickers had sold Leila to Emilio Leóne and his prostitution ring.

When Emilio realized Leila was too defiant to break or bend to his will, he'd auctioned her off to the highest bidder, Brian Kolthoff.

The FBI had knocked down Emilio's door only hours before Leila was about to be shipped to the enigmatic figure known as The Shark, and only Zane and Amelia's quick thinking had gotten them to the meeting.

Technically, they hadn't broken any laws in their interrogation of Emilio Leóne, but Zane wasn't quite as confident that their actions would stand up under scrutiny.

Just the thought of having a lawsuit brought against him by such a scumbag pissed him off in ways he couldn't currently express.

Clenching his jaw, Zane focused back on his boss, waiting to learn why she was here. SAC Keaton's expression was casual, even relaxed. The ire he'd expect to see if she had come to serve them with a lawsuit was nowhere to be found.

He took a deep breath and leaned back in the cushioned office chair.

The metallic squawk that followed the motion drew the sudden attention of both women in the room. Amelia's eyes were distant at first, almost as if she'd been yanked out of a trance. More than likely, she'd been contemplating the same thing as him.

With a less foul curse, he thumped the armrest with one hand. "These chairs. My god."

Though faint, a flicker of amusement passed over Amelia's face. "Chair graveyard."

SAC Keaton surprised them with a bark of a laugh. "I'll see what I can do about getting you guys some real chairs. You know how fast those types of requests move, but I'll try to speed it up a little."

Zane gingerly leaned forward, reaching for his pen on the table. Despite his effort to avoid another distraction, the chair squealed louder, exaggerating his movement, drawing out the high-pitched noise as he retrieved his pen. By the time he had reclined back, both women were glaring at him.

He shrugged in lieu of an apology. "One of my monitors broke when I was in D.C., and it took me almost two weeks to get a new one. We'll just have to get used to all this squeaking in the meantime."

Or bring a can of lubricant.

Or exchange these heinous chairs for the ones at their old desks in the middle of the night.

The corners of SAC Keaton's eyes creased as she grinned. As much as Zane respected her no-nonsense demeanor and her ability to command the attention of an entire room, he respected her for having a sense of humor almost as much.

Jasmine patted the manila folder. "So...the Leóne family. As you both know, we have unofficial task forces for the San Luis Cartel and the Russians. Each task force has two or three agents from Organized Crime, along with a few agents from the Violent and Cyber Crime divisions."

No lawsuit. Zane breathed a silent sigh of relief.

"Even though they're each technically 'unofficial,'" she raised her fingers to add the air quotes, "it's a much more cohesive approach to what we do in Organized Crime. Now, neither of you are rookies, but you're both still fairly new to this office, so I've been waiting to assign you to a task force of your own. And considering the good work you did in the Leila Jackson turned Emilio Leóne case, I think I've figured out where to put you."

"We had something like that in D.C. too." Zane glanced at Amelia. "What about Boston?"

She nodded. "Yeah, a similar system. No one was really a jack-of-all-trades. We each had our specialties."

SAC Keaton offered them an approving smile. "Good, then you're already familiar. If either of you have any objections to working on the Leóne family, then I'll certainly hear you out. My goal here isn't to stick the newbies with the shitty job. You both proved yourselves more than competent. Emilio might have only gotten a nickel, but at the end of the day, you still put away a Leóne capo."

Zane appreciated the words of praise, but it still rankled that a living turd would get away with his crimes so easily. "That's not how it feels most days, but I suppose you're right. I've got no objection." He shifted his eyes to Amelia. "What about you, Storm?"

"No objection here. What about the rest of the task force?"

"That's to be determined." SAC Keaton glanced at her buzzing phone before slipping it back into her pocket. "Once we get more of a feel for the scope of the Leónes' influence in Illinois and beyond, we'll fill in the blanks accordingly. And since you two are the first ones assigned to the task force, you'll get a say in how we proceed."

No one had mentioned money, but Zane felt like he'd just been given a promotion.

The SAC looked back and forth between them. "Any questions? Comments? Concerns?"

Scooting forward, Zane waved a hand at the whiteboard. "What about this case? How do we handle it now that we've got a specific assignment?"

As she rolled her chair away from the table, ignoring yet another squeak, SAC Keaton's gaze moved along the text and pictures that Zane and Amelia had spent the afternoon compiling. "We're sure the case belongs in Organized Crime, right?"

"Positive." Zane put all his confidence into the word. "There are too many similarities to labor trafficking to be a coincidence. Traffickers target undocumented immigrants, especially underage kids and women. Everything we've found so far fits."

SAC Keaton turned back to face them. "Okay. There hasn't been much new Leóne activity since Emilio went down. Since Vivian Kell came to you specifically, I'm giving you a week to look into the Flores case. Figure out who's behind this."

Lacing his fingers together, Zane clenched his jaw. A week to discover the criminal organization behind a forced labor trafficking ring was a hefty task, especially considering the only information they'd gathered, so far, was circumstantial. Zane didn't want to think that he and Amelia had been set up for failure, but they faced an uphill battle.

He swallowed a curse. "What happens after a week?"

"If we can figure out who's behind this, then we'll go from there. If the Russians are responsible, then we'll hand it to that task force, and if the San Luis Cartel is behind it, then we'll hand it to them."

Zane nodded slowly. "And if it's the Leónes?"

SAC Keaton's eyebrows arched as a sly smile spread across her face. "Then it's all yours."

"And what happens if we don't find out who's behind it?" Amelia's grim tone sharply contrasted the atmosphere of the room.

The SAC tapped the manila folder with an index finger. "This isn't new casework. It's a compilation of files the Bureau has kept on the Leóne family. They've been laying low since Emilio went down, but we need to use this time to our advantage. If we want to build a RICO case against them, then we need to start looking into past cases, whether they ended in a conviction or not."

The Racketeer Influenced and Corrupt Organizations Act, or RICO, gave them the ability to dig into the history of a criminal organization in order to prove a pattern of behavior. Though RICO had been used in more and more civil disputes in recent years, the statute could still be leveraged against the groups for which it was intended —the mob.

"Look." SAC Keaton folded her hands atop the table. "I know that isn't exactly what either of you want to hear. I know it sounds like you're abandoning an active case to go digging through old files, right?"

Zane and Amelia exchanged a knowing look before he responded. "Yeah, that's what it feels like."

"I get that. I was a field agent once too." She lifted a finger. "But here's the thing. We know some of what the Leóne family is involved in. We know that the longer they operate at full capacity, the more people will get caught in their web. We know people will be hurt, and we know people will die."

She was right, but passing off Javier's case after only a week's investigation still sat wrong with Zane.

Keaton gestured to the folder again. "We have an opportunity to do something about the Leóne family. Getting a

RICO case started isn't as glorious as chasing down an active lead, but in the long run, it's just as meaningful."

Silence descended over the three of them like a smothering shroud. Logically speaking, SAC Keaton was right. Shortsightedness on the part of law enforcement was part of what allowed organizations like the Leóne family to flourish. While the Bureau played whack-a-mole, the criminal enterprises adapted and altered their tactics.

Unless they adopted a long-term strategy, all the Bureau would continue to do would be to chase its tail while the Leóne family grew.

After what felt like a full fifteen minutes, Amelia's voice put a merciful end to the tense silence.

"What about Brian Kolthoff?" She looked up expectantly at SAC Keaton. "Any update on him? Or anyone who's following up on him?"

SAC Keaton pushed to her feet. "His lawyers are still throwing out roadblocks at every opportunity. But right now, it's looking like solicitation at the absolute worst. Chances are good his lawyers will whittle that away too."

Zane rubbed his temples. "How does the guy go from almost buying a sixteen-year-old sex slave to not even being slapped with a solicitation charge?"

SAC Keaton planted a hand on her hips. "I've asked myself the same question, Palmer. I'm afraid I don't have a real answer for you. And the answer I do have is probably one you already know."

"Money." Zane tempered his expression of distaste as he propped his elbows on his knees. "Money to buy a fleet of yachts with helicopters that allow him to visit each one whenever he likes." He growled low in his throat. "What about following up on it? If he was about to buy an underage sex slave, then I think odds are good he's got some other shit buried in his closet."

SAC Keaton's mouth was set in a hard line as she shook her head. "There's no follow-up. Not yet."

He opened his mouth to reply, but the SAC raised a hand to cut him off.

"There's no follow-up yet because there's no basis for one. But from what you've both found so far, there's a good chance that Kolthoff had dealt with the Leóne family before Leila came along." She pointed to the folders. *"That's* why I need the two of you to start working on a RICO case. If Kolthoff worked with them, then there has to be a trail somewhere. We find the trail and use RICO to nail his ass to the wall."

Which was exactly what Zane intended to do.

His attention shifted back to Javier and Yanira's faces on the board. He wanted to find them too. Would one week possibly be enough?

As if she was reading his mind, Keaton pinned him with her dark stare. "Remember...after a week, either hand the Flores case to the appropriate task force, or it goes to Violent Crimes. It's not ideal, and I realize that. But I trust you to do the best you can."

Zane and Amelia both nodded slowly.

With only seven days to work, Zane hoped that their best would be enough for Javier and Yanira.

5

Clasping the metal railing of the catwalk with both hands, I leaned forward to survey the warehouse floor. All the workers who had met their quotas for the day filed through to return equipment and log their work hours. Not that I cared how many hours they spent out in the fields each day, but I had to maintain some semblance of professionalism.

Even from my second-floor vantage point, I could smell the sweat and dirt that always followed them through the doors.

Forcing the foulness from my nostrils with a long exhale, I straightened and turned to face my second-in-command. "How many more are we waiting on?"

Carlo's brown eyes snapped down to the main floor. "When I was down there a minute ago, there were only about fifteen left. Matteo's got Dean helping him log their hours, so it shouldn't be much longer. Maybe ten minutes 'til they're cleared out of the building."

I hated waiting, especially in this stifling building.

Reaching to loosen my tie, I almost chuckled. It wasn't there. For a moment, I'd forgotten which life I was living.

Having two lives could become confusing, after all. One in the city and one in this filthy place. They should have been easy to distinguish, but one bled into the other from time to time.

Rather than the Armani suit I preferred when I was at home in Chicago, here, I dressed down to match the men under my command. I had to admit, as great as it felt to wear a tailored suit, I'd grown accustomed to the more casual attire I reserved for my workdays on the farm. The dark jeans, button-down plaid shirts, and work boots were far from the most stylish clothes I owned, but they were comfortable.

Carlo leaned against the sturdy handrail. "Sure would be easier if we could just deal with the slackers in front of all the other ones, you know?"

"Maybe. But in the long-term, it'd just make our jobs harder."

As Carlo nodded, I watched a woman with long, glossy black hair amble across the dusty concrete to disappear through the wide doorway. If I remembered right, her name was Ava. Mid-twenties, single, no children.

Her older sister, on the other hand, had two preteen daughters.

A few weeks earlier, one of Ava's bunkmates—desperate to return herself to my good graces after she'd failed to meet her quota for four days straight—had come to tell me that Ava planned to leave without fulfilling her contract.

Since taking over the management at this farm, I'd treated deserters with all the fire and fury that had burned inside me since I was a child.

At first, I'd been surprised by many of the workers' fortitude when confronted with their own mortality. I had to remind myself that plenty of them came from war-torn countries, and their memories of death and despair were still fresh.

But when I involved their families—their children, nieces, siblings, anyone I could find—the narrative changed.

When I'd taken Ava to the basement and presented her with her youngest niece, a sweet little thing named Camila, she begged for leniency and pleaded for no harm to come to the girl. She'd tried to claim she'd already paid her debts. When that didn't work, she offered to take her niece's place in front of the camera.

Ava Fernandez was a beautiful woman by just about anyone's standards. With her doe eyes and flawless hourglass figure, I was sure she'd drawn the attention of plenty of hot-blooded men over the years.

If I hadn't seen the way Carlo was ogling her that night, I would have turned her down. Grown women like Ava didn't make half as much money as the younger girls.

Then, of course, there was the matter of my personal preference, though Carlo didn't share the same interests as Matteo and me. Rather than pleasure, Carlo was involved in our side production to make money.

So, in a rare break from my usual mode of operation, I'd accepted Ava's plea and offered her to Carlo. As long as she made herself available to him and continued to meet her quota, her niece would remain untouched.

Once the door had clicked closed behind Ava, I returned my attention to Carlo. "It'd be easier to deal with them all at once in the short term, but it's not sustainable for the long term. If there are workers here who're productive each day, there's no point in interrupting their routine. They'll continue to be productive, and if they slip," I shrugged, "then we discipline them in front of the other problematic workers."

Lips pursed, Carlo's expression seemed oddly thoughtful. "That's true. Makes it easier to keep the place looking professional too. Chances are good none of them are going to try anything with the cops, but if they don't have anything to report, then they *definitely* won't go to the law."

I liked when people understood me right away. "Exactly. This system has been working for us for the past four years. The guy who ran this place before me did it differently, and it didn't end well for him. The boss doesn't take kindly to us drawing attention to ourselves."

The boss also didn't know about the business I conducted in the basement. Still, I was more than careful to cover my tracks.

When the girls who starred in my videos grew too old, I handed them off to the men who ran the syndicate's prostitution ring, or I put them to work in the fields. For the most part, I had no trouble molding the younger ones to be subservient.

Now and then, however, their time ended with a bullet.

As the thought crossed my mind, my gaze fell on the distant shape of Javier. For the second day in a row, he'd been lined up with the men and women who'd failed to meet quota. How was it so damn hard to de-tassel corn, pull weeds in fields of soybeans, or pick fruits and vegetables? Maybe that was why I was up here, and they were down there.

Uncrossing my arms, I clapped Carlo on the shoulder and gestured to the stairs. "Looks like Matteo's about done. Shall we?"

A faint smirk flickered over the man's unshaven face. He knew that after the punishments had been doled out, I'd let him go find Ava.

Carlo fell in beside me as we strode toward the end of the catwalk. "Hey, I forgot to ask, but how was your sister's wedding?"

I reached out for the lever door handle. "It was good, I guess. The parts I was there to witness. Everyone seemed like they were having a nice time, so I suppose that means it went well. I've never really cared about weddings one way or the other."

With a grin, Carlo raised his left hand to flash his white gold wedding ring. "Me neither, boss. Me neither."

I snorted out a genuine laugh as we started down the concrete steps. "She married up, so that's good news for me and my brother. It's a little harder for the boss to give me shit when my youngest sibling's last name is Vallerio."

Carlo nodded as we neared the landing. "Right in time too. With Emilio doing a nickel upstate, word has it that Adrian Vallerio will become the family's next capo. You used to work for Adrian, didn't you?"

"I did." I lifted my head proudly. "You know, I used to hate the guy. When I was working for him, I thought he was such an asshole. Any time he saw me or Matteo playing cards instead of working on unloading those shipments..." I snapped my fingers, "he pounced."

"Yeah. Vallerio was on us just like that too." Carlo mimed the same snapping motion with a chuckle. "It's like the guy had eyes in the back of his head."

"But now, after being in a management position for the past few years, I have to admit that I kind of like the guy, and I *definitely* respect him. He's not someone I ever want to piss off, so I'm glad his little brother is my brother-in-law now."

Carlo's laughter tapered off as we approached the set of metal double doors that led to the warehouse floor. By the time I shoved the doors open, any semblance of good humor had dissipated from both our faces.

We made our way toward Matteo and his second-in-command, Dean. Both men waited with a group of eleven workers who had been lined up along the wall. I reached behind my back to brush my fingers against the textured grip of a nine-mil. Satisfied with the weapon's presence, I stopped just short of Matteo.

I didn't even have to ask the broad-shouldered man if all the other workers had been dismissed. We'd gone through the same routine so many times over the past few years. All Matteo had to do was nod.

Sweeping my gaze over the lineup of eleven workers—seven men and four women—I waved to Dean. "Close the doors, would you?"

Dean slid one wooden door along its track and then moved to the other. A sharp crack reverberated through the space as the doors slammed into one another.

The silence that followed felt as if the warehouse itself was bracing for what was about to happen.

In the sudden absence of light, a fluorescent fixture above the double doors buzzed to life. I stepped forward to scrutinize the employees.

A few faces were familiar. Repeat offenders. They'd either stood in this line for three out of the last five days, or they'd been brought to my attention for behavioral issues other than poor work performance.

My gaze drifted to Javier.

White light caught the beads of sweat on his forehead as he tried to avoid eye contact, shifting his gaze meekly to the dusty floor.

I savored the moment, smiling as he weakly cowered for all to see. "By now, you all know why you're here, don't you?"

Satisfaction poured through me as I noticed a couple of the women exchanging nervous glances.

I slowly paced the line, stopping every few feet to issue a hard stare and enjoy the resulting terror filling a worker. Once I reached the end, I turned and began again, taking slow, measured paces that echoed around the empty warehouse. This time, I chose to stop in front of the boy. Javier. He looked as if he might faint. He'd have his time in the spotlight soon enough.

I waved a hand at the lanky man standing next to the boy. "Hector." The scared man jumped as his name echoed around the empty warehouse. I liked it when they jumped. "You have to know it's bad when I remember your name, right? How many days has it been since you hit quota?"

Hector dropped his gaze. "Si...yes, sir. I know. My leg, it is healing, yes. My numbers are getting better. Soon...very soon, I will be back to normal."

The warble in his voice fed my soul.

I paused in front of Hector and Javier. Only ten feet separated me from the group of workers, but I was flanked on either side by Matteo and Carlo. For good measure, Dean had locked the double doors and now stood beside the only exit.

Nine months had passed since the last wannabe hero had tried to fight, and part of me almost yearned for another display of obstinance. For a chance to make my position of power clear to any who thought to doubt my capabilities.

My little sister was a Vallerio now, and no one could touch me.

With an outstretched hand, I beckoned Hector forward.

His Adam's apple bobbing with a hard swallow, Hector struggled for anywhere to set his gaze. He glanced back and forth, terrified eyes shifting from Javier to another woman in line and then to the floor. Anywhere to avoid looking directly at me.

I let the silence continue unabated as Hector took his first unsteady step forward. He favored his right leg, but the injury meant little to me. I could have looked past the lower performance on account of his injury, but this week wasn't the first time he'd been short of his quota.

The man wasn't an efficient worker, and he had no family in the United States. I had no way to make money from him outside of what he contributed to the farm.

I shifted my right arm behind my back as Hector approached.

He might have been a poor worker, but he still had a purpose.

"When was the last time you met your quota for an entire week straight?"

Gesturing to his leg, Hector opened his mouth to jumble another half-assed explanation, but I cut him off with an upraised hand.

"I don't give a shit about your leg right now, Hector. Answer my question. When was the last time you met your quota for an entire week?" As I settled my grasp on the nine-mil, I waved my free hand around in circles. "Think on it, but don't take too long. I've got plans tonight."

Javier dared to look up. His momentary defiance didn't surprise me, and I met his brown eyes with a hard glare. The boy snapped his gaze away, but not before the color drained from his cheeks.

"Well?" My impatience turned the word into a growl. "You got an answer for me?"

"I-I…I'm n-not sure, s-sir." Hector wiped the sweat from his brow. "I'm g-getting older, and-and my memory isn't w-what it used to b-b-be."

His stammering explanation earned an annoyed scowl. Rage at this man's petulance ran through me as I pulled the silenced nine-millimeter free.

"How long has it been, Matteo?" I kept my gaze on the trembling man as I asked the question.

"Four weeks," Matteo responded flatly.

"A month?" I held my arms out at my sides, one hand gripping the nine-mil. "It's been a month since you met your quota. No, no. I'm sorry." My balls tightened as we drew closer to my favorite part. "It's been a month since you've done your damn job, is that right? Is that what Matteo's telling me?"

A couple of the women's eyes widened, and I thought I heard a quiet gasp. But the other ten workers remained quiet.

When faced with a gun, they were all well-behaved. I'd grant them that.

Hector's shoulders trembled as he shook his head. "No, no, I—"

"Are you calling Matteo a liar?"

The thin man's mouth gaped open. "No, of course not. But—"

"But?" I arched my eyebrows as I speared him with a look that demanded to be answered. "But what, Hector? If you can't do the job I hired you for, what good are you to me? All you're doing is bleeding me dry from having to feed you and put a roof over your head. I wouldn't keep a lame horse around, would I?"

Satisfaction shot through me as I raised the nine-mil to take aim. Right now, I was the most important person in this pitiful man's entire pitiful life. I was god. His god. From the look in his eyes, Hector recognized it too.

With a strangled cry, Hector jerked both hands up in front of his face as if the flesh and bone could stop the bullet soon to head his way. He managed a few pleas, but I paid them little attention.

"No, I wouldn't. I'd put a lame horse out of its misery."

I lined up the sights with Hector's face, enjoying the feeling of immense power as I squeezed the trigger.

Though Hector had attempted to cover his head, the bullet ripped through the heel of one hand and tore a hole just below his eye. The entry wound was no more than a circle of red, but blood and brain matter splattered the concrete at Javier's feet as the back of Hector's head exploded. Crimson droplets stained the bottoms of his jeans, as well as those of the woman next to him.

The force of the weapon's recoil buzzed up my arm, but the shot was no louder than a whisper. As the brass shell casing dropped to the ground with a metallic clink, I lowered the nine-mil and leveled my stare on the remaining workers.

"I hope my message is clear to the rest of you." I waved the silenced handgun at Hector's crumpled form. "I won't hesitate to put any of you down if you aren't doing your jobs and meeting your numbers. I'm not just some dipshit manager, and you damn well ought to know that my threats aren't empty."

Shadows moved along Javier's face as he clenched his jaw. The kid's eyes flitted between Hector's body and me.

I gestured to Hector again. "Hector didn't have any family members in the United States, and El Salvador's a hell of a drive."

Carlo's snort might have been a laugh.

"But the rest of you, you've all got family members in the States." I pointed my free hand at the woman beside Javier. "You've got a son and two daughters. Aria, Aaron, and Anna." I paused and shook my finger with mock amusement. "I see what you did there. Their names all start with A."

To her credit, the woman's expression was pinched but remained even.

"Next time." I waved at the body on the floor between us. "This'll be Aaron, you understand?" The two daughters were fourteen and sixteen—older than I preferred, but still young enough to turn a respectable profit.

As I returned the handgun to its spot behind my back, I let the space lapse into silence so the workers could digest what I'd just told them.

When I spoke again, my voice cracked through the still

air like a whip. "The three of you." I pointed to the three workers to Javier's left. "Clean this mess up." I glanced at Carlo. "Do me a favor and make sure they don't screw this up. Then go treat yourself."

An eager smile stretched across Carlo's mouth.

Chances were good Carlo would kill Ava when he finally tired of her. Even though losing a competent worker would grate on my nerves, Ava's death would mean that her niece was fair game.

"The rest of you, get the hell out of here." Javier caught my gaze as he turned to leave. "Except you."

The boy looked like a deer caught in headlights.

Circling the halo of gore around Hector's body, I clamped a hand down on Javier's shoulder and jerked him away from the remaining workers.

"I-I'm sorry." The kid swiped at the tears that threatened to spill down his cheeks.

Digging my fingers into his shoulder, I leaned forward and lowered my voice. "You remember what I told you, don't you? That your work here determines how your sister is treated? You do good work, and she's treated well, remember?"

His whole body trembled as he attempted to nod. "Yes, yes. I remember." He swallowed, and I could tell he wanted to add more. An explanation, maybe. An excuse.

Not that it mattered to me. I didn't care why he'd missed his quota for the past two days. And sob stories only shortened my patience.

Javier squeezed his eyes closed. "It won't happen again. My ribs are healing, and I'll meet my numbers tomorrow."

I flashed him a grin and shook his shoulder. "Good. You must be a quick learner because you seem to have figured out that I don't like excuses."

His head bobbed again.

Adding gravel to my voice, I tilted my head down until my mouth was level with the kid's ear. "Because if you don't meet your numbers, I'm going to hand your little sister over to Matteo when I'm done with her. And if you so much as *think* of trying to go to the cops..."

I released his shoulder and took a step back. I wasn't usually worried about any of the workers turning to law enforcement—most, if not all of them, were undocumented.

Regardless, I liked to cover all my bases with the slippery ones. More and more, I began to suspect that Javier's age and soft-spoken nature were deceptive. The kid was smarter than I had realized, and I didn't care for clever workers.

"If you try to go to the cops, or if *anyone* even thinks about going to the cops, I'll slit your little sister's throat from ear to ear. Understood?"

With another hard swallow, Javier nodded.

Turning on my heel, I walked away.

It was good to be god.

6

By the time six o'clock rolled around, Amelia had leafed through the online social media profiles of so many teenagers she felt like a crotchety old woman. She liked to share artwork and pictures through Pinterest, but otherwise, the purpose of most other platforms eluded her.

Javier Flores and his friends, however, were present on almost every social media site the internet had to offer. All Amelia wanted was to establish a timeline and a routine for the young man, but she'd waded through countless photos and posts to get there.

They were on day two of the seven they'd been allotted for the Flores investigation, and though Zane had been at her side for most of the day's slogging journey, he'd checked out a half hour earlier. Amelia had tried to tease him about a hot date, but he dismissed her playful verbal jabs with a confession of his disdain for dental checkups.

Amelia was still puzzled by the man's Friday evening plans. A dentist's office wasn't where she'd expected someone like Zane Palmer to spend the start of his weekend. With his outgoing nature and consistent upbeat demeanor, she imagined him spending his Friday nights at a bar, surrounded by friends.

On second thought, maybe she wasn't the only one whose entire life was consumed by their career.

Not that she minded. Her social life had been wrecked by ten years of military service. Still, she'd rather see her friend out having fun than living the same reclusive existence she did.

As she leaned back to stretch her legs, Amelia winced at the grating creak of her chair. Attempting to keep her body still to avoid other noises, she tapped her index finger against the armrest and turned her focus to the whiteboard.

They'd carved out separate spaces for Javier's timeline and the list of friends he interacted with most frequently online. Although social media had the potential to be a treasure trove of information, especially during a criminal investigation, she hadn't stumbled over any unexpected peculiarities on Javier's accounts.

No suspicious friends had recently been added. She found no posts about *where* Javier's new job was located. There hadn't even been a mention of the fact that he'd *gotten* a job. He hadn't updated any of his profiles in close to two months, but the timeframe lined up with what they'd been given by Vivian.

At least we can rule out Javier and his sister going on a surprise vacation.

Draping a hand over her face, Amelia groaned at the inane thought.

In truth, she wished that Javier's Instagram page had been filled with photos of him waterskiing and shotgunning beers with his friends. A party-happy sixteen-year-old was a far better alternative than one who'd been lured into a forced labor trafficking ring.

Other than confirmation of Vivian's timeline, the social media undertaking felt fruitless.

Amelia hated wasting time. In her job, less than a minute could be the difference between life and death.

On that depressing thought, Amelia rose to her feet and stretched both arms above her head. The tips of her fingers almost touched the drop ceiling.

She'd take her laptop home over the weekend and dig into Javier's online life a little more, but for the day, she had exhausted all her mental bandwidth. Her only goals for the rest of the night were to take a long, hot shower and watch television with her cat.

Once she'd tucked the matte silver laptop into its padded travel bag, she packed up her trusty tote, turned off the lights, and headed to the elevator.

For almost the entire workday, she and Zane had stuck to the repurposed interview room they'd been given by SAC Keaton. As much as Amelia hated the collection of broken office chairs that crowded one corner of the room, she'd grown fond of the privacy. Apparently, being named part of a task force came with a distinct set of benefits.

White fluorescent light glinted off the face of her watch as she double-checked the time. Amelia adored the surprisingly stylish yet practical gift her sister-in-law had given her for her twenty-ninth birthday, but she wasn't entirely happy with what the pretty watch told her.

It was six o'clock on a Friday evening. With any luck, Chicago's traffic was likely on the decline, but Amelia was in no rush to sit in her car for a forty-five-minute journey home. Even though she'd spent the day in a cramped, windowless room, she couldn't recall if she'd left any personal items at her usual desk on the sixth floor.

She shrugged to herself and jabbed the button to summon an elevator, hoping that a detour to her desk would provide enough time for the last of the brutal traffic to disappear. "Better safe than sorry."

As she waited, Amelia pulled out her phone to look for missed calls or text messages. She hadn't expected any, but she found a notification indicating that three had somehow slipped by unnoticed during the workday.

Her first thought was that Zane *really* hated visiting the dentist and that he'd sent her a series of messages to complain about his experience. But as she opened the text app and saw who had sent them, Amelia barely suppressed a groan.

They were from her sister.

Lainey had been quiet for the past few weeks, but the no-contact streak had just come to an abrupt end. Amelia only got to the second sentence of the first message before she selected all three texts and tapped the delete button.

Her heart ached with a pang of guilt, but she swallowed and pushed aside the sentiment. Amelia's younger sister might have claimed to need help leaving her boyfriend, but Lainey had played the same old song and dance for the past year and a half.

As convincing as her pleas could be, Amelia knew beyond a shadow of a doubt that each word was a lie. Lainey was an addict, and her piece of shit boyfriend was too.

Sometimes, the only way to help a loved one was to cut them off completely. Tough love. Hopefully, Lainey would one day come to a point where she could no longer stomach the person she'd become. But if Amelia enabled her financially or otherwise, that day would never arrive.

The elevator came to a halt with a cheery ding, stealing her focus away from the negative thoughts. Silver doors slid open with a mechanical hum, and Amelia charged through, nearly running straight into the man standing inside.

She barked out an embarrassed laugh before stepping to the side. "Oops...sorry."

With one hand tucked into the pocket of his black slacks, Joseph Larson held a beige folder in the other. Under the recessed lights in the elevator, his dark blond hair was closer to a caramel brown. His close-cropped cut had grown out over the past couple months, and Amelia noticed for the first time that his neatly brushed hair sported a slight wave.

As the intense expression melted away from his clean-shaven face, Amelia couldn't help but wonder what had been on his mind.

"Hey, stranger." He offered her a slight smile before hovering a thumb over the panel of buttons. "You headed out for the day?"

Amelia wrinkled her nose. "By way of the sixth floor first." The button was already lit but Joseph punched it anyway. "Thanks. Just need to check my desk before leaving. After nine hours of going through social media and public records, I'm ready to let my brain take the rest of the night off while I watch something stupid on Netflix."

He tapped the button to close the doors and chuckled. "No Friday night plans?"

"Nope."

The atmosphere inside the elevator changed when Joseph took a small step closer to her.

She met his intense gaze full-on, refusing to back away. "What? What's that look for?"

Joseph looked away, and Amelia could swear that he was feigning innocence.

Amelia wasn't in the mood for a serious conversation and decided to let humor be her friend. "I've seen that look before. The same one you use when you're about to try to convince me to eat some weird olive salad you brought to work." She raised a hand, resisting the urge to poke him in the center of his chest. "I hate olives, Larson. I *hate* them, in any form. And an entire salad made of them sounds like one of the worst things on the entire planet."

The corners of his pale eyes creased as a grin spread over his face. "No olive salad, I swear. My mom was Greek, and that's her family's recipe. I'm telling you, if there's ever going to be a time for you to like olives, it'll be eating that salad."

Amelia's lip curled into a disgusted sneer. "No. Nope. Not a chance in hell."

With a loud sigh of feigned exasperation, he threw up his hands. "Okay, Storm. Fine. I'll stop trying to share this delicious side dish with you. Even Palmer likes it, okay?"

She waved a dismissive hand. "That's because he likes olives. That guy eats at least one muffuletta sandwich a week, I swear."

Joseph crossed his arms and shrugged. "Sounds like he's got a good palate."

Until that moment, Amelia wasn't sure she'd ever heard Joseph utter a positive word about Zane. As much as she wanted to make a sarcastic observation about the almost-compliment, she wasn't ready to go down that spiral. Not at six o'clock on a Friday evening after she'd worked all week.

Brushing aside her feelings of annoyance, she returned her attention to Joseph. Before she could ask what he'd actually been contemplating, the elevator came to a stop on their floor. With another cheerful ding, the stainless-steel doors slid open.

Amelia readjusted the tote and followed Joseph out into the hall. Before she could get no more than two steps away, his hand came down on her shoulder. "Hey, you're on your way out, right? You want to go grab some food, maybe a beer or two?"

Socialization hadn't been in Amelia's plans for the night. All she'd wanted to do was veg out in front of the TV.

As if he'd sensed her trepidation, he dropped his hand back to his side. "The Cubs are playing tonight. We can go to a sports bar, and I can watch you eat a mountain of nachos again. *Without* olives."

Amelia's face warmed at the memory of just how many of those chips she managed to consume. "I didn't know a full order of super nachos was that big, okay? I'd only been back in Chicago for a couple weeks, and I'd never even heard of that restaurant before."

He grinned. "Yeah, but we were staking out a warehouse. I've never really thought nachos were good stakeout food."

He wasn't wrong. Amusement quirked at the edge of her lips. "Sometimes you've got to switch it up a little. I just figured I'd deviate from the typical burrito or sandwich. It's not my fault that order of nachos weighed three pounds."

He held up a hand as they started down the hall. "I told you to get the half order, remember? I said that their portions were massive."

"I was hungry." Amelia half shrugged. "I ate it all, didn't I?"

With a chuckle, he nodded. "That's true. Honestly, it was pretty impressive. Even I can't finish a full order of nachos from that place."

As they neared the turn that took them to the cluster of desks belonging to Organized Crime, Amelia patted her belly. "High metabolism. I think it might be starting to slow down, though. Or maybe it's just the combination of me slacking on my workouts and all this Chicago food I missed when I was in the military."

Joseph flashed her a knowing smile. "Don't worry. It happens to the best of us."

Amelia came to a stop beside her desk and ran through her options.

She didn't *want* to go anywhere other than home, but at the same time, she didn't want to blow off her only work friend aside from Zane. Besides, what had she planned to eat for dinner? She was in no mood to cook, so odds were good she'd either order takeout or toss another frozen pizza in the oven.

"Okay." She added a smile to give the illusion that she hadn't just agonized over her decision. "Where do you want to meet up? I've got to go home and feed my cat first."

His face brightened, and he held up the manila folder. "I've got a couple things to finish up before I leave, anyway. How about Madison's? I remember you saying you'd been there before. Something about their cheese curds, if I recall."

The man had the memory of an elephant. "I don't remember that conversation, but I have been there before. And the comment about cheese curds sounds like something I'd say. They *are* really good."

He reached out a hand and gently grazed her forearm with the very tips of his fingers. "So, Madison's then? Seven-thirty or eight?"

The hairs on the back of her neck prickled to attention, and Amelia wondered if the rush of anxiety was due to her being sorely out of practice in social situations or if her subconscious was throwing up a warning signal.

She shrugged away from his reach and took a quick peek at her watch to make sure she'd have enough time. "Let's split the difference and make it seven forty-five. I'll see you there."

THOUGH VIVIAN KELL had worked from home for the past two days, she still rejoiced in the day's end as she submitted her most recent article for *The Chicago Standard*.

The Standard had once been a newspaper, but the owners hadn't hesitated to move into the digital realm to keep up with the times.

Thanks to their penchant for embracing change rather than fighting it, *The Standard* had retained its entire workforce while other newspapers had been forced to lay off hundreds of reporters. Vivian was thirty-four, and she'd landed her position at *The Standard* just before the news world was rocked by the full force of the digital age.

Glancing around her little home office, she blew out a long sigh.

Her boss, Charles Langbourne, was flexible with their work from home policy, but Vivian couldn't help but feel she'd betrayed Chuck's trust. She'd cited bad allergies as her reason to stay home the last couple of days, but in truth, she was almost too anxious to leave her apartment.

Chewing her bottom lip, her vacant stare drifted to the waning sunlight piercing through the room's only window, and she slumped down in her chair.

She hadn't told Chuck about Mari Flores or the woman's two missing children. In fact, aside from Vivian's long-time friend and coworker, Felicia, she hadn't told anyone.

Well, anyone aside from the FBI.

Vivian cringed at the memory. Mari had pleaded with her not to go to the police, but Vivian hadn't taken long to determine that finding the woman's missing children was far more than she could handle alone.

Gut instinct told her that Javier and Yanira were in trouble, and since she couldn't help them, she turned to someone who could, the FBI.

Each time Mari's pleading voice echoed in her head, a wave of guilt and anxiety threatened to drown Vivian. She picked up her mug, wishing the Chai tea were something stronger.

Sooner rather than later, she would have to call Mari to tell her that the Federal Bureau of Investigation had taken on

Yanira and Javier's case. She'd need to be sober for that conversation.

After a deep breath, she sipped the tea and turned back to her two monitors. In a couple clicks, she pulled up the body of a piece she'd started almost six months earlier.

Returning the mug to its spot beside her glowing keyboard, Vivian propped both elbows on the wooden desk.

Like the contact from Mari Flores, the only person who had seen the piece was her friend Felicia. As a seasoned investigative journalist, Felicia knew the dangers of prematurely publishing a controversial article.

Even now, Vivian thought she'd be better off if she published the piece independently. At least then, *The Standard*—her employer of almost twelve years—wouldn't be raked over the coals if the article ruffled the wrong feathers.

For six long months, she'd dug into the nitty-gritty of a national labor contractor, Premier Ag Solutions, LLC. Premier specialized in farm labor, and their services were utilized by a number of mid-sized agricultural businesses, as well as a handful of industry giants.

Among Premier's largest clients was Happy Harvest Farms, Incorporated, a multi-billion-dollar company that produced food, ethanol, and seeds that were sold worldwide.

At the helm of the corporation was Illinois Senator Stan Young.

To avoid the appearance of a conflict of interest, Young had handed control of Happy Harvest Farms over to his oldest son when he'd first taken office. The entire gesture was a farce, but the leadership change had been enough to appease the United States Senate.

After twelve years in investigative journalism, Vivian didn't often buy into massive conspiracy theories. But with Premier Ag Solutions, the so-called rabbit hole never ended.

According to her most trusted source—senatorial candidate and former immigration lawyer Ben Storey—the executives of Premier Ag Solutions stuck their hands into more cookie jars every year. Aside from the usual influence on local and national politics, Premier had been fined on three separate occasions for their negligence in vetting their workers' citizenship.

All three instances had gone virtually unnoticed by the American public. In fact, Vivian doubted that the average citizen even knew Premier Ag Solutions existed, much less their seedy business model.

Vivian was no forensic accountant, but Premier's profit margins were almost double that of their competitors. Competitors who hadn't been powerful enough to escape being fined for unlawful employment of undocumented immigrants.

The profits themselves were suspect, but when she added the recounts of Ben's clients, Vivian painted a grim picture of the labor contractor.

On some level, Premier profited from forced labor trafficking.

Even if the company didn't actively house labor trafficking rings—and Vivian hadn't ruled out the possibility—they recruited a significant portion of their workers from forced labor traffickers.

The evidence went beyond mere conspiracy theory. Between Ben Storey's clients' personal experiences with the company, the inconsistencies in Premier's yearly tax reporting, and their heavy-handed method of navigating American politics, there was clearly more to Premier Ag Solutions than met the eye.

In spite of all the red flags that cloaked Premier Ag Solutions, the purpose of Vivian's article wasn't necessarily to delve into the criminal element of the business.

All she wanted to do was shed light on the sleazy business

practices in order to garner support for legislation to regulate the industry. She was sure that such a policy would earn support from both sides of the political aisle, but first, she had to make sure that Americans knew about the problem.

Rubbing her eyes, Vivian stifled a yawn. She still had one more thing to do before she could call it a day.

She hated to let people down, and she hated to betray someone's confidence even more. Especially when that someone already had to deal with the sudden disappearance of both her children. But it was time to deliver the bad news to Mari and let the poor woman know she'd broken her promise to keep Yanira and Javier's disappearances to herself.

Had Vivian not spent six months looking into a corporation with ties to labor trafficking, she might not have recognized Javier's predicament for what it was. In fact, chances were good she'd have kept the case to herself.

In hindsight, maybe she should have.

She didn't know for sure that Premier was behind Javier's so-called job, but the possibility was real. If she'd conducted her own investigation, she could have included a criminal element in her article. Then she'd be sure to capture the attention of the average citizen.

Now that the FBI had taken over, the details would be shrouded in the bureaucratic red tape of the justice system. Chances were good that she'd never learn the specifics of the investigation.

She flattened both hands against the wooden desktop.

"No." She shook her head. "No, I can't think like that. I did the right thing. Agent Storm and Agent Palmer have guns and badges, not to mention some of the most comprehensive databases in the entire world. I'm just one person. If Yanira and Javier are in danger, they need to be the first priority."

As she took in a deep breath, she repeated the mantra in

her head. It wasn't her job to save the world, and asking for help didn't make her weak. There were some problems Vivian couldn't solve on her own and others that she couldn't solve at all.

She reached for her cell at the base of one monitor.

Rip the band-aid off. Don't sit here and look at the phone for half an hour. It's already quarter 'til nine. If you sit here and agonize over this, you'll never get ahold of her before she goes to bed.

Swallowing against the barren desert in her mouth, Vivian unlocked the screen and pulled up Mari's contact information. Even though she kept her air-conditioning at a comfortable seventy-three degrees, a sheen of sweat had made its way to her forehead.

Before she could spiral into the abyss of what-ifs and doubt, she dialed the woman's number.

On the third ring, the line clicked to life.

"*Hola.*" Mari's voice was thick with sleep, and a new pang of guilt burned its way through Vivian's chest.

Great. I woke her up.

Vivian cleared her throat. "Hi, Mari. It's Vivian Kell. I'm so sorry, did I wake you?"

"*Nō nō.* It's okay." The tired drawl had all but disappeared as she switched from Spanish to thick English. "I fell asleep too early. I still must get things done. Thank you for waking me."

Vivian shoved her hair back from her face. "Okay, that's good. I still feel a little bad, but I'm glad it works out okay for you."

Mari's chuckle was equal parts strained and tired. "*No me importa.* Have you found anything? Is that why you are calling?"

As Vivian swallowed, she could have sworn her throat

was lined with gravel. "Well, yes and no. I have to tell you something first, though."

"*Dios mío!*" Mari's voice was pinched with worry. "What is it?"

"I think that Javier and Yanira were taken by traffickers. I don't know who, and to be honest, there's no real way for me to find out."

When Mari didn't reply right away, Vivian forged ahead.

"But I took the case to someone who *can* find out. Someone who *will* find out." Though her life revolved around words, she had difficulty with them now. "If we're dealing with traffickers, and I'm almost one-hundred-percent sure we are, then it needs to be reported to the right people. Because Javier isn't the only person they've hurt, and they'll keep hurting more people until someone stops them."

She thought she heard Mari's swallow over the phone. "Who?"

"The FBI is looking for Javier and Yanira now." Vivian's voice had become quiet, almost solemn.

In the silence that followed, Vivian went as far as to pull the phone away from her ear to check that the connection hadn't been lost. Or, rather, to ensure Mari hadn't hung up on her.

But the call timer ticked away, and as the seconds wore on, the tension in Vivian's muscles grew.

After more than a full minute, Mari broke the silence. "Do you think a cartel took them? *Por favor querido dios, no.* I have read about them. *El Cartel de San Luis* from *México.*"

Running a hand through her shoulder-length hair, Vivian shook her head. "I don't know, Mari. I'm sorry. But if a cartel did take them, then it is best we let the FBI investigate. Cartels can be extremely dangerous."

"I know, I know." Mari's voice trembled. "You are right,

and I see you are doing your best. But, I worry. Will I have to speak to them? The FBI people?"

Vivian couldn't imagine living with so much worry.

"No, I don't think so. I told them everything you told me, so they'd have no real reason to come question you. If they want to talk to you, they can contact you through me, okay? Until then, if you can, keep staying somewhere else. That way you won't have to worry about the traffickers or the FBI."

"*Ojalá*." A portion of the energy was back in Mari's voice. "Okay. I am not in my home. I ask my friend if I can keep staying here."

"Good, I'm glad to hear that." Vivian paused, releasing a heavy sigh that carried no relief. "And Mari...I'm really sorry. I just didn't think there was any way I could find them on my own. And, well, I know this isn't what you want to hear, but I think they're in danger."

Mari's breath hitched, and the phone went silent for a moment before the woman responded. "I understand." There was so much sadness and fear in those two words. "I try to ignore my mother's instinct, but it tells me the same thing. I pray, *Ave María purísima*, the FBI people will find my *bebés*."

Tears burned like acid in Vivian's eyes.

"Me too, Mari. Me too."

7

As Joseph reached for the fresh pint glass, a flicker of movement drew his attention to the entrance at the other end of the dim bar. In spite of the wall-spanning series of windows to his right, the dark tint blocked out all but a fraction of the waning sunlight. The glass door swung open to admit the newest patron to Madison's Sports Bar, and Joseph's pulse quickened.

He'd half-expected Amelia to text him with a last-minute cancellation, but he knew he shouldn't have worried. From what he'd gathered in the year and a half they'd known one another, Amelia stayed true to her word. If she said she was going to do something, she did it. Even if it was something she found unpleasant.

Did she find him unpleasant too?

He scoffed, knowing he was just being ridiculous now. They were friends.

Pushing her sunglasses up to rest on the top of her head, Amelia's green eyes flicked over the tables and booths until she spotted him. Joseph raised two fingers from his glass and tried not to look too eager to see her.

With a quick wave, Amelia weaved her way across the dark wooden floor. The hem of her burgundy shorts ended less than halfway down her thigh, and as she moved, threads of gold fabric shimmered in her loose-fitting t-shirt.

On the side of one thigh, he caught the shape of a tattoo, though he couldn't make out the details in the low light. Dark brown bangs framed her pretty face, and in the amber light, he thought he spotted a streak of blonde in the braid that ran from her temple to the band of her ponytail.

Ever since he'd first seen her in shorts, he'd wondered what it would feel like to run a hand up the smooth skin of her legs. Then higher. Everywhere. Explore her sweet...

Taking a long drink from the glass in his hand, he pushed the notion out of his head. Amelia was a keen observer, and unless he wanted to get caught in an awkward lie, he'd be best served by keeping the racy thoughts at a safe distance for the rest of the night.

Well, at least for the rest of their time at Madison's. Who knew where the night would take them after they left the sports bar.

As Amelia set down her handbag and slid into the cushioned booth, Joseph pushed a second pint glass toward her side of the table.

"I couldn't remember what you drink, so I just got you one of these." He held up his glass for emphasis. "It's a seasonal summer brew, made right here in Chicago."

Setting her phone atop the wooden table, she reached for her glass. "Thanks. Yeah, I love trying new craft beers, especially the local ones. They're flavorful, especially compared to the standard beers on tap."

He leveled a finger at her. "Hey, let's not knock the staples, okay?"

She scrunched up her nose. "No, actually, I think I will.

That basic stuff does not get along with my stomach. Or my taste buds, for that matter."

Chuckling into the pint glass, he took another drink. "Okay, okay. Let's just put that subject to rest before someone's feelings get hurt."

"Your feelings, maybe." Amelia gave him a quick wink to let him know she was teasing before raising the glass to her lips. She took a slow sip and let the liquid roll around in her mouth before swallowing. Another much quicker sip followed. "This is good. Thanks again."

He forced himself to look away as she licked foam from her upper lip. "No problem."

She set down the glass and cast an awkward glance at her shirt before looking up to meet his eyes. With a heavy sigh, Amelia folded her arms on the wooden table.

Joseph lifted an eyebrow, wondering at her puzzled expression. "What?"

She gestured back and forth between them. "I feel like I'm really underdressed right now. I didn't figure you'd still be in work clothes. You know, with the suit and tie and whatnot."

He tried to suppress his grin but failed. "It's not my usual style when I'm headed to a sports bar, but I didn't have time to stop at home and change." He lifted a finger. "But, if it makes you feel weird, I can try to dress down a little."

The puzzled expression deepened, though a smile tweaked at the corners of her mouth. "Do you need to go find a phone booth so you can change?"

Joseph froze midway through shrugging out of his black suit jacket. Now, it was his turn to fix her with a puzzled glance. "A...phone booth?"

Though slight, a touch of color rose to her cheeks. "Oh. Never mind, sorry. That was a weird joke. I meant a phone booth because that's where Clark Kent would change into his Superman cape."

"Oh." He felt like a moron for not catching the reference immediately but tried to play it off. "I was always more of a Batman kind of guy."

Grinning, Amelia lifted her beer and began to sing the *na-na, na-na, na-na, na-na* part of the *Batman* theme song.

Hating himself, Joseph shrugged free from his suit jacket. "Okay, got rid of that. Now the corporate noose."

As he loosened the black and silver tie, Amelia's expression brightened. "You really don't have to do that. It was just unexpected. I won't care how you're dressed once I have a pile of nachos and a basket of cheese curds in front of me."

"No, it's okay." He unbuttoned his cuffs. "I really hate wearing a tie anyway. If I hadn't been in a hurry to get out of the office, I would have taken it off before I got here."

In the middle of rolling up the sleeves of his white dress shirt, a young woman stopped by the table to ask if they planned to order. True to her word, Amelia requested an order of nachos and cheese curds. Though not much healthier than Amelia's artery hardening selections, Joseph opted for a burger and fries instead.

Once both sleeves were tucked in place at his elbows, Joseph spread his hands. "Okay, this is about as casual as I can get, unless I take off my shirt."

But it'd be better if you could take it off for me.

Kicking aside the unsolicited imagery, he plucked at the white fabric. "But they might kick us out if I do."

Amelia's laugh was more like a snort. "That's true. Better safe than sorry."

Rubbing the military tattoo on the inside of his forearm, Joseph met her forest-green eyes. "You have a tattoo on your leg. I've never noticed it before."

She shifted in her chair and crossed her legs. The question made her uncomfortable. He didn't have a problem with that.

She recovered quickly. "Well, that's because I don't usually wear shorts to work."

He raised both hands in surrender. "No, of course you don't. If you did, you'd get hypothermia and die. The Bureau keeps that place at a frosty ten-below-zero."

The tension in her shoulders appeared to ease, and she took another sip of the brew. "Exactly. I'm glad I'm not the only one who's noticed." She paused, glancing down at her side. "I got it while I was still in the military. It's a panther."

After one last drink, he pushed his glass toward the edge of the table. "Is there a story behind it?"

"Does there need to be?"

He was instantly annoyed. Why did all women have to be so touchy?

Joseph forced a smile. Maybe he was feeling a little touchy too. "No, I guess not. I don't really have a story for this one." He patted his arm. "Just that I was in the military."

Try as he might, he couldn't tell if the way Amelia's mouth lifted at one corner was sarcastic. "I've never really been one of those people who think that every tattoo has to have a story. None of mine have stories, aside from this one." She pushed up her sleeve and gestured to the tiger lily on the inside of her bicep. "You might not be able to see it, but right here," she pointed to the foremost petal, "says 'sisters.' My sister-in-law, Joanna, has the same tattoo on the inside of her left forearm."

"You have more than just those two?" He raised his eyebrows, hopeful to see a little more of her body.

Leaning back in the booth, she lifted a shoulder. "Sure. You can blame Joanna. She's got a full back piece and an entire sleeve, plus a whole bunch of others."

He propped both elbows on the table and leaned forward. "Really? I had no idea you even had one tattoo, let alone several."

This time, he knew without a doubt that her crooked little smile was sarcastic. "I know you didn't. That's because I made sure I could cover them all with a t-shirt and jeans."

He could have taken her subtle rebuff as a personal affront, but instead, a smile crept to his lips.

Amelia Storm was physically attractive, but her quick wit and strong will put her on an entirely new level.

Though Joseph was confident in his looks, and though his two ex-wives could have passed for models, he couldn't help but wonder if Amelia was unattainable for him.

As she turned her head, he took the opportunity to let his eyes drift down the front of her semi-sheer shirt. She wore a camisole top underneath, but the shape of her body was still clearly defined.

Joseph's normal mode of operation didn't include lusting after women in the FBI office. His last fling with one of the pretty forensic analysts hadn't ended well.

Michelle…damn.

He and she hadn't been on the same page. He'd operated under the assumption that their relationship wasn't exclusive. They'd meet up at her place or his place a couple nights a week, drink a little, order takeout, and have sex. In his mind, the writing on the wall was clear—they were just fuck buddies.

So, when he'd started to spend the occasional night with a bartender from a trendy spot downtown, he hadn't felt as if he was in violation of a social contract.

Needless to say, the forensic analyst had discovered pictures of the other woman on his phone when he'd made the mistake of letting her use it to order food. If the bartender hadn't picked that exact moment to send a text message, who knew what bizarre turn their relationship would have taken.

But Amelia was different.

She was his peer.

Just because they were off the clock didn't change that little fact. He needed to be smooth. He needed to be careful. To that end, he made sure to pull his eyes away from her chest before Amelia's gaze returned to him.

No, she wasn't unattainable. He'd just have to work a little harder than usual.

She was his. She just didn't know it yet.

AS THE FIRST breath of night air washed over her, Amelia was grateful to feel the clammy late July humidity on her skin. Tightening her grip on the Styrofoam to-go box, she glanced at the man at her side.

Before tonight, she'd viewed Joseph Larson as a close work friend.

Back during her rookie days in the FBI's Boston field office, she and Larson had worked a drug trafficking case together. The suspects had ties to Chicago and Boston, so both FBI offices had combined forces to conduct the investigation.

Despite her and Joseph's obvious differences—namely Joseph's taste in music compared to hers—they'd gotten along from the start.

They shared the same brand of oddball sarcastic humor and were both dedicated to their work at the FBI. Though in recent months, Amelia had a progressively more difficult time appreciating Joseph's sense of humor.

Maybe the pressure of the last couple investigations had gotten to him. Maybe he needed a vacation, or maybe he'd needed a night away from all things FBI. She still wasn't sure.

Tonight had been like old times…mostly.

For the two hours they'd spent at Madison's Sports Bar,

Joseph had reverted to a version of the man she'd met in Boston. She should have been glad to see her friend's good spirits return, to see him animated in a way that wasn't brooding or irritable.

But Amelia hadn't missed Joseph's lingering glances when he thought she wasn't looking at him, nor had she been oblivious to the lust-filled glint in his pale eyes. She was almost thirty, and she'd dealt with the creepy stares of plenty of men in her life.

Years of experience had taught her to tell an innocent glance from the roguish leers of men trying to undress her with their eyes. Over the past two hours, Joseph had firmly placed himself in the latter category.

In a normal friendship, she would have been tempted to broach the topic, face it head-on, right there on the sidewalk outside the sports bar. And she wouldn't have cared if she embarrassed him or if their conversation was overheard.

Joseph wasn't a normal friend, though.

He'd been an important part of her transfer to the Chicago field office—to her *home*. If Larson hadn't stepped in to put in a good word for her with SAC Keaton, Amelia's return to Illinois would have taken much longer.

Maybe she was just paranoid. Maybe her lack of socialization over the past decade had left her unable to tell a friendly interaction apart from a man's effort to take her home with him.

Even as the rationalization occurred to her, she knew the truth. Amelia swallowed a resigned sigh. She knew what she'd seen in Joseph's leering gaze. She'd felt the weight of his eyes on her since the moment she'd walked into the damn bar.

As Joseph scanned the parking lot, Amelia unzipped her handbag. She was exhausted, and her goal was to get the hell out of here before he thought to make an awkward advance.

She could think up a gentle way to let him know she wasn't interested after she got home safely. Otherwise, the next time she caught him leering at her chest or her butt, she'd be liable to tell him to go to hell.

Joseph's pale eyes returned to hers. His hand came up behind her and rested on top of her shoulder, his fingers digging lightly into her skin.

Amelia shrugged away from the contact, pretending to dig her keys from the bag. *What the hell?* Clamping her hand around the fob, she feigned a pleasant expression as guilt and worry gnawed at the back of her mind.

Had she misinterpreted his intentions for inviting her out tonight? Would she come across as cold if she confronted him?

What if I do and I'm wrong?

Amelia struggled to keep her smile from faltering. At the same time, his gaze made her wish she'd worn a snowsuit or a pair of coveralls instead of her usual summer attire.

She sensed she was about to lose the battle to maintain her amiable expression and quickly turned her gaze out to the rows of parked cars.

Before she could offer a polite goodbye, Joseph's voice cut through the relative stillness.

"If you want, there's a pretty nice rooftop bar a few blocks from where I live." He reached out again, this time aiming for the to-go box in her hand. "You could put your food in my fridge, and you wouldn't have to worry about driving home."

For a split-second, Amelia was convinced she had fallen asleep back at the FBI office, and her interaction with Joseph was either a dream or a new installment of *The Twilight Zone*.

Blinking away the haze of disbelief, she yanked her hand and the to-go box from his reach and took two automatic steps back. Lifting her chin, she met his gaze. "Excuse me. Is that a not-so-subtle way of getting me to go home with you?"

The words tumbled from her lips before she could rethink the question.

So much for a gentle letdown.

Though she hadn't intended to blurt out such a direct question, she maintained her unwavering stare. If she had looked away, she would have missed the fleeting hint of entitled annoyance that passed over his face.

There it is.

It had only been a split-second, but she'd caught the feigned shock in his widening eyes. The confirmation that she wasn't crazy. That the man she'd considered a friend for over a year was interested in no more than what was between her legs.

With a nervous laugh, he held up both hands and shook his head. "No, no. I'm sorry. I didn't mean for it to sound like that. I just…" He raked a hand through his light brown hair. "That did sound bad, didn't it? I'm sorry."

She appreciated the apology but only nodded in reply. If she tried to formulate a response, she was sure the reply would be filled with four-letter words.

Heaving a sigh, he lifted a shoulder. "It's a new bar, and I haven't been there yet because…well…I don't enjoy going to fancy places like that by myself. If I'm going to drink alone, I'll go to a dive, you know?"

She kept her expression carefully blank. "I go to bars and restaurants by myself all the time. It's not as bad as it sounds. You should try it sometime." Though she was convinced that her friend and fellow agent had just tried to play her, she hoped she'd kept most of the annoyance out of her tone. They still needed to work together after all.

He scratched at his temple. "I think I might do that right now, actually. Go get good and toasted and forget about that time I accidentally asked you to go home with me."

The task was Herculean, but Amelia managed a placating

smile. "Don't beat yourself up about it. It is what it is. Was it awkward? Yes. Will it make a funny story to gossip about in the breakroom on Monday? Most definitely."

She could only hope she was better at playing off her anger than Joseph was at pretending to be embarrassed.

"Yeah, that's true. I guess I just didn't think it'd come across that way since we're friends." Keys jingled as he dug in his pocket. "Maybe we don't tell the guys at work, though."

When she was younger, she might have been stricken with a wave of guilt at his simple explanation. But tonight, she saw the manipulative tactic for what it was.

Gaslighting.

He wanted her to feel bad for the alleged misinterpretation.

Amelia ignored the remark altogether. "It's okay. Miscommunications happen." She gestured to the parking lot. "I'm going to call it a night and head home."

He made a show of avoiding eye contact with her. "Fair enough. Drive safe."

"You too. See you at work, Larson."

As she turned to make her way to her distant parking space, she readjusted the handbag on her shoulder. She could sense Joseph's lingering gaze on her back, but she didn't turn around until she reached her car.

With one last wave, she fell into the driver's seat, closed the door, and groaned. She held in the slew of expletives until she could no longer see the bar's sign in her rearview mirror.

Smacking the steering wheel with the palm of one hand, she spat out so many four-letter words that she half-expected the Electronic Software Rating Board to magically appear in her passenger seat and slap an M rating on her forehead.

The entire drive back to her Lincoln Park apartment was a blur. Almost all her focus had been spent on checking to ensure she hadn't been followed while belting out the words to an angry song she'd picked up from Zane's playlist. She hardly paid any attention to the road itself.

Though she wasn't in pursuit of a suspect or in the midst of a combat zone, her brain had reverted to the state of hyperawareness she reserved for either of those two dangerous situations.

As she strode up the sidewalk to the entrance of her gray stone apartment building, her eyes danced along the shadows that cloaked the grassy courtyard.

When a dog in a ground-floor apartment barked, Amelia's muscles tightened as adrenaline rushed through her veins. With a deep breath to steady her frayed nerves, she hurried inside, up a set of stairs, and into the quiet darkness of her second-floor apartment.

After she'd locked the deadbolt and set the chain in place, she stepped out of her canvas shoes, strode across the cool hardwood of the living room, and set her handbag at the edge of the breakfast bar.

A blur of white, orange, and black appeared in the short hallway just past the kitchen. Pausing mid-stride to stretch, Hup's luminescent eyes shone in the meager glow of the stovetop light.

Giving herself a mental shake, Amelia massaged her temples in an effort to relax some of the tension. "I knew I should have stayed home with you instead."

Hup's reply was a meow that sounded closer to a chirp.

"You're right. I should always choose the cat over social situations." Amelia rested both hands on her hips. "This is how it starts, isn't it? This is how I become a crazy cat lady?"

In response, Hup rubbed against her mistress's legs.

Since the cat was being a good listener, she continued to rant. "I didn't know Joseph was like that. How dare he try and lay a finger on me. The nerve."

Hup rolled over, showing her furry belly in a plea for attention.

She narrowed her eyes. "No. I did not invite him to pet me."

The little furball was relentless. She batted her paws in the air and let out a loud mewl as her bright green eyes locked on to Amelia.

How could she resist such a request? The anger and anxiety beginning to drain from her, Amelia knelt and ruffled the fur of Hup's belly. "Maybe that's why he's a dick to Zane and not to me. He didn't want to have sex with Zane, but—"

She left the sentiment unfinished and groaned.

Her and Joseph? For a moment, she allowed her mind to even consider the two of them being together. His hair soft between her fingers. His lips on...

Nope.

She couldn't get any further than that.

Bile actually churned in her belly at the thought.

There was more to Amelia's paranoia than just the realization that a man wanted to sleep with her. She'd turned down men in the past, and seldom did the conversation elicit such a visceral reaction.

But visceral was the only way to describe her sudden bout of anxiety.

"Maybe I'm overreacting." Amelia dropped her hand to her side and looked down to Hup. "Maybe the whole Leila Jackson case just still has me on edge. Dealing with an underage prostitution ring will do that to a lady, right?"

Hup rolled to her side and started grooming one of her white paws.

Amelia's stomach twisted as a realization settled into her thoughts. The nagging sensation had been in her mind all along, but until now, she'd worked to push it deeper into the recesses of her psyche.

Her sixth-grade history teacher, Mr. Davids.

The unease that had threatened to overwhelm her all night was the same trepidation that had rung so many alarm bells in her head almost two decades ago.

Mr. Davids had offered her an opportunity to stay late after school to earn extra credit, but Amelia had declined. Her grades had been terrible at the time, but for reasons that had eluded her eleven-year-old brain, Mr. Davids had made her skin crawl.

As she discovered a year or so later, her anxiety about Mr. Davids had been well founded.

Trust your instincts.

The old adage was among the few pieces of worthwhile advice she'd received from her father during his days of binge drinking.

In sixth grade, she'd come within an inch of falling victim to a child predator. Her history teacher at the time had been a normal guy. The students adored him, and parents spoke highly of their interactions with him in parent-teacher conferences.

Beneath the polished veneer was a predator—a wolf in sheep's clothing, as the saying went. When the FBI had broken down Mr. Davids's door, they'd discovered evidence that he'd abused hundreds of children over the course of ten years, many of whom had been his students.

Amelia swallowed in an effort to rid her mouth of a sudden bitterness.

Her brain was overreacting.

Just because Joseph had made a very clumsy pass at her didn't mean he was anything like Mr. Davids. Chances were good that Joseph was a prick, but he wasn't a predator.

The FBI ran some of the strictest background checks of

any employer in the country. If Joseph had a pattern of abusive behavior, the Bureau would have noticed.

Amelia headed to her bathroom and turned on the cold water in the sink. Tonight was only the second time she'd been in Joseph's company outside of work, so it was no small wonder she hadn't picked up on his boorish behavior until now. But she had his number. She would not give him another opportunity to come on to her again.

Blinking down at Hup, Amelia pulled her shirt off and examined the faint red dots on her skin where Joseph's hand had tightened on her shoulder. She hadn't just overreacted. He'd actually been forceful. The marks pissed her off.

"I've got that asshole's number now," she told Hup when she jumped up on the counter and started batting the stream of water with her paw. "I won't be giving him another opportunity to manhandle me again. Mark my words, Hup. Joseph's a douche. No wonder Zane doesn't like him."

Back arched, the longhaired calico stretched both front paws out in front of herself.

Joseph was an asshole, and that was all.

Maybe if Amelia repeated the phrase enough, she'd eventually believe herself.

8

The weekend passed uneventfully, but Monday thrust Agents Palmer and Storm back on the clock. They only had a few more days to get to the bottom of the Flores case. After going through social media accounts failed to provide them leads, Zane suggested he and Amelia try to meet some of Javier's friends in person to see what they knew about the summer job.

Zane eased his foot down on the brake as the traffic light switched to red. Squinting at the rusted Chevy Cavalier that had just sped through the intersection, he leaned back in his seat and sighed. He and Amelia had followed the sedan for close to forty-five minutes as the driver made several stops to pick up four teenagers.

Several of the kids lived with parents or relatives whose citizenship was questionable. Since their goal was cooperation and not intimidation, rather than visit each kid's house to ask them about the missing young man, Zane and Amelia chose to meet the kids on neutral territory outside of their homes. As long as they were careful to let the teenagers know that they were only there to ask for help to find Javier, the interaction wouldn't be in violation of any ethical or legal boundaries.

Zane turned to Amelia, who sat gazing at her phone in the passenger seat of his Acura. "You're sure they're going to the mall, right? Because they've just been driving around for almost an hour."

Amelia looked up wearily from the small screen in her hand. "Yeah, I'm sure. I spent all day Friday looking through Javier's friends on social media, and a group of them regularly check in at the Upper Ridge Mall."

Zane knew from their social media pages that they normally rode together, and that the driver was almost always a kid named Martin, which was why he and Amelia had staked out his house early that morning.

Rubbing a small patch of stubble he missed while shaving that morning, Zane nodded. "Kids from the city heading out to the burbs to hang out at the mall. Been there, done that."

Though he expected a sarcastic comment, a joke, or even a question about his high school years, Amelia remained silent. He'd grown so accustomed to their banter that he couldn't help but feel like they were working together for the first time.

He looked back to the road as the light changed to green. "Are you okay?"

In the short silence that followed, he braced himself for a rebuff that could have been a middle finger, a reminder of how her personal life was none of his business, or just a weary groan.

She pushed a piece of hair behind one ear. "Why would you think I wasn't?"

He tapped his thumbs on the steering wheel. "Because we've been stalking a bunch of teenagers, and there are at least fifty jokes you could have made about it by now. But I haven't heard a single one of them." Resting a hand over his heart, he spared a glance to her. "That's why I offered to drive, Storm. I knew you'd need all your brainpower to think up puns and references to early 2000s horror movies."

As the start of a smile crept to her lips, cautious relief edged its way into his thoughts.

Before she could speak, he held up the same hand he'd rested over his heart. "If you don't want to talk about it, you don't have to. Nothing wrong with that. But if you do, you know…you can. No judgment either way."

With a sigh, Amelia's head fell back against the headrest. "Thank you. You're so…boundary respecting." She rubbed the bridge of her nose. "Have you ever considered giving lessons?"

What the hell? Of all the compliments he'd received from Amelia Storm, a remark about respecting personal boundaries was unusually personal and shockingly unexpected. How many people in her life had failed her in that way?

Before he was forced to come up with a response, he gestured to the familiar Cavalier a block or so ahead of them. "There they are. We've got a little ways to go to the mall still, maybe ten minutes. But this is the quickest way to get there, so I think it's safe to say that's where they're going."

She laughed. "Are you going to ignore my question?"

So much for ducking and weaving around their previous subject. He shrugged. "I just have a healthy respect for personal boundaries, no lessons necessary. I figured it was something everyone ought to do."

She chuckled and propped an elbow on the doorframe. "You'd be surprised. Friends are usually well-meaning when they push those boundaries. You know, asking what's bothering you or trying to get you to talk about something you don't want to talk about. Friends and family usually mean well, but it's still frustrating."

Zane hadn't ever really thought about it too much. "It's

nice to know that you can talk to someone if you want to, that those friends and family are there if needed. For most people, anyway."

Twisting a piece of dark hair around her finger, Amelia blew out a breath that made her lips flutter. "Can I ask your opinion on something?" She paused and sucked her bottom lip in between her teeth. "I don't know if you'd call it dating related, but it's in that ballpark."

He had to fight to keep his eyes from widening.

Turning to her and then back to the road, he nodded. "Shoot. Just a disclaimer, though, that's not exactly my area of expertise. But I'll try."

"That's okay. It's not my area of expertise, either." She offered him a quick smile. "So, say a guy is out with a female friend. Just something casual, like going to a bar for some food and a drink. They're friends and all, but this was only the second time they've ever gone anywhere outside of work, just the two of them."

Zane didn't have to prod to know the woman in Amelia's hypothetical story was her, but he was less sure of the man's identity.

She waved a hand as if she was shooing away a bug. "Anyway, at the end of the night, the guy asks his female friend if she wants to come with him to a new bar that's close to his place. He even offers for her to stay there if she drinks too much. What do you make of that? Do you think he's trying to get her to sleep with him?"

Zane didn't have to think it over very long. "Yeah. If it's only the second time they've hung out…just the two of them like you said, then that definitely sounds like the move he's trying to make. There's a chance that he might just be awkward, but that's actually pretty smooth."

Amelia wrinkled her nose. "Smooth?"

"Yeah, in a gross way. The guy's got plausible deniability if she says no or asks what the hell's wrong with him. Kind of sleazy, in my personal opinion, but, well..." he glanced at her and shrugged, "sometimes it be like that."

Her expression brightened as she grinned. "Right. Some-times it be like that. Do you mind if I ask why you think it's sleazy?" The smile fell away, and she began to examine her nails. "I mean, I agree, and I'm just curious."

Zane didn't like how the normally self-possessed agent had turned inward during the conversation. He needed to dig deeper, find out what was messing with her head so much. And right now, they didn't have much time.

The Cavalier was only two cars ahead of them, and the distance to the mall had dwindled. He smiled as they pulled up to a red light. "Well, it's different if it's on a date. On an actual date, it's pretty standard, and there's no added pressure of trying to maintain a friendship. No one feels obligated to do anything to appease the other person."

Amelia nodded. "Yeah, that's true. It's a different context when you're on a date."

"Exactly. But when you're talking about a friend you don't know that well, it's sleazy because it's manipulative. Guys who do that are just trying to save face. If they get turned down, they play it off like they're just her friend. Plus, there's the whole angle where they're playing the friendship card to get her alone in an unfamiliar environment where she'll be vulnerable and more susceptible to his advances."

Amelia let go of her hair and fixed her wide eyes on him. "Wow. I, uh, I didn't expect an answer that was quite so *thorough*."

He'd actually surprised himself. Well, in for a penny, in for a pound.

"The part that pisses me off the most." He shot a quick glance her way. He had her full attention. "Is how this scenario leaves the woman questioning her judgment and feeling off balance and…" He sought a positive word.

Amelia had no such qualms. "Stupid?"

His mouth tightened. He hated that word, but…

"Yeah. Not that she is, but the mind game her so-called friend thrusts her into makes her feel that way. Uncertain. Makes her wonder if she did something wrong to lead him on. Makes her wonder if she failed to read the situation correctly."

At his side, Amelia sank back into her seat, her hand coming up to play with her hair again. The strands were a tell, but more than that, a security blanket. Zane hated to think about what she'd gone through to need to self soothe in such a way.

"How did you get so smart?"

He smiled. This part was easy.

"My mom. She was a hedge fund manager." He glanced at Amelia to make sure she remembered him telling her about his family. When she nodded, he refocused on the road. "She was a really good hedge fund manager. She made a lot of money, and she retired when she was forty. But she didn't want to do your typical rich person gig, you know? Didn't want to buy a massive yacht, a multi-million-dollar house, or a handful of politicians."

She turned in her seat to study him, and he could tell that she was curious as to where the story was going. He needed to get to the point.

Zane scratched at his temple, a nervous tic he fought to hide unless he was in friendly company. He wasn't normally inclined to share personal experiences aside from the stupid stories of his younger years.

But friendship went two ways. He couldn't expect Amelia to confide in him if he wasn't comfortable doing the same.

He cleared his throat. "Her dad, my grandpa, he wasn't a

great dude. He abused my grandma, my mom, and her brother too." Rage stirred in his gut at the memory. "So, when my mom retired, she decided she'd try to help other people who were going through abuse. Instead of buying a yacht or a senator, she started a nonprofit. It's called A Helping Home, and they've got locations all over the East Coast now."

From the corner of his eye, he saw Amelia's jaw drop. "Wow."

He smiled. It really was special. "And as you'll also recall, I've always been a mama's boy. She was doing volunteer work when I was still in high school, while she was still in the financial industry, and it took me a while to realize that everything she taught me about patterns of abusive behavior wasn't common knowledge. Like the guy in your story. A lot of people think shit like that is normal, but it's far from, honestly. At least it shouldn't be."

Amelia was quiet as they pulled away from the traffic light. When he shot her a quick glance, he noticed some of the brightness return to her expression. "Every time you tell me more about your mom, she gets cooler and cooler."

The anxiety that had plagued him since the start of the conversation finally bubbled up in the form of relieved laughter. Most people tended to focus on the wealth instead of the wisdom. "Yeah, she's pretty cool."

He flicked on the blinker to signal their upcoming turn onto a looping stretch of road that led to the mall parking lot. They were still two cars behind the Cavalier, but the distance was purposeful. Just because he and Amelia were following a group of teenagers didn't mean they could throw their usual diligence to the wayside.

Drumming his fingers against the steering wheel, Zane debated his next question as they waited for the cars ahead of them. He didn't want to get on Amelia's nerves, but at the same time, he wanted to know the outcome of her not so hypothetical story.

"Not trying to pry or anything, but was the woman in your story you?"

With a heavy sigh, Amelia slumped back in the seat. "Unfortunately, yes."

"When did that happen? Was that this weekend?"

"Yep." The word was almost a groan.

"Damn." He rubbed the back of his neck. "That sucks. Who was the dude? Unless you'd rather not say."

She massaged her temples. "Someone from work."

His gut began to burn. An employee of the damn Federal Bureau of Investigation should know better. Then again, an employee of the damn FBI would know exactly how to manipulate a person.

He pushed his anger down. "Okay, I know you praised me for respecting boundaries before, but workplace gossip is a totally different beast. I just can't help myself. Now, in my defense, the stuff I usually like to talk about is almost all positive. People running marathons, kids getting on honor roll, stuff like that. But if someone at work is a jerk, well…"

He left the thought unfinished and shot her a knowing glance.

To his relief, she seemed to smile with true amusement. "Who exactly do you talk about this stuff with? Because I've never heard you mention it to me before."

"Honestly?" He hesitated, wondering how much he should actually reveal. Amelia continued to stare expectantly in his direction. *In for a penny, in for a pound.* Zane knew that, if he wanted to continue to build her trust, he needed to let it all out. "The cleaning crew. When they're doing their thing, people just keep talking like they aren't even there. Even after all the security seminars we have. I don't know what it is about offices that does that to people. It helps that a bunch of the cleaning crew are Ukrainian and I speak Russian."

"Wait, you speak Russian? I had no idea." She tapped herself on the chest. "I speak Russian too. My mom was from the Soviet Union. She wanted me and my siblings to be bilingual, so she taught us when we were really little."

"I took Russian in college, and I made friends with a couple exchange students from Moscow. I honestly think that even though I'm fluent, I speak Russian the best when I'm drunk." He chuckled at his own self-deprecating humor. "Because that's when I'd speak it the most, when I was still learning it."

"It's a psychological thing." Amelia tapped her temple. "I learned about it from NPR."

Zane waved a dismissive hand as he steered the car onto the gently sloping road that led to the mall. "Okay, but we're way off topic." He narrowed his eyes. "It wasn't Spencer, was it?"

Her eyebrows went up in surprise. "Spencer? No, he's married."

Zane snorted. When did a wedding ring stop a pervert from being a pervert?

"*Was* married," he corrected. "He filed for divorce a few weeks ago. I guess you haven't seen him much since he stopped wearing his wedding ring."

"Wow, I guess not. That sucks. I don't know him that well, but he seems like a good guy."

"He is." Zane nodded. "That's why I was going to be pissed if you said it was him. He said he was going to hang out with a female friend of his this weekend, so I had to check. Okay." He patted the air with his free hand. "As long as I know that my boy Spencer isn't out there being a creep, I can live with it. I'll stop bugging you now."

Twisting the end of her ponytail around a finger, Amelia

shook her head. "No, you're fine. It might make me feel better to tell someone, actually, but I can handle it on my—"

"Larson." The name shot out of his mouth like a bullet. He didn't know how he knew, but he'd caught the way the other agent looked at her.

Her silent shock was the only confirmation he needed. After a full thirty seconds went by, she sighed. "Good guess, but I'll handle it myself." Her gaze burned into the side of his face. "Got it?"

He didn't confirm or deny.

"What happened?"

"Friday night, we went to grab some food and a couple of beers. He was the one who invited me, for what that's worth. And all night, he was just." She left the recollection unfinished and wrinkled her nose.

Zane thought about the new rumors he'd heard. "I thought he was seeing some chick in forensics?"

Amelia did a double take. "Wait, really? Did he tell you that?"

He flashed her a sarcastic smile. "Workplace gossip, remember? One of the cleaning crew guys who works on our floor saw them together and thought they looked cute, so he told the rest of us about it."

Covering her mouth with one hand, Amelia laughed. "Oh my god, your workplace gossip is adorable." She paused to clear her throat. "Really, though, I didn't know that. But I think it's safe to say he's probably cheating on her, or at least he's trying to."

"Wow." Zane thumped the heel of one hand against the steering wheel. He'd had his suspicions about that man from the beginning, and this confirmed it. "What an asshole." He pulled into a parking spot one row down from the Cavalier. "If you ever want me to kick his ass for you, well...I wouldn't do that because it's unprofessional, but just so you know, the sentiment is there." He made a show of flexing his muscles. "I'm pretty sure I could take him."

Zane worried that his peculiar brand of humor had come across as aloof or uncaring, but the smile returned to Amelia's lips, confirming they were on the same page. "I don't know. You probably shouldn't get too cocky. Larson *was* in the military for seven years."

A chuckle slipped from Zane's lips before he could stop it. "The military isn't the only place you learn to fight."

The flicker was slight, but Zane didn't miss the hint of suspicion that flitted across Amelia's face. He thought to expound—to lie—about the cryptic statement, but more than likely, he'd just dig himself a deeper hole if he tried to lie to his fellow agent.

But if he told her the truth, he'd be in violation of more Department of Defense statutes than he could count.

As far as she and most everyone else knew, he'd learned to defend himself during the near decade he'd spent at the FBI. To be sure, the Bureau provided some of the best hand-to-hand combat training in the country. But Zane's former employer of ten years was on an entirely different level.

The FBI trained its agents in fighting tactics intended for use in law enforcement. The Central Intelligence Agency, on the other hand, taught its agents to defend themselves by killing their adversaries.

As he turned the key to kill the engine, Zane glanced at Amelia.

She hadn't specifically said as much, but he guessed her military experience was a cut above the average serviceman or woman. Few women made it through Special Forces training, but he could see Amelia being one of them. Like they did with the CIA, the United States government spent a lot of money to teach the military's specialized warfare factions how to kill.

He pushed the thoughts out of his head, having closed that chapter of his life when he'd handed his resignation letter to the Agency's Deputy Director. Now, he could only hope that none of the ghosts he'd left behind had figured out how to follow him to his new home.

Zane counted five teenagers exiting the Cavalier before he turned back to Amelia. "Really, though. It sucks when you find out that your friends are trying to use you."

Amelia shrugged. "It's okay. Honestly, I found out the easy way. That poor woman in forensics is the one getting the short end of the stick here. Someone should tell her."

"I can give you her name when we get back to the office. It's Michelle something or other. I'll have to look her up in the directory to jog my memory."

"Yeah, that sounds good." Amelia's nod appeared a little too overeager, but Zane couldn't fault her for it. "I'll figure out a way to talk to her that doesn't make me look like a total creep." She pushed open the passenger side door. "Ladies have to look out for one another, you know. Especially with jerks like Larson running amok."

Snorting a laugh of agreement, Zane stepped out of the car and into the warm rays of late morning sunshine. "Running amok is probably the best description anyone's ever used to describe what most men do in their personal life."

As they shoved their doors closed, Zane fished his sunglasses from where they hung around his neck. After almost an hour in an air-conditioned car with tinted windows, the full force of the sun's warmth was like stepping directly under a heat lamp.

He glanced at Amelia and then to himself. They'd both abandoned their usual office attire to better blend in with a crowd of late morning mall shoppers. Rather than her typical black slacks and blouse, Amelia had donned a pair of dark jeans and a loose-fitting t-shirt that draped off one shoulder.

Zane had kept the dress shirt and slacks, but he'd left the matching suit jacket and tie back at the office. After rolling up his sleeves, he was tempted to throw on his trusty black zip-up hoodie for good measure, but the heat would roast him to the bone. Dressed this casually, he hoped to pass for a store manager instead of the plain-clothes FBI agent he was.

Unclipping a pair of oversized sunglasses from the front of her shirt, Amelia stepped around the car to stand at his side. "So, how do we want to do this? Chances are good we'll spook them the second we say we're FBI."

Rubbing his chin with one hand, Zane casually peeked over to the group of high schoolers. "That's true. Anyone with 'Federal' in their job title will probably scare the hell out of them."

"Let me take point here." Amelia pushed the sunglasses onto her face. "Silvia Calleja Torres? That's the girl you couldn't find, right?"

"Yeah, that's her. She's the girl with the blue in her hair." He lifted a shoulder as they started off in the direction of the teenagers. "Just because I couldn't find a social doesn't mean she's here illegally. She's a sixteen-year-old kid, so she might not show up in the system yet."

Amelia nodded. "I grew up in a neighborhood where no one talked to cops or anyone of authority. One of the first things I remember my dad telling us after we moved to Englewood was, if the cops tried to talk to us, we were allowed to tell them we didn't want to talk without our parent present."

"Ironic, isn't it?" Zane flashed her a grin.

"A little." She chuckled. "The most important thing with these kids is to make sure they know we're here because we want to help their friend."

"We just need to make sure we stop to talk to them some-where they won't be inclined to run before we've had a chance to get that far." He gestured to the tall, arched entryway to the mall. "This is the entrance to the food court, so here's hoping we get lucky and they decide to grab a bite to eat. They might be a little more hesitant to take off if they've got a bunch of food in front of them."

As he and Amelia passed the last parking spot, the group of teenagers pushed their way through the center set of double doors. A girl's laughter echoed off the arched metal awning.

Through the floor-to-ceiling wall of glass, Zane kept his eyes fixed on the kids as they stepped to the side of the main walkway to check their phones. When he and Amelia reached the set of glass doors, the girl with blue hair, Silvia, was holding her phone out for the others to see.

Zane and Amelia stuck close to the teenagers as they ordered gyros and fries from one of the food vendors. They pretended to be focused on their phones as they covertly watched the group from a safe distance.

After the kids sat down to eat, Zane leaned in. "They're at the far table, right by the railing that looks over the floor below this one."

Amelia looked up to confirm the location. "There are a couple open seats at the end of the table. I say we just go sit down with them and lay our badges on the table so we avoid making a scene. If we make a scene, then chances are they'll be even more reluctant to talk to us."

"Good call." He palmed his badge. "Try not to look at them while we're walking over. We don't want them to know we're there for them until we sit down."

"I guess I'll look at you, then." She batted her eyelashes at him as they made their way through the tables and chairs.

Without so much as a sideways glance to the group, Zane pulled out a chair beside one of the teenage boys. As he dropped to sit, Amelia stepped around the edge of the table to claim her spot beside Silvia Calleja Torres.

All five sets of eyes were glued to the two of them and their apparent lack of self-awareness.

The boy to Zane's side looked from him to Amelia and back. "Hey, uh…mister. We're already sitting here. Sorry, it's just kind of weird." He waved a hand at the cluster of empty tables. "There are lots of free spots. Could you, I mean. Would you mind moving?"

A pang of guilt prodded at Zane's stomach. The poor kid had phrased his question more politely than most adults Zane had met in his life, and now he and Amelia were about to scare the hell out of him.

He slipped his badge onto the laminate table. Locking eyes with the surprised teenagers, he kept the gold shield and eagle covered with his palm. When Amelia pulled a hand from her tote, he slid his badge forward, swept his gaze over the kids, and lifted his hand.

Amelia didn't bother with the same dramatic reveal as she flipped open the worn leather case to reveal her FBI ID card.

Silvia sucked in a sharp breath and clamped both hands down on the edge of the table as the muscles in her forearms tensed.

"Hold on." Zane raised a hand and met her shocked stare. "We aren't from immigration, okay? I'm Special Agent Palmer, and this is my partner, Special Agent Storm. We're with the Federal Bureau of Investigation, *not* immigration."

Amelia gestured to the little group. "None of you are in trouble. None of your families are in trouble. We're here to ask for your help. That's all."

Despite the faint voices and the normal hustle and bustle of the mall that drifted over to them, the silence that followed Amelia's words was suffocating. Zane met the frightened eyes of each teenager, watching jaws and hands clench as he searched for the telltale tension that preceded a sudden movement.

The last thing he wanted to do was to be forced to chase down one of Javier Flores's friends. The clock was ticking, and they had only five days to figure out who had taken Javier and Yanira, and that was only if they counted the rest of today. If one or more of the teenagers ran, then their ticking clock would be set back even more than it already was.

Zane met each of their stunned gazes in turn. "Your friend, Javier Flores, and his younger sister, Yanira. Their mother reported them missing, and we're trying to find them. We have reason to believe that they're in danger, and we need to get to them as soon as we can. That's why we're here."

Silvia and another girl exchanged nervous glances as the kid to Zane's side—Martin, if Zane remembered right—ran a hand through his hair.

Martin looked down at his shoes as he shook his head. "We haven't seen Javier."

Zane bit back a knee-jerk sarcastic response. "That's why we're here. No one's seen him for over a month. A few days ago, his little sister disappeared too."

Martin's expression turned crestfallen as he glanced at the girl to his side. "I don't know. We haven't seen him, and no one's heard from him." The kid's Adam's apple bobbed as he swallowed. "We thought he'd been deported."

"No." Zane pointed to his badge. "We'd know if that was what happened."

Amelia spread her hands. "From what his mom said, he'd started a summer job a couple months ago. It would have been right around the end of the school year. Do any of you remember him saying anything about it?" Her expression was the closest to pleading Zane had ever seen. "Any little detail can help."

Another silence descended as the kids looked to one another before Martin cleared his throat. "We didn't know about it."

Zane propped his elbows on the table. "No disrespect here, Martin, but maybe we ought to go from person to person so we can hear from everyone."

Martin's gulp was almost audible, but he nodded. "Okay. Well, I don't know anything."

The girl to his side gnawed at the end of her fingernail. When Zane's gaze fell on her, she dropped her hand to her lap. "I don't know, either. I remember him saying that he was looking for a job, but I never knew if he'd found one or not."

"Do you remember any names he might have mentioned?" Amelia rested her hands on the table and relaxed her fingers, keeping her palms open for all to see. "Places or people he was going to talk to about work? Or even the type of work he was looking for?"

"No." The girl shook her head.

As he and Amelia went around the table, the next two muttered the same, "I don't know," as the others.

When Silvia's turn came around, Zane finally caught the orange symbol on the front of her t-shirt. "Wolfenstein." He lifted an eyebrow. "You play Wolfenstein?"

Her gaze flicked down to the shirt, and she picked at the puffed fabric paint at the edge of the logo. "Yeah."

"Have you played the new one?"

She nodded.

He leaned back in his chair, adopting a more relaxed posture. Years of experience had taught him that if he wanted to earn someone's trust, he not only needed to sound nonthreatening, he also needed to appear as approachable as possible. Body language was key to this. "I've been playing those games since the first one came out. Is the new one any good?"

Silvia opened and closed her mouth a few times and swallowed hard before she finally answered, "I...I like it."

A genuine smile warmed Zane's face. "That's good to hear. At least I won't leave here today completely empty-handed. Now, what about your friend? Do you remember anything about Javier's job?"

To no one's surprise, she didn't.

Nor did any of them remember Javier talking about new friends or mentioning strange phone calls or connecting to anyone outside their little circle. In fact, they drew a blank regarding all the questions he and Amelia peppered them with.

Zane figured the gesture was fruitless, but he and Amelia handed a business card to each of the five teenagers before they took their leave.

Five days left, and they were still on square one.

By MIDNIGHT, Zane had moved his work laptop from the dining room table to the couch. His eyelids had grown heavier in the last fifteen minutes, but he was worried that if he drank any more coffee, he'd be stuck awake for the next twenty-four hours.

Now, if he fell asleep in front of his computer, at least he'd be on the couch instead of in a wooden chair.

Rubbing his eyes with one hand, he flicked on the television and turned down the volume until the speaker was barely audible. As he dropped into the center cushion of the gray sectional, he let his head fall backward until the textured ceiling took up his field of vision.

After the fruitless endeavor at the Upper Ridge Mall, he

and Amelia had paid a visit to the Chicago Police Department. They'd obtained digital copies of missing persons case files over the past year, and they'd talked to a few detectives about potential labor trafficking rings that the Chicago PD might have come across.

They could have dug through the old reports using one of the FBI's databases, but he and Amelia thought they might glean a useful piece of information from a face-to-face discussion with a detective who'd worked one of the cases.

A grizzled veteran detective had pointed them toward a couple cold cases that matched the circumstances of Javier's disappearance, but each file was more barren than the last.

Whoever the traffickers were, they made sure to cover their tracks.

The next step had been to compile dates and locations of any missing persons reports with characteristics similar to Javier's. Though they'd established a pattern—more people of Latin descent were reported missing at the start of spring and summer than at any other point during the year—the new information was next to useless.

They already knew they were dealing with human traffickers, and the majority of victims caught up in forced labor were made to work in jobs like agriculture and construction. Both industries took off in the spring and summer, so the pattern only confirmed what they'd already suspected.

Just as Zane's eyelids drooped shut, a telltale buzz snapped him away from the edge of sleep. Taking in a sharp breath, he straightened before reaching to the coffee table for his phone.

He squinted at the number, but even though he recognized the Chicago area code, the caller ID simply read *wireless customer.*

Although he expected it to be a spam call, he swiped the

green key and raised the device to his ear. "This is Agent Palmer."

"Hi…I'm, um." The girl's voice was familiar. Zane massaged his temple as he worked to place her identity.

As he pictured the chunks of blue in her ebony hair, he froze in place. "Wolfenstein. Sorry, Silvia, is that you?"

She made a little squeaking sound, as if his memory of her name surprised her. "Yes, I'm…it's me."

The girl's quiet voice forced the remaining fog of sleep from his thoughts. "Are you okay? Is something wrong?" He squinted at the digital clock below the television. "It's quarter after midnight."

"I'm okay." She paused, and Zane had to check to make sure the line hadn't gone dead. "I'm calling about Javier. I know I didn't say anything in front of my friends earlier, and I'm still not really sure if I should be talking to you, but…"

The hairs on the back of his neck prickled to life. Zane clenched and unclenched his hand, but he made no move to break the newest silence.

"I'm really worried about Javier. I was with him when he got his job, and…I think…maybe…I should talk to you about it. To the FBI, I mean. If he's really missing and wasn't deported, then I feel like something bad might have happened to him."

"Okay." He pulled his laptop closer. "Let's talk."

"I can't right now." Her voice was hushed, her cadence hurried. "I had to call you when my parents were asleep. If they knew I was talking to you, they'd be pissed."

He nodded to himself. With it being summer break, he didn't need to worry with her school schedule. "Right, okay. The sooner, the better. How about tomorrow? My partner and I can meet you. We can buy you lunch or something like that."

"Yeah, okay. Tomorrow. There's a diner close to the mall

that I go to so I can sit and read sometimes. It's quieter there than trying to read at home. It's called The Oak Diner. Do you know it? Would that be okay?"

"That's fine. What time can you be there?"

"My parents go to work at seven in the morning, but their shifts aren't always the same. Can I meet you at noon?"

Pinning the phone to his ear with a shoulder, Zane opened a new text document on his laptop and typed in the name of the diner.

"We can do that." He deepened his tone, making sure it carried the urgency he felt. "Silvia, this is really, really important. I'm not trying to scare you, but Javier could be in real danger. My partner and I *need* you to be there tomorrow, okay?"

"I will. Javier is my friend. I want to help him."

A touch of determination had edged its way into her voice, and Zane's anxiety loosened its hold, if only for a moment.

The clock was still ticking.

Four days.

9

Vivian had turned the investigation of the missing Flores children over to the FBI, but she found she couldn't go back to her usual routine. Not while Mari Flores was overwhelmed with worry for her kids' safety and fear of deportation.

Mari's world was crumbling. The poor woman had come to Vivian for help. She couldn't sit on her ass just because she'd gone to the authorities. Vivian had no intent to muck up the FBI's case, but she *could* help.

Mari had given Vivian a key when they'd met up for a secretive lunch a day earlier, so she could look around the family's house before the wheels of the legal machine granted Agents Palmer and Storm access.

Without Mari's permission, either the Bureau would have to obtain a court order to compel her to come forward as a witness, or they'd have to gather evidence for a search warrant.

And besides, a search of the house could wind up as a massive waste of time for the FBI. Javier hadn't been abducted from his home—he'd been lured into a forced labor camp, and Yanira had vanished on her way home from soccer practice. Chances were good that the Flores household was low on the Bureau's priority list.

As she approached the Flores home, Vivian fished in her messenger bag for a pair of blue vinyl gloves. Normally, she used the gloves when she chopped up spicy peppers or dyed her hair, but they would keep her from leaving fingerprints inside the house.

They weren't professional gloves, but as Vivian had been reminded so many times in her career, she wasn't a professional detective.

Investigative reporting seldom involved snooping around empty houses for evidence. When she wrote an in-depth piece, she interviewed the detectives, compiled notes and evidence from primary and secondary sources, and analyzed the information.

At no point was she supposed to be doing the hands-on work.

After donning her gloves, Vivian eased the wooden front door open and then gently closed it behind herself. She half-expected to trip an alarm that would announce to the entire neighborhood that she was an intruder, but the home remained silent.

Swallowing against the dryness in her mouth, she flicked the deadbolt into place. With a deep breath to steady her frayed nerves, she forced herself to turn around to face the interior of the Flores residence.

A plastic rack to the left of the closed door held a collection of shoes and sandals. When Vivian's gaze settled on a sparkly pair of silver ballet flats, a pang of hopelessness stabbed at her heart.

Mari Flores had told Vivian that her daughter loved two things above almost all else—cars and glitter.

Yanira had been gone for almost a week. Statistically

speaking, a kidnapping case with no leads, no new developments, and no messages from the kidnapper after a week was bound for a cold case shelf. The same rang true for many crimes, but there were elements unique to kidnapping that made the passage of time even more insidious.

There was no telling what the people who had taken Yanira had done to her over the course of so many days.

No one had demanded ransom, no one had claimed that the crime had been committed as retribution against Mari, and the Feds had discovered no meaningful evidence. Or if they had, Vivian had been kept out of the loop.

Determined to create her own loop, Vivian straightened her shoulders and made her way up a short set of carpeted stairs.

Pushing a lock of hair from her eyes, Vivian returned her focus to the dim living space. Judging by the fact that the vacuum marks on the living room carpet were undisturbed, Vivian was the first person to step foot in the duplex since Mari had gone to stay with her friend. Heavy navy blue curtains blocked out all but a glowing sliver of light from the room's picture window. A television remote and a gaming controller sat atop a faux driftwood coffee table, in the center of which was a three-wick candle.

The flat panel television against the far wall wasn't on the cutting edge of technology, but the fifty-inch screen was more than adequate for Javier and Yanira to sit on the loveseat behind the coffee table to play video games together.

To the side of the entertainment stand and the television was the start of a hall cloaked in even more shadow than the living room.

Vivian took in another long breath of the stale air as she started across the plush carpet, heading for the kitchen. Through the meager strip of visible window, between two curtain panels, she spotted a couple of cars outside. Vivian stopped and squinted, trying to get a better view. Both were parked across the street, but neither looked to be occupied.

From her viewpoint, the neighborhood was quiet. At ten on a Tuesday morning, traffic in the residential area was practically nonexistent.

Prying her eyes away from the window, Vivian rubbed the back of her neck. Ever since she had spoken to the FBI, she had been overcome by an unshakeable paranoia. It was as if she were being watched.

Of course I'm paranoid.

She was snooping around looking for evidence to help the FBI find a teenager and his sixteen-year-old sister who were probably kidnapped by human traffickers.

That's a pretty good reason to be paranoid.

Vivian blew out a shaky sigh. "Touché, brain. Touché." Though her voice was hardly above a whisper, the sound cut through the tomb-like silence like the wail of a siren.

Rather than bite her tongue to keep from ruining the stillness again, Vivian added a little more volume to her voice. "This is creepy, but I refuse to let a house freak me out."

She waited for a phantom to reply, telling her to be frightened, but no such response came.

Nodding to herself, she picked her way past the couch and into the gloomy hall. Family pictures hung to either side, but Vivian kept her eyes ahead. She didn't need more reminders of how high the stakes had become.

As she approached the first closed door, Vivian reminded herself that her visit to the house was legal. None of the duplex had been cordoned off as part of a crime scene, and she'd received Mari's permission to look around.

"I'm saving the FBI some time." She swallowed the wave of doubt. "If I find anything that looks important, I'll take a picture and take it to them as soon as I can."

As she twisted the knob with her gloved hand, Vivian held her breath and pushed open the door. Though not quite as dim as the living area, most of the sunlight was blocked from the room's window by a set of plain gray curtains.

Vivian glanced over a handful of video game and anime posters that decorated the beige walls. Tucked in the corner beside the window, the bed's forest-green comforter was smooth, and the matching sheets had been tucked neatly into the full-size mattress.

Stepping around the bed, Vivian pushed one curtain aside to peer out onto the street. The same two cars were visible, and an older woman had emerged from a nearby house with a beagle on a retractable leash.

Just as Vivian was about to blow out a relieved sigh at such a normal sight, a black sedan crept into the edge of her vision. The speed limit on a residential street was low, but the lazy crawl of the passing vehicle struck a chord of alarm in Vivian's head.

Though Mari had worked hard to keep her and her kids in the quiet family neighborhood after her husband died, and though most of the houses and parked cars were well-maintained, the new model Lexus stuck out in the sea of ten-year-old Toyotas and Hondas.

She could have sworn she'd seen the sleek car when she stopped at a gas station just outside the neighborhood. Plenty of people drove a black Lexus in Chicago, but the unblemished shine and the overly darkened tinted windows gave the vehicle a certain level of distinction.

Goose bumps spread over her arms as she peered at the driver's side window. Hard as she looked through the shadow of the tint, she could make out little more than the shape of a person's head.

More than likely, the driver's slow pace was due to their unfamiliarity with the area, but Vivian didn't feel especially lucky. As she pulled out her smartphone, she decided to take down the plate number and laugh at her paranoia later.

Before the Lexus disappeared out of her field of view, Vivian pulled up her phone's camera, zoomed in, and snapped a picture.

She was confident the driver wouldn't have seen her through the tiny slit in the curtains, but she wanted to cut the remainder of her trip as short as possible. Pocketing her phone, she returned her focus to the tidy space.

Javier's room was cleaner than the bedrooms of most adults Vivian knew, and she said a silent thank you as she tiptoed over to an olive-green writing desk. Aside from the bed, a dresser, and a single nightstand, the desk was the only other piece of furniture.

Renewed purpose drove Vivian's swift movements as she checked under the bed, looked over the pictures and vinyl figures on top of the dresser, and even slid open the closet door to peek at the clothes and shoes inside. She braced herself for what might be in the drawer of the nightstand, but all she found were clean socks and phone cables. No false bottoms to be found, and not any loose floor or baseboards that she could locate.

She was about to end the fruitless search when she picked up a notebook from the writing desk. Blowing out a sigh, she flipped open the cover to a blank page.

"Dammit," she muttered.

In a last-ditch effort to come away from the house with any semblance of worthwhile evidence, she flipped through the notebook. Less than halfway in, she spotted a blur of writing.

Every now and then, when Vivian was caught off guard by an important phone call, she would pop open the nearest notepad to take down information she might otherwise forget. Sometimes she landed on the first few pages, and sometimes she wound up in the middle or the end. In those moments, she cared little about maintaining organization. She just wanted to ensure she didn't forget what her caller told her.

As she read over the sloppy penmanship, she could only assume Javier had done the same.

Excitement rushed up her spine as she retrieved her phone to take a picture. All he'd written was a name and phone number. There was no guarantee that the information was even relevant to the people who had taken him. But Vivian was nothing if not thorough.

After glancing around the room, she returned the notebook to where she'd found it. "Okay. I think that's it. And I'm still alive."

She pushed thoughts of the black Lexus from her mind as she made her way back to the foyer. Once she had locked the front door, Vivian turned to the street and took in a deep breath of humid air.

To avoid drawing attention to herself, she'd parked a block away, and she had to fight to keep herself from sprinting for her trusty Mazda. At the edge of the sidewalk, she went through the perfunctory motion of checking both directions before crossing the street. As she peered over her shoulder to the right, Vivian froze in place.

Four houses down, parked between a white pickup and a red SUV, was a black Lexus.

Vivian swore under her breath.

It's broad daylight. Don't panic. There are plenty of people at home in these houses.

No matter the identity of the Lexus, she didn't want to be seen gawking. With a shaky hand, she grabbed her phone and pretended to send a text message.

Maybe they found the house they were looking for.

Then why were they still in the driver's seat?

Maybe they're waiting for someone.

Maybe, but for the time being, she would operate on a worst-case scenario basis. As she stood and watched the Lexus from the camera app on the screen of her phone, she tapped the video recording button. Despite her best efforts, she couldn't calm the tremor in her hands. She was sure all the images would be too blurry to be useful.

But she would try.

A whirlwind of questions whipped through her mind. Were the traffickers here to look for Javier's mother, or had they learned that Vivian brought the case to the attention of the FBI?

Worse still, was there truly an organized criminal conspiracy at the helm of Premier Ag Solutions? Had the executives sent a thug to threaten her into withholding her piece about the company?

When she swallowed, her throat felt like twenty-grain sandpaper.

She needed to get out of there fast. Once she was safe, she could call Mari to warn her. And if she could muster up some bravery to leave her apartment again, Vivian needed to bring the license plate number and the video she'd just taken to the FBI.

The black Lexus could be unrelated, but Vivian had never been much of a gambler. She was, however, a reporter with a slew of new information that needed to be reviewed. Storm and Palmer could sort out the information. They were, after all, the FBI agents.

With a hesitant sigh, Vivian turned her back to the luxury sedan and started off to her car. Clenching and unclenching her jaw, she fought against the urge to break into a run.

If the traffickers hadn't known about her involvement before, they knew now.

She never should have come here.

10

Though Amelia had expressed some doubt about Silvia Calleja Torres showing up to The Oak Diner at the agreed upon time—or at all, if she was honest—neither she nor Zane had time to second-guess the girl's conviction.

Two minutes before noon, Amelia spotted the familiar head of blue and black hair as Silvia pushed her way through the set of glass double doors.

"Huh." Amelia leaned back against the leather booth and glanced at Zane. "I'll be damned. She's here."

From where he sat across from her, Zane turned his head toward the door and raised a hand. "I told you, she sounded sincere. She's worried about her friend."

Recognition lit up Silvia's face as she returned Zane's wave and readjusted her canvas messenger bag.

Amelia lifted a shoulder. "I'm just saying, I would have understood if she'd skipped out on us. The poor kid has to be scared shitless about coming to talk to a couple FBI agents when she's an undocumented immigrant."

With a wistful smile, Zane nodded. "Yeah, I agree."

As Silvia drew nearer, Amelia scooted until she was next to the burgundy drywall. Waving a hand to the empty space at her side, she tried to look as reassuringly neutral as possible. "Have a seat."

Silvia took in a deep breath as she slid into the booth.

"Hi, thank you." Her dark eyes flicked from Amelia to Zane. "I'm sorry. I'm out of breath." She paused to fan herself with one hand. "I ran from the bus stop because I didn't want to be late."

Amelia's expression softened. "It's okay. Take a minute. Catch your breath. Have some water. It's already ninety degrees outside right now, so it's important to make sure you stay hydrated."

Situating the messenger bag beside her feet, Silvia managed a slight smile. "That's what my mom told me before she left for work. She knows that I get really nasty headaches when I'm dehydrated."

Zane passed a menu to Silvia. "So do I." His gaze shifted between the two ladies. "I've usually got something like three different drinks at my desk when we're at work. Agent Storm always asks me if I want to move my desk beside the vending machine."

Amelia shrugged and rolled her eyes. "I just think it would save you some time."

Silvia chuckled and relaxed back into the padding of the booth's bench seat.

Though the use of self-deprecating humor to put a witness at ease wasn't listed anywhere in the FBI's standard operating procedure, the tactic was effective with teenagers and younger kids.

More often than not, Amelia and her fellow agents wanted to appear as put together as possible when they interacted with a victim's friends or family. But she didn't need a doctorate in child psychology to know that kids weren't usually interested in top-notch professionalism.

Especially not frightened kids. Frightened kids wanted to know that the person behind the badge cared about them and that the person behind the badge was a real human being.

Zane returned his water glass to the beige tabletop. "Thank you for coming, Silvia. I know this wasn't easy for you, but I promise that we're here to help."

Some of the anxiety returned to Silvia's expression as she nodded.

Folding his hands atop the menu, Zane's lips curved into a warm smile. "We want to find Javier and Yanira so we can bring them home to their mother safely. That's our first priority, and after that, we want to make sure we hold the people responsible for their disappearance accountable."

Truth be told, Amelia was surprised that a tall, physically fit man in a tailored suit could exude such an air of wholesome comfort. His amazing mother must have played a large roll in how well he turned out.

Unless it was all an act, of course.

Silvia rolled her silverware bundle under one hand, her gaze shifting nervously between the two agents' faces. "What will happen once you find him?" Her brown eyes drifted down to the table. "Will he be deported? Will his mom and sister be deported?"

"No." Amelia shook her head. "Since he's a victim of a crime, we'll be able to get him, his mom, and Yanira each a visa. And once the case and the trial are over, they'll be able to use that to apply for permanent residency."

Zane squeezed lemon into his water. "The FBI has a division called Victim Services. We'll make sure he's set up with an agent who'll help them sort out all the legal specifics."

Silvia released the silverware roll as she nodded. "Okay. I've been worried about that. Thank you."

Though Amelia hadn't been sure how to broach the subject of Silvia's citizenship status without coming across as hostile, she spotted the window of opportunity on the heels of Zane's reassurance. "If you're worried about yourself and your family, we can help you apply for a visa too. It would include your parents and your siblings, if you have any."

She swallowed hard and dropped her head. "That's okay." She began to pick at her fingernails. "I don't think my parents would like that. Ever since my uncle was deported back to El Salvador, they haven't trusted the American government. My uncle, he was…doing sort of what I'm doing today. He was trying to help the police with something, but then one day, he was just gone. He did a video call with my mom and me a week later and told us that the case he was helping out with had been dismissed, and his visa application was rejected."

As Amelia met Zane's gray eyes, she fought to keep the surprise from her face.

Jaw clenched, he shook his head in a silent request that they not press the subject.

Silvia prodded at the roll of silverware with one finger. "It's okay, though." With a sudden smile, she looked at Amelia, then Zane. "My grandmother has lived in America for fifteen years, and she just became a citizen. She helped my mom and dad apply for permanent residency a couple weeks ago. We just have to wait for them to process it now."

Amelia breathed out a silent sigh of relief.

Even to a Federal employee, the American immigration system was complex and difficult to navigate. She knew a little about the process to become a permanent resident from her mother, but laws changed so often, she couldn't be sure if her knowledge was up to date.

When she'd slogged through government websites to learn about the S-Visa that was available to witnesses in criminal cases, she'd come within an inch of ripping out her hair. She was glad to know that Zane and Silvia were more knowledgeable about the subject.

They paused the line of discussion as a young man stopped by the table to take their drink orders. While Zane and Silvia went with iced teas, Amelia ordered coffee. She was pleasantly surprised when the server returned with an entire stainless-steel pot and a ceramic mug.

Ever since SAC Keaton had given her and Zane the ticking clock for Javier and Yanira's case, she'd averaged about five hours of sleep per night. Plus, she'd spent the past two days at the FBI office looking over her shoulder like she was a spy in a secret society.

Though she'd avoided Joseph Larson since their awkward dinner, she knew their time of reckoning would come sooner rather than later. Even with her and Zane's shoebox of a conference room, she couldn't avoid Larson forever.

Amelia gritted her teeth and forced thoughts of that man out of her head. Nothing could take up the brain power she needed to focus on bringing home the missing children.

After the server returned for their food order, Amelia took the first tentative sip of her newest cup of coffee. "Silvia, did you want to talk before we eat or after?"

Silvia sipped at her tea and lifted a thin shoulder. "Before, I guess. I'm kind of nervous, so maybe that way I don't have to worry while I eat."

With a nod, Amelia fished in her handbag for a pen and a notepad. "Good thinking."

The girl's brown eyes shifted back and forth between the agents. "What did you want to know?"

Zane's expression was unreadable as he folded his arms at

the edge of the table. "You told me that you were with Javier when he got his job. Is that right?"

"Yeah." She used the straw to stir the ice in her drink. "We were both looking for a job. But." She glanced around the restaurant, her nerves practically jumping through her skin. "But neither of us have the paperwork to get jobs in America. We couldn't apply at the same places as our friends. Places like restaurants or grocery stores."

Though steady, Zane's voice was gentle. "How did you hear about the job?"

"Online. It was one of those sites where you can buy and sell stuff, and where you can pay people for some kinds of work. Like Craigslist, but not as popular." She peered up from her tea to meet Amelia's eyes. "It said that they were looking for help doing work out on a farm and that you didn't have to be a citizen to get a job with them."

Amelia scribbled down a few words to jog her memory later. "Did they have a company name that went with the job post?"

Silvia turned her gaze skyward for a moment, as if trying to recall. "No. It was just a description of the job and a phone number. I tried to look for the listing again, but it's gone."

Zane tapped the table with an index finger. "You said that you were there when Javier got his job. Does that mean he was offered the job in person? How did that work?"

A new light of determination flickered to life in Silvia's eyes. "Yeah, I was there. We both went to the interview together. The guy said that they didn't usually do group interviews, but he'd make an exception for us since they needed the help so badly."

Amelia's pulse picked up at the mention of an in-person meeting.

Before she could open her mouth to pose a follow-up question, Zane spoke. "We're going to come back to the man you two met with, but first, what was the interview like? What sorts of questions did they ask?"

Silvia pursed her lips and tapped the glass of iced tea. "Just some questions about what type of work we'd done in the past, what kind of pay we were looking for, stuff like that. I mean, I've never been in a job interview before that, but my friends have told me about theirs. It all seemed really normal to me, honestly. He took down notes on a laptop during the whole thing."

Apparently, the traffickers put forth an effort to come across as a legitimate operation, at least to those who were young and unfamiliar with the American job system. But from what Silvia had revealed so far, the traffickers could have fooled most teenagers.

After a long pull of iced tea, Zane pushed the emptied glass toward the edge of the table. "Where did the interview take place?"

Silvia's cheeks grew a few shades darker, and she looked miserable as she shook her head. "I...I'm not sure I remember. I don't drive, so Javier borrowed his mom's car. It was a house, somewhere in the Lower West Side. It looked really run down, but the guy said that they were doing remodeling."

To the best of Amelia's knowledge, the Lower West Side wasn't controlled by any single criminal organization.

She turned the ballpoint pen over in her fingers. "You said he hired Javier. Did he give you a reason that he didn't hire you?"

Fidgeting with the straw in her drink, the girl breathed out a long sigh. "No, he hired both of us at the end of the interview. He said that he just had to put our paperwork through and that he'd call us later in the week with more details." Her gaze fell to the table. "I was talking to one of our other friends about it, and my mom overheard me. I didn't think anything was wrong, so I wasn't trying to keep it a secret or anything. But when I got off the phone with my friend, my mom freaked out."

Zane frowned. "Why'd she freak out?"

"She said that the man who gave us the job was a con artist, and she made me rip up the number he'd given me. Plus, you know." Her shoulders sagged. "She didn't want me to get a job, even just over the summer. She said that I should be focusing on school so that I don't have to work low-paying jobs like she and my dad do."

The determination in her eyes had faded, and when she finished speaking, her voice was quiet and solemn.

"What happened after that?" Amelia made sure to match Silvia's hushed tone.

Rubbing her forehead, Silvia let out a breath that more closely resembled a sob. "My mom told me to tell Javier that the job was a scam, but I thought she was overreacting. I was mad about it, and I didn't want to ruin Javier's chance to get a summer job just because my mom yelled at me. So, I told him about how my mom freaked out, but I said I didn't believe her." A single tear slid down her cheek. "I guess he didn't believe her, either."

Though slight, Zane shook his head. "Don't blame yourself. It's not your fault, and it's not your mom's fault. Agent Storm and I have both dealt with people like that man before. They're clever, and they've tricked many, many people before you. It's their fault, and only their fault."

"Yeah, I guess." She lifted her chin. "How are you going to find Javier? I don't even have the phone number the hiring man gave me."

Amelia tapped her chin with the end of the pen, trying not to look disheartened by the dead end while she searched for another angle to explore. "I think we ought to circle back to the man you and Javier met with. Did he give you a name?"

"Yeah. He said his name was Vince, but his friends called him Vinnie."

The name was such a surprise that Amelia froze midway through writing. As she dragged her eyes up to meet Zane's, she tightened her grip on the pen. Zane shot her a *what the hell* look, and she lifted her shoulder a millimeter.

She doubted that anyone in the Russian mob or the San Luis Cartel went by Vinnie.

Vinnie was such a common Italian nickname that it had become an expected part of any mob television show or movie.

Zane gave the girl a comforting smile. "Vinnie? What did he look like? Did he have any tattoos, piercings, anything memorable about his appearance?"

Was he wearing a tracksuit and a gold chain?

Amelia was stereotyping, she knew. But stereotypes were created for a reason.

Silvia stared at her water glass, her brows drawn together in concentration. "He was tan, and I think he was white or Latino. It's summer, so it was hard to tell. He had black hair and dark brown eyes. About the same color as mine, I think. I'm pretty sure he had a tattoo on his arm." She rubbed her right forearm. "Right around here. I was trying to figure out what it was, and I think it was a mermaid. I might be wrong, though. It was kind of faint, and his arms were hairy."

Even as Amelia scribbled down the girl's description, she was surprised by the level of detail. Then again, most witnesses only caught a glimpse of a suspect. Silvia had sat across from the man for an entire interview.

"Oh." Silvia tapped her chin. "He had a cleft chin too."

Rubbing his cheek, Zane nodded. "Did he have an accent? Not just an accent from a different country, but did he have a Jersey accent like me? Or a Southern accent? Anything?"

"No, not that I could tell." She shrugged. "But I don't have an accent, and I was born in El Salvador."

That was disappointing. Amelia wrote out the word *accent*, circled it, and drew a slash through the middle.

Their collective attention shifted as the server approached the table with three plates of food balanced on his arms. Amelia pushed aside her notepad to make room for a platter of French toast.

Once the three of them were alone in their corner booth again, Amelia fixed Zane with a hard stare, hoping he might hear her telepathic plea. Since Silvia had called him the night before, she figured he would have better luck asking the girl to come back to the FBI office with them.

Bringing Silvia in to work with a sketch artist hadn't been on their agenda for the day, but with the girl's detailed description of the man named Vinnie, they had to take the chance.

Zane set his fork beside the plate of eggs and hash browns and picked up the pepper shaker. "Silvia, I know we were just going to meet here to ask you some questions, but I think you might actually be able to help us more than you realized."

The girl blinked up at Zane before she turned to Amelia. "What do you mean? Was that not helpful enough?"

Amelia's heart squeezed, and she wanted to hug the girl. "You've been extremely helpful, which is why we think you might be able to do us another favor. We need to know everything about this Vinnie guy that we can, and if we could have a picture for reference, it'd be a huge help."

"Oh." Silvia tightened her grasp on the fork and stared at them like a deer caught in headlights. "You mean like a lineup? Or a sketch artist? Or a—"

Amelia held up a hand. "A sketch artist would be perfect, but only if you're up for it."

To her surprise, she didn't have to lay down the sales pitch she'd started to craft in her mind.

The fire of determination had returned to Silvia's eyes. "Okay. Yeah. I remember what he looks like pretty well. If it helps you guys find Javier, then I'll do it."

It was a start.

Though the name Vinnie and the lack of an accent had all but convinced Amelia that the man was Italian, they would need more than an educated guess to convince SAC Keaton.

11

With a quiet exhale, Zane folded the printout of the composite sketch Silvia Calleja Torres had helped create the day before.

Based on the man's physical appearance—dark eyes, black hair, and a tan complexion—he and Amelia had decided to take the image to the Organized Crime Division's cartel task force to see if one of the agents would recognize him. Though there was a possibility that Vinnie could be Russian, his physical characteristics pointed to Latin roots.

That left them with the San Luis Cartel or the Leóne crime family.

Stifling a yawn with the back of one hand, Zane tucked the piece of paper into his black suit jacket. The Organized Crime Division—including the cartel task force, the Russian mob task force, and all others—shared the same floor, but finding the agents at their desks was a challenge in and of itself.

He glanced around the rows of empty cubicles nearest the wall of tinted windows and then across the room to the empty desks that belonged to him and Amelia. At quarter 'til eight in the morning, the only sound was the faint hum of the building's air-conditioning.

His intent had been to swing by the cartel task force before the agents dispersed to the field or to different parts of the expansive FBI building. Based on the black screens of the computer monitors, no one in the row had been to their desk yet today.

Shaking his head, he headed to the breakroom.

In his rush to get to the office to catch the agents of the cartel task force at their posts, he'd neglected to brew himself a pot of coffee at home. He'd contemplated swinging by the drive-thru of a coffee shop near his apartment, but the line of cars had been wrapped around the little building.

Now that he realized his effort to get to work early had been for naught, he wished he'd braved the long wait to get a latte or a Frappuccino. Amelia would have given him hell for the blended coffee beverage that was closer to a milkshake, but he would have gladly endured her teasing for the rest of the day if it meant he didn't have to drink the dreaded breakroom sludge.

As he flicked the switch to bathe the breakroom kitchenette in white fluorescence, he yawned into the crook of his elbow. Maybe the first pot of sludge wouldn't be so bad.

"Famous last words," he muttered to himself.

But caffeine was caffeine, and beggars couldn't be choosers.

He wrinkled his nose at the thick black slime at the bottom of the pot. "Nasty." Opening the slot for water, he closed it quickly before opening it up again. No wonder the coffee tasted so bad, no matter the time of day. "When was the last time this thing was cleaned?"

Slipping off his jacket, he set to work, grumbling to himself the entire time. If he hadn't been so desperate for a cup of joe, he would have thrown the entire machine away.

When an initial scrub did little to scrape off the thick black coating, Zane squirted soap into the pot to let it soak for a few minutes. Still grumbling, he grabbed the television remote and began flipping through the channels. He paused the surfing when he spotted the shape of a familiar woman striding toward him. Special Agent Kavya Bhatti looked every bit as awake as Zane felt.

White light shone on the long, glossy black hair she'd fashioned into a neat braid that draped over one shoulder. Aside from SAC Keaton and a handful of women in other departments, Kavya was one of the few agents who wore colorful attire on a regular basis. Today, her gray slacks flared slightly at her feet, and her yellow blouse was trimmed with black. Her matching mustard yellow flats were silent against the carpeted floor as she approached.

Much to his relief, Agent Bhatti was one of two agents from their department who had been assigned to the San Luis Cartel task force.

Zane raised a hand in greeting as she neared the open doorway. "Morning, Agent Bhatti."

Rubbing her tan forearms, she stepped across the threshold and nodded. "Morning, Palmer. Why is it always two degrees above freezing in here? I've worked at this office for the past four years, and I can't figure it out."

He shot her a grin. "My partner asks me the same thing at least once a day. Maybe you two should team up and figure out who in the hell sets the thermostat around here." He gestured to his black suit, pastel blue tie, and crisp white dress shirt. "I mean, *I'm* fine. You ladies seem to be getting the short end of the stick, though."

Kavya pulled out a chair across from him. "That's true." She lifted an eyebrow. "Agent Storm is your partner, right? You guys are the new Leóne task force?"

It was Zane's turn to raise an eyebrow. "As opposed to the

old task force?"

"No, not since I've been here, at least." Agent Bhatti leaned back in her chair. "But task forces come and go as they're needed."

"Right, like the Irish task force. They were reassigned after that big bust we made earlier in the year." Zane stood and headed over to where the coffee pot was soaking. "I decided to save us all from botulism. Give me a minute, and I'll see if I can brew a decent pot. Want some?"

With a chuckle, she nodded. "I do, actually. I've been trying to save a little money by drinking coffee here instead of going to one of those overpriced shops."

Zane nearly cheered when the glass came clean. Well, mostly. Putting the machine back together, he loaded it with water and one of the premade coffee packets. "You know, I think it'd almost be preferable to rack up a bunch of credit card debt to avoid drinking this stuff every day." He pressed the start button. "Let's see if this pot is any better. We're tossing it if it isn't."

She crossed her fingers. "Here's hoping."

He grinned as he pulled open a white cabinet door to fish for a couple mugs. "I usually brew my own coffee at home before I come to work, but I tried to make it in early today. I was actually hoping to catch you or Agent Alvarez this morning."

"Glad you caught us. As soon as Alvarez gets here, we're headed out to a crime scene. Double homicide, one of the victims is a cartel lieutenant."

Zane's eyebrows shot up. "Really? Someone's going after the Cartel?"

Kavya pursed her lips. "It's starting to look like it. We don't know who...yet."

Rubbing his chin, Zane dropped back to his seat. "Well, Storm and I will keep our ears to the ground."

"Thanks. Whoever's been picking these fights has to be a heavyweight in Chicago if they think they can go toe to toe with the San Luis Cartel. We can't rule out the possibility that it might have something to do with the Leóne family or even the D'Amato family."

Zane's stomach turned. A war between an Italian crime family and one of Mexico's largest drug cartels was the last thing the city of Chicago needed.

"Storm and I are looking into a kidnapping. Well, two kidnappings, actually." He reached into his pocket for the sketch. "How much do you know about the Cartel's involvement with human trafficking?"

Propping her cheek in one hand, Kavya's chocolate brown eyes shifted to the ceiling. "Not much, really. As best as we can tell, their main focus right now is carving out territory to push heroin and meth. They hit our radar a few years back, but they've only really *shown up* within the past year."

The coffee pot began to hiss and spit, a sure sign it had almost finished brewing. "Shown up as in racked up a body count?"

Kavya nodded. "That's not to say that they *aren't* dabbling in human trafficking. But if they are, we don't know much about it. It's a big business for their rival, the Veracruz Cartel, but the San Luis Cartel doesn't have much of a history with it."

Another check in the Leóne box.

He slid the paper across the table to Kavya and rose to pour what he hoped would be two decent cups of coffee. "We think our first victim was lured into a forced labor camp, and this is a witness sketch of the guy who recruited him." He set one of the cups in front of Kavya and tapped the edge of the picture. "The witness said his name was Vince, but he went by Vinnie. He had a tattoo of a mermaid on one arm, and he didn't speak with any accent that the witness could tell."

A crease formed between Kavya's brows as she studied the sketch. After a few moments, she shook her head as she reached for the steaming mug. "I don't recognize him. The name and the tattoo aren't familiar, either. The Cartel has a few tattoos that are specific to their operation, like two crossed sabers or a black sunburst. But a mermaid doesn't have any significance."

A sudden movement in the doorway stole Zane's attention.

Blue and white lunchbox in hand, the newcomer blinked a few times as he made his way into the room. Even with the pressed suit, Zane could tell that the man maintained a muscular physique. If memory served, one of his arms was tattooed with a full sleeve, and the other sported a handful of different pieces.

Kavya's gaze shifted to the bleary-eyed man. "Hey, Alvarez."

Stifling a yawn, Agent Alvarez pried open the refrigerator. "Morning, Kavya. Palmer."

"You sound like I feel." She chuckled and waved at the half-full pot. Pour yourself some coffee. We've got a double homicide to get to before nine."

Alvarez rubbed his eyes and shuffled over to the counter. "It's too early for murder."

Midway through a drink of the semi-respectable coffee, Zane fought against laughter. The comment was so similar to a remark Amelia would make, he had to double-check to make sure he hadn't imagined Agent Alvarez in Amelia's place.

Once Alvarez had filled a mug, Kavya waved him over to look at the sketch. "Do you recognize this guy? First name, Vince, but goes by Vinnie."

Agent Alvarez set his mug on the laminate table and moved to stand behind Kavya, and he took a moment to review the sketch before shaking his head as his partner had done before. "No, he doesn't look familiar. Is this someone you're looking for, Palmer?"

With a nod, Zane took a long drink of coffee. The temperature had dropped just below molten lava, and he was impressed with how much better it tasted while trying to not think of all the nastiness he'd consumed with the dirty pot over the past days and weeks.

"Vinnie, huh?" Alvarez took a seat at the end of the table. "Sounds Italian."

"It sounds very Italian." Zane lifted a shoulder. "But I can't say he's a Leóne just based on a name, you know?"

Kavya drummed her fingers against the table. "Well, just because Vinnie sounds Italian and doesn't have an accent doesn't mean he's *not* Cartel. The San Luis Cartel is a big operation, and there's no way me and Alvarez know every guy in it."

Zane didn't bother to hide his disappointment. He heaved a sigh as he returned the sketch to his interior jacket pocket.

Kavya offered a sympathetic shrug. "But I can tell you that it significantly decreases the likelihood that he's part of the Cartel."

"That's true." As he rose to stand, he rapped his knuckles on the laminate surface. "I appreciate it, Agents. Any information is better than no information."

Maybe the sentiment was true, but as Zane left to return to his and Amelia's base of operation, he didn't feel much better.

How in the hell could they have a detailed, lifelike sketch of a man they knew for certain had been involved in Javier's disappearance and still be no closer to uncovering the culprit?

Something had to break. He just hoped it would break before their time ran out.

12

L eaning back in my office chair, I sipped at the latte I'd picked up on my way out to the farm that morning. Though the acreage was more than two hours outside the city of Chicago, I kept the commute short by renting an apartment in a town that was only a half hour drive. As much as I missed the city, I had to admit that the little town's café was a cut above most chain coffee shops.

Besides, the city didn't have the collection of pretty little things I kept in the basement.

Amidst all the hustle and bustle of Chicago, hiding an operation the size of my pet project would have been next to impossible.

A knock pulled my attention back to the dull gray walls of my office. I straightened in my seat and set the paper coffee cup on the rich wooden desk. Even though I knew that only my men had access to the section of the warehouse that held our offices, I didn't need Dean or Matteo to see me kicked back in the cushioned chair, half-awake.

I cleared my throat. "It's unlocked. Come in."

The lever handle turned, and the door swung inward

with a faint squeak. As Carlo's dark eyes met mine, he offered me a slight nod of greeting.

Carlo's mouth was set in a hard line as he eased the door closed behind himself. His expression left me wondering which piece of shit was about to hit the fan this time.

Carlo was notorious in the Leóne family for his good humor. If he'd been driven to anger—or even just to seriousness—I wanted to know the reason.

"Have a seat." I gestured to the two armchairs that faced my desk. "Something's on your mind."

Running a hand along his thinning hair, Carlo slumped down into one of the chairs. "Yeah, I figured you'd be able to tell."

Was I going to have to pry the story out of him? "Business or personal?"

"Business. I just got back from the city. Had to visit the wife and kids, you know?"

I didn't but nodded anyway.

As he leaned his head back, he let out a sigh. "While I was there, the boss called me. He wanted me to bring you a message."

My mouth went dry hearing he'd spoken to the boss, and my pulse rushed in my ears like a tidal wave. Still, I fought to keep my expression blank.

The business I ran in the basement wasn't sanctioned by my superior, nor any other capo in the family. In fact, none of them knew the operation existed. Any time they wound up at the farm, I kept the basement door locked. So far, no one had asked questions.

I swallowed as I tried to chase away the bitterness on my tongue. "What's the message?"

Dropping his elbows to the armrests, Carlo met my curious stare. "He said there's someone who's been looking around those Flores kids' house."

This wasn't good. "Someone? The cops?"

"No, not the cops. Some reporter." He scratched his bearded chin. "It didn't sound like a big deal to me, but the boss wanted you to know about it. He said he's had guys following her to see what she's up to."

I shrugged, hoping that I appeared more relaxed than I felt. "Sounds more like an annoyance than anything. If someone reported one of those kids missing, it could just be that the nosy bitch is trying to find her fifteen minutes of fame. Not much we can do from here, anyway."

Carlo nodded. "That's what I thought too."

"What about the girl, Yanira?" Such a pretty little thing. "Is she still not eating?"

As he crossed his arms, Carlo groaned. "No, she's not. I tried to force her, but it didn't work."

I gritted my teeth. At first, Yanira had seemed like one of the most promising girls I'd filmed to date. She had obeyed instructions without hesitation. A rare but valuable trait.

But, over the past couple days, the girl had stopped eating. No matter the type of encouragement I'd used to coax her to consume so much as a piece of toast, she'd refused. I'd threatened her with violence, threatened her brother, even threatened her mother—though I still wasn't sure where Mari Flores had disappeared. Yanira didn't know that, though.

No matter what I said or how colorful the threats became, she only stared back at me with dead eyes.

My rising star had turned into a thorn in my side, and if she didn't correct her behavior soon, my hand would be forced.

The thought of losing such a pretty little thing so soon after her debut was infuriating. If I actually knew where Yanira's mother was, I'd drag the woman down to the basement to straighten out her daughter's attitude.

Family was always the best motivator. At that thought, realization clicked in my head. I knew exactly how to get Yanira to cooperate.

I turned my attention back to Carlo. "We'll try something else."

Carlo raised a dark eyebrow. "What's your idea?"

My mouth twitched as the idea formed. "She hasn't seen her brother for a little while, has she? Maybe we ought to bring him downstairs for a little family reunion."

Scratching a bearded cheek, Carlo shrugged his broad shoulders. "I'm not sure, boss. I tried telling her I'd kill her brother if she didn't eat anything, and it didn't make a difference."

Sometimes, I thought I was surrounded by idiots. Maybe we needed a few courses on Coercion 101. "True, but maybe she didn't believe you. She might think her brother's already dead. I think we just need to show her that he's alive but that if she doesn't start to cooperate, he *will* be dead. Or worse. And that his death will be all her fault."

A portion of my sly smile manifested on Carlo's face. "That's perfect. I'm sure Matteo wouldn't mind taking a few more swings at the kid."

Willing myself to be patient, I held up a finger. "No, that's not quite what I had in mind. I'm not sure that'd get the point across. Not permanently, anyway. We'd probably have to bring Javier down there every other day to rough him up to keep her in line."

Tapping the armrests with his two forefingers, Carlo nodded. "That's true. She's an obstinate little shit, isn't she?"

"She is. We've had to deal with a few of these in the past, and most of the time, they end up with a bullet between their eyes. That's what I'm trying to avoid here." I could almost see the dollar signs flush down the toilet. "Besides, Javier's met his numbers for the past two days. After the beating he took, it's honestly impressive. The kid's a workhorse."

Carlo cocked his head. "True. I've had my ear to the ground. You know, listening to see if he's stirring up any shit, but he's not. He's been quiet as a church mouse."

I leaned back and crossed my arms over my chest. "Exactly. I don't want Matteo to beat the hell out of him and ruin his productivity for the next week."

Rubbing his hands on his thighs, Carlo looked up expectantly at me. "What's the plan?"

I loved being the smartest man in the room. "As luck would have it, there's a market for incest porn. I'd say it's a niche market, but you'd be surprised at how much I've stumbled across." I spread my hands. "She eats and starts to cooperate again, or she gets fucked by her older brother, and I make a shitload of money off it. It's a win-win."

Though only for a split-second, apprehension flickered behind Carlo's dark eyes, but the sentiment was gone as soon as it had appeared.

I pinned my second-in-command with an intent stare. "If this isn't your cup of tea, you don't have to participate. I'm sure Matteo would love to split the profits three ways instead of four."

Our fourth wasn't around the farm as often these days, but his contribution to our enterprise was still invaluable. As a detective in the Chicago Police Department, the man had his hands full.

Expression blank, Carlo met my gaze and shook his head. "No, nothing like that. It was just unexpected. I think it'll work, though. And you're right. I think it'll work *permanently*."

"I know it will."

And if the threat itself didn't work, if Yanira was *still* stubborn, then she and her brother would put on a show.

13

As he combed the fingers of one hand through his slicked-back hair, Joseph Larson glanced to the pricey watch on his wrist to check the time. Quarter after nine.

He blew out a breath as the digital counter beside the elevator keypad reached twelve. The stainless-steel doors slid open with a cheery ding. He'd spent the previous night working out his sexual frustration on a pretty redhead he'd met at the trendy bar near his apartment. Her first name was either Heather or Holly, and he didn't think they'd even bothered with surnames.

It was almost too easy. Flash them his killer smile and mention the badge. Nothing gets a woman wetter than learning they're with an FBI agent. After a couple drinks and a casual mention of his handcuffs, he had Heather right where he wanted. They headed back to her apartment for a little undercover work.

The instances where he stayed out past one a.m. on a weeknight were rare, but he'd been out of sorts ever since his and Amelia's awkward departure outside Madison's Sports Bar.

At the thought of the willowy special agent, he clenched his jaw and stepped into the quiet hallway.

Try as he might, he couldn't figure out how the interaction with Amelia had spiraled so far out of his control. Since their return to work two days earlier, he'd only caught sight of her once. She'd been alone but was out of earshot.

If Amelia had noticed him, she'd been careful to ignore his presence.

Any time he went over their Friday night conversation, he cringed. She'd called his bluff, and he doubted she believed a word of his backpedaling.

He was sure he'd been within an inch of bringing her home. The image of her lithe body, naked and sprawled out across his bed, faded into the void. What he wouldn't do to that woman. Her tight ass, those perky tits, and those lips. He bet she knew how to use 'em too. If only she hadn't shot him down. They'd have gone all weekend, and she'd beg him for more.

As Joseph strolled down the hallway, he casually adjusted himself in an effort to hide his growing erection.

Even just the thought of Amelia bent over was enough to threaten the tethers that bound him to reality. If she only knew the things he would do to her, the things he'd do *for* her, she'd change her mind. Of that, he was certain.

All she needed was a little chemical encouragement.

If they'd ever made it back to his apartment on Friday night, he could have given her that encouragement.

Molly, of course, not Rohypnol. He wasn't some dipshit frat boy. He wanted his women awake and coherent enough to enjoy themselves. He'd slept with plenty of women who had willingly, *knowingly*, taken Molly to enhance their experience. Hell, he'd even partaken in the past.

Rubbing his eyes, he shook himself away from the

thoughts and turned the corner to the section of desks that belonged to Organized Crime.

If he was smart, he'd forget about trying to sleep with Amelia Storm. For all the same reasons he found her irresistible—her strong will, her wit, her physical prowess—he'd be wise to steer clear.

He clenched and released his fist. Chances are, she'd probably already slept with Palmer, anyway.

Women were slippery like that. They'd act polite when they turned a man down and then slip off to sleep with his friend.

Or his rival, in Joseph's case.

Normally, Joseph would take note of any potential flaw to leverage against and eliminate a man he viewed as competition, but there was a cunning behind Zane Palmer's scrutinizing glare that made the hairs on the back of his neck prickle. He'd seen the man in action when they took down the Irish gangsters who'd captured Fiona Donahue, and he was man enough to admit that he'd rather avoid a physical altercation with Agent Palmer.

In an effort to ground himself, to remind himself that he was at the FBI office, he paused to look over the rows of cubicles. A couple agents sat or stood at their desks, and on the far side of the room, he spotted Fiona Donahue's coppery hair as she conversed with Spencer Corsaw.

Straightening his black tie, Joseph glanced to the open doorway on his other side. He'd thought the dim copy room was empty, but he froze in place when his eyes settled on a familiar figure.

Amber light caught the polished silver band of her watch as she brushed a piece of hair from her forehead while checking her phone. Her unlined face was calm, even serene. As he followed the curve of her neck down to her collarbone, he spotted the subtle shape of the cup of her bra.

Her white dress shirt was buttoned well past the point of cleavage, but she always found some way to tease him, didn't she?

His rational mind told him to keep walking and stop staring at Amelia's alluring figure, but as soon as he'd spotted her, Joseph couldn't help himself. He stepped into the doorway and rapped his knuckles against the metal frame.

A muscle in her cheek twitched the moment she locked eyes with him, but otherwise, her expression was unreadable.

He ignored the telltale sign of irritation and forced a smile to his lips. "Hey, Storm."

She pocketed the phone. "Morning, Larson. How's it going?"

Her tone was amiable enough. The hour was early, and maybe he'd jumped to conclusions when she'd tightened her jaw. Most agents in the building were about as good-humored as an aggravated badger before they'd had their morning caffeine.

He finally let his hand relax as he crossed the threshold. "I'm fine. How about you? What brings you to the copy room at nine in the morning?"

She grabbed a sheet of paper off the nearest laser printer. "Printing things, actually. Well, one thing."

Before he could ask her a follow-up question, she held up a black and white sketch of a man with tousled black hair, dark eyes, and a slight cleft in his chin.

"Do you recognize this man?"

With another step closer, he peered at the lifelike drawing. "He doesn't look familiar." He shifted his gaze back to hers. "Why? Who is he?"

Glancing at the picture, she lifted a shoulder. "That's what I'm trying to figure out. We're pretty sure he had something to do with Javier Flores's disappearance, but we can't seem to pin down an identity."

Joseph's eyebrow quirked up before he could stop it. "We? You and Palmer?"

"Yep." Her lips curved into a smile, but he didn't miss the hint of impatience in her gaze. "Looking for another trafficking ring, it would seem."

"Traffickers get old fast, don't they?" He remembered when he'd first asked her the question in the Boston field office. As far as he was concerned, her stint on the East Coast might as well have happened in another lifetime.

She folded the sheet in half. "They sure do."

As the space lapsed into silence, he glanced over his shoulder to ensure they were alone. When he turned back to Amelia, the amusement had disappeared from her face so thoroughly that he wondered if the good humor had been there at all.

He stuffed a hand in his pocket and sighed. "Can we address the elephant in the room?"

The muscle in her jaw ticked again, and her eyes burned through him like a pair of green embers. "What elephant? I don't see any animals aside from the human ones."

Though he let out another defeated sigh, the truth was, he'd been over this conversation in his head at least thirty times. She'd already seen through to his true intention, and he could either continue the lie he'd started on Friday night, or he could try a new tactic.

Spreading his hands, he opened and closed his mouth a few times before he spoke. The feigned trepidation was all part of the act.

"Okay, look. I'm sorry about Friday. I just." He raked his fingers through his hair. "It's been a while since Megan and I got divorced, and I'm not great at, well…reading women, I guess. I haven't been with anyone in quite a while, and I thought you were interested in something else, and I was wrong."

Her eyes narrowed, but she was quiet.

"And that's totally fine." He lifted his hands and offered her a nervous chuckle. "Totally fine. I'm just an idiot, and I'll deal with that on my own time. Like I said, it's just been a while, and I guess I'm, I don't know...*dense*."

He expected a snarky reply, a side-eye glare, or simply a sigh as she dropped her hands to her hips. Instead, she just blankly stared.

Confused by her response, his temper got the best of him. "What?"

Rolling her eyes, she folded the sketch a second time. "You, that's what. You're a pretty good liar, you know that?"

"I'm sorry, come again?" Annoyance rolled over him as he fought to keep the disbelief off his face. "Why do you think I'm lying?"

As she pocketed the paper, she rubbed the bridge of her nose. "For the love of god, Larson. I don't have time for this shit. I know you're sleeping with Michelle Timmer. Look, I'm not one to judge people's sex lives, really. As long as everyone's having a good time, that's fine. But this..."

She gestured back and forth between them.

"We work together, bud. Not just in a call center or something, but in a job where we might actually get shot at. Where we might actually need to have one another's backs in a life or death situation. I thought we were friends, but you've been throwing one lie at me right after another, and I'm getting sick of it."

Dammit all to hell.

"Michelle Timmer? How'd you know about that?"

Another eye roll. "FBI or not, we're in a giant office building. People talk."

Michelle Timmer, the pretty Yale graduate. She had an ass he could bounce a quarter off of. If he was honest with himself, part of him missed Michelle. She'd been a great cook with an impeccable sense of humor and a body made for sin.

A body not much different from Amelia's.

He gritted his teeth and pried himself away from the recollection. Amelia clearly knew Michelle's name, but he doubted she knew everything about their circumstances. He'd have to find the right angle to work with to avoid digging the hole he was in any deeper, or he'd never have a chance to play out the dirty fantasies in his head.

"I'm sorry." He heaved a genuine sigh. "I don't...I don't really know what to say right now. I've told Chicago PD everything I know about the case. And I pray they find the bastard."

"Hold up. The what now, with who?"

Her reaction was confirmation enough that Amelia was operating on little more than rumors. This, he could work with.

"Michelle Timmer. Look, yes, we went out on a date. Not the smartest move, I know, but nothing happened." He paused and took a long breath, sending his eyes down to the floor, hoping to give off an air of deep embarrassment. "I was walking her home, and she kept looking over her shoulder like she thought someone was following her, so I asked about it."

He paused again, glancing up just long enough to see if Amelia was buying his story, and quickly scrubbed his hands over his face in mock frustration.

"Go on."

Joseph wanted to punch the smug look off her face. Instead, he peered down at his shoes again. "I should have done something. She was clearly scared, but I felt like she was just trying to find a way to end the night without...you know...inviting me inside for coffee. She didn't come in to work the next day."

Amelia stood in stunned silence, staring at him.

"I feel terrible, so I'm trying to follow up some leads and work with Chicago PD to find her."

"Well, I hope they do find her, and not just so you can have a second date. You don't shit where you eat. And furthermore, how could you just ignore a woman clearly feeling threatened or fearful? It's that kind of thinking with the wrong head that gets people hurt."

Not the reply he was expecting, but at least she seemed to have accepted the story. Joseph dropped his gaze again, watching his shoes as he shuffled from one foot to the other. He had to make sure his body language sold the impression of guilt he was trying to convey. "I know. I'm sorry. I was stupid. I'm trying to make up for it."

If she had any sympathy for his remark, the sentiment didn't register past the wicked fire in her voice.

"That's...whatever. Let me make a few things perfectly clear, so I can get back to doing my job and find these poor kids." She held up one finger. "First, I'm not interested in fucking you. Not casually, not in a relationship, not at all." Another finger. "Second, since men always seem to get hung up on this when they're rejected...no, I don't think you're unattractive. You're actually pretty handsome, at least until you open your mouth. I don't sleep with every man I find attractive, so let's put that to rest before you get your panties in a bunch, okay?"

He held up both hands as if to show he was unarmed. "Okay. I get it. Shit, Storm, I'm sorry." He rubbed his forehead. "Can we talk about this somewhere that isn't the copy room in the FBI building?"

Her gaze shifted to the left, toward the doorway at his side.

Gritting his teeth, Joseph turned to face the newest disturbance.

SAC Jasmine Keaton stood in front of the open door.

"Storm. There you are." She extended a hand to beckon Amelia forward. "You've got a visitor. Relevant to your case." Her steely gaze drifted to Joseph, and she offered a quick nod.

"Morning, SAC Keaton." He looked to Amelia, hoping to convey earnest sorrow in his gaze. "Catch you later, Storm. Think about what I said."

She flashed him a thumbs-up, though her expression made him think she would have preferred to stick a different finger in the air. "Yeah, sure."

The dismissive gesture should have made him angry, but as he watched the two women disappear from his field of vision, he craved Amelia even more.

He was playing with fire, and he knew it. Joseph chuckled to himself.

The game was half the fun.

As the heavy wooden door creaked open, Vivian jerked her head toward the familiar woman who stepped into the room.

The corner of Amelia Storm's mouth twitched in what might have been a smile, but there was an unmistakable flicker of annoyance in her forest-green eyes.

FBI agents were never happy to deal with journalists, were they? Vivian tightened her jaw and rubbed her arms over the sleeves of her gray cardigan, attempting to push past the wave of defensiveness. "I'm sorry, Agent Storm. I know it's early. I wanted to stop by yesterday afternoon, but…" She trailed off and merely shook her head.

But I was being followed, and I didn't want them to tail me to the FBI office.

Waving a dismissive hand in the air, Amelia pulled out the

wooden chair across from Vivian and dropped into the seat. "There's no reason to apologize, Ms. Kell. Please, call me Amelia."

"Thank you, Agent…uh…Amelia." She cleared her throat. "Call me Vivian."

"Maybe some other time. Not while we are in the building or discussing an official case. Have to maintain a sense of professionalism when on duty, you know." She paused and snickered as if privy to an inside joke. Her expression lightened as she shook her head. "Sorry. It's just been a frustrating morning, completely unrelated to your visit. Honestly, I'm glad you're here. SAC Keaton said you might have found something that could help on the Flores case."

As Amelia's irritability faded, a flush rose to Vivian's cheeks. "I found something, yes. Well, a couple things, technically. I'm not sure how helpful it'll be, but I wanted to make sure you knew about it."

With a nod, Amelia flipped open her notepad and pulled off the cap of a ballpoint pen.

Agent Storm and her partner, Agent Palmer, had been nothing but kind and professional since she first met them. Too often, the ball of anxiety that lived in Vivian's head liked to convince her she was a burden, even when her logical mind told her she was anything but.

And for the past twenty hours, Vivian's anxiety had taken over her rational mind. On her way home from the Flores house the day before, she'd spent more time with her eyes on the rearview mirror than she had on the cars in front of her.

She'd considered contacting Agent Storm or Palmer as soon as she'd arrived home, but her instincts told her the black Lexus would know if she went to the FBI office right away.

Instead, she had closed all the blinds and curtains in her

apartment, turned off the lights, and spent the rest of the day and night in the living room with a twelve-gauge shotgun at her side. She'd bought the weapon a few years earlier when an ex-boyfriend began stalking her. He'd eventually moved out of the city to be with a new girlfriend, and Vivian could only hope that woman was safe.

Once her hands had stopped trembling, she mustered up the courage to call Mari. Though Vivian couldn't be entirely sure who was behind the wheel of the black Lexus or who *they* were truly interested in, she had to at least give Mari a warning to prepare herself for the worst. Vivian hadn't asked for Mari's location, for safety's sake, but by now, she should be miles away from the city.

Vivian shook off the memories and fished in her handbag for the printouts she'd brought. "Mari Flores, Javier and Yanira's mother, gave me a key to the house when I met up with her a couple days ago. That was before she knew that the FBI was investigating, and she wanted me to have it so I could go look around for something that might help me find her children."

Amelia's eyebrows arched in curiosity. "You didn't mention that, but, since neither of the kids went missing from their home, a warrant hasn't been high on our priority list. I take it you found something?"

Vivian swallowed against the desert in her mouth and nodded. "Yeah. I thought that maybe if I could take a look around, and if I found anything, it would save you and Agent Palmer the hassle of having to get a warrant."

Tapping her pen against the notepad, Amelia's expression turned thoughtful. "I suppose it could. What did you find?"

As she smoothed out the printed photo of the phone number in Javier's notebook, Vivian took in a steadying breath.

She met Amelia's expectant gaze as she slid the picture

across the wooden table. "It's just a phone number and a name. Vinnie. When I looked up the phone number last night, I couldn't find anything. But I figured you guys probably have access to some more sophisticated databases here at the FBI."

"Yeah." Amelia scribbled the number in her notepad. "We'll run it through our system and see what we can find. Did you call it?"

Running a finger over the crease in the center of the second piece of paper—the printout of all the information she'd found about the black Lexus—Vivian shook her head. "No. I didn't. I was worried that an unsolicited call might tip them off, provided they're involved in Javier and Yanira's kidnapping."

"Good thinking." After setting her pen down, Amelia folded her hands. "Not to be rude, but I've seen people in the middle of panic attacks who looked less worried than you do right now. You look about as comfortable as a whore in church."

Heat rose to Vivian's cheeks at Amelia's choice of words. She'd first met the agent when they had both been working different angles of a prostitution ring case. Of course, she was only doing journalistic undercover work, but the correlation was not lost on her. Vivian dropped her gaze to the license plate number she'd already memorized.

"It's that obvious, huh?" Vivian coughed into her fist and fought to push against the anxiety. No use falling apart here. Vivian lifted her head and met the agent's eyes again. "To be fair, I haven't made it a point to hide it since I got here. But yeah, you could say I'm nervous."

Vivian reached back into her handbag with one hand and slid the sheet of paper across the table with the other. "That's the license plate number for a car that was following me yesterday. It's a black, late-model Lexus ES 350, at least as well as I can tell." She produced a flash drive from her purse. "I took a video, but most of it is blurry. My...my hands were shaking pretty badly. I was able to make out most of the license plate, but I couldn't figure out the last number."

Lips pursed, Amelia studied Vivian's notes. "You said this car was following you? Can you tell me a little more about that?"

With a nod, Vivian launched into her recollection of the nerve-racking trip to the Flores residence the day before. She went over all her sightings of the black Lexus, including how she'd double and triple checked to ensure she hadn't been followed to the FBI office that morning.

As she wrapped up the story, Vivian wrung her hands in her lap. Her heart clamored against her chest, and her mouth felt like it had been stuffed with cotton balls.

Her intent had been to provide all the information she'd gathered from her trip to the Flores house, but she couldn't help the pang of guilt when she thought of her piece on Premier Ag Solutions.

The possibility that such a big player in the labor contracting industry might be tied up in organized crime was a stretch, but it *was* a possibility.

As confident as Vivian was that no one—aside from her friend Felicia—knew of the exposé's existence, she couldn't be certain. Until recently, she'd backed up the article on a cloud-based server.

Clouds were hacked all the time. Who was to say Vivian's online storage had remained secure?

And who was to say that Chuck, her boss, hadn't seen it in her working folder and mentioned the piece to one of his colleagues at *The Chicago Standard*?

"There's one more thing." Vivian was surprised her voice didn't crack.

As Amelia's green eyes fixed on her, Vivian wondered how long the room had been quiet.

Vivian flopped her hands back onto the table and sighed. "It probably isn't relevant. I think they were following me because I'm looking into Yanira and Javier, but there's one more possibility."

Though she remained silent, Agent Storm's gaze remained fixed on Vivian.

"It's a piece I've been working on for quite a while. Six months, maybe longer. It's turned from more of an article into an exposé, almost. I've even wondered if I should just keep going with it and write a book." Vivian brushed a piece of dark hair from her eyes. "It's about labor contractors. Specifically, those that contract labor out to agricultural businesses. There's one company I was interested in, Premier Ag Solutions. They've been fined multiple times for employing undocumented workers."

Amelia's silence and expression were unreadable.

Vivian cleared her throat as the familiar thrum of anxiety worked its way down to her bones. "Only a couple people know about my article, but it's still possible that Premier could have found out somehow. It's possible that's who was following me."

She half-expected Agent Storm to laugh aloud or to wave away the concern with a roll of her eyes.

Instead, she set down her ballpoint pen and nodded. "Do you think that Premier is involved in Yanira and Javier's disappearance? Or is this an unrelated circumstance?"

Truth be told, Vivian wasn't sure how many times she'd asked herself the same question. But no matter how many times she ran through the what-if scenarios in her head, all she could offer Agent Storm was a shrug. "I don't know. But I can't ignore my gut, and it's telling me I should mention the company, in case it is related."

"Okay." Amelia nodded again. "If you don't mind, could you send me your article? It seems like a bit too much of a coincidence that Premier would have people following you for writing that article now, of all times. Our main priority is to find Yanira and Javier. But, like you said, we can't rule out the possibility that the two are connected."

Vivian dropped her gaze to her hands. "Yes, I can send you the article." Her heart kicked into overdrive at the thought of having to share the article with the FBI, of all agencies. She wasn't as worried about sharing the unfinished piece as she was about the prospect that a company the size of Premier could be involved with kidnapping and extortion.

As much as she'd wanted to dig up dirt about the contractor over the last six months, Vivian suddenly hoped Premier's extracurricular activities were limited to those of the white-collar variety.

"Good, thank you." Amelia's tone sounded empathetic, at least. "Now, in light of the fact that you've seen someone following you, I'm going to get ahold of the Chicago Police Department to set you up with a little security."

Vivian reflexively opened her mouth to protest, but Amelia cut her off with an upraised hand.

"I know. No one's all that keen on having a cop follow them around, especially in a line of work like yours. I don't blame you. But considering the fact that we might be dealing with a powerful group of traffickers, I think we ought to take a little precaution."

As she swallowed the lump in her throat, Vivian fidgeted with the hem of her gray sweater. Agent Storm was right, but she couldn't help but wonder if a security detail would only draw *more* attention to her involvement in the case.

With a steadying breath, she looked up. "What kind of security?"

Amelia leaned back in her chair and spread her hands.

"Nothing too intense. I'll just put in an order to have an officer in the area drive by your apartment building every half hour or so. Honestly, since we don't know *who* we're dealing with yet, it'll be hard to get the CPD to do anything more. They're stretched thin enough as it is."

"Oh." Vivian blinked a couple times. She'd expected Amelia to suggest a uniformed police officer follow her around morning, noon, and night. "Okay. Yeah. That sounds good. Thank you."

Pulling a business card from the pocket of her black slacks, Amelia gave Vivian a reassuring smile. "Here's my card. My email address is on it, and you can send the article there whenever you get a chance."

Vivian's stomach churned with unease. She kept her expression even as she accepted the business card. If Premier Ag Solutions's criminal roots went to a deeper, more sinister place, then Vivian had just painted a target on her back.

14

D espite the effort Amelia put into following up on the information she'd been given by Vivian the day before, she'd managed a full eight hours of sleep for the first time in over a week. She'd been relieved to have gotten the conversation with Joseph Larson out of the way. Telling him off had been cathartic.

She blew a raspberry into the still air of her and Zane's windowless workspace. Though she was certain Joseph had deserved every word and then some, she couldn't help but wonder if she should have been more diplomatic.

After all, as she'd so pointedly mentioned to him, they *did* work together at the FBI, and chances *were* good they'd have to watch each other's back at some point in the future.

Rubbing her temples, she forced the thoughts out of her head and returned her focus to the glowing laptop screen. At a quarter after six in the morning, Amelia was alone in their so-called war room, and aside from a couple members of the cleaning crew, she hadn't run into a single person since she'd arrived at the office a half hour ago.

She and Zane had gone through Vivian's photos and

video the day before, but they hadn't been able to pin down a useful image of the person behind the wheel of the black Lexus. Due, in part, to the sun's glare and the tint of the car windows, the driver's face had been obscured in each picture.

The license plate number should have been more straightforward, but neither she nor Zane had located a match in the DMV database. They'd tried every combination to fill in the final blurry digit in the photos, but none were associated with a black Lexus.

Once Zane had finished spitting out a slew of four-letter words at their newest dead end, and after Amelia had finished laughing at his colorful expletives—it was either that or weep at their failure—Zane printed out the highest quality image of the license plate and the driver. Both pictures now hung on the whiteboard, just below the sketch of the mysterious Vinnie.

Amelia propped her elbows on the table, leaned forward, and rested her chin on her knuckles. She stared at the whiteboard as if trying to will it to give her answers it simply didn't have.

All recent Illinois license plates ended in a series of numbers, and since only the final digit in Vivian's photos was obscured, they were left with ten possibilities. Of the ten, three vehicles were no longer operational, and of the seven that remained, the closest make and model was a navy-blue Mazda sedan.

None of the seven drivers had reported their license plates stolen, and the probability that the criminal organization had manufactured counterfeits so realistic they could fool cops out on the street was next to nil.

She was missing something. Something obvious.

Eyes narrowed, she zoomed in on the image she'd opened on the laptop. Had they misread one of the numbers or a letter? Confused the Illinois design with a different state?

No, Abraham Lincoln was clearly printed on the left side. There was no doubt that the license plate belonged to Illinois.

"Land of Lincoln," she muttered to herself.

For what might have been the five-millionth time, she stared at the series of letters and numbers. There was no question that the first was the letter A, and the second was a Q.

With one finger hovering above the plus key, Amelia froze in place. "Wait a second."

Rather than zoom in closer, she adjusted the color saturation to make the color red, the shade of the text on an Illinois license plate, stand out from the background.

After the adjustment, the tail of the uppercase Q didn't pop out like the rest of the letter.

The mark wasn't red, and it wasn't part of the plate number.

Amelia's eyes went wide. *The starting letters are AO, not AQ.*

A rush of excitement brought a tremor to her hands, but she ignored the sensation as she opened the Department of Motor Vehicles database. The first AO result belonged to a pickup, but Amelia closed the window and opened a new search in record time.

She came across a Camaro, another Mazda, and finally, a black Lexus sedan. The vehicle was registered to a woman, but when Amelia spotted her last name, she nearly cheered.

Brandi Dalessio.

Over the next forty-five minutes, Amelia traced Brandi Dalessio's background, her family, and her social connections. She was so absorbed in her search that she hardly glanced away from the laptop.

When a faint beep and a metallic click jerked her out of

the trance-like state, she sucked in a sharp breath and almost leapt out of her chair.

Zane's gaze was fixed on the hall as he slipped through the doorway, a stainless-steel thermos in one hand. As he turned toward the room, Zane cursed, his hands coming up to fight.

"Jesus!" He pointed his thermos at her. "You scared the shit out of me! Since when do you get here before eight?"

Amelia waggled a finger at him. "No, *you* scared *me*. Didn't you see me jump just now? I'm pretty sure my ass left the cushion." The momentary surprise faded, replaced by Amelia's excitement to share the new information she'd discovered. She waved him over and pulled one of the few functioning office chairs up to the worn table. "Come look at this."

He accepted the offered seat. "You got something?"

"Yep." Amelia slid the matte silver laptop closer to him. "Look at this. This is the original picture of the license plate, and this…" she tapped a key, "is the same image, but with the saturation cranked up. Anything look off?"

"The Q." He set his coffee on the table and scooted forward. "No. It's not a Q. What the hell is it?"

Amelia shrugged. "I don't know. Could be a piece of dirt, could be a bug. The rest of the car was clean, so I'm leaning more toward a bug. It might be a cicada, honestly. I've heard those things every night."

"Then we're looking for an AO plate." He gestured to the screen. "I'm assuming you already looked that up? How long have you been here? Did you even go home last night?"

Plucking at the fabric of her teal blouse, she shot him a look of feigned indignation. "Yes, Mom, I did. I slept really well, actually. That's why I got here so early."

He gave her a grin so big his dimples showed. "Okay,

okay. Well, based on that look, the license plate wasn't a dead end. What did you find?"

"Brandi Dalessio." Amelia clicked over to the woman's picture. "She's married to Frank Dalessio, whose brother is Joe Dalessio."

Zane rubbed his chin. "Joe Dalessio? That sounds familiar. Leóne Capo, right?"

Amelia nodded. "Right."

He leaned back, the chair screeching in protest. "So, we think Frank was the one driving the car and following Vivian?"

"We do." She held up a finger. "But that's not all. I was just looking through their social media profiles. Check out what I found on Brandi's."

As his attention flicked back to the laptop, Zane straightened.

"She was at a wedding recently. One of Joe's cousins, Isabella, married a man named Nicolas Vallerio. From the looks of it, it was a pretty extravagant event." She clicked through a couple photos from the wedding before she landed on the image she sought.

Zane took in a breath through his teeth. "Is that?"

Hovering the cursor over the leftmost man in a group of three, Amelia nodded. "Yep. That's Vincent Piliero, also known as Vinnie. You remember Emilio's fiancée, Ileana Piliero? Vinnie is her older brother." She pointed to the taller man in the middle. "That's Joe again, and then this younger guy on the right is one of Isabella's older brothers, Alton Dalessio."

"Shit." He drew out the word until it was closer to four syllables than one. "This is like a who's who of the Leóne family. Where the hell were our invitations?"

Clasping Zane's shoulder, Amelia painted a look of disappointment on her face. "Honey, the only Leóne invitation we'll ever get is to a funeral...our funeral."

His lips parted in a grin. "I'd be willing to attend for a couple of those caviar-topped canapes. You see that?" He pointed to the screen. "They had lobster. That's got to be worth...what...at least a misdemeanor, right?"

Amelia snorted and gave his shoulder a friendly shove. "First of all, how do you know what caviar canapes are?"

Though she was normally hesitant when physical contact was concerned, she'd spent more time around Zane Palmer over the last couple months than any other person she knew. They'd had plenty of time to get to know each other during their undercover work on the Leila Jackson investigation.

She and Zane had posed as a wealthy couple in order to access the so-called VIP section of a nightclub that fronted part of a prostitution ring. After the night full of feigned lewd glances and groping, a friendly touch didn't bring on any of the usual anxiety. Plus, she had to admit that part of her had enjoyed the purposeful touches that night.

Zane shrugged. "What can I say? I'm a man of good taste."

"Who is easily bought by the promise of a good meal. I'll remember that."

"We all have our price."

Amelia's jaw was starting to hurt from smiling. Zane was disarming like that. And he seemed to enjoy finding new ways to make her crack up.

Amelia hadn't bothered with men since an amicable breakup with a Naval Intelligence Officer shortly after she'd left the military. Between his promotion to Lieutenant Commander and her start with the FBI, their lives had taken them in different directions. They'd been together for three years before they split, and now, even a casual fling didn't seem worth the effort.

The relationship had always felt light and airy, almost like they were both there to enjoy time away from the dating world. When the day had come to move on, a couple tears had been shed. But more than anything, they'd wished each other well and promised to stay in touch.

Maybe the two-year gap explained why Amelia's stomach had flip-flopped the first time Zane had brushed his hand along her leg when they were at Evoked.

With his flawless smile, his lean but muscular frame, and those slate eyes that seemed to take on a hint of the color that surrounded them, there was no denying that Zane Palmer was attractive. Some people might have been put off by his self-deprecating comments and slew of embarrassing middle school stories, but his recollections always helped to keep Amelia grounded.

He was nice to look at, but more than anything, Amelia was glad that she could call Zane her friend. And right now, with Joseph—a man she'd *thought* was her friend—and his attempts to sleaze his way into her pants, plus the rat that lurked somewhere in their office, Amelia was grateful to have someone she could trust.

Zane stood and shrugged out of his jacket, tossing it over one of the more broken chairs. Amelia jerked her attention back to the windowless room.

Picking up his coffee from the scuffed table, he lifted his eyebrows. "What's the plan?"

Amelia leaned back in her chair, one of the few that didn't screech like a pissed off alley cat when it moved. "First, we need to confirm that Vinnie's our recruiter. We can either bring Silvia here for a photo lineup or stop to talk to her."

He nodded. "I'm not sure if that by itself will be enough to get a warrant to search his place. *We* know that he's part of a mafia-run trafficking ring, but we don't have anything to prove it. The way a judge will see it, we've got an eyewitness who confirms Javier went to an interview for a job that probably hires undocumented workers. But we've got no employer name, no location, nothing else."

"Maybe not a warrant to search his entire house," she flashed him a knowing grin, "but I think it'll be more than enough for us to get a warrant for his business's employment records. He's off the grid, so it's not like we can subpoena them, you know?"

With a chuckle, Zane dug his heels into the carpet and wheeled his chair away from the table. "No, I suppose we couldn't." He raised his hand. "You start on the warrant, and I'll go talk to Silvia."

She smacked his palm with hers. "And then we go talk to our pal Vinnie."

15

As grateful as I was to be back in the city, the reason for the unplanned visit left a foul taste in my mouth. First, Carlo had brought me the message about that damn reporter, and now I was in Chicago to meet with my boss about an urgent security matter.

I didn't believe in coincidences.

Before I even pushed open the elaborate wooden door to the boss's office, I was confident that the reporter *was* the security matter.

The boss's dark eyes snapped up from where they'd been fixed on a sheet of paper atop his mahogany desk. Without an ounce of greeting, he beckoned me forward.

Glancing around the handmade bookshelves built into the beige walls, I eased the door closed behind myself. If there had been plastic on the floor, I would have turned tail and run. Still on alert, I headed to one of the two squat armchairs and dropped into the seat.

Rubbing the dark stubble on one side of his cheek, the boss finally smiled. "Good to see you again. It's been a while. How was your trip into the city?"

The greeting was a tremendous relief, and I hated myself for having those few moments of uncertainty. "Terrible. About what I'd expected from Thursday morning rush hour traffic in Chicago. As much as I miss being in the city, I sure as hell don't miss that."

With a chuckle, he nodded. "Can't argue with that. How's work out at the farm going?"

"Honestly?" I tapped the fingers of one hand against the armrest. "It could be better. We had that kid, Javier, try to take off about a week ago, and then we lost another worker a couple days later. It's getting later in the season, and we need as many people working out in those fields as we can get. Plus, we've got the pesticide guys spraying the crops today, so that always slows the work down for a few days."

As he nodded again, he pushed a stray piece of dark hair away from his forehead. With his neatly parted slicked-back hair and tailored suit, Joe Dalessio looked like he could have been a 1960s adman. "We'll need to hire some more. How many do you think you'll need to keep production on track?"

I rested my shoulders against the stiff cushion. "Four or five should do it."

He scribbled out a few words on a yellow notepad beside the sheet of paper his eyes had been glued to before I arrived.

"Okay." His gaze flicked back up to me. "Four or five. I'll get ahold of Vinnie and have him get started on it. You should have your new workers within a week or two."

It was difficult to keep my body and face perfectly neutral, when what I wanted to do was close my eyes and dream of what might come in this next shipment. I always looked forward to the new additions to the farm. With each new worker came the possibility for me to expand on my collection of pretty little film stars.

More money for me and those loyal to the empire I was creating.

I wasn't stupid enough to pocket the entirety of the profits from my side business, of course. When Matteo, Carlo, and I had started the venture, we'd dedicated a certain percentage of the money to be invested back into the family. The number was the same the Leónes used for all our other operations.

In the unlikely event someone like Joe Dalessio discovered what we'd been up to, we could easily point out all the cash we'd made for the family over the past few years. Not to mention the girls I sent to Emilio Leóne's prostitution ring before the Feds caught up to him.

The thought of Federal law enforcement snapped me back into the moment. I turned my attention to Joe. There was no way he had called me all the way back to Chicago for an in-person meeting just to check on my workforce. The reporter Carlo had mentioned the day before popped into my mind.

Might as well get it over with. "So, what's the real reason I'm here today, boss?"

Turning the ballpoint pen over in his fingers, all semblance of welcome slid from Dalessio's face. "I'm so glad you asked. It seems we've got a problem."

The accusation in his tone confirmed my suspicions. "The reporter?"

He nodded. "That's right. Her name's Vivian Kell, and a couple months back, she published an article about prostitution in Chicago that mentioned a couple of our spots."

My eyebrow quirked up. "Just ours? What about D'Amato's?"

His lip curled, and he waved a dismissive hand. "The D'Amatos haven't been in the street business for a while. Alex Passarelli moved all of that behind closed doors. Literally. You know, I hate the Passarellis, but Luca's kid is damn good at making the D'Amato family money." He dropped his pen, letting it clatter to the desk, and leaned forward. "But that's not what I called you here for, either."

I gulped hard and reached a hand up to loosen the collar of my button-down shirt. The way the boss looked at me, I felt as if I had a noose around my neck, and he was ready to string me up with it. And I knew the reason why. "Carlo said something about this reporter. She was looking into Javier and his sister."

"She is. She was at that Flores kid's house a couple days ago, so I had someone tail her for a while. She didn't go anywhere until the next day when she went to work. She's probably just looking for her fifteen minutes, but I don't like nosey reporters snooping around too close to my business. We don't know what she knows or if she's working with anyone. That's too many questions without answers. I don't feel too comfortable with that lack of information, do you?"

"No, boss. You're right, of course. It's not good. Especially if you're thinking she might know something she shouldn't."

"Why am I the only one thinking this?" Dalessio arched an accusing eyebrow as he stared me down, daring me to answer the obvious trap of his question. When I didn't, he sighed. "This is the kind of thinking that gets you opportunities to advance. I shouldn't have to tell you. You should have jumped the moment you learned about this nuisance. But since you didn't, here's what you're going to do. Irregardless of what she knows, make sure she doesn't have any opportunities to share information with anyone else."

As the room lapsed into silence, I kept my eyes on the boss and refrained from correcting his grammar. Didn't he know that using words like "irregardless" made him look stupid to his men? Capo or not, I'd known the man for almost my entire life, and I could tell when he was holding back. I knew when there was more to his story than he'd been willing to reveal.

Joe Dalessio was ten years my senior, and he'd taken me under his wing when I was still in high school. Truth be told, he'd been more of a father to me than my biological father, at least in terms of integrating me into the León family.

My old man died a few years earlier, when I was twenty-four. He'd been a drunk who shook down the local business owners for protection money.

Not that any of them required much shaking. Everyone in this city knew who the León family was and knew better than to get on our bad side.

Unless, of course, they were aligned with the D'Amato family.

We'd had an uneasy truce with the D'Amatos for the past five years, but who knew when the ceasefire would come to an abrupt end. The only reason we'd stayed out of each other's way was because the D'Amatos had shifted much of their enterprise into the digital realm.

Despite their departure from the more traditional illicit businesses—street prostitution, selling drugs, running guns —only a fool would believe they'd gone soft. Before the unofficial ceasefire, some of the men in the León family had learned that lesson the hard way.

There was a reason Alex Passarelli was referred to as The Surgeon, and it had nothing to do with a medical degree. The man was precise, diligent, and meticulous.

I still wasn't convinced that he was even human.

When I realized that Joe had no intent to elaborate on his cryptic statement, I crossed both arms over my chest. "With all due respect, Joe, this doesn't make any damn sense. She's a reporter, and she's going to write a story about two missing kids. Big deal. There's no witnesses, no evidence, nothing. And even if there *was*, it's not like she can go back to her apartment and process a DNA analysis, you know?"

Joe clenched his jaw.

Before he could get pissed, I went on, "Like I said, I'm not trying to disrespect you or your order, but you're the one who taught me to keep my eyes open when things don't make sense. And right now, things definitely don't make sense. If we chased down every reporter who wrote about something we were involved in, we'd never get anything else done."

Joe's expression looked as if it had been carved from stone. His brown eyes were flat and emotionless, his mouth a thin line. When he scrubbed a hand over his face and tilted his head back to laugh, I fought to keep the confusion out of my expression.

"Sometimes I forget that I'm the one who taught you about this world." He shook his head. "And you saying shit like that would piss me off if it didn't make me proud."

I fought against a sigh of relief as I returned his grin. Though I regarded Joe as family, he was notorious for his volatility.

Tapping the sheet of paper with the pen, Joe propped his elbows on the heavy mahogany desk. "We've got bigger problems with this reporter than just her writing an article about a couple missing kids. That family is broke, so it's not like anyone would care even if it got published. But this." He pushed the document toward me. "This is a different level."

I scooted closer and scanned the text. "Premier Ag Solutions?" I looked back up at Joe, not bothering to hide my shock. "How in the hell did she figure this out?"

"We don't know." He held up the pen. "But we need to find out. She hasn't published this yet, and we need to make sure it never sees the light of day. Otherwise, our friends at Premier won't be happy with us. Last time, they got fined to the tune of four million. If they get hit again, it'll be closer to ten."

"I'll find her. You know I will." I gestured to the article. "How'd we get this, anyway?"

As Joe's mouth pressed into a hard line, I realized I was close to overstepping my bounds. "A friend of a friend. Someone on the government's payroll."

A cop, maybe even a Fed.

I thought through my options. "Carlo's downstairs. We can take care of this while we're in town. It's our operation she's threatening, so we'll handle it."

"Good." The expression on his face turned deadly. "I thought we might have to find someone else in the family to take care of it, but now I know our little problem will be in good hands. Find her and make sure this article about Premier never sees the light of day."

I rubbed my hands together, not caring to let my excitement show regarding my new assignment. I loved this shit, and I knew exactly how to handle this problem.

I loved this city.

16

As the digital clock in the center console ticked over to one o'clock, Zane pulled his sunglasses from his face and dropped them in the cupholder. Over the course of the thirty-minute drive to Vincent Piliero's two-story house, a sheet of dishwater-gray clouds had moved in to obscure the afternoon sun. And even if the sky hadn't been overcast, the residential neighborhood was filled with towering oaks, cottonwoods, and maples. Aside from the center of the road, almost the entire area was cloaked in shade.

Slowing the car to a stop at the crest of the sloping driveway of a brownstone residence, Amelia threw the gearshift into park.

Zane examined the area. "Nice neighborhood. How much do you think houses around here cost?"

"More than I want to know." Amelia didn't look impressed. "No car in the driveway. You think he's home?"

Craning his neck to peek at the attached two-car garage, Zane lifted a shoulder. "Hard to say."

"You got the warrant?"

Patting his black suit jacket, he grinned with anticipation.

"Sure do. You ready? I doubt the people around here are used to seeing the Feds serve search warrants to their neighbors."

Though slight, the corner of her mouth turned up. "Make sure to shout 'FBI' real loud. We want everyone to hear it."

He opened his door and tapped his Adam's apple. "I'll use my most manly voice."

The summer scorched grass crunched beneath their feet as they crossed the yard. Zane was first up the wooden stairs that led to the covered front porch. He reached for the warrant tucked inside his jacket. Amelia was only a step behind, but she moved to the side of the door and away from any windows.

Breaching a home could quickly become a dangerous situation, and he was grateful for the Kevlar vests they'd both pulled on. Amelia rested her hand on her weapon, her eyes scanning the area, her ears almost looking like a cat's as she went on high alert, listening for any sound.

A couple potted ferns sat beneath the window to the left of the front door, and a geranium hung from the edge of the awning. The plants rustled as a humid breeze wafted past them.

After a quick glance at Amelia to make sure she was ready, Zane pulled open the screen door and pounded three times on the contemporary five-panel mahogany door that probably cost more than several of his paychecks combined. Out of an abundance of caution, he stepped to the side, lowering his exposure in case Piliero decided a shootout might be fun.

Projecting his voice, he called out, "Vincent Piliero. This is the Federal Bureau of Investigation. We have a search warrant. Open the door."

The volume of his "command" voice was just below an outright shout and projected a good long way. Zane imagined any neighbor within earshot was pushing their curtains aside to get a better glimpse of the Piliero's porch.

Amelia did a turkey peek to glance inside the picture window. She shot him a look, frowning.

For the second knock, he balled his hand into a fist and pounded on the heavy door like he was a caveman beating a drum. "Vincent Piliero. FBI! Search warrant. Open the door."

A muffled voice replied, but the speaker was a woman. "Hold on. Just…just a second."

"I don't have a good feeling about this," Amelia murmured and walked to the end of the porch. "I'll keep an eye on that garage."

Without warning, the front door swung inward. A short woman with long, caramel brown hair looked at them in harried confusion. "I'm Donna Piliero, Vinnie's wife." She fidgeted with her hands, twisting the diamond wedding band around her ring finger. "What do you want?"

Zane removed the search warrant from his pocket and explained the proceedings. "Please step aside. Where is your husband?"

"He's in the shower."

Zane crowded Donna Piliero even tighter. "Please step aside."

She looked frightened as hell, but she didn't move. "I'll go get him. I just need a minute."

If she denied him entry, it was within his right to use force to enter the home. "That's not how this works. I'm entering your home. For the last time, step aside."

Though her expression appeared neutral, her darting eyes belied the anxiety she tried so hard to conceal. "There's no need for that. I'm sure he'll be out in just a couple minutes."

The woman wore tight yoga clothes that couldn't have concealed a weapon if they tried, but something was wrong.

Risking a glance at Amelia, he nodded toward the back of the house. She nodded back and jumped the railing.

He pushed into the home, and Donna took hold of his arm. He shook her off and backed a few steps away, giving him the response time he'd need if she attacked.

"Mrs. Piliero, lying to a federal agent isn't a good idea."

Her eyes flicked back and forth like windshield wipers in a torrential downpour. Opening and closing her mouth, she shook her head. "I...no, no, of course not." Her nervous laugh sounded more akin to a cough. "He'll be right down, I pro—"

"FBI! Stop!"

It was Amelia's command voice, and though the tone was much higher pitched her words carried just as far. It was coming from the back.

Pissed to his core, Zane shot Vinnie's wife a withering glance. "Once we catch up to your husband, this warrant will be served. And so help me god, if you're gone, I will personally put an APB out to every police precinct in a sixty-mile radius, you understand?"

Her mouth gaped open, but she managed a nod just before he took off out the door. Since Amelia had gone right, he went left, jumping the railing, and bolting to the back of the house.

According to the records Amelia had sifted through earlier in the day, Donna and Vinnie had two children—a son who was six and a daughter who was three. Between the pointed instructions and the little kids, Zane was confident that Donna would stay put. At least until backup arrived.

Sirens rang in the distance. Good. Amelia had already called them in.

Gun out, he came around the corner low and tight. The expansive yard was empty, but he spotted the top of a man's head over the privacy fence. Zane had little doubt that Amelia was right behind the bastard.

Zane searched for the best angle of interception.

About four blocks east of the Piliero house was a creek, and the only nearby bridge to cross the steep ravine was on a major street to the north. Zane doubted that Vinnie would make a break for any area where he'd be easier to spot, and he could only hope that the man didn't find a way to slip away from Amelia.

Dammit, Vinnie, why'd you have to run?

Almost every house in the well-to-do neighborhood boasted a fence around their front and back yards, and to his chagrin, each privacy fence was flush with the barrier at its side. Unless he wanted to scale one six-foot wooden hurdle after another, he needed to stick to the sidewalks.

With a burst of speed that would have made his track coach proud, he sprinted for the front of the house and down the street. As he approached the end of the next block, Zane cast a quick glance to check for cars before sprinting across the intersection. After a half mile, the more expensive wrought iron and wooden fences finally gave way to chain-link and cheap pine.

He took in a sharp gulp of air as he hopped the curb and continued toward an expansive red maple with leaves and branches that blocked out the sun like an umbrella. Gritting his teeth, he ducked his head to the side, narrowly avoiding a low-hanging branch. Despite the distance he ran every night to maintain his training, flames began to lick at his lungs with each breath and muscles at his side ached in protest at his continued pursuit.

A chain-link fence ran along the perimeter of the corner lot. Zane pushed the discomfort from his mind. Without slowing his gait, he used the forward momentum to haul himself over the five-foot barrier in one swift movement. The metal dug into his palms, but like the stitch in his side, he paid the sensation little attention.

He took the grassy yard in a few long strides, and the deep bark of a golden retriever followed him as he scaled the fence at the other end of the yard. The sound of a man's voice followed, but he couldn't make out the words over the pounding of his pulse.

Pausing on the sidewalk, he turned to peer down the new street, but aside from a distant figure pushing a lawnmower, there was no movement. The voice drifted over to him again, and he offered the homeowner little more than a sideways glance before sprinting across the street.

With less imposing fences to stop him, Zane cut through the neighborhood at a sharp angle. After a few more jumps, a couple barking dogs, and a surprised teenager, he emerged on the sidewalk below a sign that read Avery Street. One more block to the north and he'd be at the bustling road that led to the interstate in one direction and downtown in the other.

Brushing at the beads of sweat on his forehead, he fought to catch his breath as he trotted to a black SUV that was parked on the street.

A designer suit and dress shoes were hardly the attire he would have chosen for a run under normal circumstances, and he couldn't help but wonder how sticky and disgusting he'd feel for the rest of the day. The temperature hadn't climbed much past eighty, but the humidity in the air was oppressive.

As he ran a hand through his sweaty hair, he stepped out from behind the SUV to look at the street to his right—the east.

In the distance, he spotted a man hurrying down the sidewalk. Based on his shuffling movements, he was putting forth some effort to appear nonchalant. With his silver basketball shorts and black t-shirt, an onlooker could have easily mistaken him for a normal resident out for a jog.

But even from the distance, Zane recognized his jet-black hair and scruffy face. Vinnie Piliero was headed straight in his direction. Where was Amelia?

Ducking back behind the Lincoln, he peeked out far enough to squint into the distance. He was so focused on his search for movement that he almost jumped as Amelia emerged from the corner of a beige house a little more than a block behind Vinnie.

Amelia had spent ten years in the military, and according to one of her sarcastic recollections, ninety percent of that time had been consumed by running. Since she was only a couple years removed from her service, Zane had no doubt that she could have caught up to Vinnie if she'd chosen. His much taller frame must have lost her with a few leaps over a few fences. Amelia would no doubt be pissed about that.

"FBI. Stop!"

Yep. From the sound of her voice, she was very pissed.

Zane prepared for attack.

Pressing his back to the passenger side of the Lincoln, Zane turned the side mirror. The image was tiny, but Vinnie was still clear.

With a glance over his shoulder toward Amelia, Vinnie increased his shuffling from trot to jog before breaking into a full-on run.

Space was tricky to gauge in the side mirror of a vehicle, but Zane measured Vinnie's advance based on a handful of residential landmarks.

By the time Vinnie passed the mailbox nearest to the black Lincoln, the cadence of Zane's breathing had slowed to near normal. He tensed the muscles of his legs as he turned to face the street. Thanks to the SUV's half-assed parking, the vehicle blocked most of the sidewalk.

Vinnie's shadow came into view, but Zane held still until the man's silhouette blended with that of the Lincoln.

Clenching one hand into a tight fist, Zane stepped out from his spot behind the rear fender. Though he liked to think of himself leaping from behind cover like a jungle cat stalking its prey, he was sure the collision with Vincent Piliero looked more like one klutz running into another.

Zane stuck his arm out straight to catch the shorter man just below the collar. The force of the collision came with a dull ache, but he tightened his closed fist as he pushed back against Vinnie's chest. With the combination of his forward momentum and the sudden halt of his upper body, Vinnie's feet flew out from under him as his back slammed into the concrete below.

With an audible whoosh, all the air was forced from Vinnie's lungs.

Shaking out his arm, Zane pulled a set of silver handcuffs from behind his back, knelt beside Vinnie, and rolled the gasping man onto his stomach.

As a shadow of a woman fell over them, Zane looked up to meet Amelia Storm's eyes.

"You got him." She hunched over for a long gulp of air, clasping her knees with both hands. "Good...good job, Palmer. Good teamwork."

"You make a good sheepdog, Storm." He smiled, hoping she'd appreciate his good-natured ribbing.

Her laugh was closer to a wheeze, but the amusement was there in her expression. "Yeah. Sheepdog." Straightening to her full height, she pushed the matted strands of dark hair from her forehead and reached into her back pocket. "Our friend Vinnie here dropped something on his run around the block. It's what slowed me down."

Zane grinned. He knew it had to be something.

Vinnie groaned, but the sound was muffled from where his face rested in the grass.

Amelia opened her hand to reveal a shiny gray flash drive.

"He tried to pitch this down a storm drain, but it landed in a bush instead."

Nudging the prone man with a knee, Zane shook his head. "Sounds like the first stroke of luck we've had since this case started." He prodded Vinnie again. "Vincent Piliero, you're under arrest…"

TWO HOURS after their return to the FBI office, Amelia was finally satisfied that she'd pulled all the splinters from her hands. If she'd known her afternoon would involve scaling decades-old wooden fences, she would have taken a pair of gloves with her to the Piliero residence.

Crossing both arms over her chest, she settled her gaze on the man responsible for her and Zane's afternoon excursion. White fluorescence reflected off the silver cuffs that bound his wrists, and as he reached up to rub his eyes, the metal clinked together before the table they were chained to stopped the movement.

After Amelia and Zane's unsuccessful attempt to glean a shred of useful information, Vinnie rudely demanded his lawyer. In the same pointed tone he'd used to address Donna Piliero, Zane had advised Vinnie that the U.S. Attorney would seek remand when arraignment rolled around the next day. Though the man had squirmed at the mention of being held in custody without the option for bail, he still hadn't budged.

They'd left him to his solitude in the interview room, and as they waited for the forensic tech to get back to them regarding the flash drive, they had nothing better to do than watch Piliero from behind the two-way mirror.

To Amelia's side, a dim amber glow caught the face of Zane's watch as he rubbed one unshaven cheek. He'd abandoned his suit jacket before they'd even returned to the office, and he'd rolled the sleeves of his white dress shirt up to the elbow. Coupled with the windblown look of his dark blond hair, Amelia had never seen him quite so disheveled.

Then again, a mile-long sprint in eighty-three-degree heat and seventy-percent humidity would do that to the most put together person.

Amelia scooted to the side and slumped into the office chair. "You think Corsaw will find anything from Vinnie's house?"

As Zane twisted the cap from a bottle of water, he walked over to take a seat beside her. "I doubt it, honestly."

Stretching out her tired legs, Amelia nodded. "Yeah, me too. He wiped his computer before he took off."

With a chuckle, Zane shook his head. "Wiped? He ripped the hard drive out of that laptop and threw it in the garbage disposal."

Amelia spread her hands and lifted her eyebrows. "Wiped...crushed...ground up...same thing. All the data's gone, isn't it?"

He tipped an invisible hat to her. "Touché, but never say never until the dudes and dudettes in the tech department say so."

"True. Those guys can work magic sometimes."

Amelia's phone buzzed, and she checked her messages. With a wiggle of her eyebrows, she pushed to her feet. "Dani in forensics has Vinnie's flash drive opened."

Zane followed her to the heavy wooden door. "Let's go see what the magicians have revealed."

She was only a few steps down the hallway when he caught her arm. When she glanced in his direction, he looked troubled. "What?"

"Did you ever get a chance to talk to Michelle Timmer?"

They were alone in the hallway, but the volume of his voice had dropped to just above a whisper.

Amelia leaned one shoulder against the cool surface of the wall and pinched her nose between her fingers. "She's officially listed as a missing person. Didn't show up for work, and no one has seen her. There's an open case for her with Chicago PD. Larson's even been in there to give a statement on the night he was with her."

She left off the part about how the hair on the back of her neck raised whenever she thought about the woman. The timing of Michelle's absence seemed far too convenient to be a coincidence. She couldn't help but wonder if Joseph might have been more involved than he had let on, but she kept that paranoid thought to herself.

Just because the man weirded her out didn't make him a serial killer.

She hoped.

When she returned her attention to Zane, his expression softened. Apparently, she hadn't done a thorough job of masking her concern. Around anyone else, the slip-up would have brought on a bout of anxiety, but Amelia had learned by now that Zane wasn't one to cast judgment.

He held his hands out to his sides and shrugged. "And you're wondering how much of a coincidence it is, her disappearing after a date with Larson? You know something I don't?"

Amelia moved her head from side to side, indicating her indecision. "I wish I could say no, but I have a bad feeling about it. I can't quite put a finger on the why, but the whole situation feels dirty."

"I know Larson's a jerk, but I really hope he's not *that* much of an asshole. You going to follow up on Michelle's case?"

She brushed a stray strand of hair from her eyes. "My thoughts exactly. I might be in trouble if he is."

"Oh?" Zane's eyebrows arched nearly to his hairline. "Why's that?"

She shrugged and pushed away from the wall. "In no uncertain terms, I told him that I didn't appreciate his advances."

Zane followed after her. "Okay, but he had it coming."

She fought against another sigh. "I doubt he sees it that way, but…"

Until I see the Michelle case resolved, I'm going to keep my guard up.

Zane gave her a questioning glance, but she didn't state the thought out loud.

For the rest of the journey to the cyber floor, their conversation shifted over to Amelia's cat, Hup. The long-haired calico had taken to sleeping on the pillow above Amelia's head, and she told of the time she woke with the dang thing's tail up her nose.

Zane was still chuckling when Amelia swiped her work ID over the card reader. A metallic click signaled that the magnetic lock had disengaged, and she and Zane entered the dim lab.

Both tech-related labs were nestled at the end of a hallway. Aside from the floor-to-ceiling glass at the front of the room, the rest of the space was gray drywall and recessed lighting.

Amelia picked her way around a set of tall rectangular tables that took up the center of the room. A woman with chestnut-colored eyes looked up from a pair of wide-screen monitors situated at the end of her laminate worktable. A smile highlighted the flawless bronze glow of her cheeks as she waved for them to join her.

"Agents, hello. Good…" she frowned and glanced at her

watch, "afternoon. At least for another hour. Four o'clock is afternoon, right?"

Amelia actually wasn't sure. She turned to Zane, who shrugged. "Sure."

With a light laugh, the tech held out a hand. "Good. I'm glad we got that cleared up. I'm Dani Fowler, but I suppose you both already knew that."

Zane flashed his trademark grin as he accepted the handshake. "It's okay. I forget names pretty easily, so it's good to have a reminder."

Amelia followed with a very businesslike two-pump shake. "Good to see you again, Dani. Thanks for taking a look at this so quickly."

Dani's smile brightened. "Of course. It's no problem." She beckoned them over to the wide-screen monitors. "Your guy didn't do a great job of protecting or hiding the data he loaded onto that flash drive. The files were password protected, but that was it."

"That's good." Zane fiddled with his watch, looking as if he were impatient to get past the small talk, but his tone remained congenial as always. "We didn't know how tech savvy the guy was, but he didn't have a lot of time before he took off."

After tucking a piece of curly hair behind her ear, Dani tapped a few keys to bring up a list of files. "Well, everything on the drive was uploaded today."

"Which means he was trying to dump the data from his hard drive." Amelia leaned against the edge of the table. "He wanted to transfer all the data to something portable so he could throw the actual hard drive in the garbage disposal before he took off."

Zane snorted. "Looks like Vinnie wanted to have his cake and eat it too."

"He sure did." Dani double-clicked on the first folder in

the long list. "This is what each of these looks like." With one red nail, she gave the screen a gentle tap. "There's a lot of data in here, and at first glance, it appears to be fairly structured. Each folder in that list has two different photos, two text files, and a spreadsheet."

Dragging the file window to the second monitor, she went back to the list and scrolled to the bottom. "And this one at the end has a whole bunch of those other little folders in it. Everything's labeled in code, and we haven't established what that is. So, unfortunately, I can't tell why these were separated from the others. We haven't run it through cryptography yet, but I know you guys needed the data pretty quickly, so I thought you might want to work with what we have at the moment. Maybe you can get something out of it while the boys in cryptography work on breaking their code." As her eyes flicked to Zane and Amelia, she lifted a finger. "There's a pretty good sized spreadsheet that I assume is a master file. If my theory is correct, that master file will tie all the little ones together."

The good humor Zane had shown only moments earlier vanished from his features. His focus became like a laser aimed at its target. He rubbed his chin with a thumb as he stared at the screen. "Yeah, that's pretty organized. What's in each of those folders? You said they're pictures. What are they?"

Even after all the time they'd spent working together over the past three months, the abrupt transformation from upbeat Zane to serious Zane never ceased to amaze Amelia.

"Right." Dani switched back to the window she'd first opened. When she double-clicked on the first document in line, the three of them came face-to-face with a young Latina woman. Her honey-brown eyes were fixed on the camera, and her lips were set in a line.

Amelia tapped her foot against the tile. "That looks like a DMV photo."

Without looking away from the screen, Dani nodded. "Because it is. It's a scan of this woman's driver's license, but all the information was cropped out aside from her picture." She pressed a key to pull up the next photo in line.

In this image, the same woman stood against a blue background with both hands at her sides and the same blank expression on her face.

Zane crossed both arms over his chest. "And they're all like this?"

"They are." Dani's gaze shifted from Zane to Amelia. "It's almost like these are employee records or something."

A chill worked its way down Amelia's spine. When she and Zane had investigated Emilio Leóne's prostitution ring, a woman named Dawn had shown them a similar list of the working girls they had available. Apparently, their forced labor operation was just as meticulous with record keeping.

She pushed aside the thought and tilted her chin at the computer. "What about the text files? What's in those?" On cue, Dani opened the third file in the list. "The data isn't labeled, but my working theory is that it's some kind of profile information. Just look at the words." She pointed to the text file.

At first glance, it appeared like a list, but the words typed down the page seemed disconnected. Central AM, Im-Stat =NoDoc, Nicaragua, 27, F, A+.

"Wow. You're right. Nicaragua, that's Central America. This person...F has to be female. She's from Nicaragua." Zane narrowed his eyes as he studied the text. "This is their immigration status, country of origin, age." The corner of his mouth twitched in a scowl. "A+. Is that her *blood type*? Jesus, what the hell is this?"

Amelia froze midway through a foot tap. "Blood type. Oh

crap." Her gaze shifted between Zane and Dani. "For organ harvesting. We saw some of it with the drug traffickers we investigated in Boston. It's not as common in the United States as it is in some other countries, but it's still a pretty big problem. I bet that's why they're keeping track of that data."

Zane's jaw tightened. "More than likely." His eyes shifted to hers. "They keep this information so they can shuffle these people around from one operation to another. I'll bet the further we dig, we'll find they've cataloged their skills, trades, employment history. A synopsis of their medical records. Probably more information than the Bureau asked for from us when we started."

Dani shook her head, looking at her screen with disgust. "I can't speak for you, Agents, but it's definitely more than they asked from me. Except for one thing." She highlighted the topmost text. "There's no name. Just a series of letters and numbers."

"Of course there's no name," Amelia muttered.

Zane pointed at the monitor. "What about the next two files?"

As she let out a breath, Dani clicked over to a new window. Chunks of text were punctuated by square images of men, women, and children of all ages.

"Their families." Amelia swallowed the bitter taste on her tongue. "I'll bet we find another file with addresses, names, employers. *Schools.*"

Zane nodded. "That's what I figured. Is there any way you can take all these pictures and throw them into one big file?"

Some of the light returned to Dani's eyes as she returned his nod. "Already done, actually. I sort through data all the time, so I did what I could to make this stuff easier for you guys to look at."

The crawling sensation along Amelia's back receded. She

squeezed the tech's shoulder in appreciation. "Thank you. That'll make this *way* easier."

"No doubt." One of Zane's eyebrows quirked up. "We're looking for one particular kid right now. Could we take a quick look at those pictures?"

Dani seemed to be in sync with their needs and tabbed over to a collage style compilation of scanned driver's license images. She scooted to the side and passed the wireless mouse to Zane. "Go ahead. Take a look. I'll go to the other table so I can start working on a hard drive I received a little earlier. I'll be here for a while, so there's no rush. Take all the time you need. Let me know if you have any questions."

Amelia and Zane thanked Dani, and as they all got to work, the room lapsed into silence.

Less than a third of the way through reviewing the compilation, Amelia uttered more than a handful of expletives before she could stop herself.

If Zane even noticed the four-letter words, he didn't react. In a few more clicks, he had Javier's folder displayed across both monitors. "There he is." Straightening to his full height, he drummed his fingers against the white tabletop. "What are you thinking, Storm?"

She dropped both hands to her hips and sighed. "I think that even though it's Thursday, we've got a long weekend ahead of us. This is a gold mine of information, but we've got to figure out how to make it useful for us."

He nodded. "We start where it has the most potential and work our way down to the little details. We can probably get names for some of these folks by looking up any address that they've got listed. Then, we can open missing persons cases and reports. The more of those we find, the more evidence we'll have."

Rubbing her temple, Amelia shook her head. "This is going to take forever."

Zane chuckled, but the sound was without an ounce of humor. "Well, at least we know that it's our case now."

The reminder didn't bring Amelia much relief. Every second they spent sifting through digital records was another second Javier and his sister were in the hands of the traffickers.

And any second could be their last.

17

A s soon as Vivian stepped away from the glass double doors of *The Chicago Standard's* lobby, a slew of goose bumps broke out along her bare forearms. Her nerves were wound as tightly as a snare drum, and the onslaught of anxiety threatened to send her into a panic attack.

With a deep breath of the heavy, humid night air, she tightened her grip on the strap of her messenger bag. Evenings like this, she wished that *The Standard* was attached to a parking garage. Instead, she had to make her way across the street and down half a block.

And, of course, she'd *had* to stay and work late. In all the events of the past few days—not to mention her constant search for a black Lexus—she'd fallen behind on her regular reporting duties. She had a weekly word count quota, and even though her boss would most likely understand if she explained her situation, Vivian still felt guilty for playing hooky earlier in the week.

A steadfast work ethic had served Vivian well in her career, but as she strode from beneath the halo of ruddy orange light, she wished she could adopt the mantra of a slacker for a week or two.

Gritting her teeth, she looked up and down the street as she made her way across. The muffled hum of the city's hustle and bustle drowned out the quiet tap of her flats as they hit the concrete. Even at quarter 'til eleven on a Thursday, Chicago didn't rest.

Though some were bothered by the constant buzz of activity in an area as densely populated as Chicago, Vivian had never minded. People were responsible for the thrum of traffic, and the thought made her feel a little less alone.

If there were cars, there were people. If there were people, there would be witnesses, so no one would want to try something shady. She would be okay.

That thought served her well until Vivian approached an alley that branched off to the left. Despite the nearby streetlamp, the narrow stretch of empty road was cloaked in shadow.

She'd caught a faint flicker of movement in the corner of her eye, and her blood turned to ice.

Someone was in the darkness.

She slowed her pace to study the area. A dumpster stood to the side of a set of rusty double doors, and a fire escape climbed up the side of the building like a metal vine.

A feral cat, maybe. Or a stray dog, or maybe even a homeless person. Vivian always gave a few bucks to the displaced men and women she came across in the blocks around her workplace, but she saw no signs that a human might have occupied the alley.

A glow of headlights spilled over the sidewalk. As the vehicle approached, Vivian's exaggerated shadow grew smaller and smaller.

With both hands clamped around the strap of her

messenger bag, she breathed in a relieved breath and hurried across the alley. If the car at her back hadn't arrived, she would have been tempted to sprint the rest of the way to her parking garage.

She expected the vehicle to pass her or to turn into the alley. Instead, the crunch of tires against gravel and the hum of an engine grew louder.

Ice water returned to her veins with a vengeance as a dark SUV pulled up until she could see the silhouette of the person behind the wheel. Their features were little more than a blur of darkness against the tinted window, but she thought the outline belonged to a man.

Vivian's hands shook as she dug her phone from the outermost pocket of her bag. The device was always within easy reach, and she was glad for her own foresight.

"Hey there, miss." The man's low voice cut through her panicked thoughts with surgical precision.

As Vivian hurried her steps, the SUV kept its pace.

The entrance to the parking garage was visible, but she still had almost a block to go. Once she got to the concrete structure, she would be safe. Safer, at least. Most criminals avoided the area because cameras encased in dark glass bubbles were mounted along the ceiling every fifteen feet.

She kept her focus fixed on the sidewalk ahead. She would make it.

Before she could break into a jog, a hand clamped down on her bicep. With a swift step to the side, she jerked her arm away, but the man's hold only tightened.

As she yelped in surprise, Vivian twisted her upper body to meet the man's steely gaze. In the relative darkness, his eyes were as black as the hooded sweatshirt that shadowed his bearded face.

No, not a beard. A handkerchief.

Adrenaline surged, and some primal part of her brain had her fighting before she even registered the need to do such a thing. Even as she swung her arm, pain flared in her neck. Like the bite of a fire ant, the sting came without warning.

Before she could give voice to what she had felt, Vivian's world faded, and she knew nothing else.

THE AIR SMELLED LIKE CHEMICALS. Acrid and overpowering.

In her dream, Vivian had been at her sister's vacation home in the Ozarks of Missouri. She'd lounged on a wooden dock with a drink in one hand and a fishing pole in the other. The air should have been crisp and refreshing. Instead, she inhaled a fetid stench of rot covered in bleach.

As the fog of the unconscious world drifted away, Vivian fought in vain to bring back the haze. She wanted to be on the docks. She wanted to watch her niece and nephew help their father at the grill. She wanted to feel the warmth of a cheery fire on her skin as the sun inched its way below the horizon.

Instead, she was here. Wherever *here* was.

An unbearable ache had settled into the back of her neck, and as the cobwebs drifted from her mind, she realized she was seated upright. Pieces of hair had matted to her cheeks. Her head hung low, and the light of the world around her was dimmed by the curtain of dark strands that had fallen in front of her face.

She squeezed her eyes closed, praying that this too was a dream. She'd wake up at any moment, safe in her bed. But the more the mental fog lifted, the more she remembered. There had been a black SUV and a man in a hoodie with a handkerchief covering his face.

Swallowing the foul taste in her mouth, she forced herself to remain still. The air was quiet, but she couldn't be sure if she was alone. Until she'd formed a plan, Vivian didn't want an onlooker to know she'd regained consciousness.

Both her wrists were bound to the arms of the uncomfortable chair, and her ankles had been tied together. The grit of the dingy floor dug into the soles of her feet as she fought to keep her breathing deep and even.

Cracking her eyes open a slit, she glanced over what she could see with her head tilted at the odd angle. Her knees were caked with a thin layer of dirt, and a scrape darkened the top of one foot.

Bile clawed at the back of her throat. What had the man done to her while she'd been unconscious?

As tears burned the corners of her eyes, she took stock of the rest of her body. Her wrists stung from the zip ties, and her back and neck thrummed with a dull pain, though she figured the ache was the result of her awkward position. Other than a bruise on one bicep and the scratch on her foot, she couldn't feel any more injuries.

Over the relentless cadence of her pulse, Vivian barely heard the rustle of footsteps. As the blood froze in her veins, she shut her eyes and held as still as she could manage.

Deep breaths. Let them think you're still asleep. You can figure a way out of this.

She could, couldn't she? She knew how to break free of zip ties, though she was less sure how to handle the binds when each arm was bound separately.

"How long is that stuff supposed to last?"

Biting down on her tongue, she took in a long breath through her nose. She'd only heard the man in the bandana utter a single sentence, but she knew without a doubt that the newest speaker wasn't the same person. His voice wasn't as deep, but there was a commanding edge in his tone that told her he was someone with authority.

When the next man spoke, her stomach clenched. "For someone her size?" Handkerchief Man paused. "A few hours, max."

"And you didn't dose her again?"

"No. Just the one shot when we grabbed her."

She thought back to the sting she'd felt in her neck before the world had gone dark. So, she'd been drugged with a syringe.

Dirty? Clean? Did it matter?

What mattered was that these men seemed to know what they were doing. They'd been prepared to cut her off on her walk to the parking garage, which meant they knew a rough approximation of her daily routine.

The black Lexus. It has to be.

"It's been three and a half hours since we left the city." The first man's voice had grown louder. He was closer.

Vivian squeezed her eyes closed a little tighter.

Before she could tamp down on the panic sending her thoughts into a whirlwind, a hand grasped her chin. Her eyes flew open, and any plan to maintain a sleeping façade went to the wayside.

With one gruff movement, the man pulled her head up until she stared directly into a pair of irises so dark they were almost black.

As the corner of his mouth turned up in a devious smirk, he chuckled. "She's awake. She's been awake this whole time. Haven't you?"

Vivian's tongue felt thick and fuzzy, and all she could do was swallow.

A low chuckle sounded out from behind him, and Vivian jerked her gaze to the source.

She knew he was the man who had worn the handkerchief. Her glimpse of his face while they were on the street was fleeting, but her instincts left little room for doubt.

Handkerchief Man's brown eyes were lighter than his companion's, and his broad-shouldered, muscular build told her that if she tried to fight him, she'd be sorely outmatched.

She was so focused on the two men that she hardly noticed the tall, shadowy ceilings and the farm equipment stacked on metal shelves along the walls. As the pieces of the puzzle fell into place, bile crawled up the back of her throat.

Javier Flores had been lured into a forced labor camp on a farm, and now Vivian was bound to a chair in the storeroom of an agricultural warehouse.

After a condescending pat to her cheek, the first man took a step backward. "Hope your nap was pleasant, Vivian. We've got a lot to talk about."

"What do you want from me?" She was surprised the words came out as anything other than a choked whisper.

Crossing both arms over his black and white plaid shirt, he glanced to Handkerchief Man. "What do you think, Carlo?"

Carlo scratched his bearded chin as he feigned a look of contemplation. "I'm not sure, boss. What do we want from her?"

As the one she now knew was the boss turned his attention to Vivian, the malevolent glint in his eyes sent a series of goose bumps down her back.

Waving a dismissive hand, he took a few steps to the side before he turned around to pace. "We'll get to it. Let's start with something simple. Vivian Kell, that's your name, right?"

She nodded.

There was no reason for her to be obstinate at such a simple query. In truth, panic and desperation had sunk so deep into her bones that she wasn't sure she had the capability to lie.

"Good." He stuffed one hand in the pocket of his dark jeans. "And you work for *The Chicago Standard*, obviously."

She expected a question about Javier and Yanira, or about the FBI, or about Mari.

When the man spoke again, her eyes went wide.

"Word's gotten back to me that you're working on something about a labor contractor, is that right, Vivian?" His stare bore into her like a laser.

This isn't happening. This can't be real. I'm dreaming.

But when the zip ties pinched her wrists, she didn't wake. "Who are you?" She hardly registered the hoarse croak as her own voice.

The man closed in so swiftly Vivian barely had time to register the movement. He lifted a hand, and in a blur of motion, swung at her.

His knuckles collided with her cheek in a dry crack as the force of the strike snapped her head sideways. Waves of pain rolled out from the site of the blow like ripples on a lake.

A cry erupted from her mouth before she could stop it.

"We'll ask the questions." The so-called boss's voice was laden with petulance and smug satisfaction. "I know that might be hard for you to get used to, so consider that a warning."

As the taste of iron crept onto her tongue, Vivian managed a weak nod before she returned her blurry vision to the two men. With a sniffle, she blinked away the tears. "Okay. Okay."

The weak concession didn't sound like Vivian.

Even though she was plagued by irrational bouts of anxiety on a regular basis, she considered herself to be a strong person who used her empathy and compassion to do what she could to make the world a better place. She'd been anxious ever since she was a teenager, and she'd used her experiences to help several of her friends as the illness reared its ugly head in their lives.

But here, in this dim warehouse that stank of chemicals and dirt, she was so far removed from her element that she might as well have been on a different plane of existence.

When she'd started her piece on Premier Ag Solutions, she thought the company might be guilty of a handful of white-collar crimes—tax evasion, hiring workers without vetting their citizenship, anything to help their bottom line.

Though the company had potential ties to groups of labor traffickers, Vivian hadn't expected such extensive involvement in organized crime. She hadn't expected Premier Ag Solutions to be *run* by the mob.

If she'd known, she never would have written the article. She'd have tried to do *something*, but that something would have involved an anonymous tip to the FBI.

She was Icarus, and her wings were about to melt.

As she looked from one man to the other, she swallowed the blood in her mouth and took in a deep breath.

Clenching and unclenching the hand he'd used to hit her, the boss brushed the stray strands of hair away from his forehead. "As I was saying, you've been working on an article about a labor contractor, haven't you?"

All she could do was nod.

He crossed his arms as he turned to face her. "What's the name of that labor contractor, if you don't mind my asking?"

She licked her dry lips and swallowed again. There was no point in lying to the men, but if she was about to spill her guts, she'd at least endeavor to sound like a version of her old self when she spoke. "It's…Premier Ag Solutions."

His face lit up with a patronizing smile. "Perfect. We *are* on the same page. Now, I've read that article, and I'll grant you this." He held both arms out at his sides. "It's really well written. It's thorough, but it's also concise. You made it simple enough to follow that some high school kid could bring it to his activist club, or whatever in the hell kids are doing in school anymore."

The compliment might have been made to put her at ease and make her more amenable to answering additional questions, but the malicious flicker in his eyes and the demeaning edge in his voice told a different story.

He was enjoying himself.

With an upraised finger, he fixed his gaze on her. "But here's the thing. If you publish that article, it's going to cause a big headache for my boss, and for *his* boss. And you know what they say, right? Shit rolls downhill." He tapped himself on the chest. "I don't want to deal with that."

Vivian shook her head. "I won't publish it. I'll delete it. I'll..." she stopped to swallow before her voice cracked, "forget any of this ever happened. I'll never even talk about Premier again, I swear."

When he smiled, she felt like a centipede had crawled down the back of her neck.

"Good." He glanced to the bigger man and then back to Vivian. "I guess we really are on the same page. Now, this next question will be a little more difficult for you to answer, but it might be the most important one. So, I'm going to need you to forget about those reporter's instincts and be honest with me. Can you do that?"

Her stomach dropped, but she nodded. "Yes."

He clapped his hands. "Perfect. Now, in that article, there are a lot of specific mentions about what supposedly happened to laborers when they worked for Premier. And there are enough of those little stories that I think you might have an inside source." He glared down at her as if daring her to give him a reason to send his hand flying again. "Who was your source for that information, Ms. Kell?"

Tears stung the corners of her eyes. She tried to blink them away, but there was no use. Vivian bit down on her lower lip to keep the tremor of emotion out of her voice. "I don't want anyone else getting hurt."

All the malice drained from his features like a switch had flipped somewhere in his mind.

He stepped forward and crouched in front of her, his hand coming around her throat. "We just want to talk to them. I'm not sure where they've been getting all that nasty information, but we'd like them to sit down and have a chat with us so we can set the record straight."

The explanation was a lie. Though the devious flicker was nowhere to be found in his dark brown eyes, Vivian knew in her gut that his placating expression was feigned.

He was lying, but she wanted to believe it as truth.

Her source for the most important parts of the article—the eyewitness accounts of human rights abuses that the laborers had suffered during their time with Premier—had been her long-time friend, Ben Storey. Vivian had befriended his wife, Iris, when she was still in college and welcomed Ben into the friend circle after they married.

Ben was a good man, a great husband, and an even better father. Before he'd won his seat on the Chicago city council, he'd worked as a lawyer for a nonprofit that helped lower-income immigrants navigate the legal system to obtain permanent residency and citizenship.

In his role on the city council, he'd developed a knack for reaching across the aisle. So far, in his campaign for the Senate primary, he'd received praise and endorsement from both political parties. He was slated to go up against the twelve-year incumbent, Stan Young, in next year's primary. If Ben's momentum continued like it had since he'd announced his bid for Senate in May, his odds were good.

As Vivian stared up at the mafia man, she attempted to

swallow around the hand slowly cutting off her oxygen. The corners of her vision began to gray as the boss squeezed... and squeezed.

Ben had access to resources that went far above and beyond an average person. He'd spent years in the United States Army, and his time as a lawyer and a city councilman had netted him a number of powerful contacts. Plus, as a candidate in the Senate primary, chances were good he'd stepped up his personal security.

If anyone could deal with the two men in front of her, it was Ben Storey.

Though there was some truth in her rationalization, guilt raked its savage claws at her heart as she attempted to open her mouth. The hand loosened just a little.

"Ready to tell the truth?"

Was she really about to do this? Did she even have a choice? She nodded.

The hand loosened even more. "Who is your source?"

"Ben Storey."

She hated herself before the words even left her mouth, and she wanted to curl up in a dark corner and hide. The searing pang of shame thudded in her chest as her stomach rolled.

I'm sorry, Ben.

He'd forgive her if he knew, but the thought brought fresh tears to her eyes.

The mafioso rocked back on his heels. "Ben Storey? The guy running against Stan Young in the primary?"

Sniffling, Vivian nodded again. "Yes."

Whistling through his teeth, the boss rose to his full height and glanced to his broad-shouldered companion. "Didn't you say your wife was going to vote for that guy?"

The one named Carlo let out a low chuckle. "She did. She's all about keeping up with politics these days." He lifted one dark eyebrow. "Do you think this bitch is lying? Storey's a popular guy right now. She could've just pulled a name out of her head."

The boss's gaze shifted between Vivian and Carlo as a smirk curled his lip. "No. She's not lying."

Cautious relief came to Vivian like the first hints of a cool breeze, but the pleasant sensation was ripped away the second she saw the sinister expression on Carlo's face.

"Please." Her eyes darted back and forth between the men as a surge of adrenaline pushed aside the guilt and hopelessness. "Please, I won't say anything to anyone. I'll delete that article and all my notes about it. I won't tell Ben about this. I won't go to the cops, I swear. Please." She trailed off as fresh tears rolled down her cheeks.

Holding both arms out wide, the boss heaved a resigned sigh. "Oh, Vivian. I wish I could believe that. But you're a reporter, you know? You can't help it. It's in your nature to find a good story. And I bet." He chuckled and wagged a finger at her. "I bet this would earn you a Pulitzer, wouldn't it? Americans *love* their conspiracy theories, especially when you sprinkle a little organized crime on top of it."

"No." She shook her head in a frantic motion that caused the room to spin. "No, I won't. I promise. I'll never say a word to anyone. I'll leave Chicago, and I'll never come back. Whatever you want. Just please, please let me go. I don't even know your name, and I don't know his full name."

He clucked his tongue and turned to Carlo. "She's all yours. Just remember what we talked about."

"No open wounds. No blood." Carlo licked his already wet lips. "Don't worry. I'm not about to ruin a pretty face like yours, sweetheart."

With a dismissive wave, the boss turned to make his way to a worn metal door. "I'll give you two some privacy. Come get me when you're done."

Bile rose in Vivian's throat, and her heart thundered against her ribs as Carlo took a step her way. He began laughing as he unbuckled his belt.

She could scream for help, but she already knew no one would hear.

18

Gritting my teeth, I swiped the screen of my phone to disconnect the call. As I let the device clatter to the dark wood of my desk, I raked a hand through my hair.

Almost three days after I'd gotten rid of the reporter, and her nosiness was continuing to throw roadblocks in my operation.

It wasn't enough that she'd spent six months writing an article about Premier Ag Solutions—the company that fronted the Leóne family's labor trafficking—but now the main recruiter for my workforce was behind bars.

I knew better than to tell myself the two events were a coincidence. In one way or another, that bitch had *something* to do with Vinnie Piliero's arrest.

Carlo glanced to Matteo, and both men straightened in their chairs.

To my surprise, Matteo was the first to speak. "That didn't sound good. What's going on, boss?"

I squeezed my eyes closed and massaged my temples. "When I was in Chicago a few days ago, I talked to Mr. Dalessio about getting us some more workers since we're closing in on the end of the summer." I turned my gaze to one of the gray walls as my anger hissed out in a loud breath through my teeth. "And he was going to get ahold of Vinnie to recruit a few more workers for us, but…"

The room lapsed into silence, and neither Carlo nor Matteo made a move to speak. They knew better than to take over the conversation when I was irritated.

Propping my elbows on the desk, I met the men's curious stares. "But Vinnie's in jail."

"Shit." Matteo spat out the word like a bullet.

Carlo's jaw went slack. "Jail? What the hell for? When did that happen?"

It was good to see the men equally as incensed as I was about this whole mess. "He was arrested three days ago. For human trafficking."

As Matteo spat out a few more choice words, Carlo dropped his face into his hands. "What the hell do they have on him? How'd he get popped for human trafficking? Holy shit." He rubbed his forehead and grumbled something I didn't understand.

What?

How?

Both were questions I needed answers to. I hated not having all the information.

"All Mr. D could tell me was that the Feds found a flash drive containing a list of all the workers we have here and at the other locations."

Carlo froze. "That's not good."

"No, it isn't." I sighed at his unhelpful and obvious reply. "Vinnie's been doing this for a long time. He keeps all his records in code and doesn't use their names. It might *seem* like a lot of information for the Feds to get ahold of, but in reality," I spread my hands, "they've got a whole lot of nothing. Mr. D said it'll probably have them chasing their tails for a little while, and I agree with him."

"Huh. Yeah, I suppose you're right." Carlo fidgeted in his seat, tapping his fingers against the armrest. "How do you think they found him?"

More questions when I needed answers. I scowled at the thought. "All we've got right now are guesses."

Matteo narrowed his eyes. "That kid, Javier."

It was a weak guess, but at least Matteo was offering something other than a constant stream of questions. "No. Not the kid," I replied.

Carlo piped up. "I've had Dean keeping a close eye on him. He's been quiet as a church mouse, and after we had that little chat with him and his sister, they've both been cooperative."

He pursed his lips and leaned forward, resting his forearms on his knees. He looked as if he were trying to think, so I gave him a moment.

"What about their mother?" Carlo finally said after moments of silence had passed. "We know that reporter was around their house. Maybe the mother contacted her, and now she contacted the Feds."

I had considered the option myself. "That, or the reporter called the Feds, which is what I'm thinking. Just because we didn't see her with them doesn't mean it didn't happen." I hated not knowing the answer. "Either way, it doesn't matter. Have we dealt with the reporter?"

"Her body's been in the deep freeze for two and a half days, boss." Matteo cracked his knuckles. "We'll take her to Chicago tonight and make it look like she was mugged, just like you asked."

Carlo nodded eagerly. "The freezer idea was smart. It should definitely throw off the time of death. They'll probably find her the next day, and it'll look like she was killed the night before."

Due to Vivian Kell's connection to a sitting city councilman, my men and I had decided to take a different approach to throw suspicion away from the motive for her murder. Under normal circumstances, I would ensure a body was difficult, even impossible to find. But with Vivian, I needed the city cops to think her death was just another senseless act of violence in Chicago's ongoing battle with rising crime rates.

"And you're certain the snatch was clean? We can't have anything tracing back to our operation." I glared at Carlo, eager for his reply.

"No one saw nothing, boss." He smiled proudly and puffed his chest. "I staked out the reporter's apartment. She had a squad car making regular rounds, so instead of waiting for her to arrive home, we snatched her from the street when she'd left work."

"And what about the reporter's car?" If those idiots left a single string for the Feds to follow, I'd have their heads.

Matteo perked up and nudged Carlo in the arm. "You're going to love this, boss." The two men exchanged glances before Matteo chuckled. "The parking garage is heavily monitored by security cameras and personnel, right? And we knew we couldn't just leave her car to sit in the garage all weekend. That squad car rolling by her house might get suspicious if she never came home. So, this genius here." Matteo nudged Carlo again. "He calls his cousin Frank, who's married to a woman who has been in our lifestyle since she was born. With a wig and a change of clothes, Frank's wife drove the reporter's car back to her apartment complex."

Carlo was smiling ear to ear, clearly proud of the plan he and Matteo executed. "Yeah. I doubt the cops will even check the security footage of the garage after we staged the wrong time of death with the freezer, but in the unlikely event they do, our bases are covered. They'll just chalk it up to a senseless act of violence. Case closed." He mimed wiping his hands clean to punctuate his point.

By establishing an alternative motive for her phantom killer, our operation controlled the narrative.

"Excellent work, boys." I clasped my hands together. "Now, normally, I'd say we would just leave Mari alone. But the fact is that the Feds got to Vinnie even though we know damn well Javier didn't open his mouth. That means Mari might be a witness. In which case…"

Straightening in his chair, Carlo took on the eager expression of a dog about to be tossed a bone. "We need to deal with her."

"We do. And we will. Frank was already following the reporter around, so he ought to know where to start. I'll call and have him track her down. And when he finds her," I lifted my shoulders, "he'll bring her back here. Then we'll get to the bottom of this whole situation."

Mari and her children had been a thorn in my side since Javier had first tried to run from his duty on the farm, and I intended to make sure she paid for every headache she and her spawn had caused me and this family.

19

Rubbing her temples, Amelia leaned back in the cushioned booth. The aroma of roasting coffee and the general chatter of the cafe employees was a welcome reprieve from the recycled air and eerie silence of her and Zane's shoebox-sized office at the FBI building. Though the hour hadn't yet reached ten, Zane had decided that they'd each earned a Frappuccino.

And if *Zane*—who teased her any time she showed up to work in the morning with what was essentially a caffeinated milkshake—was the one to suggest it, they really needed a break.

Despite the tedious nature of the weekend research into Vinnie Piliero's flash drive, Monday had come far too soon. They'd made it through roughly three-quarters of the information, and their goal that day was to wrap up the review of the remaining fourth.

Morning sunlight caught the face of Amelia's watch as she dropped both arms back to the wooden table. "How many of the people on that flash drive do you think we've even been able to identify so far?"

Midway through a sip of his white mocha Frappuccino, Zane lifted his eyebrows. His face was free of the usual stubble, and Amelia couldn't help but wonder if he'd cleaned up for a special occasion.

She reached for her own drink. "Ten percent, maybe? Or do you think we got closer to fifteen?"

He paused, rubbing one cheek thoughtfully. "Maybe somewhere in the middle. Twelve or thirteen. Looking people up by address can be useful, but it has its limits. And we have to limit the time we spend on each person unless we want to be sifting through this data for the next six months."

She'd hoped Zane's outlook would be a little more positive. With a sigh, Amelia rested her chin in one hand. "Right. Better to turn our focus to the people we *were* able to identify. But only a handful of them had even been reported missing, much less kidnapped."

He nodded. "We've pulled two open cases out of all that data so far." Blowing out a long breath, he tapped a finger against the plastic cup. "Neither of those turned up any leads and they're both cold cases."

"Yeah, one from two years ago, and the other from three years ago. Who knows what kind of timeframe we're looking at? Five years? A decade?" With a groan, she leaned all the way back into the chair and rubbed the bridge of her nose. "This is the most useless data cache I've ever found."

She shouldn't have been surprised. The Leónes had made their share of slipups during their time at the top of the city's criminal hierarchy, but there was a reason they'd held their position of power for so long.

Any records of their illicit enterprise would undoubtedly be in code, much like the names on Piliero's flash drive. The code wasn't unbreakable, but after only a single weekend, neither Amelia nor Zane had been able to catch on to a discernable pattern.

Zane lifted his shoulders in a resigned shrug, and the shadows beneath his eyes seemed more pronounced. "I've seen some that were worse, but not by a lot. There's not much else we can do right now, though. Vinnie's about as cooperative as a brick wall when you try to ask it questions."

Amelia absently stirred her drink with a tiny straw as she struggled for a new angle to approach the problem. "A lot of those people probably aren't even from Chicago. They might be from out of state or out of the country." Searching for people by single entries would have them chasing their tails for weeks or even months. But knowing how the entries fit together, it might make things a lot easier. "Maybe we ought to change our approach a little."

He raised an eyebrow. "Oh? You've got an idea, I take it?"

"Something like that." Amelia tilted her head, not fully committing to a nod yet. "Obviously, the Leónes are good at keeping their data coded. But if we could decipher their code, it'd make our lives a lot easier, and not just for this case."

Zane leaned in closer, folding his hands on the table. "That's a good idea. You think we should hand that data over to someone in forensics? There's a couple of analysts who specialize in cracking codes. They've usually got their hands full with court dates and training, but we're a task force now." His smile returned as he grabbed his cup for another sip. "I bet we could get the department to lend us someone for a little while."

Amelia let out a chuckle that was fueled by equal parts relief and amusement. Zane was always the more upbeat of the two of them, but even his posture that morning had been resigned. She was glad that some of his normal demeanor had returned.

"Well." She swirled the caramel drink in her cup. "That's true, but if we're really going to devote ourselves to breaking the code that the Leónes use for their record keeping, I don't know how far we'd want to spread that, you know? We still don't know who tried to rat us out to the Leónes when we were looking for Leila, and even though I doubt it is anyone in forensics, still." She left the thought unfinished and shrugged.

He rubbed his chin and slumped back in his seat. "Yeah, that's also true. If I had to guess, I'd say that's part of the reason SAC Keaton gave us our own room. To keep things secure." He met her gaze. "What if we give ourselves a deadline to figure it out, and then we go to one of the analysts if we haven't had any luck?"

As Amelia opened her mouth to reply, a pronounced buzz jerked her attention to the smartphone she'd placed near the edge of the table.

"That's not a bad idea. Hold on." She lifted a finger, pausing the conversation so she could check her phone. The caller ID didn't list a name. She swiped the green answer key and raised the phone to her ear. "This is Agent Storm."

"Agent Storm." The man's deep voice was professional, but there was a slight strain in his tone. "This is Detective Floyd Yoell with the Chicago Police Department."

Amelia silently groaned. An unexpected police call was never good news. "Good morning, Detective. What can I do for you?"

He cleared his throat. "My partner and I are out at Old Pines Park. We got a call from a civilian who was out for a jog. They found a woman's body hidden down in a creek bed. Your card was in her back pocket."

Midway through pushing her Frappuccino around in a circle, Amelia froze as tendrils of adrenaline slithered down her neck. "Do you have an ID for her yet?"

"We do. She had an ID on her, but all the credit cards and cash were gone. Her name's Vivian Kell."

Amelia stiffened in her seat as her pulse thundered in her ears. Despite the physical reaction to the news, she kept her voice level and cool. "She's a Federal witness. My partner and I will be there as soon as we can."

"Roger that," Detective Yoell replied mechanically. "We'll be waiting for you."

"Thanks." Amelia watched her phone as the screen went dark.

Zane pushed to his feet. "Where are we headed?"

Dropping the phone back into her tote handbag, she stood on legs that didn't want to hold her. "Old Pines Park. The Chicago PD found Vivian Kell. She's dead."

20

A puffy white cloud moved in to obscure the sun as Zane shoved open the driver's side door of his silver Acura. He always had the option to drive one of the Bureau's many sedans, but he preferred his smaller coupe. Besides, the Acura was more fuel-efficient than the black Town Cars that the FBI kept on hand.

As he and Amelia stepped into the shade of a tall evergreen at the end of the rounded parking lot, he looked over the gentle hills of the park. The detective had sent Amelia an approximate location of Vivian's body.

Donning his aviators, Zane spotted a cluster of people in the distance. He raised an arm to point to the small crowd. "Down there, off the walking trail, right by the creek."

Amelia's gaze followed along the line he pointed. She heaved a sigh and tipped her sunglasses down from her head to cover her face. "Well, it's only ninety right now." She glanced at her watch. "At half past ten in the morning. This should be pleasant."

His chuckle sounded more like a quiet snort. "No sarcasm there. All right, let's go."

"No, no sarcasm at all. I love August." She stepped over the cement curb.

In silence, they cut across a patch of grass to reach the sidewalk that wound around the outskirts of the park. Neither of them had spoken much on the trip from the coffee shop, and Zane suspected they were both coming to terms with the news Amelia had been given by Detective Yoell.

Though they hadn't known Vivian Kell well or for long, the death of a witness or an informant always felt like a personal failure.

He glanced at Amelia. "I know we don't have much to go on yet, but what are you thinking? Leóne hit?"

"That was my first thought." Brushing a flyaway hair from her face, she nodded. "She said she was being followed by a black Lexus, the one that Frank Dalessio was driving. We'll have to see what's at the scene, but it might be worth looking into him if we don't have anything else."

"We had a police detail on her, didn't we?" Zane was careful to keep his tone neutral and non-accusatory.

Amelia had done her best to keep Vivian safe, and the last thing he wanted was to inadvertently lay the blame at her feet.

She let out a long sigh. "Yeah, I had a patrol car drive by her place every half hour or so. We didn't know who we were dealing with at the time, so it was the best I could do."

He nodded. "Right. We'll have to check with them and ask if they saw anything out of the ordinary."

She stopped dead in her tracks and looked him straight in the eyes. "I'm not blaming myself, Palmer. I know I did the best I could. At the time, I thought I was going overboard. Even Vivian thought I was going overboard. I'm pissed that this happened to her, but I'm not going to beat myself up over it."

"Good. Because you shouldn't." He brushed at the sheen of sweat that had formed at his hairline. "And honestly, when you told me about giving her a security detail, I thought it was a little much. But I trust your judgment. You knew what you were doing."

She seemed to relax at his confirmation, a dead giveaway that she did blame herself, at least a little.

They followed the sidewalk as it looped around a thick patch of evergreens and sloped down toward the creek. At the edge of the cluster of trees, two picnic tables were shaded by a square gazebo. A pair of middle-aged women sat at the table closest to the sidewalk, both focused on the buzz of activity at the bottom of the gentle hill.

As Zane and Amelia approached the throng of civilians that had gathered on the grass next to the sidewalk, they produced their badges.

Wide-eyed and slack-jawed, a couple college-aged kids, an older man, and a young woman with fiery red hair all stepped to the side to make room for the newly arrived FBI agents.

Zane lifted the crime scene tape for Amelia to duck under it. He followed behind, scrutinizing the gathering for anyone who seemed out of place.

The old adage of murderers returning to the scene of their crime was well known for a reason.

As Zane scanned the small crowd, all he saw were curious onlookers. None matched the dark eyes and hair of the Leónes and their Italian lineage.

Jaw clenched, he turned away from the civilians as he followed Amelia to a man and woman who stood beside a thicket of tall grass.

Once the searing light of the sun was blocked by the rows of tall trees that lined the creek, he breathed a sigh of relief.

Their journey hadn't been long, and even though they'd walked downhill, sweat was beading on his forehead.

Brushing at his temple, Zane nodded a greeting to the two detectives.

Detective Yoell's pale blue eyes shifted from Amelia to Zane and back as he extended a hand. "You must be Agent Storm."

Amelia tilted her chin at Zane as she accepted the handshake. "I'm Agent Storm, and this is my partner, Agent Palmer."

To Detective Yoell's side, a tall, willowy woman with rows of neat braids pulled into a low ponytail nodded but made no move to offer her hand. "I'm Detective Natasha Reyman. Sorry, I don't do handshakes. Too many germs."

Zane smiled back, appreciating her candor. "Fair enough. What have you found so far?"

Detective Yoell glanced at his partner. "It looks like the vic was mugged, to be honest." He gestured to a steep slope behind the thick tangle of grass, weeds, and tree branches. "We found her bag about twenty feet downstream from the body. It was caught on a rock, but my guess is that the perp tried to toss it so it'd be washed away by the creek."

Zane glanced to Amelia, noticing her contemplative expression, and wondered what she might be thinking. With a deep breath, he crossed his arms and turned back to the detective. "Cause of death?"

Detective Reyman answered this time. "It's hard to tell. There's some light bruising around her neck, so it could have been strangulation. The coroner will be here any minute, but we wanted to wait so we could make sure you two had a chance to get a good look at the scene."

Waving a hand in front of himself, Zane nodded. "Let's take a look."

The detectives led them to a spindly ash tree. To the side

of the trunk, the mess of vegetation had been tamped down to form a path.

Detective Reyman's chocolate brown eyes flicked back to Zane and Amelia. "Be careful. We've had a couple people almost go headlong down into the creek."

From where he stood at the edge of the steep decline, Detective Yoell tapped himself on the chest. "Including yours truly. There's a couple rocks you can use to keep your balance, though."

Zane took stock of Amelia's shiny ballet flats as he arched an eyebrow.

She narrowed her eyes. "I caught Vinnie Piliero in these shoes. I'll be fine. They're more durable than they look."

He shot her a knowing grin.

Though the detectives' caution about the treacherous ravine was well-founded, all four of them made their way to the rocky bank without incident. The quiet babble of moving water was barely audible over the buzz of cicadas.

To his relief, the tangled mess of plant life at the top of the ravine thinned out to give way to the gray stones that lined either side of the creek. Zane had grown up in the heart of Jersey City, and he'd never been much of an outdoorsman. Not in the summer months, at least.

Thanks to a number of trips in his younger years, plus the time he'd spent in Russia during his tenure with the CIA, he could navigate a wintry forest with relative ease. However, chopping through vegetation with a machete was a little too far out of his wheelhouse.

As he blinked the salty perspiration from his eyes, he almost wished he was back in Russia.

Almost.

The Midwestern summer hellscape of heat and humidity was a small price to pay for the confidence that he'd wake up the next morning.

Not to mention an improvement in the company he kept. He'd take Amelia Storm over Russian oligarchs any day of the week. Even though there was a mole in the FBI office—or a rat, as Amelia preferred to say—he felt safer in Chicago than he had at any point since he'd joined the agency a week after his twenty-first birthday.

Plenty of men and women made their careers in the Central Intelligence Agency, but Zane wasn't one of them. He'd grown tired of the constant hyper-awareness and paranoia that had come with his time behind enemy lines. Specifically, from his time infiltrating the Russian government and aristocracy.

That chapter of his life was closed. Finished. Never to be reopened.

Not that anyone in his current life knew about that chapter or how he came to be with the FBI now. They couldn't know.

Pulling himself from the reverie, he shifted his focus to the oppressive humidity and climbing temperature of the August morning.

As he accepted a pair of vinyl gloves from Detective Yoell, Zane caught the first glimpse of the body splayed on the rocky ground. One of Vivian's hands was only a foot shy of the water, and her unseeing eyes stared straight up at the branches and leaves that arched over the ravine.

The vibrant shade of her light blue irises had clouded over, but otherwise, signs of decomposition were minimal. Aside from dried blood that was caked to a small cut on the side of her face and the faint shadow of the ligature marks on her neck, there were no obvious injuries.

Had her eyes been closed, an onlooker could have fooled themselves into believing she'd merely fallen asleep.

A couple crime scene techs milled about the rocky bank

with their cameras, and when he looked over his shoulder, Zane spotted another pair twenty or so feet downstream.

He jerked a thumb at the distant techs. "That's where her purse wound up?"

Detective Yoell nodded. "Yeah. The CSU measured the distance already. Twenty-six and a half feet, give or take an inch or two." He waved a gloved hand at Vivian's body. "It's a good thing we haven't gotten any rain in the last few days, or she'd have probably wound up in the water. We think the killer pushed her body down here after she was dead, but again, the M.E. will need to confirm that."

To Zane's side, Amelia shook her head. "Who pushed her down here? The Incredible Hulk?" Her comparison might have been sarcastic, but her tone was flat and humorless.

Glancing up the steep incline and then back to Vivian, Zane snapped the first glove onto his right hand. "She's right." He pointed at the gap between the body and the side of the ravine. "Vivian's body wouldn't have made it out this far if the perp had just shoved her over the edge. Someone threw her. Vivian's on the slender side, but she's also five-ten. I seriously doubt that one man would have been able to lob her body down here."

Detective Reyman tilted her head at her partner. "That's what I said earlier. I think we're looking at more than one killer."

Amelia knelt down but stayed a few yards from Vivian's body. Like Zane, she wouldn't want one of her stray hairs to fall into the scene. "You said you found my card in her back pocket, right?"

"Right." Detective Yoell nodded. "We took pictures of the scene, and then we checked her for identification. That's when we found the card."

Something wasn't adding up. "Two killers, huh? In a

mugging?" Zane scratched his cheek with his ungloved hand. "That seem weird to anyone else?"

"Yes, actually." Detective Reyman hunched down next to Amelia. "Look at her knees."

"They're muddy." Zane narrowed his eyes. Aside from the dried dirt caked to her knees, Vivian's dark wash jeans were clean.

Detective Yoell offered an appreciative nod to his partner. "Like I said, Agents, it hasn't rained in the past four days. They don't water the grass here, and the ground up above is just about as dry as it gets. Either the killer, or killers, robbed her down here, or—"

"Or the body was dumped." Amelia rocked back on her heels.

Yoell nodded again. "Exactly. We'll know more once the medical examiner takes a look at her. Right now, all we've got are educated guesses. No witnesses, no murder weapon, nothing."

"Vivian Kell was a Federal informant for an investigation into a human trafficking ring run by the Leóne crime family." Zane scowled, knowing what the lack of evidence suggested. "And now she just so happened to be mugged, leaving zero evidence at the scene? Conveniently, without any witnesses?"

Amelia's lips pursed. "Vivian was paranoid. She knew someone was following her. There's no way she'd decide to go for a stroll in a wooded park when there were no other people around."

As he pulled on the second glove, Zane looked to the detectives. "This sounds like a hit, if you ask me."

21

F or the second time in the last five days, I found myself knocking on Joe Dalessio's office door. Unlike the previous visits, every muscle was already tense in anticipation of this meeting.

When I'd received the phone call to summon me to Chicago, Joe had spoken almost every word through clenched teeth. I still wasn't sure what had caused his obvious irritability, but I had a suspicion.

"Come in."

I almost jumped at the sudden disturbance in the otherwise still house. No one officially lived at the location, but we used the lavish residence for large gatherings and meetings. None of the Leóne capos liked to conduct business at their homes, and none of them wanted to live where they conducted business.

Taking a deep breath, I pushed open the wooden door and stepped over the threshold.

As soon as Joe's dark eyes fixed on me, his unshaven face darkened. He pointed to the set of chairs. "Sit."

It wasn't a suggestion.

With a slight nod, I shut the door and complied.

Dropping to his leather office chair, Joe raked a hand through his hair. "You know why you're here, don't you?"

I gritted my teeth. "The reporter?"

A muscle in Joe's cheek twitched as he clenched and unclenched his jaw. "The reporter." His glare finally landed on me. "I'm going to ask you this once, and I expect you to have a good answer, you understand, Alton?"

My back went rigid. No matter how big a chunk of this world I carved out for myself, Joe's anger still made my blood turn to ice. Though he'd taken me in as his protégé, Joe had a reputation.

A reputation for breaking necks first and asking questions second.

I swallowed and nodded. "I understand."

He dropped both arms on the mahogany desk. "I got a call this morning to tell me that the cops found Vivian Kell's body at Old Pines Park, down by the creek. They're saying right now that it looks like she was robbed, but let me tell you a little about that, kid."

A spell of silence followed, and if looks could kill, I'd have been dead a hundred times over.

Leaning forward, his glare didn't so much as waver. "Staging a scene to look like a robbery isn't easy. You know why?"

As the pervasive quiet returned, I shifted in my seat.

The next words came through clenched teeth. "Because if someone's staging a robbery, chances are, they had a motive to kill that person. And the second the cops find something wrong with that fake scene, they'll look high and low for that motive. That make sense to you?"

I gulped at the knot forming in my throat.

He laced his fingers together. "Now, I know you're only twenty-eight, so let's hope that this winds up just being a learning experience for you. But here's my question. You ready, kid?"

This time, I cleared my throat. "Yeah."

If Joe was going to rip me a new one, I'd face him like a man who was worthy of his status in the Leóne family. I was sure I'd made the right call, and I would stick to my decision, come what may.

Without breaking his gaze, Joe leaned forward and lifted an eyebrow. "What in the *fuck* were you thinking?"

My heart beat a merciless cadence against my ribs, but I kept my expression cool and impassive. "You told me to stop her from going after Premier *and* sticking her nose in the Flores kids' case. You wanted me to make it go away and ensure the article she was writing never saw the light of day."

The sharp crack of Joe's fist against the wooden desk split through the air like a gunshot. Despite my best effort, I jumped at the sudden report.

"You didn't have to fucking kill her!" Joe's voice was one step below an outright shout.

I fought to keep from cringing at the venom in his tone. "With all due respect, Joe, I disagree."

Though I braced myself for a harsh rebuff, his next words were deathly calm. "Do you? Care to tell me why?"

Taking in a deep breath, I spread my hands. "She's an investigative journalist. I've dealt with one of those before. You remember that, right?"

Joe's glare hardened.

I jabbed an index finger at the arm of the chair. "I know how reporters work. When they're that deep into something like she was with Premier, there's no turning them away from it. They might leave town if we tell them to, but they can publish their articles from anywhere in the world. As soon as the freshness of their encounter with us is gone, they'll be right back at it. And you can't tell me that hasn't happened before."

Propping his elbows on the edge of the desk, he managed a slight nod. "Maybe so. Then why in the hell did you let the cops find a body? Staged robbery or not, what the hell were you thinking?"

As the tension of my muscles eased, I tapped the armrest. "To throw suspicion away from us. If she'd just up and disappeared, the cops would think for sure that we had something to do with it. They'd be knocking down our doors by the end of the week."

"And what makes you think they won't do that now? Especially since they have a body?"

"Because we were thorough." I met Joe's intense stare. "No murder weapon, scraped under her nails, wiped her skin down before we dumped her, the works. And we kept her body in a freezer over the weekend, so as far as the cops are concerned, she was killed last night. We all have alibis for the entire night."

Joe held my gaze as the seconds ticked away in a silence so prominent, it was deafening.

In those moments, I wasn't honestly sure if he would congratulate me on a job well done or leap across the desk to bash my head into the carpeted floor.

Unclasping his hands, he pushed away from the desk and leaned back in his chair. He rubbed his eyes and let out a long sigh. "You'd better hope you and your guys were as thorough as you think, and you better hope the medical examiner doesn't look for freezer burn at the cellular level." Joe dropped his arm to the side. "In the meantime, stay the hell out of Chicago. You've got work to do, anyway. We'll get someone to fill in for Vinnie in the next few days."

I wanted to let the self-satisfied grin make its way to my face, but I was still stuck on his comment about freezer burn.

Could an M.E. tell that she'd been frozen? I hoped the hell not.

But I couldn't worry about that right now. The past was the past. I needed to focus on my future. I'd do what he told me to do and stay away from Chicago. I didn't need to go there to get to Mari, anyway. I'd go back to the farm and wait for Dean to deliver her.

Then, I'd make her understand what a grave mistake she'd made by going to the reporter for help.

And everyone on the farm, including her two brats, would get to watch.

22

B y the time Amelia stepped out of the passenger side of Zane's silver Acura to face the medical examiner's office, the sunlight had taken on a golden hue. Their shadows were long as they made their way to the two-story cement fortress.

Though Chicago's medical examiner was near a cluster of sleek, state-of-the-art hospitals, the M.E.'s office resembled a prison. A row of windows ran along each floor, but the sills were built far enough back in the concrete structure that they were perpetually dark.

Frowning, Amelia brushed the stray hairs from her sticky brow. Aside from the hour and a half at the site of Vivian Kell's body, she'd spent the entire day in air-conditioning. Yet, somehow, her forehead was *still* sticky.

With all they'd gleaned during their review of Vivian's financial records, their phone calls to her friends and coworkers, and the time they'd put into reviewing security footage of the businesses and other buildings around *The Chicago Standard*, Amelia might as well have gone home to take a shower.

After almost seven hours of focused investigation, they had no additional evidence to support their theory that Vivian had been the victim of a Leóne hit.

Security cameras in a parking garage down the street from the *Standard* showed that Vivian had made the trip to her car without incident on Thursday night. Amelia had reached out to the officers who had patrolled Vivian's neighborhood. They'd confirmed that her car had been parked at home that night, and based on their patrol records, it hadn't moved since.

Old Pines Park was within walking distance of Vivian's apartment, and though the officers hadn't seen her leave home, with their patrol being a thirty-minute interval, it was possible they simply missed her.

So far, Amelia and Zane had nothing more than a hunch to support their theory.

If Amelia hadn't seen the look of fear and paranoia in Vivian's eyes when they'd met up the week before, she wouldn't have suspected the Leóne family was responsible. But her gut said otherwise, and she had learned to trust that instinct.

Their entire case was in the hands of the medical examiner, and if SAC Keaton hadn't taken it upon herself to contact the powers that be, they might have had to wait a full day for the results of the autopsy.

A wave of cool air washed over Amelia as she and Zane made their way through a set of double doors. Breathing a sigh of relief—even though they'd parked right in front of the entrance—Amelia turned her attention to a square waiting area with three rows of cushioned seats and a wall-mounted television. The outside of the building might have looked like a fortress, but the interior reminded Amelia of a dentist's office.

She'd been to visit with the medical examiner a couple

times since moving back to Chicago, but the striking difference between the inside and outside of the squat building never failed to surprise her.

"*House Hunters.*" Zane's voice cut through the quiet air.

Surprised by his oddly chosen words, Amelia turned to her partner. "What?"

He tilted his chin at the television. "That's what's on TV. *House Hunters.*" They continued on toward the glass partition that separated the staff from the waiting room. "I used to watch it with my mom when I was home from college. She'd always make fun of how snooty the people were."

From behind a long, wooden desk, a young man with a crop of sandy brown hair straightened in his seat. His gray eyes flicked from Amelia to Zane as he retrieved a clipboard. "Hello. Can I help you?"

With a small nod, Zane retrieved his badge and identification from his black suit jacket.

Whenever Amelia watched him produce an item from a hidden pocket, she couldn't help but wish she wore men's clothes. At least during the winter months, she could get away with a peacoat or a heavy cardigan, but not in August. Not unless she wanted to sweat out half her body weight in one afternoon.

Zane flipped open his badge as Amelia pulled hers from the depths of her handbag.

"I'm Agent Palmer, this is Agent Storm."

On cue, Amelia flashed her ID to the receptionist. "We're here to meet with the medical examiner."

The young man's face brightened with curiosity.

Aside from the Violent Crimes Division of the Chicago office, federal agents weren't frequent fliers at the M.E.'s building. And then, agents in VC weren't half as common as city cops. Federal jurisdiction in murder cases didn't occur as often as the media liked to portray, even in a city the size of Chicago.

"Oh, that's right. The M.E. is expecting you." The receptionist pushed a clipboard through the slot at the bottom of the glass barrier. "Just sign in here, and I'll buzz you in."

She and Zane complied, and the young man—Sven, according to his nametag—rolled his chair to the end of the desk. With the press of a button, he admitted them to a bright hallway that led into the heart of the building.

They followed Sven's directions down to the basement morgue. Exam Room A was the first door on their left. After a heavy knock, they were beckoned inside by a muffled female voice.

To Amelia's surprise, the bespectacled woman who greeted them couldn't have been much older than thirty.

"You must be Agent Storm and Agent Palmer. Nice to meet you. I'm Dr. Sabrina Ackerly." Her silvery blonde hair was pulled away from her face in a low ponytail, and the corners of her pale blue eyes crinkled as she offered them a smile.

Blinking a couple times, Amelia politely accepted the woman's handshake. "You're the new medical examiner for Cook County?"

"I sure am." Sabrina nodded. "Arthur, I mean, Dr. Landen retired a couple months ago."

Dr. Landen had been a competent medical examiner. He'd spent years as a surgeon just down the street before transitioning to the world of forensic autopsies.

She wanted to ask the M.E. how long she'd even been out of med school but stopped the question before it could rudely pass her lips.

Even though Amelia liked to think she looked past most common misperceptions, her immediate assumption that Dr. Sabrina Ackerly was young and therefore inexperienced and less competent than her predecessor was based on nothing more than stereotypes. Clearly, she still had work to do.

Amelia expected Zane to step in with one of his usual charming smiles and an introduction, but he remained silent as he shook the doctor's hand.

Though her imagination might have gotten the better of her in those seconds of awkward silence, she could have sworn that Zane and Sabrina's eyes lingered on one another for a beat longer than normal.

Clearing her throat, Amelia ignored the part of her brain that insisted the two of them could have been cousins. Based on the doctor's fair skin, light hair, and taller than average stature, she shared Zane's Nordic roots.

Dr. Ackerly's attention shifted to the chart in her hand, like she'd been yanked out of a trance.

"Sorry, it's been a long day." Sabrina gestured to the covered body resting on a stainless-steel exam table in the center of the room. "You're here to talk about Vivian Kell, correct?"

Before Zane could reply, Amelia answered, "Right."

Sabrina snatched up a blue nitrile glove. "Well, I'm glad you came to the office for this one, Agents."

Amelia stepped over to the other side of the table. "Why's that?"

As she pushed her cat-eye glasses up on her nose, Sabrina's pleasant countenance vanished, and Dr. Ackerly showed up, ready to work. "There's a lot about Ms. Kell's final hours that don't add up."

A twinge of hopeful relief edged its way into Amelia's thoughts, followed by a pang of guilt.

The doctor adjusted the UFO-shaped exam light before she switched on the bulb. "Her time of death was a little difficult to pin down, but there wasn't much in the way of decomposition or insect activity. Between the environmental factors and her body temperature, I'd normally estimate that she was killed last night between six in the evening and midnight, but..." she held up a finger, "her body temp was much cooler than it should have been for August. I'll be studying her cells at a molecular level to look for blood cell ruptures and any intracellular fluid leaks."

Amelia felt like she was listening to Charlie Brown's teacher talk. "What does that mean?"

The doctor lifted a shoulder. "It means that something is off, and I need to look into it further."

Zane crossed his arms as his eyes shifted between Vivian's body and the doctor. "Do you know her official cause of death?"

"Manual strangulation." Pulling down the white sheet, Dr. Ackerly gestured along Vivian's neck. "Have a look at the marks. See how there are several different imprints?"

As Sabrina pointed out three distinct sets of bruises, Amelia's eyebrows lifted. "She was strangled more than once?"

"Exactly," Dr. Ackerly replied.

Amelia turned to Zane, hoping he had come to the same realization she had. "Doesn't sound much like a mugging, does it?"

He shook his head. "Nope."

"There's a contusion above her left temple too." Sabrina settled the sheet just below Vivian's collarbone. "Once I saw the injury on her head and the multiple sets of strangulation marks around her neck, I looked at a sample of her brain tissue. Early on, in med school, I was considering neuro-surgery, so I studied the brain quite a bit. When a victim's cause of death doesn't seem to add up, I always go back to the brain."

As each minute went by, Amelia was more and more impressed with Dr. Sabrina Ackerly. The woman had been an aspiring brain surgeon. No wonder she'd landed a position as the medical examiner at such a young age.

Sabrina looked down to Vivian, and a flicker of sadness passed behind her pale eyes. "When I examined her brain cells under a microscope, the neurons looked odd in a way that makes me suspect that she likely fell unconscious multiple times before she was finally killed."

Amelia could only imagine the horror Vivian had gone through. Sadness and anger gripped her heart. "She was tortured."

Sabrina's nod was solemn. "She was also raped. Brutally, and more than once. There was no semen, but I found a couple hairs inside her, and I don't believe they are hers. I've sent those, along with everything else, over to the FBI's lab."

Ice water seeped into Amelia's veins. Since they were dealing with the León family, the sexual assault didn't come as a surprise, but the development sank like a stone in her stomach all the same.

Sabrina lifted one of Vivian's hands up to the bright examination light. "It gets more disturbing, believe it or not." She held out Vivian's pinky finger. "The nails were scraped. I confirmed with the coroner and the Chicago PD and none of our guys at the scene did it. Which means her killers did it to remove evidence. See? This mark goes up into her cuticle, but there's no blood."

Zane blew out a sigh as he turned away. "No blood because they did it after she was dead." For a moment, he looked like he was going to be sick, but his composure returned nearly as fast as he'd lost it.

"Exactly. Her skin was clean too." Sabrina waved at Vivian's forearm. "Whoever they were, they wiped down most of her body. Other than the trace amounts of dirt we found on her knees, there's no sweat, no grime, nothing. And considering what she endured, that's virtually impossible."

Squeezing his eyes closed, Zane rolled his head to stretch the tight muscles. "Tell me there's some good news in here somewhere?"

"There is."

Zane's eyes popped open, and Amelia jerked her head toward the doctor.

As she replaced Vivian's arm, she moved toward the head of the gurney. "Her entire body was wiped off, but they didn't wash her head. I found residue and dust in her hair and on her scalp, so I sent that to the FBI lab for analysis. I'm no geologist or chemist, but I noticed that the samples had a faint chemical smell to them, and so did her clothes."

A crease formed on Zane's forehead as his brow furrowed. "What kind of chemical?"

Sabrina held her hands out, palms up. "Like I said, I'm not a geologist, and my understanding of chemistry is mostly medical. But if I had to guess? Since the smell is in the dirt, it could be a pesticide."

Amelia sucked in a sharp breath as she glanced at Zane. "A pesticide."

He clenched his jaw and nodded. They were both thinking the exact same thing, she knew.

"We need to push that analysis through as fast as they can do it." He was already tapping away at his phone. "I'm not usually the gambling type, but I'd put money on the fact that Vivian was killed in the same area where they've been keeping Javier and his sister."

AFTER A DINNER OF CHINESE TAKEOUT, another fruitless run through the parking garage security footage, and a half-dozen stories about how Hup had taken to flushing the toilet in the middle of the night, Amelia was overcome with cautious optimism when she and Zane received an email from one of the Bureau's forensic chemists.

Though they were closing in on midnight, the young man who greeted them at the entrance to the lab looked as if he had just downed a quad-espresso.

Like Sabrina Ackerly, Oliver Jeffries appeared young for someone with the title of forensic chemist. But, just like the medical examiner, Oliver was brilliant. Amelia and Joseph had worked with him during their investigation into the Irish gangsters during the Fiona Donahue undercover agent fiasco.

Thanks in no small part to Oliver's diligence, most of the men involved with the drug trafficking ring had received hefty prison sentences. Not only had the gangsters been slapped with charges for the drugs that were in their possession during the FBI raid, but Oliver had tied the chemical makeup of the bricks of heroin to an entire network of drug sales that had been ongoing in the city for months.

Stifling a yawn with the back of one hand, Amelia shifted her focus to the dim corridor. In the center of the second floor of the FBI office, there were no windows aside from those that looked out onto a hallway.

Maybe that was how Oliver had maintained his chipper attitude. He didn't know how damn late it was.

The young chemist had a brilliant grin that revealed straight white teeth. He pulled open the glass and metal door and ushered them into the lab. "Hello, Agent Storm, nice to see you again." Red thermos in one hand, he tilted it at Zane. "And you're Agent Palmer. Nice to meet you too."

"I've heard good things about you, Oliver." Zane flashed his trademark grin.

Oliver let out a quiet chuckle. "Well, here's hoping I can live up to expectations." He gestured to the computer at the end of a lab table spanning the length of the wall. "I just got back from refilling my coffee, but I've got everything pulled up on the computer already."

As she and Zane followed Oliver to the dual monitors, Amelia tugged at the bottom of her purple dress shirt. "Thanks for working on this so late, by the way. It's really important that we chase after this lead as quickly as we can."

Oliver set his thermos beside the edge of one monitor and offered her a warm smile. "It's no problem at all. I actually work the third shift, so I started working on these samples as soon as I got into the office at six." He tapped a key as the computer hummed to life. "I like the overnight hours, honestly. I get a lot more done when it's quiet around here. Plus, everyone else hates third shift, so it's not like I had to fight for it. The only time it gets iffy is when I have to be in court during the day."

He waved a dismissive hand and typed in his password.

"But anyway, you guys aren't here to chat about work schedules. And I'm guessing you want to go home sooner rather than later."

Pulling up an office chair to sit at Oliver's side, Zane rubbed his eyes. "It's been a long day. We're hoping you can tell us a little more about the type of chemicals that were found on our victim's body."

Rather than snatch another cushioned seat, Amelia leaned against the sturdy lab table. If she plopped down into a comfortable chair, she worried she might never want to leave.

"Right." Oliver clicked through a couple windows to pull up a colorful image of microscopic crystals. "This is my main find from the samples that the M.E. sent over." He glanced to Zane, and then Amelia. "This is probably what she smelled on your victim's clothes and hair."

Amelia glared at the glowing monitor. "What is it? It looks like stained glass under a microscope."

Nodding, Oliver clicked over to a text document. "It does, a bit. It's an insecticide called Nitenpyram."

Amelia's lethargy disappeared as she saw the pieces falling into place. She speared Zane with a look of victory. "We were right."

Zane leaned in closer, pointing to the screen. "What can you tell us about it?"

Oliver propped his elbows on the table. "Well, Nitenpyram has been around since the mid-nineties. It's classified as a neonicotinoid because of how it works to kill pests. Basically, it binds to the nicotine acetylcholine receptors in insects, which causes central nervous system failure and death. But when mammals come into contact with it, it's relatively harmless."

"Low toxicity in humans." Amelia's mind was whirling. "How common is it?"

"Anymore? Not very." Oliver shrugged. "It's a first-generation neonicotinoid, so it's been used an awful lot in agriculture, but nowadays, it's mostly used to treat animals with fleas. It's still effective, but it's been used less and less over the years."

Amelia straightened and smoothed out the front of her shirt. "Any idea why it isn't used as much anymore?"

"The newer variants of this family of pesticides are still popular around the globe, but there's been some controversy recently. When plants that pollinate are treated with a neonicotinoid, the chemicals are transferred to butterflies and honeybees. In Illinois, at least, there's been a trend for farmers to move away from them ever since they were banned in Europe back in 2018."

Zane tapped his index finger against an armrest. "Looks like our people aren't following that trend."

"If it makes a difference, Nitenpyram is cheaper than the newer variants." Oliver looked back and forth between them.

"Plus, it's highly soluble in water and less toxic to humans than those newer insecticides."

As Zane crossed his arms, his eyes flicked back to the monitor. "Is there any way to tell who's used Nitenpyram recently?"

"There is." Oliver's expression brightened.

Excitement raced through Amelia's cells. "Did you just say that there *is* a way to locate the places that have been using Nitenpyram?"

With a proud waggle of his eyebrows, Oliver turned back to his computer and opened an internet browser. "I did. That's another thing I looked into before you guys got here. I'm already familiar with sifting through chemical companies, suppliers, and buyers, so I figured I'd save you a little time."

For the first time that day, a hint of cautious optimism crept into Amelia's mind. Though they'd learned a great deal about Vivian's final hours during their trip to Sabrina Ackerly's office, none of the developments so far had pointed in a definitive direction. Aside from confirmation that the site of Vivian's body was probably staged, they'd been left with more questions than answers.

Keys clacked as Oliver's fingers flew over the glowing keyboard. "I started by looking for local suppliers of Nitenpyram. Specifically, the suppliers who sell it for agricultural settings. The form that's used to help your pets get rid of fleas differs from the stuff they spray on crops."

One of Zane's brows quirked up. "Does Hup have fleas? Maybe Oliver can help find her some flea treatment if she does."

Crossing both arms over her chest, Amelia rolled her eyes. "Hup doesn't go outside. No, she doesn't have fleas."

As the sarcastic smile crept over Zane's face, Amelia felt as if she'd finally returned to the real world. She'd spent almost the entire day in *The Twilight Zone*—a place where muggers scraped their victim's fingernails and cleaned their grimy skin. To say she was glad to return to some semblance of normalcy was an understatement.

Aside from a flicker of amusement in his eyes, Oliver didn't react to their banter as he continued to type. "Here we go. See?" He turned to Amelia as he pointed to a spreadsheet. "One of my friends is an intelligence analyst upstairs, and she taught me how to import the data into a spreadsheet like this. Then it's really easy to sort through it. Of course, it helps that the FBI has software that does most of the work. I don't have to worry about writing out lines of SQL code or something."

She nodded, not quite sure what SQL was, but knew better than to interrupt when he was on a roll.

"I took those suppliers and filtered down to who does business in Illinois. I also threw in Indiana but didn't get any results. This supplier here..." He highlighted a cell. "Bright Star Chemicals LLC, they're a supplier for insecticides, herbicides, all kinds of pest control. Now, the EPA monitors anyone who's selling large quantities of things like fertilizer, pesticides, anything potentially toxic or volatile like that."

Zane rested his elbows on the armrests and leaned forward. "Ever since the Oklahoma Bombing by Timothy McVeigh, regulations on all that stuff have tightened up."

"Exactly." Oliver shot him an appreciative smile. "And considering the damage that these types of insecticides can do to bees, the EPA has been keeping a close eye on them. So, I just hopped over to their database to see which locations were buying Nitenpyram within the past few months."

Amelia didn't realize she'd been holding her breath until an ache burned through her side. "And you're sure this is the stuff that was in the victim's hair? And on her clothes?"

Oliver nodded. "One-hundred-percent sure. I don't have

the exact chemical makeup of this specific batch since there are teeny, tiny variations in each batch, but I can say without a doubt that it *is* Nitenpyram."

He pulled the spreadsheet to the second monitor to reveal a map of Illinois. When he pressed another key, two red dots lit up—one just southwest of Chicago, and another down at the southernmost point of the Illinois-Missouri state line.

Amelia and Zane's attention was rapt, and in the seconds that followed, the only sound was the hum of the building's air-conditioning.

With the mouse, Oliver circled the northern dot. "This is a farm about an hour and a half southeast of here, just on the edge of Kankakee County. The other one is a farm that's just a few miles away from the Mississippi River."

Pushing to his feet, Zane kept his focus on the screen. "Oliver, let me ask you something."

"Sure."

"Maybe I'm getting ahead of myself. And if I am, just tell me." He leaned closer to the monitors. "Would you be able to tell if the pesticide on our victim's body was the *exact same* as a sample taken from one of those farms?"

Scratching his temple, Oliver tilted his head and thought for a few moments while Amelia held her breath again. "Well, I could confirm without a doubt if the chemicals came from one of these two locations. But there were some dust and dirt samples too, weren't there?"

Zane nodded.

"With those," Oliver smiled as he glanced between the two agents, "plus the Nitenpyram, I think one of my geologist colleagues and I could confirm if that's the location where your victim was killed."

23

Though Zane had initially worried that the evidence they'd collected from Vivian Kell's murder wouldn't be enough to satisfy the sometimes stringent requirements for a search warrant, he'd been pleasantly surprised when Amelia had returned from the courthouse that morning. The warrant was specific to the collection of dirt and pesticides, but he'd take it. If the FBI lab could match the samples to what was found on Vivian's body, they'd be able to obtain a more thorough warrant for the property.

Then again, with the Leónes, nothing was ever straightforward.

Zane was no stranger to gravel roads—Russia had plenty —but they'd been on the same bumpy path for so long that his hands were going numb from the vibration of the steering wheel.

Slowing the car for an upcoming turn, he glanced to the rearview mirror as a black SUV crested the hill. From the modest distance, Zane could barely make out Spencer Corsaw and Joseph Larson.

The plan was for the two men to act as backup while

Amelia and Zane served the warrant. Once the area was secure and they'd determined how cooperative the people in charge of the farm would be, they would reach out to a couple forensic technicians who had posted up nearby.

The four special agents were more than capable of taking dirt and chemical samples. However, in the likely event that the sprawling acreage was the location of Vivian Kell's murder, Amelia and Zane wanted their case to be ironclad. Trained crime scene technicians left no room for a defense lawyer to pull a motion from their hat to suppress evidence on the grounds that the samples had been improperly obtained.

Amelia pointed out the window. "There's the farmhouse."

Zane squinted at the pristine siding and the covered porch that wrapped around half the building.

Like a king watching over his domain, the two-story residence was perched atop a hill that overlooked fields of corn and soybeans stretching off into the late morning sun. He wouldn't be surprised if all the crops they'd passed since hitting gravel were part of the land run by the occupants of the lavish farmhouse.

Just before the start of the fields, four warehouses were spaced evenly along the bottom of the hill. In the distance, sunlight glared off a pair of metal silos.

Blinking against the bright spots of light, Zane turned his attention to the two cars parked in the driveway of a detached, two-car garage—a gunmetal Audi and cherry red sports car. "Pretty nice place for being in the middle of nowhere. Nice cars too."

With a snort, Amelia retrieved the paper copy of their warrant from the handbag at her feet. "I guess you make a lot of money when your labor force is the result of modern-day slavery."

He pulled in behind the sports car and threw the gearshift

into park. "Tell Larson and Corsaw to stay by the garage. That way, if these assholes try to run, it'll be on foot."

Amelia nodded as she dropped her phone into the tote. "Already done."

Turning the key back to kill the engine, Zane patted the service weapon holstered beneath his left arm. "I think it's best we operate under the assumption that this place is run by Leónes. Just because Emilio went without a fight doesn't mean these guys will. We didn't have a murder to pin on Emilio, so who the hell knows how the guys who run this place will act when we say we're investigating a homicide."

As the black SUV approached, Amelia scooted forward to readjust the Glock at her back. "If Vinnie Piliero was any indication, we've got a lot of running ahead of us." She gestured to her dark jeans and black high-top trainers. "I'm prepared this time. Dry weather or not, I'm not running through a field in ballet flats."

Shoving open the driver's side door, he groaned. "Don't remind me. I've still got a bruise on my arm from clothes-lining that jackass."

The faint sound of voices, along with a whiff of cigarette smoke, drifted over to them on a humid breeze. As Amelia's eyes met his, she tilted her head toward the house. "Sounds like they're outside. They must be on the side of the porch we couldn't see."

He pulled his badge from the pocket of his black suit jacket. "It'd be nice if they didn't notice us, but it'd also be nice if money grew on trees."

Blowing out a sigh, Amelia stepped around the front fender to stand at his side. "That's almost exactly what I was thinking. Is it sad that we've only been on this task force for a week, and we're already this jaded, or is it normal?"

He rubbed his unshaven cheek as they watched Spencer

pull into the driveway behind the Audi. "I'm not sure. I'll have to ask Kavya Bhatti the next time I see her."

The hum of the SUV's engine came to a halt, and Spencer stepped out onto the pristine concrete. Zane didn't miss the way Joseph Larson's pale eyes went straight to Amelia as he emerged from the other side of the Lincoln.

Based on the tic in her jaw, Amelia hadn't missed his stare, either.

Zane jerked a thumb over his shoulder. "They're on the other side of the porch."

Spencer moved so that he could see around the side of the house. "We'll wait here. We won't have a visual on you, but if they decide to run, we can at least make sure they don't get to their vehicles."

With a curt nod, Zane turned to make his way to the house, Amelia at his side. The wooden steps hardly made a sound as they ascended to the relative shade of the porch.

When they passed a picture window, Zane caught a glimpse of the fields in the reflective surface of the glass. Though the figure was distant, he was sure he'd seen a person emerge from the nearest rows of corn. Whether they were a worker or another member of the Leóne family, he couldn't be sure.

Clenching his jaw, Zane pulled his attention away from the window.

The rat in the FBI office still hadn't been identified, and he wondered if they were about to walk into a trap. Until they'd piled into their vehicles to head out to Kankakee County that morning, he and Amelia had been the only two who knew about the details of Vivian's murder.

He could only hope that meant the Leónes were in the dark.

As soon as he and Amelia rounded the corner, three sets of eyes snapped up to meet them.

The men were seated in cushioned chairs around a circular table, and right away, Zane recognized one of the trio. He'd been featured in a number of photos on Brandi Dalessio's social media accounts.

They'd operated under the assumption that the farm was run by the Leóne family, and now they had confirmation.

Though the chill of adrenaline crawled down Zane's back like a set of icy claws, he let a cocky smirk find its way to his lips. "Morning, gentlemen."

The bald man's brows furrowed at the upbeat tone of Zane's greeting, and the other two exchanged unsure glances.

Clearing his throat, a broad-shouldered fellow with a neatly trimmed beard—Carlo something-or-other, if Zane remembered Brandi's Instagram tags correctly—set down a handful of playing cards. "I'm sorry, can we help you?" He waved a hand at Zane and Amelia. "Based on those clothes, it looks like you two might be lost."

Zane's smile widened. "No. We're exactly where we need to be." He shifted his gaze to the man with the full head of hair, and as soon as their eyes met, he knew they'd found their perps. "Alton Dalessio, it's nice to finally meet you. I hope you had fun at your sister's wedding last week."

Alton's dark eyes narrowed. "Who are you? Feds? What the hell are you doing here?"

To Zane's side, Amelia flipped open her badge. "Good guess, Dalessio. I'm Special Agent Storm, and this is Special Agent Palmer. Now, as much as we'd love to join in that game of Go Fish you've got going on, we're actually here for business."

A muscle twitched in Carlo's forearm as he clasped the edge of the table.

Baldy held a lit cigarette in one hand while the other was clamped into a fist.

Alton's elbows were still propped on the glass surface.

Pocketing his badge, Zane gestured to the three of them. "Let's keep those hands right where they are, gentlemen. We aren't here to arrest anyone, but at the same time, I'm not stupid enough to think the three of you are unarmed. We know who you are, and now you know who we are."

"What do you want?" Alton's words came through clenched teeth.

Amelia unfolded the warrant. "We're here about Vivian Kell. We have a warrant to—"

Three distinct thuds sounded out as each man's chair tumbled to the floor of the porch.

Zane hadn't even blinked before Baldy leapt over the wooden railing. Carlo hopped down the set of steps beside their table with Alton close on his heels.

"Shit!" Adrenaline seared through Zane's veins. His feet were moving before he'd even committed to the action. Glancing over his shoulder to Amelia, he waved a hand toward the Leóne men. "They're splitting up! Radio Corsaw and Larson, tell them I'm following Carlo, the guy with the beard."

He barely saw Amelia's nod before she disappeared around the corner.

Glock in hand, Zane sprinted over the manicured lawn until he reached the stretch of gravel that led to the first of the four warehouses.

To his chagrin, Carlo was headed straight for the sea of tall corn. Gritting his teeth, Zane slowed his sprint to avoid pitching head over heels down the bottom of the hill.

He and Amelia had dealt with Vinnie Piliero when he'd tried to escape into the depths of Chicago, but a rural chase was a different beast. Zane could outmaneuver his query in the maze of a city but in a cornfield…?

Not so much.

If Baldy or either of his friends made it into the endless

rows of corn, there was a real possibility that they'd be able to get away. Provided, of course, that *they* knew how to navigate such a landscape.

If Zane wound up in the field, he wasn't so confident.

He'd spent most of his life either in populous metropolitan areas or the frigid Siberian hellscape of Russia. Even there, he'd primarily stayed in cities. The Central Intelligence Agency had little need for its operatives to spy on bears in the Russian wilderness.

In fact, he realized that he'd never even *been* in a cornfield.

There's a first time for everything. The sentiment left a bitter taste on his tongue.

Once the ground flattened, he resumed an outright run, ignoring the burn in his lungs as he passed the side of the warehouse. The distance from the house to the fields hadn't seemed like much, but he felt as if he'd been running for half a marathon.

He lost sight of Carlo, but as soon as he passed the edge of the warehouse, he jerked his attention to a flicker of movement.

There, roughly twenty feet from Zane, Carlo had come to a halt at the edge of a veritable wall of leafy stalks.

Zane caught the unmistakable shadow of hesitancy that passed over his bearded face. He didn't want to traverse the corn, either.

Before Zane could raise his weapon or yell for him to stop, Carlo disappeared into the shadows of the tall stalks.

Taking in as deep a breath as he could manage, Zane tightened his grip on the Glock as he came face-to-face with the wall of nine-foot plants.

With one last glance over his shoulder, he stepped into the labyrinth.

By the time Amelia sprinted through the door on the side of the warehouse that faced the cornfield, she'd lost sight of Zane, the bearded man he'd been chasing, and Alton Dalessio. Spencer Corsaw had taken off after the third man, but Amelia figured the odds that Spencer would catch the guy were about fifty-fifty.

The only saving grace was that, if Baldy tried to make a run through the cornfields, Spencer was well-suited to follow. For the first eighteen years of his life, the Supervisory Special Agent had lived in rural Indiana. And according to Spencer himself, Indiana was comprised almost entirely of corn.

Amelia, on the other hand, was a city dweller through and through. The only rural-ish areas she was familiar with were the Iraq and Afghani deserts. She was about as equipped to follow a perp through a cornfield as a fish was to climb a tree.

Back before he'd chosen to view her as a sexual conquest, Joseph Larson had told her horror stories of kids and teenagers daring one another to venture into the tall rows of corn in his native state of Missouri. After less than ten minutes of aimless wandering, the adolescent in the field would lose their sense of direction, panic, and scream for their friends' help.

Clenching her jaw, Amelia paused just inside the tall doorway. She glanced around the rows of shelves to her right, the catwalk above her head, and the open floor to her left.

Nothing was stirring. The only sounds were the drone of the overhead fluorescent lights and the faint buzz of cicadas.

Raising her nine-mil, she kept the weapon close enough to avoid her shadow giving it away as she maneuvered. Head on a swivel, Amelia quickly peeked around the corner, looking for any sign of movement, and waited long enough to listen for any sounds of feet shuffling. Safe in her own assurance that the coast was clear, and with her finger grazing the trigger, ready to squeeze, she stepped around the end of the first shelf.

Amelia's gaze fell on the unexpected and shadowy shape of a woman. A jolt of adrenaline tore through her body like an electric shock.

The woman's dark eyes were wide with fright. Her jaw went slack, and she threw both hands up in the air above her head. "Please, don't shoot!"

Gritting her teeth, Amelia lowered the Glock a couple inches. Based on the layer of dust on the woman's dark jeans, her long-sleeved shirt, and her heavy gardening gloves, she was a worker. Not a Leóne.

Amelia took in a deep breath. "Who are you?"

An unmistakable tremor ran through the woman's hands as her eyes flitted back and forth. "I'm...I work here. On the farm." Her words were tinged with a Spanish accent, but even with her obvious anxiety, she was articulate.

With a curt nod, Amelia pulled out her badge and flipped it open. "I'm a special agent with the FBI. I'm here to serve a warrant. Alton Dalessio, he's a person of interest in an investigation I've been working on, and I saw him run this way."

Before Amelia had finished the explanation, the woman's eyes welled with tears. "You are here for them? You are *actually* here for them?"

Glancing over her shoulder to the two tractors and the still warehouse floor, Amelia nodded. "Yes. We are."

After pulling off one glove, the woman pushed the matted strands of hair back from her forehead. "My name is Ava Fernandez. Many other workers are frightened of being deported, but I do not care any longer. I learn my English when I came to this country because I want to be a citizen." With a snort of derision, she shook her head. "But I would rather go back to El Salvador than stay here with these... these...horrible men."

Ava raised an arm to point out a glowing exit sign.

The shape of a door was partly obscured from her view by the pair of tractors parked against the wall to the left of the entrance. Amelia groaned, frustrated that she hadn't noticed the sign when she'd run into the warehouse.

Ava's eyes burned with pure, unadulterated hatred as she looked at the door. "The man you are looking for. He went through that door. It leads to the managers' office and the basement of this warehouse. It is also connected to the silos." She waved her hands as if trying to paint a picture to go with her words. "Each warehouse has a basement with a path to the grain storage. Everything is connected."

A shadow moved at the edge of Amelia's vision. Without thinking, she spun, leveling her nine-mil for a headshot.

Her finger was a twitch away from squeezing the trigger when she recognized the man who belonged to the shadow. "Larson, what the hell?" Brushing at the sheen of sweat on her brow, she let out an explosive breath. "Say something! I almost shot you!"

"Woah. Sorry." Joseph held his hands up in surrender. His alarmed gaze shifted between Amelia and Ava as he slowly lowered his arms to his sides. "I yelled when I was coming around the corner, but it must have been muffled by the building. The Kankakee Sheriff's Department is on its way. The deputy said their ETA is about fifteen minutes." He gestured to Ava with his free hand. "Who's she?"

"A witness." Amelia waved at the door as she crossed the dusty floor. "She said that Dalessio went through this door. It leads to the basement and connects to the silos. That's got to be where he's headed."

As she came to a stop beneath the red glow of the exit sign, Amelia scanned the concrete wall and the doorframe. Satisfied that there were no tripwires or other nasty surprises, she pushed down on the silver handle. When the lever didn't budge, she spat out a series of four-letter words. "This door is locked, and it's heavy. We can't kick it down, and I'm not about to start shooting at metal with a nine-mil."

Joseph was at her side in a flash. When the locked metal door wouldn't budge for him, he ground his teeth and shot a glance over his shoulder to Ava. "What do they keep in the basement? Do you know?"

After a few steps in their direction, Ava paused. She swallowed hard, and the embers of resentment in her expression morphed into fear. "I have an idea, but I've only been down there once."

Though slight, Joseph narrowed his eyes. "What's down there?"

Ava's knuckles had turned white where she grasped her work gloves. "Children. My niece."

"What's her name?"

Tears filled Ava's eyes. "Camila. Camila Morales."

The hairs on the back of Amelia's neck stood on end. She uttered another curse and turned to look around the area, searching for anything that might help her get through the gray, rust-specked door. As she met Joseph Larson's gaze, all the recent memories of his sleazy behavior had been tossed into the figurative back seat. "Go get me something to open this damn door."

He just stared at her for a long moment. She scowled at him. If he didn't do something helpful, and quick, she'd use his head as a battering ram.

He opened a nearby cabinet. "Like what?"

Amelia opened a drawer on the opposite side of the room. "I don't know. A lock pick, a shotgun, some fucking C4! If there are *kids* down there, and if *he's* down there, only god knows what he's liable to do."

With a determined nod, Joseph backed up past the first tractor. "There's no C4, no lock picks as far as I know, but we *do* have a twelve-gauge. I'll be back in a second." Turning on his heel, he sprinted toward the rays of daylight that pierced through the wide doorway.

Her morning had gone from serving a warrant for soil and pesticide samples to blasting open a locked door with a shotgun.

Nothing with the Leónes was ever straightforward. And just when Amelia was sure she'd reached the depths of their depravity, they proved her wrong.

24

Zane wasn't lost in the corn field, but he had no idea where he was going. He'd kept tabs on the location of the sun, and even though he could determine basic cardinal directions to find his way back to the warehouse, he didn't have the first clue how to efficiently navigate the labyrinth.

Not to mention, Zane had only spotted the occasional glimpse of Carlo since he'd first followed the man into the dense vegetation.

Zane had taken off in Carlo's direction at first, but as soon as a leaf had sliced through the skin of his cheek, he'd slowed his pace. Apparently, the disorienting claustrophobia of the narrow rows wasn't enough of a challenge. Corn plants had to have leaves like razor blades too.

Though the temperature of the field was at least ten degrees warmer than the already uncomfortable August morning, Zane was glad he'd worn long pants and sleeves. If he hadn't been clad in a suit jacket and slacks, his arms and legs would have been shredded by now.

His fear of becoming irreversibly lost in the towering stalks and knife-like leaves had waned, but he still hadn't figured out a method to locate his bearded query. He'd kept an eye on the soil to watch for footprints, but there were more than a few impressions on the dark earth. Zane hadn't paid enough attention to Carlo's shoes to discern which tracks might have been his.

Cutting through rows of corn, Zane had zigzagged through the field in the approximate direction he thought the road might be. He hadn't stopped moving, but he was still no closer to discerning whether the corn ever ended.

Of course it ends, you idiot. This isn't a Stephen King novel.

He hoped.

A faint snapping sound ripped him out of the feeling of dread the thought created. Gritting his teeth, he glanced to his left, then his right.

Nothing.

He held his breath and stared straight ahead, straining to make out any discernable sound. A breeze rustled the tops of the tall plants, but other than the soft murmur of leaves, the area was still.

With one last look over his shoulder, Zane pushed his way through a wall of stalks. Each movement was measured and diligent, making as little sound as he possibly could.

He'd heard *some*thing. A bird, a worker, a damn plane. *Something.*

After a painstaking effort to remain silent, he stepped onto the soft dirt. Like a kid preparing to cross a busy street, he'd checked up and down the newest row before he emerged.

Flexing his grip on the nine-mil, he crept forward. He'd only managed four steps when a shadow moved at the edge of his vision.

Rather than spin around to level the Glock at the source, he pretended to pay the disturbance no mind as he continued his sluggish advance.

His previous tactic to catch up to Carlo by matching the man's pace hadn't worked. As long as Carlo *knew* Zane was hot on his heels, he'd continue to fight his way through the field.

Which meant it was time to try a different tactic.

So far, Zane had shouted for Carlo to stop, and he'd repeatedly reminded the man that he was a federal agent. Each reminder had likely spurred Carlo's desire to put distance between the two of them.

But if Zane pretended to slow or lose track of his prey, then maybe the Leóne man would lessen his pace.

Zane didn't have to be right on Carlo's ass when they came to the edge of the field. He only had to have the man in his sights.

Since repeated orders for Carlo to stop had gone unheeded, and since by now, the man was most definitely guilty of a crime, Zane would be well within his right to give the next order as he stared down the sights of his Glock.

When Zane heard another faint rustle, a surge of adrenaline accompanied his pounding pulse. The rush was a reminder to keep his focus grounded in the present.

Not only had the disturbance been out of time with the wind, the sound was close.

He didn't move. Didn't turn to face the noise, didn't even let on that he'd *noticed* the noise. His mind raced through all the possibilities, and none of them were good.

His eyes flicked to the fractured rays of sunlight that danced along the ground. A whiff of woodsy cologne drifted past him as a man's shadow overtook the shape of the swaying corn plants.

Shit.

He was screwed. If Zane tried to turn and bring up his gun this far away, Carlo would take him down before Zane could get a bead on the man.

Right now, Zane was nothing but a sitting duck.

Think. Think. Think.

This wasn't how Zane had wanted to catch up to Carlo, but he'd have to make the situation work in his favor. He just hoped that Carlo wasn't the type of man to shoot a person in the back.

With Carlo behind him, Zane knew his only hope to win this battle was to do something crazy...let Carlo get as close to him as possible. He needed Carlo within arm's reach if he had a prayer of disarming him.

Zane also needed Carlo to lower his guard. To that end, Zane bent and put his hands on his knees, forcing himself to loudly cough and gag. If he pretended to be on the verge of throwing up, he might be able to get Carlo to come within fighting distance.

Crunch.

Crunch.

Crunch.

His prey was behind him now. Just a little closer.

Crunch.

Zane straightened, and as if on cue, a metallic click sounded as cold steel parted the back of Zane's hair.

Zane didn't have to see. He knew Carlo had pulled back the hammer of the weapon pressed against the base of his head.

Jaw clenched, his eyes fixed straight ahead, Zane wordlessly raised both arms out to his sides, though he didn't let go of his Glock.

When Carlo's gravelly voice cut through the still air, Zane focused on the movement of the man's shadow and practiced his takedown maneuver in his head.

"I don't want to hurt you, Mr. Fed. I'm not exactly in the business of killing cops, and neither are my friends." Carlo blew out a long breath. "And I don't know what you think I did, but I'm not going to prison."

An image of Vivian's colorless face flashed across Zane's mind. The onslaught of adrenaline was all at once frigid and searing.

Zane had been twenty-three the first time someone had pointed a gun to the back of his head and threatened to pull the trigger. In the eleven years since, he'd need both hands to count how many times he'd endured a similar event—not to mention the times he'd stared down the barrel of a gun or been shot at.

The Russian mob, and even the Russian *government*, operated on an entirely different plane of criminal activity than an organization like the Leóne Family. The Leónes stuck to the shadows, but when the Russian Mafia was on their home turf, they didn't need to hide.

But no matter his unsettling familiarity with the sensation of a gun barrel at the back of his head, Zane was always pointedly aware that each time could be his last.

Carlo cleared his throat. "I'm going to need you to drop that Glock of yours, Mister."

The man was clearly nervous. The way his voice cracked as he made the request was proof enough of that. But nerves made people unpredictable, and that was a double-edged sword.

With a muffled clump, Zane's nine-mil tumbled to the ground.

As he studied the shape of Carlo's shadow, Zane held his tongue. He could have tried to reason with the man or maybe offer him a deal. He could have brought up his position as a federal agent, the fact that killing him would catapult Carlo and all his co-conspirators onto the FBI's Most Wanted List.

The rational side of him leaned toward using the olive branch of diplomacy, but Zane was sure Vivian had tried to reason with Carlo and his friends before they'd raped and murdered her.

"Here's what's going to happen." Carlo paused, and the pressure of the barrel lessened. "I don't want to kill you. I know you think I'm some kind of monster, but believe it or not, me and mine have never been in the business of killing cops. But I can't have you following me out to the road, you know?"

One wrong move now, and Zane was dead. His window of opportunity was about to slam shut.

His gaze flicked back to the shape of Carlo's shadow. "Maybe we ought to talk this through. If you're not guilty of anything, then you don't have to do this."

The Leóne man laughed mirthlessly. "I don't—"

There it was. The opening Zane needed. Carlo's posture eased ever so slightly as he laughed. With a swift step sideways, Zane spun on his heel, moving his head free of the handgun's aim.

Leaving no time for the Leóne man to react, the moment Zane finished his rotation, he brought one hand under and clamped his other on top of Carlo's wrist.

The muscles in Carlo's forearm tensed. His finger was still on the trigger.

Hands clamped in position, Zane pushed down hard with his right hand and rotated enough to send the muzzle of the gun pointing to the ground. With his left hand, Zane forced Carlo's wrist up. The combined pressure forced Carlo's wrist to bend at a painfully sharp angle while his finger was wrenched painfully back.

Zane's height had always worked to his advantage. He held firm, shoving Carlo's wrist as high as he could.

Even through the obvious pain in his eyes, Carlo tried to fight.

With a frustrated yelp, any movement was excruciatingly futile.

The moment Carlo stopped fighting, Zane tweaked Carlo's wrist to the right, just enough to let pain do the rest of the work. As expected, Carlo struggled. At that angle, and with his weight, Carlo's wrist cracked and popped like a dry twig before the idiot finally gave in to the momentum.

With practiced efficiency, Zane pulled the gun from the toppling man's hands and had it leveled at Carlo's head by the time he recovered from the fall.

Carlo stumbled to his feet, cradling his limp right hand. He should have stayed down. A smart man would have. But Carlo didn't appear to be the brightest crayon in the box. He threw a clumsy punch with his left hand.

Zane leaned back to avoid the strike, planted his back leg, and sent his foot straight into Carlo's knee.

Along with the howl of pain that erupted from Carlo's mouth, Zane not only felt the crack of cartilage, he heard the joint give way as clearly as if someone had opened a can of soda next to his ear.

Carlo sank to his knees.

Not wanting to shoot the man before he faced justice, and unwilling to see him pathetically try to get up again, Zane balled his fist for one last finishing blow. Knuckles connected with Carlo's cheek, sending the man's head sideways.

Zane enjoyed the momentary win as Carlo hit the ground and stayed there.

The handful of blows he'd dealt weren't a fraction of what Vivian had endured, but at least one man responsible for her death would know what powerlessness was like.

Admiring Carlo's handgun, Zane whistled. "This is a nice weapon, friend. Let's see, does it have a serial...nope, it does not. No serial number, how about that?"

Carlo spat out the blood in his mouth. Jaw clenched, his gaze slowly shifted to the abandoned Glock.

Clucking his tongue, Zane strolled over to the matte black handgun laying in the dirt. "No. This is mine. You're right-handed anyway, aren't you?" He chuckled and retrieved his Glock. "Pretty sure that's the one I broke, isn't it? Doubt you'd be able to fire this thing worth half a shit even if you got to it."

With the back of one hand, Carlo wiped blood from his bottom lip. "Are you going to arrest me?"

Zane met the man's eyes for a beat before he holstered his sidearm and tucked Carlo's handgun behind his back. "I sure am, bud."

Carlo's gaze flicked to the rows of corn at his side.

"Unless you run again." Zane waved an index finger. "Then I'm going to shoot you."

The man's Adam's apple bobbed. "Who the hell are you? You don't sound like any Fed I've ever seen."

Producing a pair of silver handcuffs, Zane flashed his famous grin. "Hands behind your back or I'll put them behind your back for you."

Color drained from Carlo's face as he complied. Zane hauled Carlo to his feet, ignoring the balding man's cries of pain, and snatched a wallet from the back pocket of his jeans.

"Carlo Enrico." He flipped the wallet closed and tucked it into his suit jacket. "You're under arrest. We've got a long list, so we might as well walk and talk at the same time."

Carlo produced a slew of colorful four-letter words.

"Well, I'll do the talking. You have the right to remain silent, and I urge you to use it." Zane none-too-gently prodded him forward. "You're under arrest for the murder of Vivian Kell, for unlawful possession of a handgun, and for filing the identification off said handgun, which is a felony all on its own. You're also under arrest for the attempted murder and assault of a federal agent. That's me, by the way. I'm willing to bet we'll have a whole mess of charges to add by the end of the day, but I think I'll leave that up to the U.S. Attorney."

As he pushed the limping Carlo toward the end of the field, Zane rattled off the man's Miranda Rights.

Only Vivian and her killers knew who had played which part in her brutal murder, but at least one of the men responsible would see prison time.

Now, he had to hope the other two men could be caught.

Moreover, he had to hope none of them would put a gun to Amelia's head like Carlo had to his.

25

After blowing the door handle off with a single slug from the twelve-gauge combat shotgun, Amelia directed Joseph to head outside to cut off Alton Dalessio. Since all the warehouse basements were connected, there was no way to tell where Dalessio might emerge. They could only hope that the Kankakee County Sheriff's Department would arrive before Alton made his break for freedom.

But Amelia wasn't willing to rely on good fortune.

As soon as Joseph had left, she'd blasted open a second door and headed down the set of concrete stairs.

Someone had to follow Dalessio.

Glancing over her shoulder, Amelia offered Ava Fernandez a stiff nod before she turned to face the drab concrete hall.

Ava had offered to help with the search, but Amelia was quick to reject the suggestion. Instead, she'd asked Ava to remain in the relative safety of the topmost landing, and she'd given strict instructions that the woman only come downstairs if she was forced to flee from danger.

Though Ava hadn't gone into detail, Amelia and Joseph

had gleaned enough from her cryptic remarks to establish that the men in charge of the farm used the basement to hold the workers' kids and younger family members captive.

The children were insurance. Leverage to ensure the loyalty of those who were forced to labor in the fields.

But based on the haunted shadow that had passed over Ava's face, the Leóne men hadn't brought the kids all the way to Kankakee County just for collateral.

Amelia ignored the stone in her stomach and tucked the stock of the shotgun tight against her shoulder. Fortunately, Dalessio hadn't felt the need to turn off the lights— not yet, at least. Gritting her teeth, Amelia flexed the fingers of one gloved hand against the pistol grip of the twelve-gauge.

The hall was wide enough for three people to comfortably stand side by side. Other than her quiet footsteps, the only sound was the gentle buzz of the overhead light fixtures.

Two doors loomed on either side of the corridor, but only those on the left were open. Still, the sickly yellow fluorescence didn't pierce more than a couple feet into the shadows of those two rooms.

Lowering the shotgun until the barrel pointed at the ground, Amelia approached the first of the closed doors. As she scrutinized the rust-splotched frame to look for a trip-wire or other trap, light flickered in a narrow gap between the door and the wall. Her gaze shifted toward the handle, and Amelia realized the door hadn't latched closed.

With one more glance up and down the hall, Amelia pulled the stock of the Benelli shotgun back up to her shoulder as she used her free hand to shove open the door, jumping back to avoid any immediate fire. When none came, she entered the room fast and low. Moving the sights of the weapon from one corner of the cramped space to the next, she forced herself to focus through the flickering light as she cleared the room.

A battery-powered work lamp had crashed to the ground at the edge of a full-sized mattress, and the bulb sputtered on and off. Shadows cloaked an alcove in the corner of the room, but Amelia made out the approximate shape of a metal toilet and sink.

Once she was satisfied that no Leóne gunmen were lurking, Amelia turned her attention to the foot of the bed.

The taste on Amelia's tongue turned bitter as white light revealed the dark splatter along the cinderblock wall. Liquid dripped onto the floor, congealing in a pool of what appeared to be chunks of brain tissue.

Amelia had seen dead bodies before. People of all ages, genders, races. She'd seen more sets of lifeless eyes than she could remember, more than any other agent in the Organized Crime Division, save perhaps Joseph Larson. But there was no way anyone could get used to the sight of a dead kid. Not a young girl who had been shot in the head before her tenth birthday.

The girl was little more than a crumpled pile of bones and skin resting on the cement floor. Her mouth hung open in a cry that could no longer be heard. Milky, unseeing eyes stared straight ahead, wide with the last moments of horror she had witnessed. At some point before her death, she'd knocked down the black and yellow work light and ripped the pastel sheets away from the dingy mattress.

She had tried to fight her assailant, but she'd never stood a chance.

Swallowing the foul taste in her mouth, Amelia jerked her gaze away from the gruesome scene to take stock of the rest of the room. A tripod had withstood the scuffle, but if it had been fitted with a camera, the device was long gone. Amelia stared into the shadows in an effort to locate any remaining electronics, but all she spotted were a handful of stuffed animals.

With a scowl, she turned her attention to the hall. The blood spatter was fresh, which meant the girl hadn't been killed long ago.

That confirmed Alton Dalessio was the most likely culprit.

The tripod and work light confirmed Amelia's suspicions that Dalessio and his men had taken to exploiting the children they'd kidnapped as collateral. Though the poor girl at the foot of the bed wasn't Yanira, Amelia knew the youngest Flores child was somewhere in this hellhole.

She didn't stop to puzzle over Dalessio's motive for shooting a ten-year-old in the head.

As Amelia returned to the drab hallway, she pushed away the thoughts. If she wanted to reach Dalessio before he murdered any more kids, she had to move fast.

Stalking to the next door in line, Amelia almost forgot she was in Illinois. Between the sickly shade of the overhead lights and the faint smell of must, she could have tricked herself into thinking she was back in an enemy bunker in the heart of the Iraqi desert.

Maybe she wasn't in the Middle East, but as she cleared the other three rooms, her mindset was in a combat zone. Her movements were precise, methodical, and fast.

She'd done this before.

Another young girl had been shot and killed in the second room on the right, but her head had been covered by a pillow before the assailant pulled the trigger. Amelia barely registered the girl.

The macabre discoveries would catch up to her. They always did. But for now, she had a singular purpose.

The hallway branched off into a T as it met a cement wall. Without pausing to weigh the options, Amelia took the corridor to her right. More light fixtures droned overhead, though the sickly illumination sucked the color from anything it touched.

As a shadowy doorway emerged to Amelia's right, she double-checked the hall before she swung the Benelli around and stepped into the gloom.

Before she'd gone more than four steps, the blood froze in her veins.

The disturbance was faint—just a light click in the tomb-like silence—but Amelia brought the twelve-gauge to bear as if she'd heard the wail of a siren.

When a series of overhead lights buzzed to life, she relaxed her death grip.

"Motion sensor lights," she muttered.

Her words were hardly a whisper, but she still couldn't help a paranoid look around to see if anyone had heard.

One fixture sputtered a few times before its glow steadied to reveal a tiled room. Orange rust stains dripped from where four stainless-steel showerheads were mounted into the wall. At the end of the tile, three backless wooden benches separated the shower area from the shelves of colorful clothes lining the wall.

Even as her unease mounted, Amelia ignored the implied use of the benches as she strode past the shelves to check a handful of bathroom stalls. The motion sensor lights had been off when Amelia arrived. That was a good indication that the area hadn't been disturbed in some time, but her prior military training wouldn't let her leave an uncleared room at her back. Especially not when she was in pursuit of an armed man who was more than willing to kill.

She was glad to leave the unsettling shower room behind once she'd swept the area, but her relief was short-lived.

As she came across four more closed doors, the cold

claws of adrenaline raked down her back. Like the rooms before, each was locked from the inside, but not the outside.

In the first room, like the previous four, she located a tripod but no electronics or storage devices.

As she shoved open the next door in line, the smell of iron wafted over to her before she saw the body sprawled out on the ground. A halo of blood darkened the dingy concrete beneath the girl's hair.

The pool was growing.

Her heart clamored against her ribs like the beat to an angry song from Zane's playlist as she went through the motions to clear the room.

She was close, but she couldn't let her guard down now.

She couldn't risk a clever ambush or leave the potential for an enemy to sneak up behind as she made her way deeper into this veritable dungeon. So, she cleared the next two rooms and set off to another T shaped intersection. For the second time, she went right.

As the hall opened up into a half-hearted attempt at a cafeteria, she spotted a machine responsible for the whir that had overtaken the eerie silence.

A dishwasher.

Why in the hell was a dishwasher running?

Without lowering the shotgun, she sidestepped past a couple circular cafeteria tables to make her way to the source of the disturbance. Dalessio must have started a wash cycle to mask the sound of his movements.

Amelia would have done the same in his position. Or…

Shit!

He could be washing his evidence…literally.

Stabbing a finger at the button to stop the cycle, she breathed out through her nose, keeping her attention on the relative gloom beyond the cluster of tables. Listening. Watching. Waiting.

Amelia was tempted to open the dishwasher door to see if her gut instinct was correct. She didn't. She had more pressing things on her mind.

Her shoulder ached where she'd tucked the stock of the Benelli, and she swore she could hear her muscles creak as she began moving again.

The soles of her shoes made little more than a whisper of sound as she picked a diagonal path through the tables and chairs. Breathing shallow, she strained her hearing to its limit as she drew closer to a hallway at the end of the open floor.

A faint scuffle echoed through the corridor, sending new tendrils of adrenaline shooting down Amelia's back.

To her left was nothing but gray cement, but to her right, she spotted two open doors. With the Benelli leading the way, she stepped through the first doorway and swung the weapon as she checked each dim corner of the makeshift cell.

Another empty tripod, a burnt-out work light, and a blood-spattered collection of stuffed rabbits and teddy bears greeted her. A rivulet of crimson trickled down the girl's dangling arm from where she'd tucked her face into her bicep.

Amelia swallowed the sting of bile and tears in the back of her throat.

Dalessio was close.

She quick-stepped across the room, brought the Benelli to bear, and hurried out into the hall.

Just before Amelia had covered the distance to the next door in line, a clatter and an accompanying smash cracked through the silence like an explosion.

"Did you or your mother have anything to do with this, you little bitch?" Alton Dalessio hadn't spoken much on the porch, but Amelia knew, without a doubt, that was his voice.

On instinct alone, she took two long strides that brought

her into a room with a layout that had become all too familiar.

The white glow of the work light caught the pieces of broken plastic that scattered across the dingy concrete as Alton Dalessio took a swift step away from the fallen tripod. He froze in place halfway between Amelia and the young girl cowering at the edge of the mattress.

In tandem, Dalessio and the girl looked straight at Amelia. Gaunt shadows had formed along the girl's cheeks. Her honey-brown eyes were wild with fear. She was one of the most beautiful things she had ever seen.

Yanira.

With the sights of the Benelli trained on Alton's chest, Amelia sidestepped along the wall to keep as much distance between them as she could manage. His posture stiffened as he continued to firmly grip the handgun.

Each movement Amelia made, no matter how small, Dalessio's dark eyes followed.

"Alton Dalessio." Amelia's voice was cold but calm. Deadly. "Drop your weapon and raise your hands slowly."

Though the motion was painstaking, Dalessio extended both arms out to his sides. Still, he didn't let go of the handgun.

There was a glint in his brown eyes that made the hair on the back of Amelia's neck stand on end. She'd seen that look before, but not in this country.

The men she'd seen with that flicker of determination had been the select few who weren't afraid to die. The few who counted their successes by the number of bodies they accumulated before they met their violent end.

Tightening her fingers against the shotgun's grip, Amelia narrowed her eyes. "Drop the weapon, Dalessio."

He shook his head, but his gaze didn't leave her. "I'm not going to prison, lady."

Brian Kolthoff's image flashed into her mind. Chances were, the man called The Shark was relaxing on one of his luxurious yachts as he floated along the edge of the Great Lakes. Chances were, he had his own personal chef, a bartender to mix drinks from overpriced liquor, and maybe even a pretty young woman to warm his bed at night.

Brian Kolthoff, a man who had come within an inch of buying a sixteen-year-old sex slave, a man who undoubtedly had an entire regiment of skeletons buried in his closet, was a free man.

Not only was he free, but his lavish lifestyle hadn't been touched.

Then, there was Emilio Leóne. The mafia capo had been sentenced to a whopping five years behind bars for forcing underage girls into prostitution, not to mention the countless sexual assaults he'd committed with the aid of his position of power.

Amelia had seen the face of one of his victims as she gave her statement. She didn't know a fraction of the hell that poor girl had lived through, but sheer terror in the girl's eyes revealed more than her testimony ever could.

When Emilio was eventually released from prison, he'd walk back into the same life of luxury he'd left behind. His family would commend him for not rolling over to law enforcement, and he'd be placed right back on his throne.

Nothing ever changed with men like Emilio and Kolthoff. They owned this world, and the only thing that would ever stop their reign of terror was a bullet.

When Alton Dalessio told Amelia he wasn't going to prison, his words had merit. He was no capo, but she was sure the Leóne family would throw money at his legal defense all the same.

She was sure the U.S. Attorney would crucify him in a

courtroom, but then again, she'd thought the same about Brian Kolthoff and Emilio Leóne.

Pressing the stock of the Benelli even tighter against her shoulder, Amelia clenched her jaw. "Drop the fucking weapon, Dalessio, or you're right. You won't go to prison. You'll leave here in a body bag, just like all those little girls you killed."

He stretched his arms wider but didn't let go of the handgun. "I don't know what you're talking about." His eyes narrowed. "You're a Fed. You can't kill me. I can stand here with this nine-mil all damn day, and you can't shoot me."

Blood burned its way through Amelia's veins. "If your arm so much as twitches, I will shoot you."

His stare remained fixed on her, but his expression was unreadable.

He was sizing her up, trying to figure out if he could aim his weapon and pull the trigger before a shot from the twelve-gauge punched through his chest.

The seconds ticked away in utter silence. Even the girl was quiet from where she had hunkered behind the edge of the mattress to make herself a smaller target.

That's when Amelia saw it.

A flicker of motion as Alton raised his arm. He'd barely lifted his foot to take a step in her direction when she squeezed the trigger.

The combat shotgun bucked against her shoulder, but her iron grip kept the weapon steady. In a concussive blast, Alton Dalessio's body flew backward, slamming into the cinderblock wall. A wide smear of blood followed his final slump to the ground. As she watched, the life flickered out of his eyes.

Good.

Then the doubts set in.

Amelia couldn't say for sure how much Dalessio had

moved before she shot him. The motion had been slight, but there *had been* movement, right?

She was sure of it.

She'd seen the look in his eyes, the look she'd seen on the faces of terrorists and mass murderers. He'd said himself that he wouldn't go to prison. Before Amelia had entered the room, he had already killed four innocent children. He wouldn't have hesitated to kill again if it meant he'd escape imprisonment. Of that, she was certain.

He'd moved. He'd tried to step forward, and he was bringing his weapon to bear.

That was it. She'd pulled the trigger because she feared for her life.

Why, then, was the pang of doubt so prominent in the back of her mind? It wasn't guilt—she'd never feel guilty for killing a man as twisted as Alton Dalessio.

But she felt...uneasy.

Lowering the Benelli, Amelia ripped herself from the contemplation and turned to the girl.

Amelia held out a gloved hand as she took a step toward the bed. "It's okay, Yanira. It's okay." She tapped herself on the chest. "I'm with the FBI. I'm here to take you back to your mother. I know there are other bad men here, but you're safe now. My friends will catch those men too. They can't hurt you anymore."

With one trembling finger, the girl pointed to the doorway. "Is he your friend?"

Tightening her grip on the shotgun, Amelia spun around, ready to fire.

Her gaze settled on a pair of familiar pale blue eyes, but rather than relief, she felt as if a phantom hand had clamped down on her throat.

"Joseph." The ground beneath her feet suddenly felt unsteady. "How long have you been there?"

He stepped across the threshold, his gaze not leaving hers. "Since right before you killed him." Joseph's expression turned grave as he waved to Alton Dalessio's body.

It was a good shot. A clean shot.

Wasn't it?

All Amelia could manage was a nod.

Was she just kidding herself?

She didn't know if she'd truly been in danger when she'd shot Alton Dalessio, but the last person she wanted to rely on to back her up was Joseph Larson.

26

The sun was dipping just below the horizon as Alex Passarelli shut down his work computer and shoved away from the sleek corner desk. Stretching both arms above his head, he arched his back until he felt a light pop.

He glanced to the black office chair as he moved to stand. "I need a better chair," he muttered.

Alex was about to turn thirty-two, and though his uncles liked to remind him how young and spry he was, compared to them, he didn't *feel* it after spending six hours in front of a computer screen.

Blowing out a sigh, he pushed the chair back into the desk and made his way to the kitchen. His work for the day was done, and like most nights, he'd go through his workout regimen and shower. Then he could relax on the couch, order some takeout, and watch the news.

As much as Alex hated the news, local segments were by far the most palatable broadcasts. He and the D'Amato family had a web of contacts to keep them updated on the happenings across the entire city, but if Alex wanted an overview of the day's events, he still turned to the evening news.

And today, there had been no shortage of events to cover.

Earlier, his uncle had alerted him of an upcoming press release from none other than the Federal Bureau of Investigation. When he'd switched over to the local channel, Alex's first thought was to look behind the woman at the podium. He hoped to spot Amelia but knew the Bureau wouldn't send field agents in front of a crowd of rabid reporters.

When the speaker—the Special Agent in Charge of the Chicago Field Office—had listed off her agents' newest takedown, Alex's jaw had gone slack.

The D'Amatos kept their ear to the ground to monitor the goings-on of their rivals, particularly the Leóne family. But they hadn't heard a single word of the impending bust of a Leóne labor trafficking ring.

Apparently, even the *Leónes* had been in the dark.

Their inside man hadn't been able to help them save the multi-million-dollar operation they'd run on an acreage at the edge of Kankakee County. No specifics were offered about the agents involved in the takedown, but Alex knew without a doubt that Amelia had been part of the operation.

Every day she was in this city, she sank deeper and deeper into the volatile world of the Leóne family. As much as Alex wanted to warn her to watch her step—*and* her back—he reminded himself of the conclusion he'd drawn months earlier.

Amelia Storm was a soldier.

Not like some low-level mafioso who liked to *call* themself a soldier. She was a real, bona fide soldier.

With a fresh glass of lemonade in hand, Alex plopped down onto the center of his gray sectional.

He let himself meld into the overstuffed cushion as he flicked on the television right in time for the eight o'clock news.

Nodding a thank-you to the middle-aged man at her side,

the younger of the two anchors shuffled through a few papers before she turned her light brown eyes to the camera. "Thank you for that update, Keith. Now, we turn to the newest development in a breaking story from Kankakee County."

The camera angle shifted, and Alex straightened in his seat.

"Earlier today, the Federal Bureau of Investigation announced that it'd made several arrests yesterday in a human trafficking investigation that turned deadly. Four victims are believed to have been killed by the traffickers. We don't have many of the specifics about the charges or the suspects yet, but we expect to learn more as this case unfolds."

Beside the young woman's head, an aerial image of a sprawling farm appeared, complete with a host of vehicles parked around a warehouse building. The caption below the picture merely read *Kankakee County, Illinois*.

"Information shared with us, so far, indicates at least sixty migrant workers had been used as laborers on the fifteen-hundred-acre farm. Details have yet to be released, but sources indicate that the majority of the workers are undoc-umented immigrants from a handful of South American countries, including El Salvador and Guatemala."

The reporter droned on, providing a high-level overview of forced labor trafficking, including other recent cases across the United States. Alex was already familiar with the illicit industry, but the rundown still brought a scowl to his face.

A photo of a man named Matteo Ricci followed. Ricci was the one suspect the Feds had been willing to identify to the public so far, but only because he'd escaped before he could be arrested. The typical disclaimer warned civilians that the man was armed and dangerous, and a statement from the U.S. Marshal Service advised anyone who spotted him to dial 9-1-1.

Stifling a yawn, Alex reached one hand to rub his eyes. Just as he was about to change the channel to a late baseball game or a rerun of an animated comedy, the news reporter called his attention back to the television.

"The land is owned by Happy Harvest Farms, Incorporated." She folded her hands on the polished black desk. "Happy Harvest Farms is a multi-billion-dollar agricultural company that produces much of the Midwest's ethanol, as well as seeds and a variety of produce. And as many of us here in Chicago know, the company is headquartered right here in the Windy City and is owned and operated by the Young family. We'll go now to Keith to discuss Senator Stan Young's response to yesterday's arrests."

Clearing his throat, Keith nodded. "That's right, Brenda. Stan Young, one of two sitting senators for the state of Illinois, was at the helm of Happy Harvest Farms until he won his first bid for Senate. His son, Josh Young, has since taken charge of the company. Senator Young is facing a fierce opponent in next May's senate primaries. Field reporter, Anita Jensen, caught up with Senator Young earlier today to ask for his take on the situation."

As the camera cut to a scene recorded outside the courthouse earlier that day, Alex hardly heard the woman's words.

Senator Stan Young—the same senator who had received a substantial amount of financial support from none other than Brian Kolthoff himself—was the owner of a stretch of farmland that had been worked by men and women in one of the Leóne family's forced labor operations.

Alex's research over the last couple months left little doubt that Kolthoff was an ally of the Leónes...but the senator?

Like a surprise slap to the back of the head, Alex hadn't

seen that coming.

And if *he*, with his network of lookouts and informants on both sides of the law, hadn't realized the likelihood that Senator Young was a Leóne puppet, then he doubted Amelia knew either.

Her job had just become ten times more dangerous, and she had no idea.

He told himself he should leave Amelia well enough alone, that he should stay confident in her ability to handle herself, and that he was overreacting. But despite all the rationalization, Alex's phone was in his hand before he'd even turned off the television.

As JOSEPH SHOULDERED open the glass and metal door to the third floor of the parking garage, he loosened the pastel blue tie around his neck. Narrowing his eyes, he glanced at the city skyline.

In August, he wasn't used to leaving the FBI office after the sun had set. But today, he'd been summoned to a hearing about the death of Alton Dalessio.

Of the four agents who had been there—SSA Spencer Corsaw, Zane Palmer, Amelia Storm, and Joseph—only Joseph and Amelia had witnessed Alton's final moments. Amelia had pulled the trigger of the twelve-gauge combat shotgun a split-second after Joseph had arrived in the doorway.

Joseph was no saint, but Dalessio and his friends existed on an entirely different level of twisted. As far as Joseph was concerned, the sick bastard had gotten what he deserved. Dalessio had been warned to stand in place, and the little shit had still tried to take a step toward Amelia.

Never mind that she'd had a shotgun pointed at his chest.

Joseph hadn't actually *seen* the movement that had sealed Alton Dalessio's fate, but he'd let Amelia and the FBI think he had.

The road back into Amelia Storm's good graces would be a long one, but he was confident he'd started in the right direction. Under oath, Joseph had backed up Amelia's recollection as if he'd stood beside her when the blast from the twelve-gauge had slammed Dalessio into the cinderblock wall.

She owed him now. He was Amelia Storm's peril.

Fishing a set of car keys from inside his black suit jacket, Joseph chuckled and shoved the memory aside. As he pressed a button to unlock the gunmetal sedan, a woman's voice jerked his attention to the double doors at the end of the row of parked cars.

Well, speak of the devil.

Though the white fluorescence was unflattering to almost anyone in the FBI office, the lighting gave Amelia's pretty face an ethereal glow. He spotted a hint of pink nail lacquer as she raised a hand to wave.

He smiled politely, returning the greeting. "Hey, Storm. How're you doing?"

She let out a sigh and shrugged. "I'm okay. Been better, but I've been worse too."

Flipping the keyring around on his index finger, Joseph leaned against the car. "Yeah, I can imagine." He lowered his gaze to the ground and shook his head. "That's not something I ever want to see again, I can tell you that much."

To his surprise, the words were truthful.

He'd left Amelia and run to the second warehouse but looped back when the Kankakee Sheriff's Deputies arrived and followed Amelia's path through the basement. As soon as he'd spotted the body in the first room, he rushed through the drab hallways searching for Amelia.

Grown women didn't quite seem like Dalessio's type, but if the little shit had so much as laid a finger on her, Joseph wouldn't have hesitated to take him apart piece by bloody piece.

Joseph gestured to the driver's side door and cleared his throat. "Well, I'm going to get out of here. I feel like I've been at this office for a year."

Pushing a piece of hair behind her ear, Amelia let out a quiet chuckle. "Yeah, me too. Look, before you go." As her eyes met his, she pressed her palms together in a gesture he instantly recognized. He almost expected her to say "namaste," but instead, she blushed. It wasn't something he'd seen before. He liked it. "I just wanted to thank you for backing me up today. I know that it's been...awkward between you and me lately, but I appreciate you having my back anyway."

"You don't have to thank me for that, Storm. Just because I'm an idiot and misread the vibe, or whatever the hell you want to call it." He waved a dismissive hand for emphasis. "That doesn't mean I'm going to stop backing you up."

Even as her face brightened, he didn't miss the flicker of trepidation in her green eyes. "You know I'd do the same for you, right?"

"Of course." Joseph cleared his throat. "I know you don't need me to tell you this, but you did a damn fine job yesterday. If it weren't for you, Mari Flores would have never seen her daughter again."

Amelia's expression tightened at the mention of Yanira Flores, and for a split-second, Joseph wondered if he'd gone too far.

"Thanks." She gulped hard but managed a slight nod. "And Camila Morales was just down the hall from where we, from where I shot Dalessio. It was close." She trailed off and dropped her gaze to the ground, and he knew she was thinking of the children they hadn't been able to save. "I'm glad we found them, though. The girls. Javier."

Her face clouded, and he could tell that she was thinking of the girls they didn't save.

Joseph pointed a finger at her and had to fight the urge to reach out and run his thumb along her bottom lip. "You made sure Yanira got home safe. And if you hadn't turned off that damn dishwasher, all the electronics that Dalessio threw in there would be completely fried."

When her gaze lifted and she met his eyes, the fleeting moment of vulnerability was gone. Like it had never even existed.

Her smile was tired, but there was no semblance of the anxiety she'd shown only moments ago. "I'm glad I did too. Hopefully, we get something useful from all those water-logged memory cards."

"I think we will." Joseph held up his keys. "Go home and relax, and drive safe. I'll see you tomorrow."

As she readjusted the handbag on her shoulder, she stepped away from the rear fender. "You too. Have a good night."

Though he was tempted to watch her walk down the row of cars, he pulled open the door and dropped into the seat.

Maybe he was closer to being in Amelia's good graces than he thought. Joseph chuckled to himself as he sat, rubbing the stubble on his cheek. Maybe the reason she'd rebuffed him so quickly was because she wanted this as much as he did, and she didn't know how to handle the desire.

As he pulled out his phone, he unlocked the screen and opened his personal email. Toward the top of the list was a bold message advising him that the round-trip plane tickets he'd been watching had gone on sale.

He glanced to the rearview mirror, and this time, he let

his eyes linger on Amelia until she disappeared into her own car.

His plan had been to take a much-needed vacation to visit Michelle Timmer along the Florida coast and to spend time with an old friend. Between the ocean breeze, the sun, Michelle's flawless body, and the company of his good friend, Joseph had been certain he'd found the perfect distraction to sate his desperate need to have Amelia Storm.

Looking back to his phone, he tapped an icon beside the email and pressed delete.

With a self-deprecating chuckle, he pulled up a secure messaging service and typed.

Hey, I thought about it some more, and I think I'm going to have to postpone that visit I had planned. I've got some shit to take care of around here. I'll let you know when I'm thinking about rescheduling. – Red

He hadn't even pocketed the device when a chime told him he'd received a response. As he scanned the text, the corner of his mouth turned up.

That must be some sweet piece of ass you're tailing. I'm stuck here in the city for a little while longer than I thought I would be anyway, so don't sweat it. – B

Joseph's fingers flew over the touchscreen keyboard as he responded to Brian Kolthoff, The Shark. His good friend owed him a big favor now, after he'd helped make sure some important evidence was "lost." *She sure is. She's the one who arrested you.*

The reply was almost instant. *That IS a sweet piece. Seems like she might be a handful. Let me know if she gives you any trouble.*

Joseph's response was a succinct *will do*. As he tucked the phone into his jacket, he shook his head again.

Amelia Storm was going to be his undoing.

27

As Zane followed Amelia through a familiar glass and metal door, he rubbed his cheekbone. The cut from the razor-sharp leaf had healed in the eight days since he'd chased Carlo Enrico, but a faint mark remained.

Even with the element of surprise and a forty-caliber handgun, Carlo hadn't landed a single blow. Zane's only battle wound that day had come from a damn plant.

Easing the door closed behind himself, he glanced to the middle-aged woman at the other end of the lab. He and Amelia had been in close contact with the technology lab manager, Portia Wingrove, over the last week. When they weren't busy chipping away at post-arrest paperwork, Zane and Amelia were consulting with either an immigration lawyer or a forensic analyst.

Fortunately, they'd been able to push through U-Visas—temporary residency cards granted to victims of crime who cooperated with law enforcement—for Javier and his family, as well as Ava's entire family. The United States capped U-Visas at ten thousand per year, so he'd been more than relieved to learn that there were still slots available.

Zane was impressed at how fast the evidence from the Kankakee County farm had been processed and examined. Today, he and Amelia would finally learn how much data the tech lab had salvaged from the damaged electronic devices they'd taken from the warehouse basement.

The corners of Portia's blue eyes creased as she offered them a smile. Rolling her chair away from the trio of monitors, she rose to her feet and extended a hand. "Good morning, Agents. Thanks for stopping down here so bright and early."

Zane accepted the handshake and lifted his stainless-steel thermos. "Bright and early has been the name of the game lately. We saw your email and figured this ought to be our first stop for the day."

Portia nodded and beckoned them to the desk nestled in the corner of the room. "Here, there are a couple chairs, so take a seat." She patted the backs of two office chairs before she took her spot behind the keyboard.

As Zane rolled a chair over to Amelia, he met her eyes. Aside from dialogue specific to their case, she'd been quiet for the last week. She still cracked a smile when he threw out a stupid joke or a sarcastic comment, but otherwise, she had seemed distant.

He didn't need a degree in psychology to explain her abrupt change. Amelia was the first to follow Alton Dalessio into the warehouse basement that had been repurposed into a dungeon. As she'd chased the man, she'd come across the freshly killed bodies of four young girls.

If the victims had been killed hours ago, the sight would have still been disturbing. But the sense of guilt, the knowledge that she'd been so close to preventing those girls' deaths, the knowledge that if she'd run a little faster, she could have at least saved one. Those thoughts were far more than just disturbing.

He'd been there before.

Raising the thermos for a quick sip of still hot coffee, Zane pulled his head back down to earth as he and Amelia took their seats.

Amelia rested her paper cup on one knee. "So, you said that you and your team finished recovering data from the memory cards and hard drives that Dalessio tried to run through the dishwasher?"

Tapping a few keys, Portia nodded. "We did. And before I get into what we found, I just want to make sure you guys have a fair warning." Her gaze shifted from Amelia to Zane. "I know you were down in that basement with the crime scene techs, but I don't even know if that's enough to prepare you for what's on these drives. This is some seriously dark shit."

Zane set his thermos on the desk. "How much progress have you made on it?"

Portia gestured to the three screens as she reached for the mouse. "Here's what we recovered."

With a click, she opened a photo of all the damaged electronics. The cameras, hard drives, and memory cards were lined up on a lab table like a group of ants headed to a picnic.

"This is the broken stuff. In the dishwasher, there were two cameras, three solid-state hard drives, six flash drives, and about seven SD cards. I say about because." She zoomed in on the image. "Your perp broke two of them in half before he tossed them in the silverware basket."

Propping his elbows on the armrests, Zane lifted an eyebrow. "What about the devices he didn't get to?"

The lab manager shook her head. "The only thing he didn't get to was a couple more cameras, and both of the memory cards had already been removed. There was a laptop and a desktop in that farmhouse, but they had been wiped already. From the looks of it, these guys stored their SD cards and hard drives separately from the other hardware. This is everything, Agents."

As Zane rubbed his eyes, he barely suppressed a groan. "Tell me there was at least something salvageable from all the shit he dumped in the dishwasher."

Portia brushed a lock of silver-streaked, caramel-brown hair from her forehead. "Honestly, it looked bleak at first. All but one of the SD cards was unusable, and only two of the flash drives survived. But…" she pushed the pointer of the mouse to a pocket-sized hard drive, "we were able to pull all the data from one of the SSDs and close to half from another. SSDs can be pretty durable, and we caught a lucky break. The perp might have been a cheapskate with the flash drives and SD cards, but he splurged on the bigger hard drives."

Turning the coffee cup around in her hands, Amelia nodded. "Have you been able to look through any of the data yet?"

The corner of Portia's mouth turned down, but she returned Amelia's nod. "Some of it, yes." She closed the picture of the broken electronics, opened a new folder, and hovered the mouse over the first file in line. "Just another disclaimer, Agents. My team specializes in analyzing footage and images from child exploitation rings, but I'm aware that you two probably aren't familiar with it. These images are cropped, and they focus on the perps, but still…"

Zane mentally armed himself. "Let's see it."

Portia explained how they'd identified Alton Dalessio—how they'd determined his approximate height, pinpointed unique marks on his body and even matched up the sound of his voice thanks to a video from Brandi Dalessio's Instagram.

Matteo Ricci was next, and though there was no wealth of social media posts that involved the bald man, Matteo had a tattoo on his chest. He'd hidden the ink with bandages, but in one video, the adhesive had come undone enough to show the edge of the tattoo.

Not that Matteo's guilt mattered. The United States Marshals had located the man two days ago. In a ramshackle hotel room in the middle of rural Kansas, Matteo Ricci had blown off his head approximately twelve hours before the marshals kicked down the door.

Though Carlo hadn't been identified in any of the videos so far, Zane couldn't say he was surprised. According to Ava Fernandez, Carlo didn't touch the girls. He preferred playing the part of cameraman.

Ava had helped the FBI track down and arrest Matteo's cousin Dean, but Portia and her team hadn't spotted him yet either.

So when Portia pulled up a cropped photo of a lanky, shirtless man, Zane clenched his jaw as he and Amelia exchanged vehement glances.

Amelia scooted forward, her expression grim. "Who the hell is this?"

Blowing out a sigh, Portia shook her head. "We don't know. We compared him to every person mentioned in your investigation. Vincent Piliero, Dean Ricci, even Emilio Leóne, but we got nothing."

Zane gritted his teeth. "Piliero is short and has a bit of a belly. Dean Ricci has three tattoos on his left arm and one on his back. Emilio even has a little ink. This guy doesn't have any we can see."

Portia closed the image. "We'll keep looking, and if we find anything, you'll be the first to know."

"Okay. That's all we can ask." Zane stuck out a hand as he pushed away from the table. "Thank you for all your hard work. You have no idea how much we appreciate what you do."

With a slight smile, Portia accepted his handshake, and then Amelia's. "Take care, Agents. I'll be in touch."

As the glass door swung closed behind them, Amelia shot him a knowing look. "Are you thinking what I'm thinking?"

"Yep." He didn't hesitate. "I think our rapist cameraman might have an idea who the other man is in those videos."

Amelia checked the time. "Not even nine yet. When do you suppose visiting hours start at County?"

He laughed. "Who gives a shit? We'll go in there and pull that prick out of his cell if we have to."

For the first time in a week, Amelia's grin wasn't wistful or strained.

METAL CLATTERED as Carlo Enrico dropped his shackled hands on the stainless-steel tabletop. The cuff that bound his right arm was positioned above the edge of a plaster cast, and Zane suddenly felt better about his corn related injury.

Enrico's dark eyes shifted between Amelia, seated across from him, and Zane, who stood leaning against a cement wall.

Though Zane wanted nothing more than to break the man's other wrist, he offered Enrico a shit-eating grin instead. "Nice to see you again, Carlo. I heard that the judge remanded you without bail, so I figured we could find you here. How's your week in County treating you?"

Carlo scowled. "What do you people want? Where's my lawyer?"

With a snort, Amelia crossed her arms. "Doubt you want your mob lawyer here for this conversation, buddy."

As Carlo opened his mouth to reply, Zane cut him off. "No, you probably don't. My guess is he'd just run back to your capo and tell him we offered you a deal, wouldn't he?"

Clenching and unclenching his good hand, Carlo shook his head. "I don't know what the hell you're talking about. I didn't do anything. All these charges are bullshit."

Zane couldn't help his burst of derisive laughter. "Sure. Especially the one where you put an illegal firearm to the back of a Federal agent's head. That one's *definitely* bullshit, isn't it? You know you can get life just from that, right?"

Carlo gritted his teeth so hard they squeaked. "What do you people want?"

Amelia tilted her head, and though Zane could only see the side of her face, he didn't miss the malevolent fire in her eyes. "We don't want anything from you. Not right now. We're just here to tell you we know about the other guy in your little kiddie porn ring."

Carlo opened his mouth, but before a single syllable left his lips, Amelia brought her hand down against the stainless-steel table. The resounding crash was enough to make him jump in his seat.

"Save it, Enrico!" Amelia's voice dripped with so much venom, Zane half-expected Carlo to fall over dead right there. "I don't have time for these stupid excuses, you understand?"

Carlo's Adam's apple bobbed, but he kept his mouth shut.

With another smirk, Zane spread his hands. "See? Just keep your mouth shut, bud. That's all we want from you right now."

Amelia pushed her chair away from the table and jabbed a finger at Carlo. "You know, I'm already sick of you, so I'll lay this out plain enough that even an idiot like you will understand."

Zane maintained his disarming smile as Carlo's gaze shifted to him. "Like my partner said. We know about the fourth guy. What we don't know is who he is. And we can't very well ask your boss or your pal Matteo about him, can we? Not unless we conduct a séance."

Carlo growled low in his throat, but his eyes flickered with uncertainty.

Zane made a show of dusting off his suit jacket. "I'm not keen on lighting that many candles. It's a fire hazard, so here's the deal. If you tell us who that man is, we'll see what we can do about getting you a sentence where you're in protective custody. I'd highly recommend you think about our offer, and I'd also recommend you keep it to yourself."

Resting both hands at the edge of the table, Amelia leaned in to pin Carlo with a withering stare. "See, Enrico, here's the thing. You know how pedophiles are treated in prison, right?" She tapped beneath one eye. "Based on that nice, fat bruise, I'd say you have some idea. And now, on top of that, both of your co-conspirators are dead. Who do you suppose the U.S. Attorney is going to want to pin with all the rest of those charges?"

Carlo dropped his gaze to the stainless-steel table.

Amelia jabbed a finger low enough for Carlo to see. "You. That's who. And with the Leónes stirring up bad blood with the San Luis Cartel, not to mention all that bad blood that's already between you guys and the D'Amatos, how do you suppose a *Leóne* pedophile is going to fare?" She straightened and held her hands out at her sides. "Maybe the bulk of this would have blown back on Alton and Matteo, but they're both dead, and you know what that makes you? The fall guy, that's who."

Stepping to the side, Zane beat a fist against the heavy door to signal the nearby guard. As a buzzer rang out in the cramped space, he met Carlo's wary gaze. "Think about it, Enrico. Otherwise, if you ask me, you're going to die in here before you ever step foot in a courtroom."

28

W eekends meant little to Amelia, at least since she'd started at the FBI. But for the first time in what felt like an eternity, she was on board the "thank god it's Friday" bandwagon. After all the hours she and Zane had poured into follow-up work over the last week, SAC Keaton had personally advised them to stay away from the office until Monday.

Before they'd departed their shoebox office, Zane had suggested that they kick off the weekend with takeout and a few episodes of a show he'd been hounding her to watch.

"I know you well enough by now that I think I can comfortably say you'll never get around to watching it unless I'm literally sitting beside you with the remote in my hand." He'd fixed her with a knowing look, and then his chair screeched in protest as he'd leaned back.

After he offered the chair a few choice words, he reminded her that they'd never arranged visitation for Hup, and he hadn't seen *their* cat since Amelia brought her home at the end of the Leila Jackson investigation.

Though Amelia's knee-jerk response was to decline, to

say she was tired from the long work week, she'd been surprised to find that the prospect of a friend's company was far more comforting than sitting alone with her thoughts.

Before Zane could launch into any more of his sales pitch, she'd nodded and asked what time she could expect him.

Now, as the digital clock of the stainless-steel stove ticked one minute closer to the agreed upon seven o'clock, she hurried through her apartment to ensure any embarrassing messes were cleared away. Not that she ever *had* any embarrassing messes, but she also rarely invited anyone over.

As Hup trotted up to her in the kitchen, Amelia held out her hands and sighed. "I don't know how to be a hostess, Hup. Is this good enough? Should I light a candle?"

The long-haired calico mewled and rubbed against Amelia's shins.

Truth be told, Amelia wasn't even sure if she should wear shorts. Ever since the uncomfortable interaction with Joseph Larson at Madison's Sports Bar, she'd gone out of her way to dress like the temperature was closer to forty than ninety.

She hated the forced modesty, if that's even what she could call it. As far as she was concerned, she *had* dressed modestly. When the air outside was comprised almost entirely of water, and the sun baked the city to a toasty one-hundred degrees, she wanted to wear shorts and a sleeveless shirt.

Screw the men who couldn't keep their eyes to themselves.

Wrapping both arms around herself, Amelia sighed. Her encounter with Joseph in the FBI parking garage had been benign enough, but she couldn't shake the nagging sensation that he still hadn't revealed the cards in his hand.

As the intercom buzzed, Amelia jerked herself away from the paranoid line of thought. Even if she wanted to change into jeans or sweatpants, she didn't have the time.

After she peeked out the window to make note of Zane at the entrance to the apartment building, she pressed a button to unlock the front door. There was a reason she'd selected a second-floor unit with a view of the parking lot—she wanted to see her visitors approaching.

Brushing off the front of her Kendrick Lamar concert t-shirt, she took in a steadying breath and flipped the deadbolt. By the time she pulled open the door, Zane had reached the landing. His face brightened when their eyes met, and despite the crippling doubt she'd just slogged through, she smiled.

Amelia stepped aside, letting him enter. As she closed and locked the door, a wave of guilt struck her. For the past week, she'd replayed the events leading up to Alton Dalessio's death over and over, but she still wasn't sure if her rendition was true.

For all she knew, she'd been lying to the man who had become one of her closest friends.

Adrenaline had surged through her body as she'd pointed the twelve-gauge at Alton's chest, and she'd been pointedly reminded of both Emilio Leóne and Brian Kolthoff—neither of whom had received the punishment they deserved.

Was that why she'd killed Alton? Had the movement she'd seen been nothing more than wishful thinking?

Or had she pulled the trigger to compensate for failing to save the four dead girls?

If she'd run faster, maybe they wouldn't have been killed. She could blow Alton Dalessio's heart out of his chest a hundred times over, and the act still wouldn't bring back those poor children.

Swallowing past the stone in her throat, she forced herself to turn away from the door.

Good timing for a breakdown, Amelia.

She should have plastered on a smile, led her guest to the kitchen, and offered him a drink.

But she was tired of the invulnerable façade and trying to pretend she was still Lieutenant Storm.

"Are you okay?" Zane's voice was hushed, but the words jerked her back to reality all the same.

With a shaky sigh, Amelia brushed some hair over her shoulder and shook her head. "No. Not really."

A shadow of concern passed over his gray eyes. "Is there anything I can do?"

Amelia knew exactly what she needed from him right then. Rubbing her temple, she lifted a shoulder. "I…" She paused, swallowing hard. Could she do this? Ask for what she needed without worry? "I think maybe I just need a hug. A real one. Not from a cat who is angling for an extra bowl of kibble."

Zane's eyes softened as he opened his arms. "I can do that."

As she closed the distance between them and stepped into his warm embrace, she bit her tongue to stave off tears. Squeezing her eyes closed, she hugged him tighter and forced the images of the week from her mind.

"It wasn't your fault." His deep voice reverberated along her cheek, but she hardly noticed the sensation.

"I could have moved faster. I stopped to clear every room I passed because I didn't want him to sneak up on me, but I should have known he was trying to get to the exit. I shouldn't have wasted time." The words slipped from her lips before she could think them all through.

He shook his head as he pulled away to meet her gaze. "You couldn't have known that. Hindsight is twenty-twenty. Right now, you know that he was trying to get to the exit. But then…" he stroked her back, "you didn't know. You did the best you could with what you had. None of us would have charged in there without clearing the path behind us."

Amelia chewed her lip and dropped her gaze to the tiled floor.

He lifted her chin with a finger. "What would you say to me if our roles were reversed?"

Her mouth hung open stupidly as she lifted her gaze and met his eyes. She knew exactly what she would say to him. "I'd...I'd say it wasn't your fault. That you did the best you could. Because I know you would have done your best, and—"

He placed a finger on her lips. "No ifs, ands, no buts. You're right. I would have done my best, just like you did. Don't sell yourself short like that. Maybe you *think* you could have done better, but that's just your brain looking at it in hindsight." He gave her arm a gentle squeeze. "You did your best, okay?"

Blinking repeatedly to chase away the sting in the corners of her eyes, Amelia nodded. "Yeah. You're right. I...I did." For the first time, she believed herself.

"I know what it feels like to think you should have done more."

She searched his face. "You do?"

With a sad smile, he nodded. "It happened right after I joined the Bureau. It was an all-hands-on-deck thing, a response to an active shooter. I don't know how I wound up so far ahead of everyone, but I was chasing this...this guy. This *mass murderer* through a subway in D.C. I had a couple potential shots as I was following him, but the whole thing was chaos. There were civilians trying to run out of the way, and I didn't think I could get a clear enough shot."

"My god," she breathed. "What happened?"

As he stepped back, Zane ran a hand through his hair. "He wound up holding eleven people hostage on one of the train cars. It took us almost four hours of trying to negotiate with him before a sniper finally took him out. But in that four hours, he killed another five people."

"That wasn't your fault." She shook her head. "You might have missed him and hit an innocent person."

The wistful smile returned as he brushed a piece of hair from her shoulder. "Exactly. It took me a long time to realize that. Trust me. Learn from my failure. That was a dark time in my life, and I don't want you to have to go through that too."

In the silence that followed, her stomach dropped as the guilt crept over her like quicksand that threatened to swallow her whole.

Maybe she wouldn't announce her doubts about Alton Dalessio to the entire Federal Bureau of Investigation, but she had to tell Zane.

Gesturing to the living room and kitchen, Amelia cleared her throat. "That's not all, but I guess I should be a host and offer you something to drink if I'm going to act like you're my therapist."

He scoffed as he stepped out of his black dress shoes and followed her out of the short hallway. "I'm not your therapist. I'm your friend."

"I know." She sighed and stopped to lean against the granite breakfast bar. "But it feels one-sided. Like I'm laying all this on you, but I'm not doing anything to help you. You know what I mean?"

Propping an elbow on the bar, he nodded. "I do. But that's what friends are for, isn't it? Give it a few months, and I might be the one saying the same thing to you. You never know."

Amelia clenched and unclenched one hand as they lapsed into silence. Try as she might, she couldn't think of a diplomatic way to phrase her trepidation about Alton Dalessio.

Then again, the harder she tried to be diplomatic, the closer she came to lying.

"I killed Alton Dalessio."

His eyes drifted to hers as he nodded slowly. "I know."

She balled her hand into a fist until her nails bit into her palm. "I don't know if it was self-defense. I-I *thought* it was. I thought I saw him move, but..." she bit her lip and shook her head, "but I don't know. I don't know if he moved or if I just *wanted* him to move, so I imagined it. I feel like I've been lying to you all week."

His brow furrowed. "Wait, wasn't Larson there too?"

She raised her shoulders. "I guess. I'm worried that he's just backing me up, though. I...I don't feel bad that Dalessio is dead. He deserved worse, but I feel like I've been lying about it."

Though she half-expected Zane to take a step back as his eyes widened in horror, his expression softened. "You thought you were in danger?"

She nodded. "But I don't know if I was. And I doubt the courts care what I *thought*. As far as they're concerned, I might have killed an innocent man."

Zane snorted. "Innocent? I think forensics has about five hundred gigs of data that says otherwise."

With a quiet sigh, Amelia pressed her hands to the sides of her face. "Okay. Maybe not innocent, but...unarmed."

Zane's stare turned flat. "Unarmed? He was holding a nine-mil."

Rubbing her forehead, Amelia blew the strands of hair out of her eyes. "Okay, maybe not unarmed, but...I don't know."

"Look." He tapped an index finger against the granite. "Maybe this isn't the most objective opinion in the world. I'm glad he's dead and won't waste millions of dollars of taxpayer money for a pointless trial when we all know the judge is going to lock him up and throw away the key."

"Tell me how you really feel." The sarcastic remark came unbidden, and she was glad when a slight smile crept to his face.

"I guess my point is this." He patted the breakfast bar. "If you thought you were in danger, then you made the right call. He'd just killed four little girls in cold blood, and only god knows what he would have done to you if he'd gotten the chance. As far as the Bureau is concerned, it's over and done. Larson backed you up. The end."

Amelia took a step toward the fridge. "Why? Why do you always make so much sense? I was trying to have a pity party over here, and you had to go and ruin it with your logic."

As Zane flashed her one of his charming grins, a sudden rush of water called their attention to the shadowy hall at the other end of the living room.

Jabbing a finger toward the bathroom, Amelia lifted her eyebrows. "See? I told you. She flushes the toilet. All the damn time."

On cue, the calico emerged, her luminescent eyes fixed on the two humans.

Zane laughed, and as Amelia joined in, she hoped her life might return to normal after all.

DROPPING his phone back to the coffee table, Joseph took a sip of bourbon and scooted to the edge of the plush couch cushion. He was filled with anticipation as his gaze fell on the sleek tablet he'd bought a couple days earlier.

Swiping a finger over the screen to unlock the device, he saw her.

Amelia was slumped back in the center of a gray

sectional, and her eyes were fixed on the flickering screen of the television. Joseph had installed the hidden camera in a vent above the entertainment stand. He'd angled the lens, allowing him to view almost the entire living area.

And what he couldn't see through the first camera, he'd covered with four other cameras strategically placed around her apartment. The only obscured portions of Amelia's home were the foyer and adjacent hall.

His personal favorite, of course, was the bathroom camera. He'd double and triple checked to ensure his only visual would be of the shower and the bathtub, and since he'd opted for a smaller, more durable device in that one room, the recording didn't capture sound.

He had to give her *some* privacy, didn't he?

For the past couple hours, he'd watched Amelia and Zane with rapt attention. Until tonight, he'd been convinced the two of them were sleeping together, but after he'd watched their goodbye, he'd laughed at his own paranoia. He didn't have to worry about Palmer.

He'd never *had* to worry about Palmer. The guy was so far in the friend zone, chances were good he'd never find his way out.

But what Joseph had found more interesting than Amelia and Zane's platonic dynamic was their conversation about Alton Dalessio.

Though Joseph hadn't *actually* seen the seconds that led up to Amelia pulling the trigger of the Benelli combat shotgun, he'd let the FBI think he had. His idea had been to back up Amelia's recollection to squeeze into her good graces, but reality was much more conducive to his ultimate goal.

She didn't know if she'd been justified in killing Alton Dalessio.

She *didn't know*, and she thought Joseph had witnessed the entire exchange. Yanira had been in the room, but the federal government wouldn't rely on the testimony of a traumatized child.

Amelia's career, her freedom, her livelihood, all of it was in Joseph's hands.

She was exactly where he wanted her.

She was his.

29

When Zane let himself into his and Amelia's shoebox office on the day after Labor Day, he expected to swap stories of their respective weekends. He knew Amelia had gone to Six Flags with her father and niece and nephew, and afterward, the four of them had planned to surprise Joanna Storm with a homemade cheesecake for her thirty-third birthday.

Like Amelia, Zane had spent the long weekend with his family. He'd flown out to New Jersey to meet up with his mother, stepfather, and two of his siblings—his older step-brother and his younger sister. He hadn't visited the East Coast since his move to Chicago, and the trip had been a welcome reprieve.

But instead of the anticipated morning banter, Amelia leapt to her feet before the door had even latched closed. Gold light from a handful of recessed fixtures reflected off her smartphone's screen as she waved the device in the air.

Confusion was clearly written across his face. "What? Did you just win something?"

She smiled slyly and shook her head. "No, not really. I just got a call."

Zane furrowed his brows. "Based on that look, it must be good news. Who was it?"

She picked up her handbag off the floor. "Carlo Enrico's lawyer. His *new* lawyer."

"*New* lawyer?" Zane felt like a parrot, but he hadn't consumed enough caffeine to concoct a better reply.

Amelia's smile confirmed she understood his morning struggle. "Yeah. They want to talk to us about the fourth person that Portia and her team found in those videos."

Zane's eyes widened.

Over the past two weeks, a select group of video analysts had combed through the data that had been recovered from Alton Dalessio's child exploitation ring. Neither Zane nor Amelia envied the task, but they'd learned that the specialists tended to pay more attention to the details of the perp and the location. Rather than take in the situation as a whole, they picked apart the scene to look for clues.

The tactic made sense to Zane, but he still doubted he'd be able to carry out even a fraction of their workload.

Despite the best efforts of Portia's team, they were no closer to uncovering the identity of the fourth man in Dalessio's operation. And so far, Carlo had been as cooperative as a temperamental toddler.

Blinking repeatedly, Zane returned his focus to the woman in front of him. "Is that why he got a new lawyer? Because he wanted to make a deal with the Feds and didn't want his boss to know about it?"

Amelia's good-humored expression faded. "That's part of it."

"What's the other part?"

She clenched her jaw, hesitating before delivering the

news. "According to Enrico, the fourth man is a detective in the Chicago PD."

The End
To be continued...

Thank you for reading.
All of the Amelia Storm Series books can be found on Amazon.

ACKNOWLEDGMENTS

How does one properly thank everyone involved in taking a dream and making it a reality? Here goes.

In addition to our families, whose unending support provided the foundation for us to find the time and energy to put these thoughts on paper, we want to thank the editors who polished our words and made them shine.

Many thanks to our publisher for risking taking on two newbies and giving us the confidence to become bona fide authors.

More than anyone, we want to thank you, our readers, for clicking on a couple of nobodies and sharing your most important asset, your time, with this book. We hope with all our hearts we made it worthwhile.

Much love,
Mary & Amy

ABOUT THE AUTHOR

Mary Stone lives among the majestic Blue Ridge Mountains of East Tennessee with her two dogs, four cats, a couple of energetic boys, and a very patient husband.

As a young girl, she would go to bed every night, wondering what type of creature might be lurking underneath. It wasn't until she was older that she learned that the creatures she needed to most fear were human.

Today, she creates vivid stories with courageous, strong heroines and dastardly villains. She invites you to enter her world of serial killers, FBI agents but never damsels in distress. Her female characters can handle themselves, going toe-to-toe with any male character, protagonist or antagonist.

Discover more about Mary Stone on her website.
www.authormarystone.com

Amy Wilson

Having spent her adult life in the heart of Atlanta, her upbringing near the Great Lakes always seems to slip into her writing. After several years as a vet tech, she has dreams of going back to school to be a veterinarian but it seems another dream of hers has come true first. Writing a novel.

Animals and books have always been her favorite things, in addition to her husband, who wanted her to have it all. He's the reason she has time to write. Their two teenage boys fill the rest of her time and help her take care of the mini zoo that now fills their home with laughter...and yes, the occasional poop.

Connect with Mary Online

facebook.com/authormarystone
goodreads.com/AuthorMaryStone
bookbub.com/profile/3378576590
pinterest.com/MaryStoneAuthor
instagram.com/marystone_author

Printed in Great Britain
by Amazon

83056830R00190